I0591350

PRAISE FOR *1836: YEAR OF ESCAPE*

"Rose Kleidon's *1836: Year of Escape* pulls off a literary magic trick, weaving the sweeping movements of history around the gripping account of a single family's desperate emigration to America. Kleidon vividly recreates 19th century life right down to the sights, smells, and sensations."
—Pete Beatty, author of *Cuyahoga*

"*1836* is as much an engaging chronicle as it is a novel. The tightly packed narrative unfolds like leaves on a family tree: opening, fading, growing, renewing with the passing of time. Detailed and direct, the author creates a world that feels as if the reader walks as a witness to a real family's journey through its generations."
—Nancy E. Turner, NYT Bestselling Author, finalist, The Willa Literary Awards, Arizona Author of the Year, *These Is My Words, Sarah's Quilt, The Star Garden, The Water and the Blood, My Name Is Resolute,* and *Light Changes Everything*

"Engrossing story, glowing prose, stunning imagery. Kleidon reminds us how history repeats itself. Or echoes."
—Steve Vogel, NYT Bestselling Author, *Reasonable Doubt, The Unforgiven*

"5 STARS! From the heart-wrenching beginning on the battlefields of the Napoleonic wars, the author has the reader hooked. With vivid narrative, compelling dialogue, and in-depth history, *1836* presents a compelling saga of trial, hardship, and hope for a better future…. Historical novels are often woven around the noble ranks of society; *1836* is a tale of equal intensity about ordinary people on an incredible journey."
—Emily-Jane Hills Orford, Readers' Favorite Reviews

"Brilliant! I can feel the ocean waves, see the distant horizon. I am sitting on a little sofa on the top floor of an old brownstone in Brooklyn with my tea, reading beautiful writing. Could it get any better than this?"
—Barbara Ellis, Unicorn for Writers

1836

YEAR OF ESCAPE

1836

YEAR OF ESCAPE

a novel

Rose Osterman Kleidon

RIVER GROVE
BOOKS

Published by River Grove Books
Austin, Texas
www.rivergrovebooks.com

This is a work of historical fiction. Names, characters, places, and incidents are the product of the author's imagination and are not to be construed as real. Where real-life historical or public figures appear, the situations, incidents and dialogues concerning those people are entirely fictional. In all other respects, any resemblance to persons, living or dead, events or locales is entirely coincidental.

Please note that some language may be culturally insensitive or offensive to some readers. The material reflects the culture and context of the era and/or of the fictional characters and not the views of the author.

Distributed by River Grove Books

Cover image: *Rotterdam Ferry-Boat*, oil on canvas by Joseph Mallord William Turner, 1833, National Gallery of Art, Washington, DC.

For historical notes and study questions, see www.rosekleidon.com.

Publisher's Cataloging-in-Publication data is available.

Paperback ISBN: 978-1-63299-610-7
eBook ISBN: 978-1-63299-611-4

First Edition

TO DENNIS

whose belief in me and my creative spirit

makes my writing possible

CONTENTS

Characters v

BOOK ONE: THE OLD LAND... 1
  1. Whichever Side, 1812 1
  2. Out of Line, 1836.. 5
  3. Near Miss 11
  4. Brigands and Thieves 15
  5. You Must Remember 21
  6. Das Neue Land 27
  7. The Necessity of This 33
  8. Barbaric!.. 39
  9. She's Strange 43
  10. It Should Be You 49
  11. Every Man a Prince 53
  12. All Liberty Requires 57
  13. Soldier-Fiddler... 63

BOOK TWO: ESCAPE 67
  14. A City Once Free.. 67
  15. The Green Bough.. 73
  16. Astonishing Speed 77
  17. Initial Curiosity.. 83
  18. Without a Blink.. 87
  19. Rotterdam Ferry-Boat... 93
  20. Chains of Europe.. 99
  21. *Enigma* 103
  22. Ice 109
  23. Paradise..113
  24. Gibraltar 119
  25. Günter..123
  26. Alameda...127
  27. Suddenly Dangerous 133

BOOK THREE: ACROSS 137

  28. Francesca...137

  29. Olympian above It All 143

  30. Stars of Gold 149

  31. Almost Lost..153

  32. Condemned to Live...159

  33. North Sea Capture..165

  34. Prophesying Woe..169

  35. First Sight of Land..175

  36. *Diamante*..181

  37. Something like a Berserker...185

  38. So Cruel and Greedy 189

BOOK FOUR: EMANCIPATION.......................................195

  39. La Punta y El Morro 195

  40. Ezmeralda 201

  41. Moros y Cristianos..207

  42. As Suspect as Spies...213

  43. Comfort in Drink..219

  44. Far from Free 223

  45. Secret Dances of Joy 229

  46. Most Singular Passengers 235

BOOK FIVE: HOME AGAIN..243

  47. The Blind Hand of God..243

  48. St. Elmo's Fire...249

  49. Matagorda Bay..255

  50. The Promised Land...259

  51. This Tattooed Tribe 265

  52. Indeed, Sir...271

  53. Perfectly Sublime 275

  54. Mississippi Delta...279

  55. The Paris of the New World..283

  56. A Proper Home 287

From the Author...291

Acknowledgments...293

CHARACTERS

1812: Niklas Kästner, age 22, in Napoleon's light horse cavalry
Hans, newborn, Niklas's son by his first wife, Angelika

THE KÄSTNER FAMILY IN 1836
Niklas Kästner, age 46, veteran, merchant, and member of the underground German Democracy Movement (GDM)
Hans, age 24
Katrina Beckmann Kästner, age 40, Niklas's second wife
Will, age15
Amalie, age 14
Lisette, age 7
Jakob, age 4

BERLEBURG, WITTGENSTEIN
Ernst Zimmermann, town constable, served with Niklas Kästner
Sepp Beckmann, town blacksmith, Katrina's cousin
Werner Schmidt, Katrina and Niklas's nephew
Horst and Berthe Schmidt, Werner's parents
Günter Erlinger, town baker, member of the GDM
Addie Erlinger, his wife
Elfriede Schuster, family friend
Elizabet Beckmann Mueller, Katrina's cousin

COLOGNE AND ABOARD *HOLSATIA*
Robert Blum* leader of the GDM
Aldo, captain of steamship *Holsatia*

CAPTAIN, CREW & PASSENGERS OF *ENIGMA*
Izak Peterssen, captain of barque *Enigma*
Richard Billings, Ship's Carpenter
Mr. Groves, First Mate
John Cutler (Cutlip), a sailor

Sean Crowley, Ship's Surgeon's Assistant
Francesca Lenzini, steerage passenger
Dr. Quentin Ward, Ship's Surgeon
Thomas Segrave, an owner of *Enigma*, shipmate of Izak Peterssen
Gideon Smith, age 13, a sailor, Mr. Groves' nephew
Methuselah, sailor, oldest member of the crew
Giovanni, an Italian sailor
Erik Thorvald, Master Gunner, friend of Izak Peterssen
Johannes Ackermann, steerage passenger, Francesca's cousin
Mr. Stephens, Master of *Enigma*

HAVANA
María Paloma Ruz Iglesias, rooming house owner
José Antonio Garcia de Cadiz Ruiz (Pepe), her son, age 15
Maria Ezmeralda Sofia O'Farril y Núñez de Castillo, age 16
Herr Kleimbach, German banker
Nicolás Cristóbal Cabrera, captain of *Augusta Ann*
Rafael Martinez, age 24, enslaved

LINNVILLE, TEXAS
Major John Forbes* of the Army of the Republic of Texas
Lennart Mueller, friend of Johann Friedrich Ernst,* founder of a German
    colony in Texas
George Erath, 1832 Austrian immigrant
Elijah Bennett,* owner of a hotel and store in Linnville
Mrs. Bennett, his wife
Juan José Benavides, nephew of Plácido Benavides,* early settler, Texas
    revolutionary
White Bear, Karankawa warrior
Major Slattery, the Army of the Republic of Texas
Lieutenant René Gravier, the Army of the Republic of Texas

*Historic persons

BOOK ONE

THE OLD LAND

"Pray if you like, only you'd do better to use your judgment."
— Leo Tolstoy, *War and Peace*

CHAPTER 1

WHICHEVER SIDE, 1812

At the same moment Hans was being born, Niklas thought he was a dead man for sure. In a melee at the Battle of Borodino, his horse collapsed, and a Russian bayonet sliced his face as he fell. As he was pulled from the battlefield, the voices around him were French, which was a relief, but whoever had him in hand piled him into a sweltering medic's tent and left. The smell of blood was everywhere.

It was 7 September 1812, and Niklas was with Napoleon's army, not far from Moscow. It was locked in battle against the czar's formidable generals, including the last man Niklas attacked, the bold, flamboyant Count Ostermann-Tolstoy. Niklas never saw the man with a bayonet who came to the count's aid.

A French Army field surgeon finished stitching up Niklas, wiped his hands on a bloody cloth and shouted, "You were lucky not to lose an eye." He turned to the aides: "Get him up! What are you waiting for?"

As a member of the renowned cavalry of Napoleon's Grande Armée, Chevau-Léger, 2nd Squadron, Niklas expected himself to rise and ride off, but it was all he could do to put up a hand and feel a face sticky with blood and a bandage across half of it. His mouth was full of blood, and he spat. It hurt to spit.

Someone had unbuttoned the top of his coat and turned the blue collar to the inside, for which he was grateful. Now he tried to turn the collar outward and do up the buttons. But he was surprisingly weak or clumsy, he whose arms could wield a sword, whose hands could control a charging horse, whose nimble fingers had unhooked Angelika's dress so easily.

"You're good at this!" she had laughed.

Damn buttons! He could feel the embossed insignia on them, but the buttonholes seemed to have disappeared.

"Come on, you. You can stand." Kind hands pushed him into a sitting position, his sword still in its scabbard, clunky, and in his way.

On this same day, far to the west, in the little town of Berleburg, where he had been born, kind hands held a screaming newborn. Kind hands held his dear Angelika, too, who had just named the child Hans. It had been a hard fight to give birth, and now, as the blood poured out of her, she had only the strength to smile and remark that her baby had his father's blue eyes. And then, in the house where Niklas had been born and now his son, in spite of the women in the room trying to save her, Angelika died a bloody awful death anyway, with no battlefield anywhere near.

In the medic's tent off to one side of the Battle of Borodino, Niklas no longer cared that he could not button his coat. He had fallen into a deep vortex, all of his attention on the gap yawning below him and his inexorable slide toward it, unable to grab hold or dig in his heels, about to slip into what he did not know. His enormous head swam, his good eye saw red, and then he knew nothing at all. All the kind hands in the Grande Armée could not keep him in the world of the conscious, so they lifted him off the operating table and laid him on the ground with the other corpses, to live or die as God wished.

The fields where the French and Russian armies fought the Battle of Borodino were a grisly sight by now. Along a long, rough dividing line lay the twisted bodies of young men, hacked and bled out, buzzards beginning to settle among them, more dead in one time and place than the world had ever known. Carnage, even on this scale, did not stop Napoleon, who regrouped his Grande Armée and marched it into the Imperial City of Moscow. Niklas came along on a stretcher. He was in a fever dream by then, but the flames he saw all around were real. The Muscovites had set the city ablaze and fled. The Czar could not be found. Russia was to be saved in a most absurd way, the czar hiding like a four-year-old under the bed and refusing to talk. In a month the invading French army was out of food, and much as it disgusted him, Napoleon had to order a retreat. It began with high hopes in spite of an early October snow, the French jubilant to loot the deserted city and start for home.

When winter set in, it brought shocking blizzard conditions and cold beyond anything the French could imagine. High spirits became desperation, and with a thousand kilometers to go, anything heavy or inedible was dropped in the snow. Winter was far more adept than Russians at killing Frenchmen. Only a few would survive Napoleon's Russian debacle, but among them, somehow, was Niklas Kästner, wearing a patch over one eye.

All the way home, Niklas talked to Angelika, telling her his troubles, vowing his love, surviving so he could return to her. When he arrived in his hometown of Berleburg, he was handed a son he did not know existed and told of her death. The cruelty of it shocked him. He deposited the boy with family and went back to the army, where, over the next three years, he watched Napoleon be deposed, endure exile, escape Elba, cross France in triumph, and be declared emperor again.

By June of 1815, Niklas and his Grande Armée cavalry regiment were on the miserable, muddy outskirts of an insignificant Belgian village named Waterloo. It had been nine years since he, at sixteen, had gone off with Napoleon's Grande Armée, and now, he did not complain at a long, forced march through days of cold rain to these miserable, muddy fields. He was a hardened veteran of a cavalry called 'The Unstoppables,' and he knew the speed of troop movement could surprise an enemy and engage him in battle unprepared. Thus, with every confidence, he guided his horse, the fourth one he had named Zimt, toward the battlefield at Waterloo.

Then, for the first time and to everyone's surprise, the famed cavalry failed. For this and other reasons, Napoleon lost. After Waterloo, Berleburgers were suddenly German, or at least no longer French, not even in name. The Allies' victory at Waterloo was celebrated wildly in the streets. Behind closed doors, some people cheered, others cried, and everyone wondered what was next. Berleburg was in Wittgenstein, which had been part of Napoleon's first foreign conquest twenty years earlier, a fate few embraced. The new victors were not like them either, being English, Austrian, or Prussian. They hoped their own prince, up the hill in his six-hundred-year-old palace, would assert his independence and come into his own at last. But they had no part to play in such things, so they dried their eyes and got on with life.

Six months later, by Christmastide, 1815, when the French army was unraveling, Niklas came home. The town had received the veterans of the Allied Army months earlier, young Berleburgers who had been conscripted. It was awkward having veterans of both armies in the same place. Niklas was a special embarrassment, his having been drafted when Wittgenstein was one of Napoleon's occupied territories and then having succeeded so well as part of the famous French cavalry. The scar across his face was an unfortunate reminder. In town, everyone hoped all this could be treated as ancient history, and whoever had fought on whichever side would forget his time in whatever army and think of himself as a Berleburger first. Those who had actually left Berleburg in a uniform found this unlikely.

Now home at last, Niklas noticed Hans, his motherless son, and he married again, to Katrina Beckmann. She was petite and slender, with a quick smile and strawberry blonde hair that caught the sunlight. When Niklas met her, his winter suddenly became spring, and he forgot to be sensible. As April turned to May, she became irresistible. He knew he was handsome in an officer's uniform, but now it was the wrong uniform, and there was that scar. Lovable little Hans, he hoped, would compensate. Whatever her reasons, and in spite of what people said about him, Katrina married Niklas, and a new life began for them both.

That summer, 1816, a year after Waterloo, came more shocking news: Wittgenstein was ceded to the Prussians. Prussia lay to the east, past the Kingdom of Hanover and a half-dozen smaller states. To Berleburgers, their own prince's acceptance of the situation was understandable, since he was no more than a pawn. Those who had fought for the Allies had been forced to do so, which was forgotten as they assumed the proud patina of victory. In contrast, the veterans of French Grande Armée, once heroes, were whispered to be "Old Revolutionaries," whose hearts still rang with the now despised cry of "Liberté, Equalité, Fraternité." It was treason, the King of Prussia said, to have any feeling at all for the French, but such treason still swirled in Wittgenstein.

CHAPTER 2

OUT OF LINE, 1836

Twenty years passed quietly, and in 1836, Ernst Zimmermann, the town constable, stared at new layers of gilt and mirrors in Berleburg's palace. Ernst had served with Niklas Kästner in the French army long ago, but after Waterloo he had embraced the Prussian victors, just as Berleburg's nobility had. Their palace, however, unnerved him with its size, its frowning portraits, and its newly gold-leafed furniture.

With a tap-tap of his cane, in came Franz, the old marshal of the household, who had overseen the palace stables and men-at-arms for years. He seated himself in a fine new chair with gold curlicued arms and lion's-paw legs. All this glitter made it awkward for Ernst Zimmermann. He had an image of himself sneaking into the palace with a chisel and flaking off that gold, a little at a time, just enough to make himself rich.

Franz startled Ernst: "Are the Kästners on your list?" The old marshal spoke a high, thin voice that belied his legendary ruthlessness. The prince, whose father had sent Ernst and Niklas off to fight for Napoleon, despised and feared Franz.

Ernst Zimmermann nodded. "Hans Kästner." A memory flashed through Ernst's mind of being yanked hard as Niklas pulled him out from under a fallen horse. Madrid, 1809, the Peninsular Campaign. Niklas had ridden back for him, grabbed his arm, and hauled him up into the saddle. Even now, all these years later, in the drafty medieval palace of the Berleburg aristocracy, in this newly golden room, Ernst put a hand to his throat. Without Niklas, the Spanish rebels bearing down on them would have cut his throat. He twisted his hand slightly, as if striking a thoughtful pose.

"The king has no further patience with traitors and radicals." The old marshal's voice rose even higher. "And about time!"

If I closed my eyes, I would think him a woman, thought Ernst. Out loud, he said, "It was the shock of Waterloo, I suppose. I mean, Napoleon losing, who could have imagined it?"

Marshal Franz snorted. He had not intended to invite a mere constable's opinion.

The third man in the room spoke, a man Ernst had never seen before. "Would the noble family like us to see to it..." He paused, glancing at Ernst, recalling the name. "This 'Hans'?"

Marshal Franz stamped his impatience. "Not now! Find the Würzburg turncoat before he goes back to university. Then bring in the Kästners, father and son. Some idiots still think the father a hero. Exactly what the king wants eliminated. Get the turncoat, the Schmidt boy, Werner, then wait until more men arrive."

The marshal turned to go and then stopped. "Say," he asked Ernst, "Isn't there another Kästner boy? How old?"

"Thirteen," Ernst lied.

"Sons," said the big man softly, "inherit the sins of the father."

"Thirteen," Ernst repeated in the same mild tone, as if he had not been heard.

"A child," ruled the marshal. "It shall not be said we kill children." He dismissed them with a wave, and Ernst and the stranger backed out of the golden chamber.

In the hallway, Ernst asked, "When do we expect reinforcements?"

"A week, more likely two."

That evening, down the hill from the palace and a day before the murder, Niklas Kästner went to find Hans, which, he expected, would mean breaking up a fight. He could hear the sounds of it already, near der Biergarten, the beer garden. On this cold night, street lanterns were already lit, and when Niklas stepped between them and the alley, he cast a long shadow over three men.

"Hallo, Pop," said one of them. "Want to help us finish this guy off?" Hans was wearing a lopsided grin, his usual melancholy forgotten.

Niklas did not recognize the big man sprawled on the ground, but when that creature reached for his son's ankle, Niklas stepped on the outstretched hand, pinning it to the ground.

"A friend of yours?" he asked Hans.

"Nein. A drinking buddy."

Niklas grabbed the victim by the arm and pulled him to his feet. "What did you do to deserve this?" he asked. If Niklas was not mistaken, that thickness at the stranger's waistband was a knife or a pistol. *Why*, Niklas wondered, *has he not used it?*

"He got fresh with Greta," Hans said.

"She's ain't but a serving girl," the stranger said. He was complaining, but his voice was soft, almost friendly.

"Don't," Niklas said, "insult our women."

"And that one more a child than a woman," Hans said.

"And next time," said Niklas, "don't pick a fight with the biggest men in town." Besides Hans, the second largest man in town was in the alley, Berleburg's blacksmith, Katrina's cousin Sepp, who always smelled of smoke no matter how well he washed. If Sepp had been doing the hitting, the man on the ground would not be getting up. The blacksmith lacked Hans's subtlety.

"I'm just here to referee, Claus," Sepp said, who always called Niklas by his childhood nickname.

"Es ist meine Schuld, It's my fault," said the stranger. "I was out of line."

Hans considered him a moment and then stuck out his hand. "Kästner. Hans Kästner."

"Kästner?" asked the big man, looking from Hans to Niklas. "Ah. Kästner." His soft, friendly voice had something else in it this time.

"And you?" asked Niklas.

The big man mumbled a name. Niklas looked at Hans, but Hans only shrugged. The moment of inattention was all the stranger needed. He shook off Niklas's grip and ran.

"Let him go," said Hans. Something about the way Hans turned to look at the fleeing man, a certain grace in the movement, suddenly reminded Niklas of Angelika, who had died giving birth to Hans all those years ago.

"You know him from university?"

"Never saw him before tonight."

"Must be from around here, though," said Sepp. "Because he asked after the Schmidts."

"Horst?"

"No. The boy, Werner. He's home from university."

Niklas's eyebrows flicked upward, but no one noticed. He spoke to Hans. "Come away. Supper waits, and your mother wants you home."

Since the wars, Niklas had become a respectable merchant. His courtly manners and frequent trips to Paris impressed the ladies and filled his shop with customers, especially when they caught sight of Katrina, who had become the most Parisian-like lady in Berleburg.

Despite the occasional whispers, few of these ladies dreamt that the king was right. Niklas had in fact never forgotten the cry of the French Republic. He belonged to the secret German Democracy Movement, a branch of the underground International Society for the Rights of Man, which fought the restoration of the monarchies. Its demands sounded reasonable enough, except to the Prussian king. As the years passed and liberty grew ever dearer to Niklas, it became anathema to the king.

The next morning, as sunlight poured into the Kästner family kitchen, fourteen-year-old Amalie blinked against the light and asked, "Where is everyone?"

Her mother's arch look was all Amalie needed to know she had overslept.

"Your father's at the shop. Hans went to work with Sepp at the smithy, and Will is mucking out the stables. When he comes in, give him and the young ones some oatmeal."

Amalie saw the steam rising from the oatmeal pot. "Can they have honey and raisins in it? I mean, please, Mama? Lisette won't touch it otherwise, and if she doesn't, little Jakob won't either."

"Yes. Just for today." Katrina Kästner settled her winter bonnet on her head and considered her daughter. Amalie was barely fourteen, still shapeless, with a pleasant enough face, if a bit plain. Right now, she was rubbing the sleep out of her eyes, but she could be counted on to take care of the children and kitchen. Amalie was a middle child, sensible, competent, and undemanding, never a problem.

A moment later, Katrina closed the heavy oak door behind her and stepped into a beatific winter scene, taking Old Kästner Lane downhill toward the river. All of Berleburg's streets slanted away from the palace like rays of the sun, fell downhill to the Odeborn creek and turned into the market square. Even now, in February, the center of the stream ran free, water rushing by, smelling of greenness, past banks thick with cattails rimed with ice. A rooster crowed as the town awakened, stoked its fires, fried its sausage.

In the civilized world of 1836, with the wars almost forgotten, the kindly people of Berleburg would have scoffed at the idea that evil was abroad in the world. In the ancient town, pinned down by its church, all the good children went to bed with full stomachs, and on any summer's evening, the comforting sounds of a fiddle might be heard through open windows. Berleburg was picturesque on its worst day, and on this bright winter morning, the half-timbered, slate-shingled homes and cobblestone streets sparkled like a snow-frosted Eden.

Katrina was on her way to the Kästner Dry Goods Shop with a lunch basket on her arm—ham rolled up in pastry, for she intended to help her husband sort through the woolens newly arrived. Niklas had gone at dawn, but she stayed to set everything at home in motion. This morning, she could not help but feel pleased. The Kästner family was well fed, something that could not be said of every family in the Germanies, and their fireside was the hub of a thriving household, more than anything she and Niklas once thought possible. They were now a handsome young family, respectable and comfortable, nay, even admired, all the turmoil of the Napoleonic era far behind them, every waking hour filled with the troubles and complications of keeping hearth and home safe and comfortable.

As she walked along, the tip of Katrina's green shawl flew loose. She caught it and tucked it in, recalling Niklas's raised eyebrows when she brought it home. A silk-and-cotton import from Paisley, Scotland, it was so admirable, so expensive. She had gone even further, snatching from the store the green-dyed leather gloves she now wore, and a green silk ribbon now sewn onto her winter bonnet and tied in a fashionably loose bow.

"Berleburg's best example of Parisian fashion," he told her, his voice heavy with sarcasm, and when she looked pleased anyway, he admitted, "I suppose it's good for business." Nothing was as chic as this new jade green color. It was fitting that she should be the first to wear it here.

From the near end of the square, the blacksmith's hammer rang out and just beyond it, her friends, Günter and Addie Erlinger, were in their bakery. She caught a whiff of fresh brötchen and wished she could stay,

but Kästner Dry Goods lay waiting, filled with the linens, silks, and woolens she loved and Niklas counted.

CHAPTER 3

NEAR MISS

In her moonlit bedroom, Katrina heard her father's voice as clearly as if he were living: "War hurts a man, e'en when it leaves him alive." He had said long before all of this happened, even before Katrina and Niklas married, and if she had not been so hard-headed, she might have taken it to heart, and her life would have been very different. But she did not, and now Niklas proved the truth of it again when he hit her in the middle of the night.

She sat up in bed, rubbing her shoulder. "Mein Gott, Niklas, you startled me."

"What have I done?" he moaned, his breath coming hard.

Katrina saw Hans at the doorway, candlestick in hand, its flame flickering off every near surface, not reaching into the corners. She raised a hand, palm flat toward him, and held it there, knowing he would understand. It was not the first time Hans had been awakened by his father crying out in the dark or her own panicked yelp.

"He'll be all right," she told Hans. "Did he wake the children?"

"I heard little Jakob start to cry, but Amalie's got him settled."

"Good night, then. Thank you." Hans was Katrina's stepson, but she was the only mother he had ever known, and they were devoted to each other. He could see that she was unhurt and his father was returning to his right mind. Hans pinched out the flame and padded away, retreating down the dark, narrow hallway, leaving them in peace.

A moment earlier, Katrina had awakened to see Niklas kneeling over her, his face furious and his fist raised to repeat the blow he had just given her. It was the dream again. Then he sank to one side, shaking in panic.

When his breath came back to him, he told her about it. "The call came in the middle of the night: 'Cossacks! Cossacks! Up! To arms, men.' I couldn't move or see clearly. The fire had gone out, and I was cold down to the bone. I struggled to rise and grab a weapon. I heard the barn door splinter and crash, muskets and pistols firing at close range, the screams of men. I was trapped somehow and could not seem to get to my feet. I felt a grip on my shoulder and with all my strength I swung, smashing my fist into a cossack."

"Ah," she grimaced. "I was a Russian again."

"Ja, only I didn't see you; I saw the Russian, and I tried to hit him. Suddenly I heard you calling me, and then I did not know at all what was going on, and I froze. My eyes began to clear, and you came into focus."

She was listening carefully, still wary, massaging her shoulder. It had been a hard punch, but not nearly the blow he thought, sleep-drugged as he was. She lay down again, pulled him to her and tugged the duvet over them both.

"That boy next to me—" he began again.

"Hush now," she said. "It's all right." She had heard often enough about the boy next to him who was killed by the cossacks and about the half-crazed lieutenant who froze to death that night and about the horse killed in the raid and which became their breakfast.

"It's all right," she told him again, and she kept repeating it. But even with her voice and the warmth of her body and even as his eyes told him they were safe in their bedroom in the house where he grew up, he shivered with remembered cold.

The dream revealed what soldiering had cost him, unfathomable horrors appearing in his sleep, so that he gave a convulsive jump or twitched or muttered hoarsely, inarticulately. Sometimes, his moans became long shuddering sobs or slid into incoherent curses. Sometimes, like tonight, he was up and slashing before he knew where he was.

As sleep beckoned, Niklas jerked awake. Katrina murmured reassurances and fell asleep again. He brushed a strand of hair from her cheek and blushed in shame at things he had never told her. Then he was hot with anger that he, when a child not yet Hans's age, hardly older than Will, should have had to endure such horrors. In the morning when he looked exhausted, he admitted it. "I knew I would not dare close my eyes for the rest of the night."

Niklas's years in the army had been full of near misses, and that particular one haunted him, but it was not as if he spent every moment thinking about army life. Quite the opposite. "Nothing, nothing," he would insist if ever anyone sympathized with the scar across his face. Or he would make a joke: "At least I got something out of it to improve my looks."

He was a rare bird to be alive at all, and he knew it. When he finally made it back to Berleburg after Waterloo, it was the strangest thing: he became distrusted and despised by those who had once admired him. He swore an oath then and there to be thankful for any morning he woke up alive.

She said, as she always did, "Maybe, someday, there will be no monsters."

"I hope so," he said. To himself, he repeated what he had come to believe, that he deserved an inch of ground on which to live and die free. And a good night's sleep.

Niklas often left for the shop before Hans came down for breakfast. Their son was, by now, the town's tallest, strongest, and handsomest man, not that he had the slightest idea of that distinction. For years, he had listened to his father's tales of army life with ill-concealed envy. It made him undertake military-style training with fierce determination, win shooting contests repeatedly, and set himself extreme physical challenges, like holding an axe at arm's length for longer than anyone else in Berleburg.

Nicklas had driven both Hans and Will through many practices, teaching them how to handle pistol, rifle, and sword, how to hunt, ride, and fight. He taught them how to read a compass, how to disappear into the woods, and how to build and sail a raft. He taught them never to carry a weapon they were unwilling or unable to use, one that an opponent might seize and turn on them. He taught them strategies of hand-to-hand combat: how to handle a shiv and how to anticipate one hidden in a boot or sleeve. One must be not as good as any opponent, he taught them, but faster, smarter, more skillful, and more ruthless.

Will received this military training with his typical vigor, showing promise, especially, as a swordsman. He might not be as quick at the parry and thrust as he liked to think, but if challenged, a peculiar expression darkened his eyes, narrowing them to a degree of determination that made others hesitate to oppose him. Hand-to-hand combat became one of his "enthusiasms," as well as star-gazing and mechanical inventions. At fifteen, girls were Will's deepest enthusiasm. Although he was still a skinny boy, pink-faced and not especially impressive, he had a headful of gorgeous, untamable blond curls—sure to be a source of trouble for years to come—and unflagging optimism, even when unwarranted.

Sepp had laughed with pleasure when he saw Will's steam engine model. "He's an inventor—perfect for these grand new days," Sepp said, and when Niklas looked surprised, Sepp explained, "Well, with a good hand that can make most anything, an inventive mind is what's needed. He's got one," he said, clapping Will on the shoulders, "a mind for the future and all that's coming."

Each of the Kästners had something of Will's joie de vivre, so hardly a day passed without laughter. They teased, they joked, they tickled the little children, and they worked willingly, often falling into bed exhausted. However, they became a sadder, quieter family after the Summer of Sickness. In 1832, as illness after illness swept through the Germanies, the house was kept hot and dark even at noon, draperies drawn, sheets tacked up where light peeked in. Katrina moved quietly from one to another, applying cool, wet cloths to fevered foreheads, lifting a child to ease a cough, cleaning up after them. Amalie, though only ten that year, recovered quickly and became her mother's right hand. Sometimes, a quarantine ribbon was stretched across their front door, but even when it was not, no one visited. Through the worst of it, Niklas closed up shop and stayed home.

The three youngest worried them most. Jan Emil, at eight the picture of his father, was a bright, thoughtful boy, the sort of child who sometimes said things far beyond his years. Lisette was six and likely the prettiest child in the Germanies, delighting all with her blueberry-blue eyes and halo-like blonde hair, and little Jacob was an infant in arms. All across the continent that summer, graves filled with small victims of whooping cough, diphtheria, scarlet fever, measles, typhoid fever. In the hills north of Berleburg, the Angel of Death sprinkled smallpox, and cholera swept through Europe for the first time. They were lucky, she was told that summer at Jan Emil's funeral, to lose only one child to The Plague among Children. "Lucky" had never been so cruel a word.

CHAPTER 4

BRIGANDS AND THIEVES

On that particular winter morning when murder was to stalk the streets of Berleburg, the cobblestones were charming but treacherous, notorious for twisting ankles and even worse when slicked with ice. Katrina, however, knew exactly how to dance along, so without a pause and almost in a pirouette, she turned at the river and swept into the town square. And stopped. Something was going on at the far side of the square, a melee of some kind. She stared, and then she heard a loud crack, and at the same moment, someone grabbed her, and a hand was clapped over her mouth.

"Don't scream, Mama." It was Hans. "Come with me. Hurry." He seized her arm and whisked her along the street quickly enough that her feet barely brushed the cobblestones. There was a clatter of a horse in its traces running wild, and she felt a spike of fear. Then the hoofbeats slowed, and she thought she heard Niklas's voice calming the horse. Inside the smithy, her cousin Sepp was staring through a crack at what was going on outside. He put one finger to his lips and motioned for them to look.

She saw someone lying in the street, his head in a puddle. *He must have slipped on the cobblestones,* she thought. *Someone has come to his aid, a big man—a Good Samaritan,* she thought. The fallen man lay still, making no attempt to rise. The big Samaritan reached for him, grabbing hold of his coat, lifting him a little, and just then the morning sun peeked over a rooftop, and she saw the face of the big Samaritan It was not someone from the Berleburg, but a stranger.

The sun moved an inch further, and something bright shone at the stranger's belt. He pulled a packet of papers from the fallen man's coat, dropped him back to the pavement and stood up. The bright something at his waist caught the light again—a pistol. The puddle glinted red. Someone called out, and now she saw another man waiting at the entrance to an alley. In a moment the two of them were gone, disappearing down the alley. *That puddle,* she thought. *That red puddle is blood.*

"That's Werner on the ground," Hans said.

"We think he's been killed," Sepp added.

"Werner? Werner Schmidt? Your cousin?" she said, incredulous.

"Yes."

Both men were studying her.

"Are you hurt?" Hans said, standing back and looking his stepmother up and down.

"No! Not at all. I was on my way to the shop when this happened. Where is your father?"

Sepp coughed. "That's him as caught the runaway."

A nervous pony hitched to an old barouche was breathing hard, stamping its hooves and blowing steam into the frosty air. Its reins had been thrown around a horse rail so recently that they were still swinging.

"Oh, oh, oh," she said. "Werner? How did this happen?" Werner Schmidt was her sister's boy, a few years younger than Hans, dark-haired, lithe and handsome, a university student.

"It was all so fast. They were waiting for him," said Hans, "but we didn't know that. They were innocent-like, warming their hands at the fire barrel."

"We didn't know anything was going on until we heard the shot," said Sepp.

A shot. The loud crack she had heard. "Who? Brigands? Thieves?" She looked for the attackers again, but they were gone.

Hans glanced at Sepp as if reluctant to say more. "They knew who he was. They were after the papers."

"Werner!" Katrina was shaking. Then she asked again, "Where's your father?"

Even now, twenty years after the wars, Niklas was still extraordinarily powerful, but on this day, he was a private citizen, no longer in the cavalry, mounted, armed and ready. The silver-handled sword he had carried to Moscow was hanging over the fireplace at home, neglected, unsharpened, a prop for war stories told only to the family.

The market square was empty, people having melted away into shops and around corners, doors closed, shades drawn. Sepp latched the back door. "Ernst will say good riddance."

"Ja," said Hans, "He'll call Werner a seditionist, a troublemaker, an enemy of the king. He'll accuse him of belonging to the German Democracy Movement."

Sepp answered Katrina: "Niklas saw it too. He was just coming out of the butcher shop when it happened."

"The butcher shop?"

"Yes. That's where he went after, too."

Hans grunted. "Rudy."

Sepp nodded.

"What was he doing at the butcher shop?" she asked, but neither answered.

Footsteps rang on the cobblestones, and Katrina looked at Sepp in panic. "Who?"

Hans grabbed her arm. "Here. In the stall. Until we know." There were two stalls for horses waiting to be shoed, both empty this morning. He held a gate open, and she ducked inside, saw a hay bale in the corner and sat, as quiet as a mouse, her arms wrapped tightly around herself, as if her shaking might be heard.

Hans disappeared out the back as two men and two boys hurried in, talking in low voices, glad to be off the street. First was Young Miller, a burly man with a bushy mustache and habitual scowl. His father, the Old Miller, found a half-barrel as close to the heat of the forge as he dared and sat down on the edge. Two shop boys plopped themselves cross-legged on the dirt floor.

"Suppose the family knows yet?"

"How could they? It's out there pretty far, where the Schmidts live."

They fell silent, thinking of the sad news to be delivered. The younger boy looked as if he might cry. The other juggled an acorn from hand to hand.

"Who were they?"

"No one we know." The Young Miller looked at Sepp, who shook his head.

This was not exactly true. Both Sepp and Hans had recognized the shooter as the stranger they met at the Biergarten, who leered at Greta and whom they had taken out to the alley and beaten. The one who had asked them about where Werner Schmidt lived.

"Kästner was there, wouldn't you know it."

"Ja. But Kästner himself, I don't imagine it bothered him, all he's seen and done." The Old Miller turned to the shop boys. "You wouldn't think it to look at him, but he took himself off to Napoleon's wars when he was no more than a whelp of a boy like you two and nearly got himself killed. Was in the Light Horse— 'unstoppable,' they were called."

"Until Waterloo stopped them hard." The Young Miller chuckled, and his father snorted in agreement.

"But whyever did he join Napoleon's army?" asked the tearful boy, who was too young to remember being French. He shuddered to think of going off with Napoleon, the Mad Corsican.

"It wasn't as if he had much choice, was it now?" the Old Miller said. "In those days, the prince himself had to give his guard to Napoleon."

"Claus could sit a horse better than the rest of us," Sepp added.

"Ja, he was a good horseman, good at everything: shoot, sail, hunt, ride, fight. But he paid a price—that scar on his face—he won't say how he got it." Here the Old Miller paused and looked meaningfully at his young listeners. He raised an eyebrow. "But there's a man who's seen a lot. Done a lot, too."

The older boy elbowed the younger until he came out with it: "Has he ever killed a man, Herr Kästner, I mean?"

"Bah!" the Old Miller spat the answer. "The only question is how many."

Katrina put her fist to her lips. She was not surprised to hear the Millers put Niklas in the middle of this. She knew some wondered whether Niklas had become an atheist radical in the wars, for all his being seen in a church pew. Most found his having been a soldier, however inescapable at the time, regrettably violent and something of an embarrassment.

"Claus ain't so bad," Sepp said, as he turned to the forge. "At least he came home after Waterloo."

The Young Miller spat in disgust. "Where else was he supposed to go?" He was leaning against the stall door, using a pocketknife to clean under his fingernails. On the other side, Katrina could barely breathe.

Sepp Beckmann picked up a thin iron rod, turning it over in his hands.

"An eel spear?" the Old Miller guessed.

"Ja," said the blacksmith. "They'll be running soon." He laid it on the hot coals.

Once a war is over, Katrina thought, *no man is forgotten faster than a soldier. Unless it's a sailor.*

"That poor Schmidt boy," the Old Miller said, shaking his head.

"Except he was a traitor," said his son, whose face was set hard at the thought.

Sepp pulled out the iron rod, its tip glowing, and picked up a small hammer. "Now you," he said to the older shop boy. "If they stop you and ask questions, you don't know nothing." His muscles seemed to bulge at the thought, and the older boy nodded and shut his mouth in a tight line.

Sepp began shaping the iron rod, his hammer ringing, metal on metal. It was enough of a hint for the Millers, who made their goodbyes, the boys following them out. Sepp watched them go, paused his hammering, and said quietly, "You can come out now." He went to the back door and motioned Hans in.

"Well," Sepp said, "while you two were out of the way, I saw Claus get into Erlinger's. They closed up, but you can bet they'll be open for you. Get on over there. He'll be worried about you."

Katrina took her cousin's big, rough hands in hers. "Danke, my dear Seppsi."

"Geh, go on," he said, but his face softened, and he almost smiled. They would never see each other again, but in that moment, neither of them knew it.

CHAPTER 5

YOU MUST REMEMBER

In a minute, Katrina and Hans reached Erlinger's bakery, where the door opened noiselessly, and they slid inside. Niklas put an arm around them and guided them to an inglenook where they could see out a window.

Addie Erlinger came over with a pot of coffee. She set cups and saucers down and poured. "Claus told us about it." She nodded at the window.

"I don't think they followed me," Niklas assured them. "Where have you been?"

"I grabbed Mother and took her to the smithy."

"I was going to the shop." Katrina turned to Addie. "Our nephew was killed, one of Horst and Berthe's boys," She heard the shot again, like an echo she could not escape.

"Claus told me."

"Then the Millers came in," said Hans, "and a couple of boys. We stayed out of sight and waited for them to leave."

Katrina looked with surprise at the basket on her arm, unable to believe that she had not dropped it. "Look at this!" She said this to no one in particular.

"Was he a criminal?" Addie asked. "This boy who was killed?"

Hans snorted.

"Werner was a nephew of ours," said Katrina. "You must remember him. In your Edzard's class."

Günter Erlinger appeared from the back, hands white with flour. "Mind if I snuff the candles?"

"I wish you would."

The two men, Günter and Niklas, were not unlike—both broad-shouldered, with thick hair and full chin beards. Günter was the fleshier of the two, as befits a baker, while Niklas had never lost the trimness and posture of a military man.

"The king? The prince?" Günter asked. It was a statement as much as a question.

Katrina stared. *What do these men know?*

"Either. Both. Not that I said so." Niklas had not taken his eyes from the window. He shook his arm, dropped his dagger onto the table, and then slid it back into his boot. It was a kinzhal, a Russian dagger taken long ago in Moscow from a man he killed. Katrina wondered why he had been carrying a dagger on such an ordinary day.

Hans shook his head in disbelief. "They're here. In Berleburg."

"I thought the prince—" Günter began.

"No. Either he couldn't stop it or he wouldn't."

"Prince Albrecht?" Katrina was astounded. "You were a favorite of his father's. Will they desert you now?"

Niklas looked at her with something odd in his eyes.

Was it anger? Or pity?

"He's irrelevant," Niklas said. "We were part of France then, subjects of Emperor Napoleon, not King Wilhelm. A different country, a different ruler."

All those years ago, Katrina thought, *old Prince Albrecht, father of the prince now residing in Berleburg's palace, sent Niklas off to war. The old prince had never expected to set eyes on him again. No one did, except perhaps she herself, a child too young to know better.*

When at last, Napoleon lost, the Prussians took over. And now, apparently, to the authorities, a body lying in a puddle of blood on Berleburg's cobblestones was not evidence of the murder of a citizen of Prussia or the unfortunate death of a promising young intellectual, or even the sad end of a loving son, but a simple matter of silencing troublemakers, maintaining order, and damping down the resistance.

"There was a second man, a driver?" Günter asked.

"I didn't recognize him," said Niklas, looking at Hans.

"Nor I. Maybe a friend from the university, maybe hired."

"He jumped off the barouche and escaped."

"Through Rudy's?"

"Ja."

Katrina looked from Hans to Niklas. For her, unwilling witness to murder, nothing was simple. She looked up at Addie and said, "I began this day with joy, with no sense of caution—"

Addie did not even try to answer her.

Katrina wrapped her fingers around the cup to keep the quiver of her hands from showing. Berthe's boy lay dead, Hans seemed to know something about it, and she had a sinking feeling Niklas was involved, his nightmares coming to life in a most horrible way.

Hours later, after the great relief of finding all quiet at home, after the usual commotion of supper and putting children to bed, Katrina paid a visit to the Zimmermann's. Ernst was not home, but Anna Zimmermann was happy to chat. "There is no danger to any of us," she said. "I can assure you of that." She gave a little flip of her hand, as if the violence of the day had not happened, and lit another candle.

By the time Katrina made her goodbyes, the stars were out. She stepped gingerly onto cobblestones silvered by starlight on ice and hurried home. When a night watchman approached, she stepped into a shadow and waited silently for him to pass, listening for his footsteps to fade into the distance, sorting out the sound from her own heartbeat. *Surely he's harmless*, she thought, *but on a day like this, that began with murder, who knows?* She started forward again, slipping quickly through the darkness to the ancient, half-timbered house at the end of Old Kästner Lane, where she gave the stout oak door a quick rap.

Niklas opened it a crack, grabbed her arm and pulled her in.

"What took you so long?"

"I couldn't let the Zimmermanns think I was in a hurry."

"I sent you into the lion's den." He was still shocked that she had talked him into it.

"Well, I'm safe and home now." She worked at the straps of her boots, shook them off and straightened up.

"What did you find out?"

"We were right—what happened today, the murder..." Her voice caught, and she coughed to hide it. "It was Werner—Horst and Berthe's oldest, from Edzard's class, a student at Würzburg."

"Ernst ought to watch out. Horst will go crazy, sue him or more likely, go after him with a pitchfork."

"Anna says Ernst is waiting for more men—a dozen, maybe more, secret police—to root out the disloyal, she says, and enforce something called 'The Sixty Articles.'" She saw no surprise in Niklas's expression and felt a spike of anger. It was a mystery why he did not tell her everything. "He's not a bad man, Ernst is, but..."

"Your 'not a bad man' will follow orders." Katrina could hear the bitterness in his voice.

"I'll give you that," she said. "The murder today may have been a mistake or at least unfortunate or premature, but Ernst was not sorry for it. Anna sounded like he was crowing about it." She paused, swallowing hard, not wanting to give way to tears. "The murderers were an advance party here to ferret out the Resistance, when—last night maybe—they overheard Werner saying he was going back to Würzburg University today."

Niklas nodded. Würzburg was a hotbed of revolution. "Which forced their hand."

"Ernst said they had to stop him getting back. But the papers they found on him—that was an unexpected coup."

Niklas winced. "We have to get Hans out of here."

"But you can't think...Ernst would never..."

He gave her that odd look again, and when she spoke it was in anger. "But you grew up with Ernst! You were comrades in arms. You saved his life!"

"Ernst and the prince," said Niklas, "need to show the crown they have no favorites, they allow no escape."

She spoke slowly. "Ernst would lose his position if he favored you. He has taken the loyalty oath."

"Yes." Then he asked, "How soon are the new men coming?" In the face of this outrage, this threat to the sanctity of their house and home, his voice was flat, almost casual, and this somehow made her even angrier.

"Two weeks. Oh, and not in uniform—they will be independent operatives, secret police."

He grunted.

As if he expected this too! She thought.

Niklas rose and paced the room. "A fortnight. They will be looking for young men like our boys."

"Well, Hans, yes, as a university student. You say we have to get him out of here? But surely not Will? He's only fifteen!"

"They'll think him better off in the army, separated from the influence of an 'Old Revolutionary.' People are too polite to call me that to my face, but the authorities will."

Katrina shuddered at what Niklas already knew: for him, if they arrested him, there was only prison, the gallows, or a knife in the back.

"What," she asked, "was in the papers Werner carried?"

He looked away. He shrugged.

She could hardly breathe. *Hans and Will in immediate danger, Niklas thought an instigator! The police would come for all three of them.*

"If we wait—" she said, but the images flooding in stopped her tongue: Hans with a bullet through his heart, Will bayonetted. *This very day, I have seen Werner killed, and over the years, I have heard Niklas's war ravings.*

"If we wait," he finished her thought, "it could be too late. This is no time for hesitation, for faintness of heart. There is not a moment to be lost."

"Ah," she said. *He has decided. My opinion is not required.*

"A man without an army," Niklas explained, "has two choices: flee or switch sides, swearing allegiance to the king of the moment."

A log shifted with a thud. They startled at the sound and saw sparks fly up. *His decision was half-made before we left the bakery this morning,* she thought with surprise, *but now it is certain.*

"Hans must go tomorrow." He hesitated.

"Or tonight?" she guessed.

"We can," he said deliberately, "wait until tomorrow, to give him daylight to get a safe distance away. It won't be easy to get him to go. It means he has to abandon the Resistance."

"Anna said the men were forced into action today. I think Ernst wants to wait for the reinforcements."

"Probably," he said. "It will take them a little time to regroup. That gives us a chance to get Hans away and a window of time for ourselves."

"Anna bragged about how Ernst would root out traitors and rid Berleburg of the stench of republican France at last."

"You understand what this means, don't you?" he asked. "We have to go, too. How we might feel about it does not matter in the least."

CHAPTER 6

DAS NEUE LAND

MONDAY 8 FEBRUARY

"Mama?" A timid voice. It was Amalie at the foot of the stairs, with a whimpering Jakob in her arms. "He's had a night terror, and now Lisette is up, too."

"You go on to bed," Katrina said, reaching for the little boy. "If you go back to sleep, so will Lisette." The three youngest slept in one room, and most nights, Amalie took care of the others. Katrina settled the boy over her shoulder where she could hear his heart beating against hers and rubbed his back.

"Mama, Mama, Mama," he crooned, as he lay his head on her shoulder.

The clock on the thick oak mantel chimed the hour, and she was surprised to see Niklas smile. There, in an honored place by the clock, was Gottfried Duden's *Das Neue Land*, and she realized the Old Country with all its culture and charms was already racing away from him. Army life, in spite of its nightmares, had bitten him with wanderlust, the desire to turn a corner and discover something utterly new. Duden's book described America's Missouri River Valley in that way, as a utopia, a wide-open frontier with cheap land, fertile soil and low taxes, or as Duden said, "too pleasant, …too strange, too fabulous to believe."

"I hope Herr Duden got it right," she said. "Or is it all tall tales? With slavery in the country, how civilized can it be?"

"In half the country," Niklas corrected her, which, considering his fervor on this point, surprised her. Niklas belonged to Berleburg's Antislavery Society, which believed slavery a sin. Most of Berleburg agreed. In this, Niklas was far from controversial or radical.

"The Antislavery Society is a cover for the German Democracy Movement." He was relieved to confess this.

"What?"

"That's why we meet here so rarely. I wanted to keep you innocent of the Resistance."

"Innocent of it? And yet here we are, and I'm in the middle of this as much as you are." She stroked Jakob's hair. "We are all involved, down to this innocent child." She shivered.

"Do you need a shawl?" he asked.

"I must write to Berthe." She handed him a very sleepy little Jakob.

"I'll put him in our bed." Niklas disappeared up the stairs.

There, in a house that had sheltered Kästners for generations, she was angry enough to cry. *If all he means is to protect me, why does it feel like an insult and a betrayal?* Chilled and feverish, excited and afraid and more than a little unmoored, she saw her life among friends and family unraveling. *Is Hans in the Resistance? Apparently. God forgive Niklas if he's dragged Will into it.* In the midst of all this, the sickening sound of that gunshot kept echoing in her ears.

Katrina was folding the letter of condolence when Niklas returned.

"You three should go tonight," she said. "Ride out of here now. If you stay and are caught up in another terror, or the boys conscripted, I should never forgive myself, and neither would you."

"*Ja*, I've considered it, but I think we can all get to America. France would be much easier, but we might not be allowed in, even with a passport."

"France is so unsettled. We would be persona non grata, chased out next year, if not this."

"In the New Land, we might have to live in the wilderness, among savages."

"That," she said, "would be almost as bad as living among the English."

Neither spoke for a moment, and then Niklas said, "If we are to stay alive, here's how." He began listing important things to do.

She was still distracted: *Can we really do this—leave everyone behind, never to see them again? Or has all my courage been just brave talk? I will never brag again,* she vowed, *but wherever we go, I will keep my family well fed, my house clean, and my garden tended.*

"Sometimes," he said, "the way to look like you are not running is to walk."

She did not understand. "We have two weeks..."

"Perhaps. Consider using one week—or even less—to depart in an 'unhurried' way."

"Ah. All the while packing as fast as we can."

He nodded. "And selling. We must sell the shop, the carriage, the horses, to have some money to ease the way."

"And secure a passport. Do you think it's possible?"

He shrugged. "It was possible yesterday. I'll have to go to Arnsberg for it."

"If they want to be rid of us, they might not care. We might be free to go."

"We should be so lucky."

"At least we would be together, and what happiness might befall us in America?" Not to be pushy, she added, "Or in France, for that matter."

He knew they would become strangers the moment they left, with no friends or family to speak for them or give them food or shelter. They would be exposed, even the little ones, to the wrath and cruelty of the secret police. To choose America meant facing the dangers of the sea as well.

He paused and looked at her closely. "You and the children might be safer here. Are you willing to risk the journey?"

She was silent for a moment. It was hard to grasp being here alone with the younger children. "Ja. But no more secrets. I must know what you know."

"Agreed," said Niklas.

"You may think you're protecting me, but the opposite is true. Your secrets endanger me and the whole family."

"Ja, ja, ja."

"Is Hans involved?"

"He knows that I am. What he does at Jena, he never says. It hardly matters. The king wants strong young men in his army, not in university."

"What about Will?" Her voice shook.

"He's as innocent as you are—or were until this evening." He paused and looked away.

"What is it?"

"Nothing. Just the image of the first man I killed. A Spaniard. When I pulled my sword out of him, he slid down the wall behind him and sat on the ground looking at me, surprised that a pup like me could be the death of him. I was only a year older than Will."

She took his hand. "More soldiers have had to kill others than not."

"Aye, but the first time sticks in the mind." He winced.

"We've done right by the children to keep such horrors, such torments, from them."

"Speak of the devil," he said, seeing Will poke his head into the room.

"Mama, sorry to bother, but could you come help?" He grinned in a lopsided way, wondering if he had overheard his dear, delicate mother saying, "whores."

"What's so funny?"

"Nothing, nothing at all." He made his smile disappear. "Hans knocked over my model in his sleep, and we need to sop things up." He looked at the ceiling and was glad not to see water leaking through. Will was always wild for some enthusiasm. He had given up star-gazing and gone on to tinkering with models of steam engines.

"Papa, this is why I need my own room. I need the freedom to work."

"Not now, Will."

"I'll help you get things cleaned up," said Katrina. "Did Hans damage it?"

"Nein, he just kicked it over. It's not as if," Will murmured, "I have a proper case for it."

When Katrina came back downstairs, Niklas had his old sword in his hands and was thinking about how best to sharpen it. "We have to do it again, Katrina—keep them safe, I mean. I don't want these boys in another of the king's wars. Especially Will."

They both knew Hans would make an enviable soldier—any sergeant would drool at his size and strength—but Will! Bright, energetic, and friendly, with a mind for tinkering and flirting and making money, he would be utterly destroyed by war, even if he should happen to come home alive.

"But we should not go to France."

"Nein. America it is."

"And none but we two should know the danger we are in. We must shield the children."

"From this instant on," he said, "we must bend every effort to make our escape as quickly and quietly as possible, before anyone is the wiser."

"Oh!" she said suddenly. "What if we have another child? Where will it be christened?"

"Katrina," he said, "there's no time for such questions. We must make our escape as quickly and quietly as possible, before anyone is the wiser."

Later, tucked in bed, she could not sleep for thinking. *Niklas might apologize, but he will be thrilled. The older boys will delight in such an adventure; Amalie will be thoughtful and perhaps pleased; the two little ones, Lisette and Jakob, will go where they are taken. At seven, Lisette will barely remember the country of her birth, and Jakob, at four, will not.* Now that Das Neue Land was about to be thrust upon them, she shivered at the enormity of it.

"And you with all your brave talk," she told herself. "Here's your chance." She knew a warning, even one as clear and dire as Anna Zimmermann's, would leave most men caught like a rabbit in a trap of their own indecision. Women watched helplessly while their husbands dithered. Niklas was not such a man. He would move quickly, and whatever was to come, she swore to be ready.

Niklas says a man must flee or switch sides, but there is a third way, Katrina thought, *one most men choose and all women are expected to. It is to hide, to ignore politics and find purpose and pleasure in family, work, nature, or God.* Women were expected to overlook inequalities, accept limitations and never look up, never consider the larger world. It was safer. It was easier. It was thought wiser. It required only wrapping one's own dreams and desires ever tighter and tighter, spiraling down inside until few knew how to be free or wished to be, even in their own minds. *Niklas will never hide, but will he ask it of me? Will he find it impossible to take us all? If I am slow or stupid,* she thought, *I might endanger us all. Until we are gone well away, every knock at the door might be the beginning of a disaster.*

CHAPTER 7

THE NECESSITY OF THIS

Katrina saw light through closed eyelids and thought it was a silver ribbon of dawn. But no, it flickered: Niklas was stoking the fireplace in their bedroom. Then she remembered. *Werner. America.* Today, daybreak was too late to begin.

Niklas saw her stir. "Mein Gott, Katrina, imagine it! Land for pennies! Or free!"

"Yes," she said, "Whispering 'liberty' here can get you hanged. There, people etch it onto their coins!"

They had talked like this months ago, before Werner Schmidt was killed, before Anna Zimmermann warned them unwittingly, before they agreed to leap into the future. But in the morning firelight, with the reality of it upon her, she said, "Tell me again the necessity of this. I hate to go. I admit it. It can't be helped—home is home, and there will never be another."

He was dressed already, and now he emptied a drawerful of clothing onto the bed. He looked at her sadly. "If we stay, I might be arrested and the boys conscripted." He chose three or four pieces, and then his fingers went mindlessly to his cheek, tracing the scar there. "Look what's already happening…"

"Yes, murder, coups, political repression—"

"It could end badly, very badly indeed, and there will be nothing fair about it. The masses won't rise up, and even if they did, the king's men will burn their houses or charge the cavalry against unarmed students and shopkeepers and farmers."

She agreed. "Are the Sixty Articles only an excuse to seize young men for the army?"

"Who knows? Only officials can read them."

"What? That makes no sense."

"There is also this," said Niklas. "Our childhood friends would have let me rot in the street. Without Hans's help, and him the smallest boy, I would have died. All the way home from Moscow I survived, Waterloo I survived, only to have my hometown treat me like a dog." The scar across his cheek became an angry red line. "I doubt we can save the country," he said at last, "but we can damn well save ourselves."

"And our sons."

"It takes money to fight wars, and the crown has all the money."

"Yes, and the taxes rise every day. The king thinks he has a right to everything." With a flash of insight, she added, "His kind always think they deserve everything."

Niklas snorted. "Even if a hundred peasants took up their cudgels and pitchforks, they could be demolished in fifteen minutes by a few well-trained, well-armed and mounted men." He did not say what he could have: *I have seen this done. I have done it.*

She nodded, "Don't you think many people right here in Berleburg who love the king and our own prince, as proud of the palace on the hill as if it were their own—"

"—I do not like to throw out the respect we have achieved in Berleburg over the years, but I cannot help but admire America's big, big market, the ways to make money almost unlimited—"

"—who blindly believe the old ways are always best and the rich are always right—"

"—Nothing but America will keep the boys out of another war."

"—And then there are those who would murder us in our beds if they were told to, don't you think?"

They had no answers for each other. Instead, he shrugged and said, "I'll bring in saddlebags. Wake him. Tell him to dress for riding."

A few moments later, a saddlebag was on the kitchen table, and Katrina was packing food as quickly as she could.

"What's all this?" Hans was dressed and carrying his coat.

Niklas had the second saddlebag in his hands. "Clothes for a few days," he said, handing the saddlebag to Hans. "Look, son, we have information that they may be coming for you next. I want you go now. Ride to Köln and wait for word from us."

Katrina handed him a scarf. "Do you have gloves?"

"Yes." He hesitated. "I love you, Mama."

She stood on tiptoes to kiss him on the cheek. "I love you, too. And listen to me. Trust no one."

Hans nodded. Niklas grabbed the saddlebag she had filled, took Hans by the arm and pulled him outside.

She could hear Hans's voice raised. "I'm not happy to desert my university studies, and I'm not afraid of being drafted, Father. In fact, I would rather like to have my own chance at army life."

"Don't you see," Niklas said quietly, "it could force us to take up arms against each other?"

There was a long pause. The voices faded as the two of them headed for the barn. She grabbed the edge of the table and sank into a chair, breathing hard, unable to grasp that he was gone.

A few hours later, Katrina made excuses to a neighbor about why she was washing on a Tuesday, and Niklas went to a cousin to bring home an extra trunk. As it happened, he was better prepared than even she knew. He had always been tight-fisted, an inclination handy at this moment. It was something he had learned as a soldier: as soon as you wave goodbye to your hometown, you need cash.

Niklas struck a deal with the neighboring shopkeeper for much less than their shop was worth, but he was glad to have it. He wrapped the gold in handkerchiefs so no one would hear a jingle in the sack he carried. Four of the new shawls from Paisley, carefully wrapped in muslin, came home with him, as well as his shoemaking tools and a brace of pistols in a fine wooden box, tucking tea and tobacco tins around them. Tea and tobacco could be a great comfort on a journey, and the paisley shawls would find buyers everywhere.

He sold their Schwarzwälder team to Günter Erlinger, with the understanding that he would hitch the Black Forest horses to the old Kastner berlin wagon and carry their trunks to Cologne.

"Cover the trunks," Niklas told Günter, "as if you were delivering grain. Afterwards, empty the barn of hay, straw and oats, tack and tools, the children's pony cart and everything else. It's all yours!" Niklas wrote out a receipt as proof of it, and Günter pocketed it.

He kept the buggy, freshly painted in blue with bright yellow on the spokes of the wheels and thin red stripes along the sides, but it still did not take long for a rumor to go flying around the neighborhood: the Kästners must be doing very well indeed. Imagine buying a new team and wagon at the same time!

"What is Günter thinking, to have loose lips?" Katrina whispered to Niklas.

He would not look at her, but shook his head, saying, "Günter is not all we could wish for. At least we can be happy the gossips guessed wrong. All the more reason to be quick."

"If nobody else talks, we should be all right, don't you think? Except I must tell Elizabet."

He nodded, and they separated, he back to work and she to the parlor, to write:

"My Dearest Cousin Elizabet,

If you love me, and I know you do, come to me as soon as ever you can.   Katrina"

After lunch, Katrina and Niklas were side by side, packing kitchen things. Niklas held up wooden spoons that had been his mother's. "She was so upset when I left with the regiment that first time. I couldn't understand."

"You were only Will's age, still imagining yourself immortal."

"It felt so right. To go off with the most powerful army in the world."

"By then, wasn't most of it from occupied territories like our duchy?"

"No, that was later. Besides, I never felt we were 'occupied territory.' We had been part of the French Empire for years. I mean, in the army I was considered German, but some of the others—"

"—were SO German!" They laughed to think of Bavarians and Saxons and dozens of others.

"And being chosen for the light horse cavalry—I was proud. My father was, too."

"All of Berleburg was proud of you." She wrapped silverware in a dishcloth and tied it tightly.

"It didn't take long for me to realize pride was no protection. But when Angelika and I married, I was still under Napoleon's spell."

"And then Angelika died."

"Ja, poor Hansi."

"Poor Angelika." She lifted a heavy iron food grinder and looked at him questioningly.

He shook his head. "No. Take more food than you think we'll need, and less of everything else. But one of the wooden spoons. We'll need it en route." His father had carved them, and his mother had used them. He was glad for an excuse to take one.

They did not discuss what they knew to be true, that after Waterloo he was no longer thought a hero, but maybe a traitor, and surely a fool. Gradually a new German nationalism infiltrated Berleburg until its people could not reconcile the 'natural' antipathy they now felt for the French. Even the good folk and 'free thinkers' who sat beside him at meetings of the Berleburg Antislavery Society squirmed about the French. At the last meeting, a member said, "But the French, now they're an odd lot, ain't they? Almost as wild as Americans."

Niklas had said nothing, but he was tired of saying nothing. To him, all men had rights by virtue of being human, and over time, he believed rationality must prevail. Katrina, he suspected, harbored a belief too radical to mention: that women deserved to be free and equal, too.

CHAPTER 8

BARBARIC!

Oh my, Katrina thought, *this letter should burn.* On Wednesday, she had risen while the children were still asleep and gone directly to her desk to make use of this quiet time. She tossed paper after paper in a basket for Will to burn at the fire barrel. It was when she unfolded a fat packet and recognized her own handwriting that she gasped. The ink had browned over the years on this letter, written to Elizabet and given back to Katrina.

"My Dearest Elizabet,

"You won't believe what's happened! I feel so stupid—it began when I went for a hike with Horst, a trek up the mountains I arranged so I could talk to him alone. It turned out you were right about him, my dear, right all along!"

Katrina had sent it when both Horst and Niklas asked her to marry. At the time, Elizabet warned her not to marry Horst Schmidt. When she refused him, he married her sister, Berthe. Now their son had been killed in the square, and the letter might look like evidence of bad blood in the family. "Not a moment to be lost," she whispered to herself as she folded it tight and tossed it into the basket of papers. For a beat longer she sat staring at it. She would tell Will to be sure these things burned to ash.

With the desk emptied, Katrina began packing clothes, a carpetbag each for Amalie and Lisette and a valise so small little Jakob could carry it. In Jakob's, she put a sweater, his beloved Kuschelbär teddy bear, and his baby blanket. Of all of Katrina's creative daring, the best examples were her quite amazing baby blankets. With each child, the blanket she spun, wove, embroidered, and quilted became more complex and beautiful. She had worked feverishly on Jakob's, as if by stitchery she could protect him. And he was safely born, her biggest baby and likely her last.

The house had once been brighter, but now, tall trees cooled the summers and sheltered the winters. She threw open a window to reach out and crush a few needles for their scent, which was still there even on cold mornings like this when snow had to be brushed off the branches.

Niklas's things nearly filled his trunk: a spare pair of trousers, a few shirts, cravats, small clothes, and a waistcoat. She added sweaters and a change of clothing for Hans and Will, but the trunk was still half empty. She put in spare bandages and string, dried medicinal and household herbs in tightly woven linen pockets, silverware, string heddles, and her best boat shuttle, a complicated affair with bobbins and a spring release. She hated to leave her loom, but they had built it together and could do so again. On top went Niklas's violin in its case.

She snapped the trunk closed and pulled an empty one to her, lining it with new cambric, enough to make a shirt when they were safe aboard. Into it went sheets and blankets and quilts and pillows, but most of their linens were left behind, including ratty old things she should have given away long ago. *Addie and Elizabet will understand that nothing is to be wasted.*

She left those first two trunks and began another. First, she opened a small wooden box ornately carved by her father, marveling at the silver inlay and the delicate clasp; it had been her mother's sewing kit and still carried a hint of violets. She twisted skeins of embroidery thread into a tight bundle, folded several pieces of aida cloth and fitted them in. She picked up a small oval frame and thought twice about taking it. Niklas had warned about extras. Then she snuggled it into the sewing kit. The box fit into a corner with knitting wool, a favorite small volume of Goethe's *Sensenheim Lyrics,* and her pearl-handled pistols, wrapped with white linen handkerchiefs embroidered with edelweiss.

"Go respectable but unnoticed," Niklas had told her, though being unnoticed was not really possible for a woman like herself. She lay her Sunday dress out on the bed. It was fine linen woven by her mother long ago, bleached white in the sun and then dyed with weld to a lovely clear, pale yellow. She had several collars for it, including one of lace; she rarely wore any dress without a collar. For travel she would wear a cotton collar with pin tucks, modest, ordinary and comfortable. Her Sunday dress had new leg o' mutton sleeves, and now only her cloak fit over it. The cloak was gray twill she had woven herself of their own sheep's wool with a lining of linen from flax grown in Berleburg. It had a warm collar of fox fur for which Günter Erlinger had trapped the foxes and tanned the hides;

Niklas had sewn them together to fashion the collar. The cloak was imminently usable, an honest piece of clothing.

She lay aside bolts of fine velvets and grosgrain, taffeta, and silk, brought home for making skirts and blouses and aprons—she had plans for every inch—but it was a comfort to know these would go to Elizabet or Addie instead. She would not have called herself a fashionable woman, not considering the excesses some people went to, but in this case, she thought it fortunate to have a decent wardrobe. It was always wise to look respectable when traveling, just as it was always wise to delight whatever men happened to be about. She packed a few more things for Amalie, extra aprons, wool stockings, ruffled white caps, a chemise and a petticoat.

Lastly, Katrina packed many handkerchiefs (her mother always said one can never have too many handkerchiefs) and lengths of good white English muslin, tucking these in wherever she could. These days, they were wealthy enough to buy most clothing, but her own were better made than what shops carried.

It was Katrina's habit, whatever she wore, to add a deft touch that made less charitable women weak with envy. To the careful eye, there it was: clear evidence in silk and wool of a certain daring. A niggling doubt crept in about what shops she might find in America. The little she had heard about fashion in America was notably unflattering:

"Barbaric!"

"Ridiculously out of date!"

"What one might have worn in the previous century!"

She added the muslin-wrapped paisley shawls, a bolt of green silk and one of serviceable blue and white checked linen.

Niklas looked in and asked, "Is all this quite necessary?"

"Jakob and the girls will soon need new clothing, you know. They are stretching out every day, nay, even as we speak."

"Yes, but if there's anyone as skinny, short and scrawny as a child..." Niklas suddenly felt himself on a dangerous path, and he reversed: "I mean to say, as delicately framed, it is you. Why, Amalie already fits your dresses. Or nearly so." Their daughter was still shapeless.

"What's that?" she asked. "Pass on my own to Amalie? Well, of course. But then it is I who must have new. Perhaps. We shall see, dear husband."

Niklas sighed and escaped the room. She glanced at him, seeing that he was glad to go. Their marriage was, all considered, superior to most. He did not beat her, and the household budget he gave her was adequate, if barely so. Her papa had indulged her with an education; perhaps this was why she was so very inclined to have opinions. She had learned quickly not to contradict Niklas in public. It was hard to bite her tongue, but to disagree or give advice was to condemn herself as a harpy and him as henpecked, something she would never do.

She folded and added to the trunk her best woolen shawl. Thinking of their own dear Waldschaf, the forest sheep whose fleece she had skirted, scoured, dyed, and spun for the shawl, she despaired of all they must leave behind. Then she resolutely counted all that would go with them. They knew how to make clothing and shoes, how to grow, cook, and preserve anything from a garden, orchard, or woods, how to raise and butcher animals. They would have their Bible, and she would teach the children, even the girls, to read and write and sing.

Into her trunk went a nightcap and nightgown, a blue dressing gown, slippers, and a special collar, a pelerine of pale blue brocade. She had cut it from a very old gown of her mother's, lined it with white silk and striped it with padded ribbon, sewn on with tiny white blanket stitches. The blue brocade reminded her of her mother's eyes, so often laughing. *The most important departures*, she thought, *have already happened: Mama, Papa, the first baby, little Jan Emil, so many others.* "I may not be everything I should be," Katrina worried aloud. "I admit to vanity and ambition, but such losses I have suffered." She blinked back tears as she closed and locked the trunk.

"Hans!" she cried down the stairs. "Bring your brother and take these trunks down." Then she clapped a hand over her mouth. *The open window! No*, she realized, *I closed it. Long ago. The neighbors could not have heard.* She looked out at the street's brown and white half-timbered houses, where she had been born, raised and married, she knew that, much as she loved Berleburg, it might be a relief to leave.

CHAPTER 9

SHE'S STRANGE

WEDNESDAY 10 FEBRUARY

As Katrina and Amalie hurried back to the house, Katrina already had a hand on their own garden gate, when she saw Elfriede Schuster waving frantically. She made her face a blank, knowing she would have to give an ear to Elfriede, to whom gossip was sustenance. "Say nothing," she whispered to Amalie.

"Katrina!" called Elfriede Schuster. One bony hand held her mob cap as she rushed forward.

Katrina took a step in Elfriede's direction.

"Your carriage sold! And your team! Has Niklas's store failed at last? Oh, la, Katrina, you can tell me!" Elfriede had known Katrina all of her life, and now she wrung her hands to think how far the Kästners had fallen.

Katrina ignored the surprise in Amalie's expression. "Not at all, nothing so desperate. We desire a little change, that's all," Katrina said.

They both knew Elfriede Schuster would not be satisfied with such an elusive answer, but in the moment's pause, a clatter of hooves rang out on the street crossing theirs. They caught a glimpse of an old bay nag being urged forward.

"That will be the Bauer boy fetching the doctor. His child-wife is lying in these three days past. The family refused a midwife, and now the girl will pay."

Katrina winced. She hated to have Amalie hear such things.

Elfriede did not notice. "My dear Katrina," she said confidentially, "Me and my Henry's got by all these years without no carriage nor even a buggy. No need putting on airs. You can tell me, now that your mama's gone."

Katrina coughed to hide the snort this comment elicited. "Thank you, my dear friend," she said, sounding shocked. "If you hear any more wicked gossip, tell the others, they're wrong!" Now she looked the old woman directly in the eye and grasped her bony hands. "Do you know anyone who works harder than Niklas?"

Elfriede shook her head, amazed: was she about to be told a confidence? "No one!" It was true: Niklas was often the first to open his shop, the last to come home again.

"Or who stays away from der Biergarten? Who never gambles?"

"Yes, but—" Elfriede began, thinking the same could not be said of Hans.

Katrina cut her off. "You see, all will be well soon enough. Just you wait." Katrina smiled, gave Elfriede's hands a quick, encouraging shake, took Amalie's arm, and turned swiftly toward home. She had only one thought as she latched the garden gate behind them and gave a last wave to Elfriede: *Can we be away before rumors spread to those better able to guess?*

Katrina knew her mother's old friend so well that she would not have been surprised if she had been able to hear what Elfriede said to her husband when she got home.

"She's acting strange, I tell you," Elfriede said to Heinrich, recounting the chance meeting. She lifted a teakettle from the fire and stood staring at it. "Not that I'll say a word to anyone."

Heinrich's eyebrows rose at this. It was impossible to imagine Elfriede saying not a word. Besides, he had always thought Katrina strange, Niklas even stranger, and Hans a big galoot, worst of the lot, menacingly large and silent. He wished Elfriede would pour while the water was hot.

"If she didn't dress so fine," Elfriede mused, "she'd have more friends." Like most of Berleburg, Elfriede found Katrina's elegance of dress off-putting, perhaps somewhat too much for the ordinary wife of an ordinary, or even vaguely disreputable, shopkeeper.

"Ain't that going it a bit far?" a neighbor had said once about Katrina, and Elfriede thought that summed it up. She turned to the kettle, and finally, she poured.

At the Kästner's, it was teatime, too, and Cousin Elizabet arrived, bringing a lovely streusel laced with currants and cinnamon. She was now a beautiful young widow; people thought she and Katrina sisters. They had a close, confidential chat as always, but she gasped when Katrina revealed their plans.

Elizabet set her teacup down. The saucer rattled against the silver tray. "Why America? The way it divides families is like a death. And you are so cultured, Katrina. Why go live among wild beasts and savages and Englishmen?" She picked up the cup and saucer, smoothed an embroidered napkin onto the tray, and replaced them, now silenced.

Katrina was folding a napkin into tiny pleats. "We leave very soon. Not a word of this to anyone, not a single word. You must swear it."

Elizabet's eyebrows rose. "What do you really know about America? What if the land isn't so cheap? Or they don't let foreigners buy at all?"

"Maybe America is not all they say," Katrina admitted. "We know there will be surprises and difficulties. We're not so young and foolish."

"Can't you go to France instead?"

Katrina's bitterness showed in her voice. "As children, all we knew was Emperor Napoleon, but after the wars, Niklas's commission was not extended. Suddenly, he was a German, and they owed him nothing. No, not France. France has too many impoverished veterans of its own to welcome those with a different accent."

There was an awkward pause. "Things," Elizabet said, "are getting better here all the time. Everyone says so! Our children are the best fed and educated of Europe. Our music and poets are universally admired. We are a great civilization! Surely, it cannot be so dangerous to stay."

Ah, thought Katrina, *we have come to the nub of it.* Aloud, she said, "The world is not what you think." She lowered her voice almost to a whisper. "If we wait, we may miss the moment when escape is possible."

"But you will be turning your back on your country!"

This made Katrina angry. "Hah! Niklas and Hans are all too patriotic. The king wants both of my boys in his army, do you realize that? And he will take them if given the chance." Katrina did not say an arrest—or an assassin—might be coming for Niklas.

"Mien Gott!" said Elizabet. "But what about family? What about Berthe?"

"Berthe is lost to me. Long ago." Katrina studied her teacup. "Look after her, will you?"

Elizabet nodded. She twisted her wedding ring as she listened.

"It hurts me to leave you. There will always a place for you with us in America."

Katrina pulled out a basket and filled it with pots of kitchen herbs and greens: French tarragon, rosemary, thyme, arugula and lettuce. She placed two books along the side of the basket, Shakespeare's *Midsummer Night's Dream* and Goethe's *Wilhelm Meister's Apprenticeship*. She said to Elizabet, "One moment," and disappeared around the corner, reappearing with a letter in hand. She tucked it into the basket. "You are to take what we leave behind. We're also giving some things to Sepp and some to Addie and Günter."

"Thank you, but this is all too much." Elizabet hesitated, and when she spoke again, her voice caught. "How often have we heard about a ship being wrecked and sunk?"

Katrina hugged her. "We'll be all right."

"I will pray for you."

"We'll be all right," Katrina repeated. *Pray all you like,* she thought, *but try to see the world as it really is, my dear.*

Outside, Will was waiting with a lantern to see Cousin Elizabet home. The wet streets were deserted, the gutters dripping with a midwinter thaw and a mist rising on the river and sneaking up the streets.

After they left, Katrina wrote a letter to Addie:

"10 February 1836

"Dearest Friends,

"As we find ourselves embarking upon a removal, thus do we wish to bestow on Herr Günter Erlinger and Herren Adelia Erlinger the contents of our larder, pantry, root cellar, dairy, and various and sundry other household goods, including such animals, grain, straw, hay, tools and conveyances, as are to be found in various outbuildings, excepting items separately gifted to Herr Sepp Beckmann, blacksmith, and to Herren Elizabet Beckmann Hesselberth, whose claims have priority. With our compliments to you and your children."

She solicited Niklas's signature and then, as neatly as any clerk, she melted a wax stick, let a few drops fall on the folded letter, and pressed a seal into the wax. In the last light before darkness, she wrapped herself in a warm cloak and carried the letter to slip under the door of the bakery. On the outside of the letter, she had written, "To be opened March 1, 1836" in hopes that the seal and inscription would be enough to keep the disposition of Kästner household and farmyard goods private until they were gone well away, far out of reach.

CHAPTER 10

IT SHOULD BE YOU

Early Thursday morning, Katrina punched down the latest batch of dough, while Niklas sharpened the sword he had carried to Moscow. He polished the silver handgrip and turned the blade this way and that, admiring its gleam.

"It's heavier than I remember," he said, "but it feels good." He stood and performed the Drey Wunder, the Three Wonders: thrust, cut and slice, the centuries-old secret skills of German swordsmanship.

Katrina looked up, smiling to see a sword in his hands again, and placed the dough in a greased bowl. She dipped a cloth into water, squeezed it out, and covered the bread dough. This batch was brötchen, a hard roll that would keep for quite a while.

"The king will never forgive us, we who were Napoleon's men, for the whiff of freedom that still encircles us."

"Like a halo," she said.

He laughed in surprise, "If it's a halo, it was awarded by Lucifer."

She was not sure what he meant, but she frowned as she scooped up flour for another loaf. There was much she would never understand about his having been a soldier.

Niklas began listing the irrevocable things he had done the day before: deeded away his share of the family farm and given away the house. She knew his family had been among the first Protestants in Berleburg, sturdy Calvinists who could on no account put up with the Pope any longer. After much prayer, part of their farm, once on the edge of town, had been chosen for the burgeoning congregation, and Calvinist families had settled near them, preferring to be within walking distance of the church. Niklas's grandfather had gladly turned to shoemaking, and although the family fed itself and its stock from a few remaining acres, they were glad not to depend solely on tenant farming and to have a shop of their own.

"The donation of the house will be our last to the church here," Niklas said. "Unless America really has streets paved with gold," he added with a grin.

Katrina smiled, but her shoulders sagged as she set the second batch aside, covered it, and pulled the flour closer to start another loaf. She had always thought it magic, how water and flour, yeast and salt could become bread, but now, she worried that she was asking too much, to have the magic work over and over again so quickly. She had no idea how much bread would be needed for such a journey. *Can my arms last through any more kneading? Can I keep the oven hot enough long enough?* At the thought of what lay ahead and all they were leaving behind, she remembered Elizabet's tears, and one fat tear fell right into the new loaf.

With their world crashing around them, the Kästners had no time to mourn, but by afternoon, they were in Berleburg's graveyard anyway, picking their footing along the cobblestone walk, trying to avoid the mud of this unseasonable thaw. Their nephew's funeral had been held at the Schmidt house, and his body was being brought here to lie with his ancestors.

Amalie heard three cheery notes and looked up to see a pair of chickadees, with their neat black caps and white masks, perched on a branch above the gravestone shared by the first Kästner baby and poor dear Jan Emil, dead and buried these four years. The bold chickadees stayed as they approached, as if welcoming them.

"Look, Mama," said Amalie, "winter songbirds."

"Yes," Katrina said, but she was deep in thought. Amalie said no more, but squeezed her mother's hand. Katrina stopped in front of the gravestone and spoke in a whisper to her dead sons: "We have to keep your father and your brothers safe now, but we will never forget you, my blessed lambs. Wherever we are, so shall you be, in our hearts forever." As she wiped away tears, she heard the sound of approaching carriages, and saw the chickadees take flight. Katrina turned to see the wagon bearing Werner's body enter the graveyard.

Horst himself was driving the wagon, and one of his sons, a boy of perhaps sixteen, sat on the bench beside him. Two buggies heavily draped in black came directly behind the wagon, and others followed, filled with cousins, neighbors, and friends. Katrina went to the first buggy as the door opened and Berthe was helped down. The two sisters embraced wordlessly. Katrina was in tears, but Berthe had exhausted hers. She looked much older, Katrina saw, and crazed with grief.

Niklas and Will stepped to the wagon to help lower the casket. The two families saw little of each other, but the Kästners were, after all, uncle and cousin of the dead boy. Horst climbed down and angrily waved the Kästner men aside. His brothers and their sons came forward to act as pallbearers. Horst was unsteady on his feet, Katrina saw.

The pastor's words were a blur in the winter wind, the casket was lowered, and it was over quickly. But when Niklas went to speak to Horst, the grieving father drew himself up as if to attack.

"Tell me, Kästner, how was it that you could not save my boy? You were there, you saw the whole verdammt thing. Where was your famous sword then? Did you even try? Or did you laugh as he died?"

"Of course not! Horst," Niklas said. "I was way across the square. I couldn't have reached him even if I had known what they intended."

"Hah, the big war hero, the man everyone fears, an insect, a worm."

"Horst…" Niklas was calm, but he noted the dozen men and boys lined up behind Horst.

"It should be you in that grave," Horst said, sticking his finger in Niklas's face. "What did you say to my boy? What poison did you pour into his ears? What traitorous, radical ideas?"

Horst spat on Niklas's boot, lurched to one side, and was pulled away, back toward the empty wagon. The Schmidt family's men closed around him.

One of Horst's brothers spoke. "He's drunk. And wild with grief, Claus."

"Wild." Niklas repeated. The veins in his neck bulged. There was a long pause as Niklas considered whether Horst might go to the authorities with his suspicions. He let out a breath. "He is in grief, and I understand grief."

He tilted his head to hear what Will whispered and gave it a moment's thought before he told Horst's brother, "We will not seek satisfaction."

Will looked at his father in disbelief.

"Then let us part in peace." Horst's brother ushered the rest of his group away.

"Berthe," said Katrina, "Niklas is telling the truth. I was there, too. It all happened so fast, none of us could have done anything to save Werner. I'm so sorry." When she put an arm around Berthe's shoulders, Berthe flinched, and Katrina looked inquiringly at her.

"When he's angry, he beats me." One hand fluttered above her shoulder.

Katrina gasped. "Oh, Berthe," she said, lifting her arm.

"I was never anything but someone to punish for not being you. It was always you, Katrina."

She murmured a shocked dissent, but Berthe was not listening.

"To lose a child like this, it's the end for me. I desire only the peace of the grave."

"Berthe, my Berthe, think of the other children." Katrina reached out to take her sister's hand, but Berthe turned away. The sisters, once so dear to each other, would not meet again.

CHAPTER 11

EVERY MAN A PRINCE

FRIDAY 12 FEBRUARY

The funeral had been terrible, and Katrina awoke with a start, worried about Horst. *How angry is he? How better to punish us than to denounce Niklas as a traitor.*

Still, it was not until she was in the stable that her feelings nearly got the better of her. She knew Will thought he and his father were only going to Arnsberg, but when she handed him a lunch bag and kissed him, her eyes were glittering with tears. Niklas had already saddled their beloved Schwarzwälders. Arnsberg was home to the district offices, where the courts had been forever, so that people who meant to sue said, "We go to Arnsberg!"

The two of them rode out of town past villages that got poorer and poorer as they became more isolated. In the least of these, some homes were smoky, mean, and wretched, crowded with children, so poor a crossbow might still be in use. The revolutions in America and France proclaimed that all people should be free to make their own place in life, but here, everyone was a tenant of the prince, and life went on as it had for generations, oblivious to revolutions. Isolation bred distrust and envy.

On Niklas and Will went, into the picturesque upland, where handsome stands of beech and spruce dappled the sunshine. On they went, into blue-green conifer forests empty of people, forests owned by the prince and for his use alone. Up high, where the mountain air was cold and fresh, they dismounted and led the horses on a narrow, barely used trail to a ridge of the Rothaar Mountains. There they mounted again and with the screech of an owl to accompany them, began to their descent into the Hochsauerland.

Here, the language changed with the landscape, and the churches changed from severe, wooden and Calvinist to gothic, stone and Catholic. As the land spread out more generously, the villages were more prosperous, and on this day, were made even more charming by a layer of snow on their roofs.

"A handsome region," said Niklas, "and filled with pious, hard-working, thrifty people."

"Who are Catholic," said Will with disapproval.

As the mountains faded to hills, the two Kästners rode for a long time beside the Wenne until it joined the Ruhr and then along the larger river to Arnsberg. Nicklas motioned to a spot off to the side of the road where a break in the trees let in a little sunshine. They opened the saddlebags and took out the lunches Katrina had packed: small, thick drinking glasses stuffed with a napkin holding raisins and dried apricots and a larger napkin full of bread and Berleburg cheese. Niklas's saddlebag held a bottle of Kästner beer.

Here, with no witness but the trees, Niklas told Will more about what had happened to his cousin, Werner Schmidt.

"I don't understand, Papa. Was Werner a criminal?"

"They will call him a traitor," said Niklas. "And he may have been carrying a seditious pamphlet, but his real crime was to want some rights for ordinary people."

The outrageousness of it began to dawn on Will. "Even so, there should have been a trial."

"One would think."

"Papa," said Will, "this Cousin Werner Schmidt, was he Hermann's brother?"

Niklas nodded. "His older brother, the one in Edzard's class." He sighed and continued. "The police are being required to enforce the Sixty Articles, although these have not been made public."

"How can we follow laws if they are not known to us?" Will's voice rose, scandalized.

"Exactly," said Niklas.

"Herr Zimmermann?" Will hated to ask.

"He wasn't there. But he will surely take part sometime." Niklas folded his napkin and brushed off his trousers. "New men, secret police, are to arrive soon. They will not have any local sympathies, and they will target anyone who might say a word against the king, anyone with friends at

Würzburg or Göttingen or Heidelberg," he said, listing the universities infamous for the failed coup of 1833.

"Or Jena?" Will said. Hans had been at Jena last year.

"Yes," Niklas nodded. "Jena may not be considered as bad as the others, but any university student will be suspect. As will anyone with ties to Napoleon."

"You and Hans might both be thought revolutionaries," Will said. He was horrified.

"We might," Niklas said. "And you might be forced into the army. That's why the passport we seek today is so important, but with or without it, we will leave."

"Leave?"

"You are going directly from Arnsberg to Köln. You'll find Hans there at a steamboat called *Holsatia,* which I have engaged. I'll bring the rest of the family. If we are not there in two weeks, you are to take *Holsatia* to Rotterdam. Buy a passage to America and go. Everything you need is here." He patted the saddlebag. Then he looked at Will severely: "With or without us. No questions asked. No delay. Do not send word. Just go."

It was a shock. Will could have imagined almost anything except being asked to go on alone, to Cologne, to Rotterdam, and across to America, never to look back and with his only hope a letter, someday. Now he knew why Hans was gone and why he was here with Father. This was a plan to save them, even if their father were caught. He and Hans had already left the only home they knew, with no chance to look around a last time or speak to anyone.

"Sophie," Will muttered. "I will have no chance to say goodbye."

"With all the time in the world, Son, you could have told her nothing." Niklas poured the last of the beer into their glasses. "Whatever we leave behind," he said, "America offers more. More opportunity. More freedom. No one will be your superior there. It's true that you'll have to make your own way, and however difficult you think it might be, it will be ten times harder. But in America, every man is his own prince."

Will raised his glass: "Every man his own prince!"

Niklas stood and raised his glass. The boy scrambled up to join him in the toast. "Every man a prince!" As they lowered their glasses, Niklas looked hard at his son. "Of the Kästner family," he said, "you and your brother are the most imperiled. Do not look back, do not forget the danger, and do not fail."

CHAPTER 12

ALL LIBERTY REQUIRES

FRIDAY 12 FEBRUARY

Hours later, cold and tired, the two Kästners crossed a centuries-old stone bridge and found themselves within the city walls of Arnsberg. Niklas looked from side to side with narrowed eyes and lay one hand casually on his thigh, putting his silver-handled sword, now polished to slicing sharpness, within instant reach. Will saw this small movement and became more alert, one eye on passersby and one on his father. They threaded their way through narrow, muddy streets.

At the district offices, a junior clerk listened as Niklas said there should be a passport prepared for them and told them to take a seat. They did, on a wooden bench worn into comfortable hollowings-out. The junior clerk spoke to a harried subaltern who began searching through stacks of papers.

"It's a long sheet," Niklas said, gesturing about its size. "It names each member of our family and gives our ages and destination."

"Amerika?" The subaltern disapproved. "Are you sure you wish to undertake such an awful long trip?"

"Jawohl," said Niklas with an almost imperceptible smile.

The subaltern shook his head sadly. "It'll be the death of you, you know."

"I hope not." Niklas slipped the subaltern a coin as he found the document and the required copy.

They paid the fee and waited quite a while again until they were admitted to see the head clerk, a bitter, officious old man who peered at the document, which already bore an official red wax stamp of approval. He looked suspiciously at the two of them. He was about to speak, his expression going from mere unfriendliness to righteous fury, when a pretty girl stepped into the room, begged his pardon, and with a sweet smile, set his afternoon tray of hard cider and pretzels in front of him. The clerk looked once at them and twice at the tray in front of him. With a dismissive wave of his hand, he pulled out a metal cylinder, inked the end of it, and marked the document, "Paid, half-thaler." He put it aside to dry and did the same to the copy.

"There," said the clerk. "You're free to go. If we ain't good enough for you, good riddance."

"Yes sir, thank you, sir." Niklas rolled the documents and tucked them into his greatcoat. On the street once again, he grinned in disbelief. "Son," he said, "I believe it's time for a beer."

Later, when they were seated in a dark inn with steins in hand, Niklas mused, "It might be that we owe our precious passport to hard cider and pretzels."

"Or a pretty girl?" said Will. "Maybe all it requires is escaping notice."

Niklas snorted. "Ja. A king whose left hand does not know what his right hand is doing."

Before they went their separate ways, Niklas told Will about the gold in his saddlebag and added to his charge: "You are to find and look after your brother, especially if you have to go on alone, especially where some arm of Europe's secret police might be watching for you, and especially in any harbor anywhere, where British press gangs and crimps of any nationality are a constant threat to any man able to stand on two feet. Never forget," he told Will, "besides the king's secret police, the British Navy is your sworn enemy. In any port, they will wait for you to get drunk, and then they will seize you." He looked with severity at Will as he said, "Make no friends. Avoid telling anyone your name, and for God's sake, avoid the police."

Hans had been told to hire on as a dock worker, no lounging about. Now Niklas repeated this instruction. "It will give you a few days' wages," he said, "and make you invisible, two ordinary longshoremen, not two wealthy layabouts attracting the attention of whores and pickpockets and getting yourselves into trouble left and right."

While Niklas was saying goodbye to Will, Amalie thought she was living another ordinary day in Berleburg. Early on, she asked her mother whether to give the little ones oatmeal or toast and apple butter or maybe both.

"Oh, both, to be sure. Give them all they would like," her mother said.

Amalie opened her mouth but closed it again. Something big seemed to be in the air. In fact, Amalie had asked Will what it was, but he had not been forthcoming—perhaps it was not his place to say, or perhaps he did not know.

"No one tells me anything," Amalie complained softly to Jakob, who was snuggled in her arms. "Everyone gives Mother all the credit while I am left to do the scullery work and expected to be there for you two day and night."

"I love you," said little Jakob. He kissed her cheek.

"I know you do, my darling, and I love you." A wrinkle formed in her forehead as she worried about what she usually worried about: *How soon will the next baby come?*

An hour later, Amalie's curiosity deepened when Katrina stood shivering outside the door with cuttings and roots in a big basket, stomping her feet to shake off the winter mud. Katrina slipped out of her garden clogs and stepped inside, stripping off her thick wet socks, unwinding the scarf from her neck, pulling off a wool cap and shaking out her long, strawberry-blonde braid. The dripping branches of apple and pear trees along the north side of the garden had left her sodden, and she shook like a dog. They always put seeds aside in the fall, but Amalie had no idea what her mother was doing now.

"You'll catch your death of cold, Mama."

"Mama!" yelled Jakob. He trotted down the hallway on an imaginary horse, broke off and came racing to hug Katrina around the knees. She set down her basket, took the little boy in her arms and kissed him.

Amalie looked pointedly at Jakob and asked her mother, "No lessons today?"

"No," Katrina said, nodding to the basket, "time enough for that later. This February thaw is a godsend, Amalie, unseasonable warmth when we need it most, a stroke of luck that I could gather cuttings and roots, a good omen."

Amalie smiled and nodded, but she still looked mystified. "Why do we need these at all, Mama?"

Suddenly, Katrina understood. "Amalie," she said, putting one hand on her daughter's shoulder. "I thought you knew. We are going to America. Sunday morning, if we can manage it. It's a secret, as deep and dark a secret as ever I have told you. Not a word, not a whisper to a soul."

Amalie looked at her mother in shock. "What? Why? And why in secret?" She clapped her hand over her mouth for asking so boldly, so directly.

"Sweetheart, do you remember what Opa used to say when someone burned the toast?"

"Oh, sure. He always made the same joke: 'There's an art to knowing when: Toast it until it smokes and then twenty seconds less.'"

"It's like the toast, dear," Katrina laughed. "If we wait 'til the toast burns, it'll be too late." At Amalie's look, she added, "Don't worry, mein Liebchen, it's going to be wonderful!"

She handed four-year-old Jakob to her astounded daughter and disappeared into the pantry, sorry to see such a look on Amalie's face. *Don't children*, she wondered, *listen around corners anymore?*

Katrina began by packing a small tin box with last fall's seeds. Dried peas and beans rattled on the bottom, topped by tiny paper packets of chard, kale, sorrel, and cabbage seeds as well as seeds of chive, parsley, dill, turnip, kohlrabi, poppy, feverfew, borage, and calendula. In a larger tin box, she layered straw with orris rhizomes and roots of thyme. "For courage, thyme," Katrina mused, "for grace, rue." She chided herself for being distracted as she packed roots of asparagus, onion, garlic and leeks, rhubarb, horseradish, grapes, and tarragon. "For patience, mint," she recited as she added lemon balm, lovage, and tansy. She sighed to think of the years it would take to bring these few asparagus roots up to enough to feed a family of seven.

In spite of what she had told Amalie, a garden could hardly be carried from place to place. She wiped clean her best gardening knife and added it. In the top tray went her last few sticks of cinnamon, a handful each of cloves and nutmegs, and all of the saleratus in the kitchen.

In the cellar, Katrina studied the rows and rows of beer and cider. She packed a dozen bottles in a straw-lined box, and looked sadly at the rest. Most would go to Elizabet or the Erlingers, and it was a comfort to know they would enjoy it, but she wondered when she would taste beer or cider she liked so well again.

Lastly, it was back outside for the best milker among the nanny goats along with a kid to keep her milk coming, and for chickens—the healthiest of the flock—enlisting the children's help to catch the hens and secure them in the crates Will had knocked together for her.

Niklas had not been at all sure it was wise or necessary to carry animals with them.

"It will be what makes us look like an ordinary family with no big plans," she had told him.

"They must be abandoned the instant we need to move quickly," he had warned.

She had nodded and let the matter drop.

Later, when she ran into Elfriede again, Katrina had a ready answer for her. "The boys," she explained, "are doing business for the family. It's time, and you should see that young Will do figures."

Elfriede looked askance at this.

"We will join them and stay awhile. The Erlinger boys will care for the animals, so don't be surprised to see them around."

"When do you leave?"

"Not for another week, I expect, but it depends on when I get the baking done!" Katrina laughed as if all she must do was to bring an almond streuselkuchen to her cousins. "But you know men—Niklas will want to leave when the weather allows." *I should be an actress,* she thought, *to hear how carefree I sound.*

"When will you be back?"

Katrina was ready for this question. "Who knows? It will depend on a lot of things." *None of this,* she thought, *is exactly a lie.* Katrina dug into her basket. "I have extras," she said, handing a bottle of cider vinegar and a jar of raspberry jam to Elfriede. "Perhaps you and Heinrich could use them?"

"Oh, yes! How kind of you."

With this small distraction, Katrina took leave of Elfriede Schuster forever.

CHAPTER 13

SOLDIER-FIDDLER

On Saturday, Niklas returned home alone. In fact, the boys were doing business for the family, traveling on to Cologne, confirming their passage on a steam-powered paddle vessel, *P.V. Holsatia,* and securing a night's lodging for them all. *Holsatia* was the only steamboat on the Rhine going all the way from Basel to Rotterdam's harbor on the North Sea. Once, while in Paris, Niklas had watched Robert Fulton's pioneering steamboat, the *Elise,* steam up the Seine.

"We read about *Holsatia*'s new schedule," Katrina said, "but of course, we have never ridden a steamboat, nor seen *Holsatia*…"

"Nor do I approve of spending so much money on the first leg of a journey."

"Are you sure these vessels are safe?"

"Are we in a position to worry about that?"

"Well, no," she said, "The alternative, unloading every night, finding an inn and hiring a local flatboat or stagecoach—"

"—would be slow," he said, "and would require explaining ourselves at every stop."

"Inviting delay, attracting attention."

He nodded, and she knew that settled the matter.

Snow fell late that night, and the wind rattled against the windows as Katrina and Niklas lay quietly together.

She asked Niklas, "Is all this God's will, do you think?"

"I can't know God's will. He will reveal it in His own time."

"Well, yes, but I think it's His will that we stay alive, since He kept you alive through the valley of death, the Russian winter."

"Yes," he said. "Besides, you are so worth saving. Quick, capable and discreet, a loving mother, which alone would endear you to all around you, capable in all of the necessary domestic arts, a master gardener and herbalist, weaver and needlewoman, cook and baker, a teacher, too, well read in grammar and orthography and philosophy, as well as in the proper care of children."

"Danke," Katrina murmured, promising herself not to forget such kind words. Still, she could not help fretting about irreplaceable lengths of wool roving never to be matched unless they could find a flock as useful as their Waldschaf forest sheep. An image of the root cellar floated before her eyes with jars and jars of preserves—raspberry, gooseberry, and blueberry jams; grape and apple and pear jellies, and preserves, conserves, and marmalades—not to mention beer, all to be left behind. "But think," Katrina said aloud, "of our ciders, raisins, vinegars, mustards, pickles, and sauerkraut. Oh! And the cheese and ham!"

"Please, let it go," said Niklas, "You will not once hear me groan about selling the lovely chestnut gelding I trained to the buggy last year. If I had only known!"

"With that white blaze on his forehead. And named Zimt again."

"And three white stockings, so neat." He sighed. "Or the buggy's new paint so dearly purchased, or our own Schwarzwälders, God love them!"

"What I know and you don't," she cried, "is that even jam jars will be hard to come by, let alone buckets and buckets of berries."

"Of course I know," said Niklas. "What we give up is lost forever."

"But," Katrina said slowly, "What we hope to gain is also beyond all value."

"Yes. And besides, our course is laid. There's no looking back, never a moment to be lost nor a careless word to be spoken." His voice dropped as he continued: "The king imprisons, tortures and kills those he sees as enemies. We cannot let him get his hands on our boys."

"Or you!"

"Nor can we know at which turn, at which moment, his secret police might lie in wait." Even though they were side by side under the covers in their very own bed in the big, dark house in which Niklas was born, without so much as a candle glowing to give them away, their voices had fallen into whispers.

The next morning, before dawn on Sunday, Niklas smothered the last of the ashes in the last of the fireplaces, straightened up and looked hard around the house they would never see again.

Passing through the parlor one last time, Katrina found something they had missed: two tiny cherrywood carvings of an accordion player and a fiddler. Her father had whittled them for Niklas, and now, she handed them to him and saw him stop and stare.

"It's not too late," she said.

"The children are already in the buggy—"

"That's not what I mean. You could go alone, bring the boys back. We could make a fresh start here."

Very deliberately, he took the accordion player from her, held out his arm and dropped it. She understood what he intended a moment before he released the carving. She saw it fall, grabbed for it, and missed. Her father's face flashed before her eyes. She saw his smile as he carved this little ode to music, a symbol of his joy in welcoming Niklas into the family, a soldier who was also a fiddler. She jumped when it hit the floor and broke in two with a crack, a sound too horribly familiar.

"No," he said. "And there's not a moment to be lost."

Katrina put the wooden fiddler in her pocket. She was glad to have one of them and glad it was the fiddler who was unbroken. With one foot, she brushed aside the pieces. She knew why he had dropped it, but it still hurt, and she blinked back tears.

The sun was not up, but the eastern sky had begun to glow. Niklas wrapped a scarf around her neck and asked, "All set?"

Katrina nodded. A moment later, outside, he handed her up into the buggy and climbed onto the driver's bench. Little Jakob was already sound asleep, his head on Amalie's lap. Lisette was curled up next to Amalie, covering her ears with her mittens against the cold of the morning.

Perfect timing, Katrina thought. *If we are to tell no lies, we ought not see anyone today.*

She took a last long look at their beloved home, where Niklas had grown up and they had lived since they married. As she pulled down the leather shade, she saw Ernst Zimmermann standing stock still at the corner, his pistol pointed at them. She grabbed the children and pushed them to the floor. Just then, the buggy lurched forward, and Niklas shouted,

"Giddap!" Almost as an echo, his whip cracked the air, and the gelding's shoes clattered on the cobblestones. No shot rang out, and Katrina dared to look again. There Ernst stood, his pistol raised to the sky. She gathered the children around her on the floor of the buggy, cooing and patting the little ones and avoiding the accusations in Amalie's eyes.

Then they crested a hillock and raced down into the safety of the vale beyond. The countryside enveloped them, Ernst vanished as if he had never existed, and the future received them into its arms.

BOOK TWO

ESCAPE

"He only earns his freedom and his life
who takes them every day by storm."
— Johann Wolfgang von Goethe, *Faust*

CHAPTER 14

A CITY ONCE FREE

Carnival came to Cologne with them. Its influx of strange faces was exactly what they would have wished for. Above the city soared the truncated towers of the cathedral, a sheer amazement, a massive structure such as they had never seen.

Niklas, the family's only sophisticate, said to Will, "Close your mouth!" and to all of them, "Come along!"

Is he embarrassed by his country-mouse family? Katrina didn't care. She could hardly tear her eyes away from the Cologne cathedral, and the children were no better. Even Hans and Will were amazed.

"It's called Kölner Dom," said Niklas, "or more properly, Ecclesia Cathedralis Sanctorum Petri et Katrinae."

"Oh, look," cried Amalie. "What's that at the top, the slanted bit?"

"An ancient crane, it is," said an amused passerby, an elderly, professorial-looking man with tufts of white hair standing up in his ears. He shaded his eyes and studied the south tower. "Left there in 1560, after three hundred and twelve years of building." He shook his head sadly. "At the time everyone thought the pause would be temporary."

Amalie stared. The old man spoke as if he had been there for it.

The passerby said with enthusiasm, "Drawings are being made even today to finish it." Then he noticed the coldness in Niklas's eye and hurried away.

"A crane!" said Niklas. "Proof its medieval builders sought to go higher. And failed."

None of them knew that deep under the colossal stones at the base of the cathedral lay the church of Louis the German, Charlemagne's grandson, consecrated in 870, and that under it lay an undistinguished church of the sixth century, and below it lay an even smaller and less distinguished Christian church, little more than a meeting room, of the fourth century. If a Roman temple of the first century had lain below that, or the singing stones of an ancient Celtic circle still lower, it would not have amazed the Kästners; such layers upon layers defined the only world they had ever known, one which they, as a rule, ignored.

Two young men approached, walking and talking so fast that Katrina saw Niklas stiffen. A moment more and he would have had a dagger at the ready.

"The king's an idiot!" said the taller one, "to think we'd give up being a free city. Does he have any idea how important Köln is? Has he never heard of the Hanseatic League?"

"Worse yet," agreed his companion, "just because he's a Lutheran, he thinks we all should be."

"Ja now, if our own prince had his say, he'd continue allowing Catholics and Jews to practice as they wish."

"You have a lot of faith in our prince!"

"What has it been, twenty years since we were ceded to Prussia?"

"Something like that. And now he decides this!"

"1816, twenty years," Niklas muttered to Katrina.

"Between King Wilhelm and that bastard Metternich…"

Katrina clapped her hands over Lisette's ears. *Such language right out on the street!*

As the impudent voices faded, Will asked, "Isn't Metternich a Rhinelander?"

"Ja, born in Coblenz," Niklas said, gesturing upriver. "But he's now the power behind the Austrian throne. I thought you knew this."

The whole town throbbed with talk of the German Democracy Movement. People openly discussed ending the monarchy and unifying the Germanies and establishing freedom of religion and speech and equality of the sexes. Men are capable of reason, Voltaire said, able to shape their own destiny and rule themselves with civility, reason and tolerance. Most said Voltaire meant women as well, but there were those who disagreed. They had formed a "League for Combating Women's Emancipation."

Niklas thought such open talk dangerous. He warned the family about the rebels' weakness, saying a few Resistance leaders had already escaped to America, one step ahead of Metternich's goons. He warned Günter, too, who was there in Cologne with them. Günter had driven the old berlin wagon to town with their trunks and animals, and it was he who led Zimt, the beautiful young gelding, away when the buggy was sold.

To Katrina he added: "By the way, I think it was your presence and that of the children, that kept Ernst Zimmerman from firing."

"Or maybe he remembered that you saved his life."

"Maybe. But if afterwards he counted it a soft moment, he might have been angry with himself."

"Niklas, would he send a rider to Köln to alert the authorities? A single man on a horse could have gotten here before us."

"Ja, it's possible. Though he likely thought we would go to Paris. Or Le Havre or Bremen. Still, some who can't pull a trigger themselves are happy to have others do it."

"I would hate to think of Ernst that way."

"He betrayed us, Katrina. He came to arrest me or Hans or both of us and was prepared—at least momentarily—to kill us. Don't sugarcoat it."

She did not reply. *Has all of Berleburg turned on us? Are we cut off, adrift, with no home anywhere at all?*

Niklas seemed to know what she was thinking: "Our present isolation is a blessing. Except for Günter, no one here knows us, not even the Kölner who bought our blue buggy."

On the street, the smells of sausage, pretzels, and gingerbread filled the air, as did the shouts of vendors in a confusion of dialects. A family passed by chattering, and when Katrina looked at Niklas, he said, "Ost Frieslanders." Another time, he said, "That's Danish."

Katrina shivered at the idea of being where everyone was a stranger speaking some odd dialect or foreign language. It was a relief to consider that everywhere, most spoke at least a little French.

"Köln reminds me," Niklas said as they turned onto a street leading to the docks, "of Paris."

She nodded, "Ja, and its university rivals that of Paris."

"Don't let a Parisian hear you say that." He smiled.

"Besides," said Will, "look at its situation!" Cologne rose on a bluff by a curve of the Rhine. "It almost has its own bay! A man could make money here."

"Even the Romans could see its favorable position," added Hans.

Katrina looked at Hans in surprise. It was rare that he spoke up. *That he should know something of the Romans!*

"It's why they chose this spot as an outpost of the empire's border," Hans added. "And after that, Köln was in the Hanseatic League for centuries, as an international trading center. It's an outrage that Prussia's taking away their status as a free city."

They walked by an ancient city wall with a fine old round tower. These old walls and several fine gates stood as a testament to the safety of living in Cologne.

"Rome?" she asked, patting a wall.

Niklas shrugged. "Whoever built them, these walls are impressive."

Against the evidence of thick city walls, the frivolity of Carnival seemed harmless, though it was laced through with sarcasm.

Amalie had taken the children on ahead, and now they heard her tell them, "We are here for Carnival! Aren't we the lucky ones!"

She had found a good spot to show the children a Carnival parade, but the strangeness of it frightened Jakob, who hid his face in her shoulder. Lisette was holding Amalie's hand rather tightly, not at all sure about the wild costumes and weird masks. She stared at the Junge Frau, the maiden.

"The Junge Frau is dressed as a woman," Amalie explained, "but it's really a man. They are just clowning around, Lisette."

It's all very well, Katrina thought, *for the children to see Carnival, but not if it frightens them so they are up half the night.*

Amalie told little Jakob, "Look, here comes 'Herr Bauer, His Heftiness.' No one's going to bother us as long as His Heftiness is here!"

A moment later, Amalie stumbled over a beggar, a pathetic wretch wearing an eye patch. He was squeezed into a doorway, not quite far enough to be out of traffic.

"Bitte, bitte," he said, holding up an open palm, "Please, please." The beggar smelled, and his one-leg body was startling, but Amalie was caught in the crowd, unable to escape, so she retrieved a copper pfennig and dropped it into his hand. Her father had said they must use money to grease the way, and this appeared to be such a moment. Amalie wondered, *Are there beggars in America? Surely not, in 'the land of opportunity.'* People were moving again, trying to see something, and pushing the family along.

A roar went up in the crowd as a regiment of soldiers approached. Like the Jungfrau, something was off. One of the soldiers skipped along, another stopped to scratch his head and wave at the crowd, and yet another stood flat on his feet, stretching and yawning. This was the Stippeföttche, a dance in which the signature move was standing back-to-back and rubbing butts together. Fancy coats and plumed hats made a mockery of the Prussian Army.

"Ach," an old Oma beside Katrina said happily, "Jede Jeck es anders!" It took Katrina a moment to parse the Kölsch: "Every fool is a fool in his own way." The woman asked, "Do you know they've been doing the Stippeföttchen-Tanz forever?" She pointed to a small bronze bas-relief embedded in the cornerstone behind them. The carved image of the dance was black with age. "Look! Here's the proof."

Katrina knew this was all in fun, but her anger rose. *I am a soldier's wife,* she thought with indignation. And yet, she knew Niklas hated the Prussians. It was confusing, and for an awful moment she had a chilling image of the Stippeföttche turning their rifles on the laughing crowd and firing real bullets.

CHAPTER 15

THE GREEN BOUGH

"Why don't we stand and fight?" Hans hissed. Moments earlier, he had been bragging about being glad to be shut of Berleburg with thalers jingling in his pockets. Then Niklas shoved him and Will into a dark alley and motioned for silence.

A half-dozen men in uniform marched by, a pseudo-military unit of the type known for arbitrary cruelty. Their uniforms were all Niklas needed to see. *These,* he thought, *are the kind on the hunt for us.* He and the boys were fully armed, a result of his insistence on the kind of martial preparation to which he had several times owed his life. Now his eyes narrowed, and his lips ran in a thin line.

"Nothing would please me more than to avenge Werner," he said to Hans, "but long ago, I learned to think twice."

"There's only six of them, and I can take all of them. Or at least three."

They were still talking in whispers, but now Niklas snapped at Hans. "And then what? One whistle will bring another dozen. The secret police are thick, and their ruthlessness is inexorable."

"I always win," said Hans, who had been in plenty of small-town fights.

"But this is war, and you don't know war." Niklas spoke patiently, but he was really annoyed. With all of the training he had given his boys, what had not sunk in is the need to choose your fight wisely. *Strategy,* he reflected, *is an old man's strength and a young man's blind spot.*

"Remember Count Krusinski," said Niklas: "Bóg da mi dobry miecz ale nie chcę mieć powodu aby go użyć, God give me a good sword and no reason to use it." For an instant, he had an image of Krusinski, a famed Polish colonel of the Chevau-Légers, back when they routed every opposing army and had never been beaten.

"Well," Hans admitted, "I know this is not a street fight."

Will laughed, and when the others looked hard at him, he said, "What? Hans says it's not a street fight when here we stand on a street."

"Hans is right. It's not a street fight, nor a battlefield either, where one side faces the other and the strongest, fiercest men win. This is a police state where well-armed, coordinated units pick off easy targets—like us. The laws are all on their side. Did you know a group like us, a group of three men, is considered an illegal gathering?"

The boys looked shamefaced. "Besides," Hans admitted, "what we must do is to get Mother and the youngsters aboard without anyone noticing."

"Yes! Now you're thinking. We can't do that if we are rotting in a Kölner jail." He lowered his voice. "Our best revenge is to get all of us safely away. It may come to a fight, and if it does, I will need you both beside me, but this is not the moment."

That evening, Niklas went alone to a tavern known for its embrace of the resistance. Günter was already there, grinning and swaying a little. When the others began the loyalty test, he answered eagerly:

"What have you in your hand?"

"A green bough."

"Where did it first grow?"

"In America."

"Where did it bud?"

"In France."

"Where are you going to plant it?"

"Here in our homeland.

"In the soil of truth, trust, unity, and liberty."

Niklas listened moodily. The recital came from the Irishmen of '98, and the thought of their failed revolution depressed him, as did the old French cheers: Liberté, Equalité, Fraternité. The French revolution had descended from democracy to Terror and then to empire.

The tavern talk was all of a widely respected theologian, the Reverend Doctor Weidig, and a brilliant medical student at the University of Giessen, Georg Büchner, charged some months ago with treason for writing *Hessischen Landboten*, a slim little pamphlet with a simple plea for justice. Dr. Weidig refused to flee; he had been arrested and imprisoned. Georg Büchner escaped, said certain well-informed whispers, whereabouts unknown. One of the men at the tavern shook Niklas's hand fervently and said in a low voice, "Denken Sie daran, Weidig und Büchner. Remember Weidig and Büchner."

The truth about Günter, and Niklas had accepted it long ago without the slightest grudge, was that he thought he would someday take up arms and beat the king about the head until he, Günter, finally got what he deserved: rights and wealth beyond his wildest imaginings and the admiration of all. This was the fantasy of a man who was kindness itself, who had never once raised anything more dangerous than a bread knife to any man on God's green Earth. In a desperate moment, it was possible Günter would prove to be the man he dreamt of being, but whether he did or not, there were many more like him in the Germanies, untested men, some of them right here, cheering in the tavern this cold winter night.

While Günter and the others celebrated their comradeship, Niklas retreated to a dark corner of the tavern with one of the most valued young men in the GDM, Robert Blum, with whom he shared more covert information than he ever felt was wise. It might be the last substantive help he could give the clandestine movement and its international umbrella, the Society for the Rights of Man.

Blum looked at Niklas skeptically. He was polite but seemed to wonder what such an old man could know. Then he hitched his head toward Günter. "Can we trust him?"

"He is absolutely trustworthy..." Niklas's voice trailed away.

"Even though he drinks too much."

Niklas shrugged. Günter's failings were obvious.

Blum sighed.

A wave of chatter rose from the cluster of would-be rebels. At the center of it, a high-pitched voice—a woman's—was making men laugh. Moments later, when Blum rejoined the laughing group, Niklas slipped quietly out the back, wrapping his scarf across his face against the night's cold and not unhappy to cover his face. Hours later, the men at the tavern would stumble into the starlit night, shiver in the cold air, clap each other's shoulders and swear to meet again on the morrow. By then, Niklas hoped, Günter would be safely on his way back to Berleburg, happy with three new horses and the old berlin wagon. He winced at what little Günter had paid for these. Not to mention the contents of the barn.

At least, Niklas thought, *Hans is not in the tavern tonight.* Even now, with all that loose talk, Niklas thought revolution was nowhere near, nor would it spread like wildfire from the halls of the universities into the cottages of the countryside, where often the sole decoration was a sepia print of their majesties and the royal children. If farmers took up pitchforks and cudgels, it would be to beat back vile, effete revolutionaries, not respectable king's men. *It is time,* he thought, *to leave the redemption of Germany to others and go to America, the only place liberty might survive.*

The family spent two more days in Cologne, waiting for a break in the winter ice. On the second day, Hans returned to their room at the inn with a troubling story.

"I can't believe what I saw. Zimt! Here in Köln! How could Günter have sold him? And to a stranger!"

"Zimt?" Niklas was stunned. "Günter loved that horse. He would never sell such a fine animal. Are you sure?"

"That blaze? The three white stockings? How could I be wrong? Besides, I called out when I saw him—I couldn't help myself—and I swear he pricked up his ears at the sound of his name."

"He's spirited, that horse, and best not distracted when being ridden."

"The man riding him wasn't at all pleased. He turned to me with a look that would have withered a rose, and then he seemed startled, as if he recognized me."

"Did you recognize him?" Niklas spoke with unusual sharpness.

Hans pondered this for a moment. "No. I can't say I did. Mean-looking, though. Not one to meet in a dark alley."

"Indeed."

Katrina was close to the window, and she studied the street, glad to see it deserted. "This makes no sense at all."

CHAPTER 16

ASTONISHING SPEED

Against the winter-gray Rhine, the smartly painted P.V. Holsatia looked like one of Will's models. A wonderfully modern, steam-powered paddle vessel, *Holsatia* had only one short mast towards the stern where a flag flew and a staysail could be raised to add steerage and stability. The sail was left flapping now, ready to be tightened when the passengers were aboard. Only a few lines of hemp held *Holsatia* to one of Cologne's docks. Hans and Will had hired on as longshoremen, and they themselves laded the family's trunks and animals when Günter delivered them, hiding their escape in plain view by blending it into the ordinary bustle of departure.

Niklas had sent Amalie to *Holsatia* hours ago with Lisette, a charming pair in bonnets and fur muffs, Amalie looking quite grown up enough in her traveling coat to accompany the little girl. In fact, he would not think of letting them go unescorted, but paid the inn's burly doorman to attend the girls and report back to him when they were safely aboard.

When their sisters arrived, Hans told Will, "It's a relief to have them aboard, but if the police arrest Pop at the last moment, we will have to take the little girls with us to America. Mein Gott!" Against this very possibility, Katrina had sewn a copy of the family's passport into Amalie's coat pocket and coins into her hems.

Back at the inn, Niklas wrapped six sandwiches in paper and stuffed them into a carpetbag. In just a few days he had become a fan of these Kölsch favorites, Halve Hahn, buttered rye buns with raw onion and thick slices of gouda cheese.

Katrina watched, glad he had something to occupy him, but feeling there was some minor injustice, when she had spent every waking hour baking, to see him so taken with what some thoughtless barmaid had slapped together. *Insignificant*, she scolded herself, but it distracted her. So did Jakob, who clung to her in distress. *What terrors lie between us and a new home, impossibly far away?* She kissed Jakob, smiled with a reassurance she surely did not feel, and placed him firmly in his cot. She needed both hands to pin her hat in place and pull down the veil. Then she picked up Jakob, set him on his own two feet, and took his hand.

"Herr Kuschelbär!" he said in panic and reached for his little stuffed bear.

"Ah, ja, Herr Kuschelbär," she said, handing it to him.

Niklas had hired a hackney carriage, which now waited outside. He helped Katrina in and handed Jakob to her, settling himself beside them. They traveled sedately through neighborhoods that became rougher and rougher, getting ever closer to the docks. They were both impatient but unwilling to make this obvious by rushing the driver and his horse.

"We should look entirely unconcerned," said Niklas, and she nodded her agreement.

They crossed through a gathering crowd and arrived at the docks, where they were now out of the hackney, bags in their arms and holding little Jakob's hand tightly. Then they stepped onto the gangplank and crossed the gap between the dock and the steamboat. Will met them at the top of the gangplank and took Jakob's hand; Hans helped his mother down the last big step onto *Holsatia*'s. deck. They looked for all the world like any small family on its way to Düsseldorf, and by the time they were safely aboard, the quay was filled with families waving and pointing at this experimental craft.

Katrina choked back tears. *What scavengers,* she thought, *will soon be going through my house? What dirt will they find when they move the furniture?* She knew immediately that this was childish and was grateful for her veil. *But Elizabet! How could I have left Elizabet?*

Niklas looked out at the crowd, searching for trouble, but not an official hat or jacket was in sight, and when he turned to Katrina, it was with a grin, as the enormity of their escape became real. "Now the adventure begins," he said.

On Katrina's other side, Hans bent to her ear and asked, "Was all of this subterfuge really necessary?"

"Yes," Katrina said to him and stifled a sigh. *Does he have any idea how many ties have been cut, how irreversible our decisions?*

"Anyway, I'm glad you're here," Hans said. "Whatever is to come, we're in it together."

Holsatia's smokestack gave a deafening blast, a puff of dark smoke rose, the gangplank was pulled aboard, the staysail raised, and the last of the dock lines flipped off the cleats and dragged on board. Soon, the cathedral towers were all of Cologne still visible as *Holsatia* steamed down the Rhine toward the Netherlands. Only one of them would ever return to this fine ancient city with its Roman walls or to the clean little town of Berleburg, but even that one had not the slightest idea of it.

Except for Niklas, none of them had ever seen anything like P.V. *Holsatia* or for that matter, had ever been on the Rhine, and Will, for one, was enchanted. A shipshape little steamboat, *Holsatia* had been in service for nearly three years. It could make an amazing speed of eight knots under its own power, Niklas said, and that was upstream! Since they were traveling downstream, it might be ten knots or even more, depending on the current. Without a breeze! Without men at oars! Without mules plodding along the towpath pulling it! *Holsatia* was indefatigable, so long as men fed the fire under the boiler, and with no reason to pause except for the darkness of night and the need to wood up. She chugged along with the whoosh of water breaking at her bow and running smoothly along her sides and through the paddle wheels. The tinny clank of halyards for her signal flags and staysail hit a high note; altogether, it was a true modern amazement.

"While it does not actually bring one town nearer to another," explained Niklas to the younger children, "its astonishing speed may make it seem as if it does."

Holsatia was an odd-looking vessel to any eye used to the ordinary river traffic of canoes and flatboats and rafts and barges and all the differently shaped and rigged sailboats. It was almost flat except for the smokestack amidships like a short, stout mainmast, braced by port and starboard shrouds and fore and aft stays, and the short, thin mast far aft. It was owned by the Prussian-Rhenish Steamship Company, called the Köln Company for short, and Niklas said the Kästners were lucky to book passage; the first Basel-to-Rotterdam run had been only four years earlier, and regular service could not yet be relied upon.

They had the cabin to themselves on this first leg of the trip, a long, spare passenger cabin, where they were glad to be out of the weather and have all of the benches. Katrina passed out napkin-wrapped ham sandwiches, and Niklas added his Kölsch favorites, the Halve Hahn, to the picnic. Three big hampers had strawberry-rhubarb jam, apple butter and their own homemade Berleburg cheese, a pale, cows' milk cheese, brushed with salt and wrapped in cheesecloth. Katrina and Amalie had baked in every spare moment, and the pantry was not bare when they began, so the hampers held black bread, sausages, pork-and-potato pies, walnuts, dried apples and apricots, raisins and prunes, soft wheat rolls to eat at first and for later, brötchen, crusty breakfast rolls, pfefferkuchen, and many, many, sweet, twice-baked crackers called zucker zweiback. On top was Cousin Elizabet's streusel, saved to celebrate their first day aboard and now saved again since they had two kinds of sandwiches.

A carefully wrapped Westphalian ham had been smoked in their attic in Berleburg, where a smoking closet was connected to the fireplace below. For much of the winter, while the hams cured, the family burned only beech or juniper, the best woods for smoking Westphalian hams. Amalie looked at the ham wistfully, and Katrina asked her what the matter was.

"I'm sure there are hogs in America, but will there be beech trees and junipers? As much as we have read about America, I don't know."

"We have a lot to learn," Katrina said. *Beech trees and junipers! Surely Americans had found a way to smoke a ham, but would it ever be a Westphalian ham?*

"It is a fine picnic," said Niklas, who was quietly smiling as Katrina packed everything away.

She asked him why he smiled, "Besides the obvious," she said, one arm waving at their surroundings.

"Ja, I am glad to be away, but I was thinking of how often, invading Spain or Portugal or Italy or Russia, we could only hope for such a feast. The supply trains often lost us, you know. They could not keep up."

"I should hope we can do better," Katrina said, feigning insult.

"You always do better, my dear," he said.

A mist rose along the riverbanks, and Niklas stared at it as he unbuttoned his waistcoat and took a deep breath. "Reminds me of cannon smoke, the way it rises. Sometimes you couldn't see your hand in front of your face for the smoke. When the wind cleared it out, you never knew what you would find—the way clear or the enemy face-to-face."

Katrina was listening closely. Like Hans, she always listened when Niklas spoke of the wars.

"Once, when battle smoke began to clear, it was mixed with this, a mist on a riverbank. I yanked the reins and wheeled Zimt around right before we went down into the river. We had mistaken the cries of men falling in for the cries of men being hit. As soon as I saw the river, I realized I had been hearing splashes as well."

Katrina had been rubbing her wrist as she listened. Will saw this, and said, "You have 'war stories,' too, Mama. Tell us the one about the apple tree."

She smiled and turned to Lisette. "I was about your age when I fell from an apple tree and broke this wrist." She held up the one she had been heedlessly massaging.

"And why were you in an apple tree, Mama?" Will teased.

She talked to the three youngest, since the others had heard this story often enough. "I was in love with your father, and I needed to see his going away."

"His going away?" Lisette had heard this story, too, but she wanted to hear it again.

"His going away to war."

"Riding Zimt, the first Zimt," added Amalie.

"You should have seen him, my darlings, perfectly splendid in his uniform, brass buttons shining like gold, his fine sword, the one you've all seen."

"The Second Regiment of the Chevau-Légers," said Will, "the Light Horse, newly formed and paid for by the prince."

"Not that he wanted to," said Niklas, "and not everything. My father, your Opa, paid for my sword, so it would have a silver handle and be finer than anyone else's."

"And no one"—Katrina paused for emphasis—"no one expected to see any of those boys ever again."

The children looked appropriately horrified.

"But your father did come home again."

"Like a bad penny," said Niklas.

"Like the hero he is, and so that you all could have a papa," said Katrina, to smiles all around and considerable relief and shoulders squeezed and hands held.

CHAPTER 17

INITIAL CURIOSITY

After the rush and uncertainty of the last few days, being on the steamboat was like a dream, as if they had dropped into a place too remote and safe to recognize. The initial curiosity of being aboard wore off, but they remained amazed to be carried so steadily along, in spite of late winter ice and early morning fog, free from the vagaries of the wind, living proof of the comfort and speed of steamboats.

Like *Elise*, the first steamboat in Paris, *Holsatia* was a stern-wheeler, after Robert Fulton's designs. It was forty-eight feet long and equipped with a reliable walking beam mill engine made in England by Boulton and Watt. Such fine engines could be dropped onto a wooden barge and paddles added to create a steam-powered boat rather easily, not that many riverboat men were so inclined. Having experienced it, Katrina thought a steamboat's advantages must be obvious, and Niklas agreed with her.

Holsatia's Captain Aldo was an ageless Dortmund native whose face was marred by smallpox and whose shock of gray hair was barely contained by his gold-banded cap. None of this mattered when he turned his ice-blue eyes toward Niklas and Katrina with a look piercing enough to make them duck. When they engaged him in conversation, they were surprised to find him kind and soft-spoken.

"I admit, I've seen my share of the world," he said.

Katrina was relieved that he kept his eyes on the river as he made gentle, continual adjustments to the wheel. He smiled at their enthusiasm for steamboats.

"Early passengers like you," he said, "are the exception. Intrepid, forward-looking people are the most likely to book passage on such a craft. Many won't even consider it."

Niklas nodded and smiled at the compliment, thinking privately that it had more to do with the price of a ticket. "I take your point," he said. "But steam is surely the way of the future."

Katrina nudged Niklas. "Remember when you suggested a steamboat?" she asked, and then she turned to Captain Aldo. "I asked, 'Are they quite safe? Isn't steam just a fad?'" She laughed, and the men laughed with her. "Now our Will, he had quite the opposite reaction."

"Our second son has always been interested in modern inventions," Niklas explained to Captain Aldo. "He even had a model of a steam engine in his bedroom."

"Good heavens! Don't ever let him keep such a thing in a house."

"It was small, a toy," Niklas assured the captain.

"I do worry," said Katrina, "what will become of us as the old ways disappear. Won't old skills be forgotten?"

"Ah, well, that's the way of the future," said Captain Aldo. "Everything old—not just technology but science, politics, wealth, commerce—is changing."

"With uncertain results," said Niklas, and Captain Aldo agreed.

Katrina asked, "Isn't a steamship being built for an ocean crossing? How anyone would attempt it is a mystery. Can this be true?"

"It's not like you can stop to wood up in the middle of the ocean," Niklas added.

Captain Aldo laughed, a deep, friendly laugh. "It's just some whippersnappers trying to break the distance record. Steam may replace wind ships someday, but for ocean-going travel, that's a long way off. Now, for harbor work, river traffic, and even coastwise travel, the advantages are undeniable, and steam is fast replacing sail."

"If an ocean crossing ever succeeds, which I doubt," said Niklas, "I suppose the future will have indeed arrived."

"The future," Captain Aldo said, "sneaks in on cat's feet, when we're not looking."

"And only if we can afford it," said Katrina.

"A sailing ship on the ocean," Niklas pointed out, "has wind for free, which is all of the fuel it needs."

"And indeed, sometimes too much," Captain Aldo said. "Some people go through life looking backward, ignoring facts. That way, they don't have to accommodate change, and it's easier to nurse the grievances of their fathers."

"Ja," said Niklas, "There are powerful people who call any change at all 'presumptuous,' against the law of nature." He was thinking of Prince Metternich, who had written something very like this.

Captain Aldo looked thoughtful. "Thus we lose or delay a thousand promising prospects." His eyebrows rose. "Metternich! A grasping Austrian upstart not above marrying his way to power."

"So many people think," said Niklas, carefully.

"I know it personally! He rebuffed my design for a vastly improved steam-powered riverboat, as well as my scheme for organized landings for wood or coal. Worse than that, he refused to see me, leaving me to the predations of one of his functionaries, who wormed the outlines of my plan out of me and then summarily dismissed me. I am watching, indeed watching very closely, for my design to emerge afloat—owned by some grasping fawn of the prince's."

His fury surprised them. "A coordinated system," said Niklas soothingly, "would help."

"Of course!" said Captain Aldo, "It could transform trade, enrich the country, and unite it."

The three of them fell to musing, each leaving much unsaid.

After a while, Niklas changed the subject: "I heard of a shipwreck last year that killed more than two hundred?"

"*Neva*, an Irish barque," said Captain Aldo, "carrying convicts, mostly women and children, bound for Australia. Two hundred and twenty-four lost."

"Gott im Himmel," Katrina said.

"Well," said Captain Aldo, "all travel is dangerous, but children at least don't deserve such a fate."

Katrina wondered what dangers of travel Captain Aldo had in mind as they steamed closer to the Netherlands every minute, sliding quickly past innumerable local officials and their awkward questions. Instead of asking him, she murmured her agreement, took Niklas's arm and returned to the passengers' cabin. The Kästner trunks and sea-bags were stowed safely below the bench, the chicken coops lashed securely to one of the trunks. Niklas sent Will to feed their goats, which were tied up on deck, their backs to the breeze. The children took turns standing at the rail in the lee of the smokestack, to watch the shores of the Rhine slide by. The motion of the boat was soothing, and soon Jakob was sound asleep on Katrina's lap, and Lisette snuggled up next to her.

Katrina pointed to a tower on the shore. "It's a castle, Lisette."

"Oh!" Lisette craned her neck to see. "Will we see more, Mama?"

Katrina was surprised to feel the sting of tears as she realized all the children would miss. *Will was meant to go to university, the church pews need us, and then there are summer picnics at the Berleburg Palace Orangery and Christmas nights glowing with candles and carolers. Amalie might think her father has lost everything and we are now poor. Or running from debt. I must find a moment alone to explain to her.* An image sprang to her mind of cloth ripping down the middle, a clear and powerful image, surprising and frightening her for a moment; she gasped at the strangeness of it. Then she shoved such thoughts aside and answered Lisette.

"Ach, nein, we won't see many castles, Mein Kind," she told Lisette. "Most are upriver, past Bonn and Koblentz." She thought of the fantastic medieval Castle Eltz and how charmed she had been when she was taken to see it as a girl. "They are quite a sight," Katrina went on, "and some have been here almost since the Romans. That's a very long time ago." *How much time has passed since the heathen Romans set up camp along the Rhine?* She sometimes mixed up the heathen Romans and the wicked Roman Catholic Church, but who did not? Thus she did not venture any historical precision. *There is just too much history,* she thought. Instead, she hurried on to her main point: "America is new; in America we can build our own castles." Katrina glanced at Niklas, and he returned her smile.

She, who knew certain horrors of war and torture would never be wiped entirely from Niklas's memory, was grateful for the softness of her own life, and became more determined to maintain the steady cheerfulness everyone counted on. She knew they were luckier than most, who went to America too poor to have any hope at all at home. Still, she could not help but think of the many difficulties ahead, traveling as they were, alone and under shadowy threats. There was the wide ocean to cross, and when at last they were exhausted and impoverished, they would face a first winter in America. Without bidding, Niklas's description of the frozen wastes of the Russian steppes came into her mind, a black and white landscape of burned rubble half hidden in snow, no hope of game or grain or shelter. *God help us,* she prayed, *Gott, hilf uns.*

CHAPTER 18

WITHOUT A BLINK

Mid-afternoon, they put in at Düsseldorf to wood up, and Captain Aldo kindly asked if they wanted to go ashore. "The Schloss Benrath is un palais de plaisir, a pleasure palace, and the pinkest building I ever laid eyes on. It was Prince Murat's, was it not, in the days of Napoleon?"

Niklas nodded assent, and Captain Aldo continued.

"And there's the MarktPlatz, where they sell beer and sausages, right here by the dock, an easy walk."

Katrina gave the captain her weakest smile, as if a shore excursion were beyond her, and the children kept their heads down.

"Let him think," Niklas said quietly when Captain Aldo walked away, "we have not a pfennig to waste on food or beer."

After a few more hours on the river, *Holsatia* tied up at the docks in Duisburg.

"Is this the ocean?" Amalie asked Niklas as the ship wound its way to a berth.

"Nein, Daughter, but the harbor is indeed huge. I have not seen another so large anywhere inland. We may well be amazed to see this, but we are not even out of the Germanies yet."

That night, Niklas lay awake, and when sleep threatened to overtake him, Katrina heard him slip out of bed and stand guard at the door. At four in the morning, he shook Hans and said, "Your watch."

Hans opened his eyes. He looked balefully at his father but dropped out of his bunk to the floor, pulled on his boots and grabbed a coat.

The long night passed without event, and the morning dawned clear and cold, the sun a gold sliver on the horizon, no warmth to it at all. They loaded wood for the voracious engine, disembarked goods and passengers, and boarded new ones. One of these families tried to start a conversation, and Katrina smiled and listened, but when the young mother asked where home was, Katrina coughed a little and called to Jakob, who looked up in surprise.

"You have to keep such a good eye on them," Katrina confided to the young mother, who immediately stepped away to check on her own children. Katrina watched her go with satisfaction. This was no moment to make friends.

When Captain Aldo delayed departure, Niklas was deeply apprehensive.

"Even without this early spring flooding, my dear Herr Kästner," an unhappy Captain Aldo told him, "sandbars and shores shift almost every day, and on a day like this, we could face collapsed banks or worse yet, 'sawyers'—half-submerged trees washed out into the river, ready to stove in a hull or catch us in their roots."

Niklas nodded sympathetically.

Captain Aldo explained further: "The conjunction of the two rivers here is treacherous, the two currents becoming confused." He could not help but illustrate with his hands, stirring the air as he explained the opposing currents.

Niklas relaxed a little. "Perhaps," he told Katrina privately, "the delay is only as our captain says, time to learn what is happening with a strong current and heavy rain. There are chunks of ice washing out from the Ruhr and many other streams feeding the Rhine."

"It's a modern city," Captain Aldo told Niklas a few minutes later. Niklas thought he was hinting that there was still time to go touring before they departed. "You can see just a little further along where Franz Haniel's shipyard is building steamships."

Will could not help asking, "What is that tall smokestack with steam or smoke rising from it?"

Niklas gave him a hard look. *The less said the better, so close to the border.*

"Ah," said Captain Aldo, "that is the Curtius Sulphuric Acid Factory. See where a streak of orange dyes the river? It's runoff from the factory, a mighty pretty color. Some say it kills the fish, but that's the price of progress, ain't it? There's plenty of fish in the sea, I say." Then he remembered to tell them, "You will smell it, too, if the wind changes. It's not the kind of modern thing to be found in Köln yet!"

"Danke," Will said, looking as if he might melt under Niklas's gaze.

As soon as Captain Aldo could dispense with polite conversation, he hung out over the railing, chatting with vessels coming up or down the Rhine. Boats going upriver had more control than those going downriver like *Holsatia*, when a boat could be almost helpless, shoved forward by a stiff current. Those that had come downriver after *Holsatia* knew more about the extent of flooding affecting the current.

Niklas kept a constant watch on the captain, aware that their lifeline was as slender as the good will of this one man, a virtual stranger. Mid-morning a pair of customs officials appeared on the docks, going boat to boat, inspecting each. Captain Aldo met them at the gangplank, spoke in a low voice and pointed to a barge down the quay. The officials hurried off in that direction, and just then a thin sun appeared and the current slowed, so *Holsatia* pushed off.

"There appears," Niklas said quietly to Katrina, "to have been no sly notification to the authorities, no greedy request for a bounty."

"No sudden betrayal," she agreed in a whisper.

He breathed a sigh of relief and went to take a much-needed nap; before he closed his eyes, he called Hans over. "Son, wake me the instant there is any unscheduled stop at all or any mid-river boarding."

The family stayed crowded in the cabin as *Holsatia* left the dock and even then, they stayed close to each other all day, watching the shores slide by with gratifying speed. All but the youngest children were worried by the rising tension in Niklas's manner.

Holsatia put in again to spend the next night at Wesel, a small, heavily fortified town where she tied up at a floating dock between Der Zitadel, the 1682 fort, and Fort Blücher, called Le Citadelle Bonaparte when Napoleon had it built on an island in the Rhine. Its name had been changed to honor the field marshal who led Prussian troops to victory against Napoleon. Off the starboard side, behind the fort and ancient city walls, two fine steeples were etched against a pink and orange evening sky.

"Blücher the Butcher," Niklas told Katrina, "roused his men at Waterloo by saying they fought for 'freedom and fatherland.' No one gained anything from the fight against Napoleon but absolute monarchy."

"And poverty," she said.

On the third day, 19 February 1836, they crossed the border into the Netherlands, an unimaginably quick and sure passage. Now, as their own Westfälischer Totleger rooster stretched his neck and crowed to celebrate the rising sun, they were on the "Rijn," as the Dutch called the Rhine; their passport was accepted without a blink by the bored Dutch officer who inspected it at Arnhem. The man, obviously a fancier of poultry, paid most of his attention to the rooster, admiring it and inquiring about it. Niklas might have sold it to the customs officer if he had not seen Katrina's hard look at him.

Amalie pointed out a steeple not far from the shore, St. Eusebius, according to a Dutch passenger, but the younger children could not be made interested. By midday, they were tired and bored, the novelty of being aboard ship having worn thin and Amalie's stock of games and songs having been run through more than once. The little ones seemed incapable of looking out and seeing all there was to see along the Rhine.

"Are we there yet?" Jakob asked Amalie. Lisette looked up expectantly, eager to hear her sister's answer. She gathered them into her arms, one on each side and told them, "Now, look. Our new home is very far away, and it's no use asking all the time. Just be glad we are together, and warm enough, and that we have something to eat." She tickled their bellies and made them both giggle.

All of the family was inside on a bench, and as time wore on, Jakob could not be still any longer. He squirmed this way and that in his seat, kicking his legs until Niklas was forced to stand up and stare in any other direction. "That child," he said privately to Katrina, "looks as if he is trying to screw his bony little bottom right into the bench."

"And this, only the first boat," she said.

Gradually, the riverside bluffs flattened into lowlands stretching out on both shores, icy puddles and rivulets reflecting the sunlight like elongated mirrors, windmills picking up the sharp breeze of the day, white-belted red cattle grazing in fields laced with frost. Farmsteads appeared and disappeared as *Holsatia* floated steadily along, their thatched-roof buildings arranged around a central courtyard, where pigs squealed and dogs barked to see a boat passing.

Amalie watched the Dutch landscape with satisfaction. *My first new country,* she thought. *The first of many.*

From time to time, a small village with a lift bridge appeared. Captain Aldo had his engineer blow the stacks well in advance of each lift bridge. At one of these interruptions, Katrina stepped out for a moment on deck and was treated to a rare sight—cranes flying north, high in the sky, vast numbers of them, their squawking audible from a very great distance.

"Evening, ma'am," said Captain Aldo, "a pretty sight, ain't it? Now, do go back in, don't catch cold."

Holsatia slowed, having to wait for a man who knew how to operate the bridge. Katrina watched, feeling a little stubborn about leaving the evening sky and honestly interested in this novel contraption, a lift bridge. Still, she tried to make herself look insignificant, while listening to see whether questions were asked (no, they were not) and whether taxes or fees were levied (yes, they were). When Hans and Will came out on deck to watch with her, she stole an admiring look at the pair of them. *Prussia,* she thought, *may be happy to let an old revolutionary like Niklas take himself out of the country on his own thaler, but it would never want to lose two such strong young men.*

More long miles slid smoothly by, and as darkness fell, they reached Rotterdam, steamed past much of the city proper and pulled at last into their berth, where their nostrils caught the smell of frying fish and sausages and sauerkraut, and for the first time, something they did not recognize, the scent of a salty ocean.

CHAPTER 19

ROTTERDAM FERRY-BOAT

They awoke the next morning full of praise for the Rotterdam innkeeper after a night in a well-furnished room with thick mattresses and heavenly quilts. The fire was well stoked and a breakfast of omelets, ham, and poffertje appeared unasked for, brought in by a pretty daughter of the house, a red-cheeked girl with blond braids and delicate blue eyes.

"Now, Papa!" said Amalie, looking around at the white-washed room so well-scrubbed and neatly appointed, "This is worth traveling for. Are you sure we need to take a single step further?"

She was teasing, and Niklas returned her happy look. But when the children were otherwise occupied, Katrina turned quietly to him and asked, "Are we really safe here?"

"We are safer," he replied, "but we must keep our wits about us. Neither Austrian nor Prussian secret police respect national boundaries, and we cannot know with what interest or fury they might discover our escape."

"Besides," Niklas added to Hans, who had joined their surreptitious conversation, "local police everywhere are easily persuaded or corrupted."

"There's the harbor town problem of crimps."

"And the ordinary problems of pickpockets and of not knowing our way."

"It would be wiser if none of us went out on the streets alone."

They agreed to make arrangements to depart as quickly as possible.

In an aside, Niklas said to Katrina, "I think the Dutch too occupied with the Belgian separatists to pay much attention to us."

"War is certainly distracting," she agreed, "but the Dutch king is a friend of the King Wilhelm and has been since what? Waterloo?"

"At least," he said.

Will was telling the younger children to appreciate all this and expect their quarters aboard to be small and crowded.

"Papa," asked Jakob as he tugged on Niklas's coat, "will there be room for Herr Kuschelbär?"

"What?" Niklas had not been thinking about cuddly stuffed bears.

"I can leave him here if it would be better." Jakob was trying very hard to be brave, but his chin quivered.

"Never in the world! Where you go, Herr Kuschelbär goes. However," and here Niklas assumed a severe face, "He can't have his own bed. He'll have to sleep with you."

"That's all right, Papa! I'll share!" Jakob could hardly contain his relief.

They were soon dressed and on the ancient streets of Rotterdam, where the salty scent of the sea competed with mouthwatering aroma of deep-fried eels sold from handcarts along the wharfs. Around them flowed Dutch, Frisian, German, French, and Danish, amid many other languages. It was chilly, and Katrina wrapped her gray shawl around her shoulders more tightly.

They ducked into a bookseller's shop, where the talkative proprietor told them, "The Spanish, then the French, and then our own Belgians take it on themselves to practice war. We Dutch need to get back to what we do best—making money."

"Ja, natuurlijk," Niklas said soothingly.

Hans held up a copy of Toqueville's *De La Démocratie en Amérique,* and Katrina asked, "But can we afford it?"

"Hmm," said Niklas, "Think of the long days of the crossing."

"And of our need to understand where we are going."

Niklas bought the book, installed the children in a coffee shop and threaded his way with Katrina along the docks. They soon found *Holsatia,* where they hoped to thank Captain Aldo and slip a gold coin into his hands.

"We appreciate all you have done for us," Niklas said.

They were standing together on the deck of *Holsatia,* and as Niklas and Katrina turned to go, the captain said, "Some say America is full of rebels and thieves, naught but criminals, debtors and heretics."

Niklas turned to listen, and the captain continued. "Don't you believe it! I think you'll find freedom and prosperity in America, a new life."

"You knew?"

Captain Aldo turned his ice-blue eyes to Niklas. "Who won't get off the boat for a pink schloss? Or a beer and a sausage? More to the point," he said, looking grim, "your scar. My son wore one like it. Infantry. Fifty-fourth. Badly injured in Spain, lost at Borodino. Your, shall we say, 'awkward status,' was why we left Duisberg when we did and why we did not stop at Arnhem, not even to wood up."

Tears sprang to Katrina's eyes. "Vielen Dank, Herr Aldo, we thank you," she said, seizing the captain's weather-beaten hands.

"For the love of liberty," Captain Aldo said in a low, serious voice.

"Which is what we hope to find in America."

"Oh, you won't *find* liberty in America. You must *bring* liberty to America." His ice blue eyes were penetrating.

Niklas and Katrina looked at him, mystified.

"Ja, the country has rid itself of kings, but what really matters— liberty, equality, brotherhood—resides only in the heart and must be taught to each new generation."

"Because tyranny," said Niklas, as he grasped the captain's idea, "seeks always to rise again and seize power."

"Exactly, but when you bring your ideals to America, you heal and strengthen her."

"Not just with ideas but with children," said Katrina, who now understood him.

Captain Aldo smiled at Katrina. "That's right. Teach your children, and they will be the living embodiment of your principles. They will carry on for you and make America stronger by their presence."

As they debarked *Holsatia*, Captain Aldo called after them: "Take the Rotterdam ferry-boat to Delfshaven. A good man and his sons sail it."

Being in Rotterdam was not enough. The family had to get to Delfshaven's deeper waters, where ocean-going ships berthed.

Soon, the family waited on the dock for the Rotterdam ferry, surrounded by trunks and bundles. Jakob laughed and danced, the happiest little boy. He tugged Katrina's sleeve. "Mama, Mama, we're going to America today!"

The goats, chickens and larger trunks were laded onto the ferry, a traditional, rather beamy, double-ender, and then dock lines were thrown off and sheets tightened. Katrina gasped as the gaff-rigged sloop caught the wind and heeled sharply to one side.

Now, with every tack, the skipper of the ferry waved Niklas and the older boys to the high side, his stern face telling them they were not to be inattentive or slow. Niklas grasped the coaming, and Katrina thought of the irony of going side to side, just as they now switched sides from the Old World to the New. Anticipation flooded her, but also worry. *We have left our country to fend for itself,* she thought, *and now have endangered all of our family with this journey, which is not a tenth completed.*

For the moment, however, Katrina could do nothing but stay out of the crew's way and hold the children as tightly as possible. She sat unmoving on the centerline, staring at the receding town, making the four of them a little knot of warmth and stability. If she were to tell the truth, which she was not prepared to do just yet, she would have said that leaving the continent made her feel undone, as if it were abandoning her. She was not sure where they belonged now or when she might feel at home again.

"Mama," said Amalie, smiling at her, "you can't hold us like this all the way to America."

She tried to return her daughter's smile, but she was deeply worried, and besides, the facts did not matter. She wanted her children firmly in her grip, even though they were not at all afraid but instead, thrilled with the ride.

"Ready about," cried the skipper, and Katrina gasped again to feel the tidy little vessel pause and flatten out, lines flying and sails flapping noisily, and just as quickly, begin to tilt to starboard, tilt and tilt and tilt to an alarming degree. The three Kästner men moved to the high side as the sails filled again, and the spunky little boat leapt forward through the waves. Will laughed with pleasure.

The ferrymen had brought her about with very little conversation, these men and boys having been over this route a half-dozen times a day for a dozen years. Now they were setting belaying pins in their proper place and coiling lines from palm to elbow, just as they had done a hundred or maybe a thousand times before.

Will and Hans sat with their father, speaking quietly in their home dialect, to the dissatisfaction, or one might even say disgust, of the first mate.

"Te Duits voor mij," the first mate muttered, "Too German for me."

"Guld is guld," replied the skipper, who was his father, "Gold is gold." His dismissive manner suggested this son could be counted on to be snappish, no matter who they carried outbound or inbound, winter or summer.

The wind picked up and obliged the crew to tighten their lines; they did it automatically, without a word from the skipper or to each other. Niklas and the boys gripped the coaming more firmly, and Katrina braced herself against the steeper tilt of the deck.

Hans's knuckles might be white where he holds on, she noticed, *and he looks cross*. She wondered if he was getting a little green around the gills, and realized she herself was not feeling at all well.

"Whoo-hoo," cried Will, pointing to a gaily painted steam-powered tug. The ferry-boat was going much faster and about to pass it by.

Niklas smiled. "It makes a steamboat seem tame, doesn't it? And it's much more interesting to be aboard a sailboat here than on the Odeborn. But really, Will, does it take no more than a little breeze and a slanted deck to make you happy?"

"It does not, Father. It's the unthinking joy of youth." He added, with a grin: "You must recall it," but the wind blew his last words away, as he hoped it might.

As they approached the dock in Delfshaven, the skipper warned Katrina: "Hold tight, now, ma'am. One hand for the boat and one for the children."

Katrina gasped as the ferryboat knocked against the dock. She looked with apprehension at the two surfaces hit again, seeing the danger to little fingers.

"Aye, ma'am, it's not water to fear so much as its hard edges."

One of the crew chimed in. "That's sailing all right—dangerous at both ends and uncomfortable in the middle." The rest of the crew laughed as they handed Katrina and the children over onto the dock, and she felt with joy the unmoving Earth below her feet again. Jakob was rubbing the wrist she had gripped too hard and trying not to cry. Delfshaven was Rotterdam's most seaward harbor, where a dazzling array of naval vessels floated: men-of-war, ships of the line, frigates, and cutters. Flanking these were merchantmen: big West Indiamen, tartans, snows, settees, sloops, barques, and brigs. Here they expected to find *Enigma,* a three-masted barque, which according to Captain Aldo, had set something of a speed record.

"There she is," cried Will. He quickened his pace to be the first at her side. As *Enigma* swung at anchor, the stern board engraved with her name showed briefly and then disappeared. In a moment they all stood staring up at her, amazed. *Enigma* made the ferryboat look like a toy. Katrina had imagined the ride on the Rotterdam ferry a good introduction to ocean life; now she was not sure there was any similarity.

"It will be much more stable," Niklas told her. He had not missed her panic aboard the ferry.

"'She,'" said Will, "a ship is 'she,' not 'it,'" to which his father said nothing. His hard look said enough.

CHAPTER 20

CHAINS OF EUROPE

When they disembarked the ferry, the skipper warned them not to go lee-ward into Delfshaven's stinking sailor town, lined with taverns and brothels. Sailor towns were notorious for crimps, the civilian press gangs ready to shanghai any male between ten years old and fifty.

The skipper pointed the other way to the Delfshaven markets, and a few minutes later, Katrina was replacing what they had eaten so far and adding as much as she could. As passengers, they were required to bring their own food for an ocean crossing of forty-five days, more or less, and Katrina was rightly worried about having enough. The shops were full of gouda and edam cheeses wrapped in red wax; rookworst, a smoked sau-sage; and bitterballen, fried meatballs. The men sampled stamppot—potatoes mixed with cabbage, carrots and sauerkraut—and recommended taking along a sizeable crock and two big sacks of cabbages and potatoes. At a bakery crowded with customers, they bought stroopwafels and oliebollen, cookies and doughnuts.

"These won't last," Katrina told Amalie, looking at their haul from the bakery, "but with Hans and Will, they would be gone in no time any-way."

"I've heard that ship's biscuits—'hardtack'—are dreadful."

"But they last, and I suppose people will eat anything after a while." Katrina sighed. She did not mention a disgusting fact: by the time they needed it, the hardtack would be full of weevils.

More than provisions were to be bought, and that included delftware, the famous pottery made in Delft and for which Delfshaven, the "harbor of Delft," had been built. Katrina turned a beautifully smooth piece over and over in her hands, admiring its lovely cobalt scenes of windmills and sailing ships, like the Dutch landscapes and seascapes around them.

"We can sell some and earn enough to have ours for nothing," Katri-na said, and to her surprise, Niklas agreed.

Some of the dinnerware, canisters and tiles had exotic Chinese scenes that Lisette could hardly tear her eyes from: tigers and dragons and people in odd robes and hats in front of exotic little houses with upturned roofs. She was especially taken with a small whale oil lantern. Amalie tried to explain the idea of China to the little girl, but she was as ignorant of that far-away country as Lisette, and for once, their father was little help, having never been any nearer China than Moscow.

"It's east," he said. "A long way east. On the other side of the world." But he pointed down as he said this, and Lisette looked up at Amalie for an explanation. "Come now, Daughter," he told seven-year-old Lisette, "Even you know the world is round."

Katrina could scarcely believe they had the luck to be here, only a few miles from Delft, once home of the Vereenigde Oostindische Compagnie, the Dutch East India Company, importer/exporter par excellence. The shopkeeper's son had enough German to speak with them. Now he turned to his father and murmured something in Dutch.

The older man waved him away. "Deze Duitsers eruit zien alsof ze het zich kunnen veroorloven," he said, "These Germans look like they can afford it." The son turned back to Niklas with a smile and held firm on the price.

Niklas said something admirable about the delftware, speaking smoothly now in Dutch, and offered to buy more—at a lower price. The Dutch boy looked back at his father, who gave a disgusted nod. At such a lovely price, they bought quite a lot of china and tile, watching as the shopkeeper's daughters appeared with lidded baskets to pack the pieces, slipping a square of felt between each plate, securing the stacks in bags of red or green baize, and stuffing straw around the bags.

There would be buyers in New Orleans, a city sounding impossibly distant and romantic. Katrina had heard it called 'the Paris of the New World,' and that gave her hope. "Besides what we can sell," she said to Niklas, "this will be a lovely start to our new home."

Niklas was not blind to the charms of delftware, but watching Katrina linger over every piece, while Lisette stared, Amalie chased Jakob, and the older boys poked and teased each other outside the shop, he muttered to himself, "More camp followers than men."

Enigma was one hundred and twenty foot of sailing majesty, her purser told them, and in fact the Bristol Ships Registry had called her an "uncommonly handsome vessel." They felt honored to be its only passengers in cabins, which were usually reserved for officers. She was a Bristol-built barque with fore-, main- and mizzenmasts, a beam of 27' 10", three decks and a square stern. In '34 she left Bristol on 28 June and made a run to Mauritius in twelve weeks, discharged cargo, laded new, and was back in Bristol by 25 January 1835. This was considered an almost incredibly short passage by those well versed in nautical affairs.

Enigma impressed their landlubber eyes with polished brass, scrubbed decks, neatly coiled lines, and gunports painted in a checkerboard pattern. She was bigger than they had expected, like a village afloat. The gangplank looked freshly painted, and at each of her three masts bright flags drooped, including the Blue Peter, whose white square within a blue field signaled imminent departure. The wind had died, and as they watched, each sail was unfurled and left hanging to dry. This made a spectacular showing, and they looked on entranced, with Lisette exclaiming at the sight of sailors climbing to the topsails and scrambling out along the yardarms.

"It smells clean," said Amalie, "like tar and hemp and polish." Even she had heard about the stink of slaver ships and was glad this ship, their ship, showed no sign of that cruel trade.

Katrina and Amalie seemed to be the only women in sight, and the salty language they heard was no comfort.

"You know how they say, 'he swears like a sailor'?" Katrina asked her daughter. "I'm afraid we shall have to learn to stop up our ears."

"Tsk," said Amalie. "How will we protect the children?"

"I do not know that we can, my dear."

As they watched, crates, trunks, sacks, and barrels were loaded, and a small menagerie was carried aboard in stout canvas slings.

"Dinner on the hoof," Niklas remarked, as cows mooed, pigs oinked and sheep baaed.

"Look," cried Will, as the Kästner goats and chicken crates were lifted aboard. They saw their trunks being hauled up, as well as crates of delftware, and bales of straw, and bags of oats and barley for the animals.

Before they boarded, Niklas directed the family to Pelgrimvaderskerk, the Pilgrim Father's Church, built in 1472 as the Roman Catholic Church of St. Anthony. The old church with its distinctive Dutch gable sat on a sidewalk along the Aelbrechtskolk Canal, which was lined on both sides with barges, canal boats, lighters, and the smaller kinds of sloops. Niklas told them that right here, in front of the church, was a special spot.

Before he could go any further, Katrina dug into her pocket, pulled out the tiny carved fiddler, and held it up to the family.

"Oh, Mama," cried Will, "you brought a little bit of Berleburg with us!"

Niklas laughed, "There's a lot more of Berleburg in each of you than in that fiddler."

"Opa made it, didn't he?" Amalie asked.

"He did indeed, my dear," said Katrina, as she tucked it away again. "We can consider it the blessing he'd have given our journey."

"This," said Niklas, looking around, "is where the Pilgrims knelt in their black robes and white collars in 1620 and prayed before setting sail on the *Speedwell* for the New World."

"With that in mind," Hans said, "this must be the most fortuitous place in Europe to embark."

"Precisely," Niklas said. "Now let us pray." As Katrina and the children bowed their heads, Niklas prayed: "Lord, whom winds and seas obey, guide us through the watery way; in the hollow of thy hand, hide us and bring us safe to land."

For a little while they spoke quietly of their hopes and fears.

Then Niklas announced: "The Pilgrims did it two hundred years ago in a leaky, unweatherly ship, landing on a rock-bound, northerly coast entirely uninhabited but by savages—and in November! If they could do it," he said, "so can we."

There on that canal street in Delfshaven, the little family gave a cheer, not being quiet for once and ignoring the curious eyes of passersby. For them, America was still a long way off, but they could already feel the chains of Europe dropping away and the wilderness of America sparkling in their hearts.

CHAPTER 21

E N I G M A

The morning they shoved off Delfshaven was a lucky Monday, 29 February 1836, the leap day of a leap year, and besides that, they were carried out on an ebb tide in a most seamanlike way. It was a complex estuary facing them, but the winds were favorable, and they were towed past the worst of it, and their Danish captain, Izak Peterssen, knew the rest well, having navigated often through its many small waterways. By Tuesday morning *Enigma* had passed the Hook of Holland, cleared the islands of Voorne and Putten, and was at last in the great North Sea itself.

The dawn was breathtakingly beautiful, the cold ocean a deep cerulean blue with crests of white showing here and there, sparkling and glittering in the morning sun, the western sky still bearing wide stripes of violet and indigo along the horizon. A pale blue filled all the dome above, with white puffs of clouds moving gently. *Enigma* would soon slip between Dover and Calais and run the length of the English Channel.

On deck, Katrina stood in the most out-of-way spot she could find, with a sick feeling. The world seemed upside down and everything wrong. Their three-masted barque was much larger than she had ever imagined, especially in height, and from the deck, she felt like she was inside a gigantic loom, lines all around taut with mysterious purpose. She had often warped a loom, but here, she was inside it, dwarfed and incapable. At the master's voice, she jumped. It was loud and harsh enough to out-holler the wind. Sailors sprang acrobat-like onto the rigging and began to climb. It was fascinating and horrifying to watch them ascend. She reached for a mast to steady herself and jumped back when the lines below her hand moved, tugged from above. From far forward, she heard a few notes of a shanty as men heaved on lines. Inside this net of hemp, life ashore seemed gone and irrelevant, while outside it, the sea stretched away to the horizon in every direction.

Niklas appeared by her side, startling her. "Do you remember how I described the steppes? Endlessly flat all the way to the horizon. Frightening openness. Like this."

"Ja, no comfort or refuge."

"But sometimes beautiful, like this sky."

With him at her side, she felt she could walk a little, from main to mizzen and back, staying away from busy men and conscious of keeping her balance. Niklas had told the family he expected they would sail south through the Channel and then west, either to London or towards Plymouth and then past Lizard Point, where the entire Atlantic would lie open to them When they came near the poop deck, Niklas called up to the captain, "Shall we put in at London?"

The tall, brusque captain with a Danish accent and long blond hair in an old-fashioned pigtail told them firmly: "We will not. In the first place," he said, his bright blue eyes flashing fire, "London would slow us down by several days and charge outrageous fees!"

"Liverpool, then? Or Plymouth?"

"There ain't nothing at Plymouth but ruffians and smugglers, who would sooner fleece you than look you in the eye. And Liverpool's completely out of the way and besides, even worse." Plymouth, a once-proud city, according to Captain Peterssen, had had nothing to say for itself since the Peace of '15. "That there's a dockyard that ain't to be saved by naught but the next good war, not that peace ain't a wonderful thing,"

Niklas and Katrina exchanged a look. She was disappointed, even though she knew Niklas would be happy to sail past England, home of his Waterloo enemies. Still, she would have liked to see London, the most modern city in the world.

Izak Peterssen added, "Besides, in '34 they had The Cholera. No, it's neither safe nor wise to put in at Plymouth."

"Cholera!" Katrina said. "An excellent reason to stay away."

Cholera had swept through Paris in '32, killing a hero of Niklas's, General Lamarque, a man Napoleon said "performed wonders." Lamarque's funeral sparked huge protests with barricades thrown up in the streets. The citizens of Paris fought for liberty in Lamarque's name, but the results were never really in question. The royal Garde Municipale put down the demonstrations without mercy. Paris still seethed with anger. Niklas said its citizens would rise again someday, oust Louie the Whatever, and make Lamarque's ghost proud. Niklas and Katrina wandered off from the captain, disappointed for more than one reason and thinking him rather rough and unfriendly.

She said privately to Niklas, "Just think, the French public still honors those who served under Napoleon."

He answered without a pause, "Yes, they do."

When the girls came on deck, Lisette asked, "Are we crossing the ocean now?" To this, Amalie could only look confused, and it was the ship's first mate, Mr. Groves, who answered the child. "It's only south we're going, along the coast. The ancients called this the whale road, so keep a sharp eye out for whatever swims."

When the Kästners were out of hearing, Izak Peterssen grumbled, "How do they expect to get anywhere if they keep wanting to stop at every little island?"

"Aye, sir," agreed Mr. Groves. "Everyone knows a ship should keep to the sea, away from rocks, shoals, and lee shores."

"And ports are the devil's playground—where ships rot and men go to hell."

"Aye, it's bad enough we have to put in at Gibraltar."

Izak Peterssen was annoyed that his passengers had spoken to him. A captain should never be bothered with frivolities, and worse yet, their questions were lubberly. Groves was not surprised to see the fury rising on his captain's face, and he sent one of the boys scurrying below: "Bring the captain a cup of hot coffee," he said with some urgency.

The ship Izak Peterssen sailed, *Enigma,* was square- and fore-and-aft-rigged, rated at three hundred and fifty-seven tons and fitted out with twelve brass cannon and a bow cannon Izak Peterssen himself had paid for, an impressive weight of gunnery for a merchantman. She had a master and first mate, a ship's surgeon and surgeon's assistant, a steward, a purser, a cook, a carpenter, a sailmaker, an efficient crew of thirty-six, room for eight cabin passengers, and eighteen hammocks recently slung on a lower deck for steerage passengers.

The Kästners occupied the only large cabin besides the captain's and were lucky it was built for eight while they had only seven. Katrina stepped in and had her first look while their trunks were still piled on the deck outside. A small sofa lined each side with curious hooks above them, and bolsters formed of rolled nets. Then she grasped that the sofas converted to bunks, and the nets were hammocks to hang on the hooks.

To one side a small mahogany writing desk and a gimbled lamp were fitted into the curve of the ship, opposite a sort of dressing table, which, she saw when she lifted the lid, hid a convenience. A table was suspended on pulleys from the ceiling beams, ready to be lowered between the sofas for meals or work, and further in, beyond a bulkhead, four hammocks hung in a space fitted to them. Under, over, and around, every crevice was fitted with lockers or horizontal bars meant to keep books, maps, and other gear in place. *How thoughtfully planned and cleverly executed!* Katrina thought as she took her father's carving of the fiddler out of her pocket and tucked it firmly in the smallest niche, where it could look out to see them and where they were going.

To one side of their cabin was another barely big enough to hang a cot. It was for the ship's surgeon, a Dr. Quentin Ward, and next to it was the cabin of *Enigma*'s Master, Mr. Stephens. On the other side, the captain's steward, Mr. O'Malley, occupied another tiny rectangle, as did the First Mate, Mr. Groves. The officers' dining saloon and the captain's aft-cabin filled the stern.

In the afternoon, the breeze freshened enough to order reefs put in the foresail and main. Some of the passengers fell sick, and others were shocked at the ship's speed and the obviously dangerous slant to the deck, like the roof of a house, which several thought they should call to the attention of the sailors, although it seemed not to worry the captain or any of the Enigmas in the least. *Enigma* was making an excellent start to its passage, seven knots, eight knots, even ten or eleven knots, watch after watch.

Among those who appreciated their brisk start was Captain Peterssen, who had been aware for some years that life at sea was not the quiet walk in the park some landsmen seemed to imagine. He seemed surprised when a little bit of heeled-over deck, icy wind and near-frozen spray was felt to be more than a temporary inconvenience by first-timers, at least if they had not been born in the tropics and were decently past the innocence of childhood. Even he, however, could not look with complete equanimity at a dropping barometer such as he saw now. He shortened sail further with each watch and was not shocked when morning dawned with a cold gray sky and a stiff breeze coming 'round to nor'-nor'-west. The temperature had dropped into freezing territory overnight, leaving the rigging rimed with frost and the deck coated with ice wherever spray landed, which was everywhere.

Enigma was now well clear of the North Sea and through the English Channel, but open to a storm building as it crossed two thousand miles of open ocean. From yesterday to today the surface of the sea had turned from pretty flecks of white to ugly white foam, salt spray flying across the deck, and cold penetrating deep within, creeping down hatchways and through oak timbers into the cabins, the steerage, and the hold.

CHAPTER 22

ICE

In the Kästner cabin, Katrina lay cold, gray and insensible, racked occasionally with spasms but otherwise mute and motionless. She would happily have thrown herself overboard if she could have dragged herself to the rail, or at least in her disordered mind, she believed she would.

Patting her hand, Niklas apologized. "What have I done, to bring you to this degree of desolation?" He had never seen her look so wretched, but he understood that their new foe, Nature, was as heartless as the old.

She waved him off and turned away, too miserable to answer.

Amalie and Lisette, never feeling the least mal de mer, bustled about, keeping blankets wrapped around their mother, sponging her face, which looked old and thin, especially in the bad light of cabin and storm. They were otherwise more worried about Hans and especially little Jakob. He lay in shocking stillness, all color drained from his baby face, smiling weakly when Amalie stroked his forehead, and at her urging, he tried to drink a little water. Not even that would stay down, and Amalie was distraught with worry.

Hans was on the deck, lashed to the rail so he could vomit overboard, his face a sickly green and blotched with two days' stubble. Niklas and Will crouched beside Hans, retching along with him for the first few hours, but now recovered and keeping him company, holding his head and keeping layers of blankets wrapped around him.

Hours passed, and Katrina slept as she rarely had, deep and dreamlessly, and awakened feeling alert and almost human.

"Mama?" Jakob was at the side of her cot, watching her closely. He was the first to see her eyes open. Hans was inside, too, having been brought in when the cold became too much, and resting at last, sound asleep.

Katrina pulled Jakob up to her cot and laid him across her chest, surprised at how heavy he was and how weak she was. Amalie was there at once, very happy to see her mother's eyes open at last and her face less green, and shocked to see her lift Jakob.

"You must try to eat," Amalie said, a pot of soup in her hands.

Katrina looked at the soup doubtfully and waved it away. "How is Hans?"

"Over the worst of it, probably. Father says we won't know till he wakes."

"How long has this one been recovered?" Katrina stroked Jakob's very blond hair.

"Oh, hours, now. He's still weak. He's been so worried about you."

Even in these few moments, it had not escaped Katrina's notice that Jakob lay so still against her. "Has he eaten?"

"Only a little zweiback." Amalie set the pot down, pushed it into a crevice to secure it, and stuffed a towel in to pin it there. "Perhaps you should start with a biscuit, too."

"Let's have another biscuit, shall we?" Katrina said to Jakob, and the child nodded. The two of them struggled to sit up a little, and Amalie handed each of them a slice of zweiback. Katrina looked around at her miserable family. *Have we gone from kettle to fire?*

Just then, Hans groaned—or growled, it was hard to tell which—and rolled over.

"He's coming out of it, I think," said Amalie.

More long hours passed before Hans staggered free of a cot and dropped to the floor, collapsing with a degree of weakness he had not anticipated. It took more long hours yet before he sat curled over a bowl of soup, talking with the other men, while Katrina, now wrapped in her gray woolen cloak, bundled the three youngest into coats and shawls and knitted caps and blankets, their feet tucked up under them as they played cat's cradle and told each other stories and occasionally curled up together and got warm enough to nap, once they were too tired to mind the shrieking of the wind and the roar of the seas.

By the next morning, vast, smooth swells carried foam-topped waves across an infinite sea, its gray blending into the gray of the sky above. Life-lines were already rigged and boats double-lashed to the davits. Amidships, men of the watch worked with chisels knocking ice off rails, lines and belaying pins. A few moved methodically from gun to gun, securing each more tightly against the rails. A few, anticipating the order to reduce sail, stamped their feet for warmth as they stood at the ready to haul in or go aloft. In the waist, Gideon Groves, midshipman and the youngest member of the crew, hid from the wind as he knotted and spliced, pausing now and again to blow on his fingertips.

As they worked, they glanced back at the master, awaiting orders; however loudly Mr. Stephens boomed them, these might not be altogether audible over the crash of waves on the bow, the mighty rush of water along *Enigma*'s sides, the whine in the rigging, and the clanking of halyards against the masts, even those that had long been hanked off properly.

The orders came at last, Captain Peterssen not being one to waste a steady blow, and one by one, sails were reefed or furled entirely. Work went slowly, despite the best intentions, with a slippery deck and lines stiff with the cold, but by midnight, the end of the first watch, *Enigma* was down to bare sticks except for a storm jib and the spanker to steady her. When dawn broke, it was with a faint weak poor glimmering not ready to warm anyone or light a Christian soul's way. The sea showed white from edge to edge, and huge great swells rolled across it. Few gulls were in sight, and such that remained whizzed past the barque, pushed by the remaining strength of the gale.

"Ain't it grand?" said Izak, as Niklas inched his way across the deck. "I love to see the barky go."

Niklas turned his face away from the frozen wind to catch his breath and wondered what idiocy caused him to venture onto this ice-slicked deck.

Izak Peterssen looked insulted. "It ain't like there's icebergs off to larboard." Then he had the temerity to laugh at Niklas. "And it ain't the Horn we're rounding, nor the Cape."

It was clear, perfectly clear to Niklas, that Izak Peterssen was a sheer raving madman.

"What's worse," Katrina said after Niklas returned fuming to the cabin, "is that he acts like a dictator."

"He is a dictator on this ship. On any ship, the captain is the law."

"A fine kettle of soup that is!"

Niklas sighed.

Fearsome as this scene looked to any ordinary eye, the trained one saw reason to hope, as the cross seas were gone, not a wrinkle of them still in view. Though sharply heeled and challenging her own noon-to-noon speed records, *Enigma* was sailing smooth again. The cabins began to stir with human voices and warmth, and the stoves were soon lit for hot coffee and breakfast.

Their course would take them coastwise along France, Portugal, and Spain, but well west to avoid the Bay of Biscay, where the current and a westerly wind combined to form one of the worst lee shores on Earth. These were heavily traveled waters, and lookouts were posted around the clock, men who could make sense of the sails and running lights all around. *Enigma* had to bear off occasionally for a ship, part of the coastwise traffic between France and Wales or Ireland, and once they ran in among a fleet of fishing boats, mere dinghies, nothing longer than forty foot, who seemed to think they owned the seas.

CHAPTER 23

PARADISE

After a week in forced inactivity in the family cabin, Will and Hans wrung permission from Niklas to learn what they could of seacraft and be of service to the crew.

"They need to be kept busy," Katrina said, "but as sailors? Gott im Himmel, Niklas, what can you be thinking?"

"I'm thinking to make men of them, Katrina. Especially Will."

Soon the boys stood before the captain, hats in hand, having made their offer. To Izak Peterssen, two more men were welcome. At least they were not sailor-town riff-raff being dragged on board drunk or beaten half to death by some crimp. It was clear Hans could be made to haul a line as well as any landsman, and since they claimed to have some woodworking skills, he assigned them to carpenter's crew. This made them "Idlers," like the cook and galley crew, on one twelve-hour shift a day instead of four-hour on-and-off watches. After a gruff talking-to, in which the captain made clear the dangers of the sea and that the boys' first responsibility was to stay out of the way, then to follow any order given them, Izak Peterssen agreed to take them on, rating them in his ledger as landsmen. Then he found them again and warned them that a call for 'all hands' included them, anytime, night or day. Lastly, he gave them a piece of good advice: "Don't get yourself kilt."

The ship's carpenter was Richard Billings, a bald, barrel-chested Devonshire man with bulging arms and such a rolling, sea-leg gait that he walked as if he had never been on land. When Captain Peterssen took the boys to him, Richard Billings did not look happy. At all.

"Brought up in service to His Majesty's Royal Navy," Billings told the boys by way of introduction. "My pappy and grandpappy were sea captains, born to the sea."

"No man aboard," Izak Peterssen nodded, "is more dedicated to the good of the ship."

With this the captain left Will and Hans, and Richard Billings looked at them with blind fury. "Useless dunderheads, nor able to speak the King's English nor tell a spar from a toe rail."

Richard Billings made no complaint to the captain, of course, not a word, nor did he need to, with his eyes narrowed to slits and his lips in a tight line. In the old days, he would have gotten the lash or the cat for an insubordinate word or even a rude look, but now, on a decidedly relaxed merchantman, he could allow his face to show his displeasure.

"*Enigma*," he groused, "ain't no godforsaken loose American ship nor some Nova Scotian with a cruel hard captain, but you'll do exactly what I tell you, neither more nor less."

To keep his new acquisitions out of the way, Billings set the boys to work shaping a rough beam into a yardarm, and had grudgingly to admit he was glad to have someone else do it, the need for spare yards always arising should it choose to blow again, which it surely would. When he inspected their work, he nodded; it could not be the first time Hans had held an adze in his hand and Will clearly knew one end of a plane from another. As they had some degree of craftsman-like skills and Niklas, who came along to translate for them, Richard Billings, a fair man at heart, began to appreciate his new acquisitions, enough that when one of his messmates made a shockingly rude remark about "them bloody Krauts," he surprised himself and stood up for them.

Niklas, for his part, spent most of his days with the carpenter's crew, happy to translate and not altogether unhappy to escape the clatter and confusion of the family cabin, persuaded as he was that Katrina and the younger children could not mind a few spare inches either.

Like any seaworthy crew, Enigmas were inclined to scorn landlubbers, most especially those who tried to make themselves useful. Knowing this, Izak sent word through his officers: these three were to be taught any word they needed, and the crew would be pleased to recall, these Prussians were paying passengers, regardless of any additional role they might now choose to play. Then he sought out Niklas to remind him that all Kästners were to feed themselves, and it was no use thinking they should get a share of the weevily hard tack or rotten salt meat meant for real sailors.

Richard Billings was soon pleased with his acquisitions and denied ever having had any other opinion. Hans had prodigious strength and was perfectly at ease putting it to use. Will proved himself as smart as a whip, picking up English and nautical jargon with surprising speed. Niklas was amiable, a landsman to be sure, but strong enough when a heavy spar needed lifting or a line needed an extra hand and unusually capable at easing linguistic tangles. Disinclined as Niklas was to give advice or seize upon a tool, he seemed satisfied to appear as the ship's namesake, an enigma, once a man of action, but now willing to stay quietly out of the way, sunning himself, reading or working at mysterious drawings.

"Unfortunately," Captain Peterssen told Niklas some days later, "we have to put in at Gibraltar's Crown Colony."

"An unwelcome complication." Niklas spoke slowly.

"Oh, aye, 'unwelcome' is not the half o' it. Making port is always damned tricky and dangerous and a curséd delay."

"A ship in any port can be wind-bound for weeks," explained First Mate Groves, "an entirely preventable problem."

"And this one," said Izak Peterssen, "will take us far out of our way, require us to run the Strait of Gibraltar, cross the Gibraltar Bay—not a little thing in itself—and cozy up into the colony's harbor, as crowded and full of hard edges as any bit of land."

"Why, then?" The two of them sounded so angry Niklas hesitated to ask.

"We must pick up *Enigma*'s owner, Thomas Segrave."

"An Englishman."

"Aye." Captain Peterssen seemed to feel no need to explain further.

"It will also," Mr. Groves admitted, "make a long ocean crossing shorter and put us on the south edge of the horse latitudes, closer to trade winds. And we can re-provision where there's a natural glut of oranges, lemons and limes for preventing scurvy."

"Still, all that for one Englishman." Niklas's voice was flat enough that Mr. Groves stared at him. The scar caught the light, and Mr. Groves said, "Oh!" and then added, "he's a young man, this Mr. Segrave, a Royal Navy man." He did not say, "Too young to have been at Waterloo and in the wrong branch of the military." He did not have to.

As the captain stomped away, grumbling about the depredations crews sink to in port, Mr. Groves explained further: "Thomas Segrave is an old shipmate of the captain's and has given him his first command as *Enigma*'s captain. I've never met the man, but I imagine the captain will take some pleasure in having him aboard."

"However. An awkward interruption," Niklas said. He had not missed the words, "first command."

Mr. Groves replied with vehemence: "Aye, most awkward."

Once they cleared France and Portugal and headed southeast along the coast of Spain for the Strait of Gibraltar, a warm southerly wind came out of the west-sou'-west, on *Enigma*'s favored point of sail, just abaft the beam, and day followed day of extraordinarily smooth sailing. The perfection of each dawn was so great, and the sea spread around them so fresh and endlessly that the family spent many long hours on deck, speaking in low tones so as not to break the spell of this lovely weather and sleeping at night with a soundness born of the rhythm of the sea.

"It is something like paradise," Katrina told Niklas, "however unexpected and brief it might be."

"Naught but deservéd after a hell of ice storms and mal de mer," Niklas said, thinking of the seasickness she had endured.

"Or is it more like Purgatory?" she asked thoughtfully. "Must we earn our passage, our right, to the strange and fabulous Neue Land?" When she recovered from being seasick, she had spoken of feeling reborn, as if she had come through a tunnel, where the past was expunged and she was given to a new life.

"Purgatory?" he asked with disapproval. "Nonsense. What Catholic idea is this?"

Katrina apologized. "It was a badly chosen word, I'll admit."

To Mr. Groves, Niklas mentioned the boats he loved to sail on Berleburg's rivers, so he was not entirely surprised when Captain Peterssen called him over one mild day and asked him if he felt he could take the wheel.

"Absolutely!" said Niklas.

"Here then. Keep that headland off your larboard bow." He watched Niklas closely to see that he understood.

"Aye, aye, Captain."

Captain Peterssen watched for a while and then dusted off his hands and went below.

It was the first of many times Niklas took a turn at the wheel, always at the captain's invitation and never when weather threatened. He was silent at the wheel, not ever giving an order and always aware that a half-dozen of the crew on deck at any time knew as well as he did how to handle the wheel. Among these was Cutlip—so the family nicknamed a certain sailor for the ugly scar across his mouth—who was permanently angry and clearly dangerous. This young-old man—it was impossible to tell which—was a sailor's sailor: nut-brown and emaciated, nothing but skin, bone and ropey muscles. His lips were sunburnt, and his long sailor's queue was bleached to a sandy brown. One arm had a mysterious tattoo, and around his neck was a kerchief in an exotic pattern. "Indie" he scowled when Katrina asked him about it.

"That is as much as we are likely to get from him," said Niklas.

"Indie?" Katrina mused. "The West Indies? Or the storied subcontinent itself?"

Niklas shrugged. "Whatever else is true, he seems to have set foot in many places."

They saw Cutlip leap into the ratlines and scale them from deck to masthead like a monkey. He danced out along the yardarms fearlessly, gathering sails in as if they were featherweight linen.

"I imagine this crew is even more motley than the army was."

"When we set out for Moscow, half the army was from occupied territories, but I never considered us 'motley.'"

"No, of course not," she apologized.

They watched the sea for a while and then she whispered, "Have you seen the tattoos?" In the warm breeze, men had stripped to the waist, tattoos over their shoulders and backs or spiraling down their arms. The faces all around were sunburnt and scarred, hard faces of men who had spent their lives aboard a ship or in a sailor-town tavern. Most were bearded and barefoot, and many wore an earring.

"It's the knives and spikes that worry me," said Niklas. All wore these at their waists, many with the points bent or hammered off, a shipboard practice to make it harder for one man to stick another.

Katrina agreed and changed the subject. "This puts me in mind of how widely you have traveled, from the deserts of Egypt and Spain, to the shores of Elba, and to Moscow."

"That damnable oriental city of Moscow."

"What do you remember most about it?"

"The sunlight, I suppose, bouncing off gold-skinned domes, and the smell of half-burnt houses mixed with disgusting Russian cooking."

"I'm sure they don't find it disgusting."

"I grant you that. They are used to it."

She brought the subject back to travel. "Are you happy to be traveling again?"

"Well, we have outrun Metternich, and that is a joy, but no ocean is ever safe." Niklas paused to think. "I like being abroad. I wouldn't mind seeing exotic lands again, feeling a hot tropical sun…"

"I thought as much. I miss Berleburg, I do. But then I imagine exotic flowers, something like, what are they called, 'orchids'?"

"Right now, I'd settle for a really good cup of coffee."

CHAPTER 24

GIBRALTAR

Captain Izak Peterssen put a big foot on the larboard rail and slung himself up into the ratlines. *Enigma* rose on the swell, and in the distance, Cabo Finisterre rose out of the waves, dark, mysterious, and unmoving. It was Land's End, the westernmost tip of the European continent, and it marked *Enigma*'s successful traverse of the Bay of Biscay. Many long hours later, she had navigated the straits of Gibraltar, rounded Tariffa, and passed promontories on either side. Gibraltar lay to the north and on the south, Ceuta, a fortress in the Spanish province of Cadiz on the coast of Tangier. Then Ceuta faded into the distance, and *Enigma* made her way across a vast bay, toward headlands entirely different from the grim Cabo Finisterre, sunny, colorful, and so inviting that Katrina felt the strongest desire to go ashore at once and abandon the very idea of America. She did not dare say this aloud.

As the last of the day's light faded, the Enigmas hove to and picked up moorings at Gibraltar. The huge bay *Enigma* crossed and the high waves in the strait made for a daunting approach between Morocco on one side and the Crown Colony of Gibraltar on the other. Now, in the harbor, hundreds of ships contested for anchor room, from massive Indiamen and sleek galleys to cutters, barges and other working boats—launches, fishing boats, lighters, and every description of small craft.

"Fend off, ye blind bastard of a bat, fend off," came faintly across the water, one of many distorted voices, perhaps off starboard, perhaps not. Just barely visible in the fading light was a long, curved stone quay, the Old Mole. It had defined Gibraltar for centuries, with its massive dockyard, quarantine island, and low warehouses on what had once been ordnance and victualing wharfs. Dr. Ward was on deck, and now he told the captain, "Nowhere do I see the yellow flag of pestilence."

"Gudskelov," said Izak Peterssen. "Thank God." It was unfortunate for the passengers that their first nodding acquaintance with Gibraltar should come as night fell, but after the many difficulties of their journey, it mattered little to anyone aboard.

"At least," said Mr. Groves to Captain Peterssen, "the dark dampens any mad rush to put ashore."

For the captain, it was a relief to be at an anchorage and need only to eat a decent supper and write the docking report sure to be required. For everything else, tomorrow was soon enough.

In the morning, the fog lifted, leaving a startling blue sky and many bright greens of spring dotting the city and the mountains behind. All around lay a harbor throbbing with action: brigs, ketches, schooners, feluccas, xebecs, pinks, and small craft. The quays were busy with stevedores bent double under their loads, pushing wheelbarrows and whipping donkeys. Small, neat houses lined up beyond the harbor, and above all, the glorious cliffs of Gibraltar drew a sharp line against the sparkling blue sky.

Hans was at work, and Niklas was in the dining saloon drinking coffee. The rest of the family stood at the rail with Mr. Groves while a warm breeze brought them a delectable floral scent.

"What perfume is that?" asked Lisette, her face lit with amazement at such lovely freshness. The sudden appearance of springtime and the scent of land were intoxicating.

"It's citrus! The scents of orange blossoms, lemon blossoms, and lime blossoms entwined for your delight," said Mr. Groves with a smile. "One of the finest scents in all the world, blooming only for two or three weeks." He turned to Lisette and Amalie, "Which makes you the luckiest girls in the world to be here for it, my dearies."

Amalie breathed in the perfume and decided they should settle in Gibraltar. She wondered where exactly they were and if Gibraltar was actually part of Europe, having often overheard the word, "Africa" as they came through the straits.

"Look," cried Lisette, "palm trees!"

Amalie knocked Will in the ribs and whispered, "They do look like something out of a fairytale."

He grinned and agreed. "I always thought he made them up."

Niklas had told them about palm trees in Spain and Egypt, and maybe Elba, and had drawn them, but until this very moment, the children had thought them fantastical. Now, a thought flickered through Will's mind: *What else have I got wrong about Papa?*

"Gibraltar is even more beautiful than I remembered," said Mr. Groves, gazing with satisfaction at the harbor and the fine ships anchored nearby. Mr. Groves was friendly and talkative in spite of his high position among *Enigma*'s officers. One star-studded evening he had confided to Katrina that the children reminded him of his large brood at home in Cornwall and that he eschewed the usual bias against women aboard. His kindliness was so consistent and welcome that when they heard him bellow orders to the crew in that booming, cursing voice, they hardly knew him.

"Look at that one, young Herr Kästner," he said to Will, pointing off to starboard. "It's a ship-rigged clipper, it is, the one with an orange hull with a black strake, American-built by the look o' her..." The ship they stared at swung on its anchor until its nameboard showed. "Ah!" said Mr. Groves. "It's the *Ann McKim* out of Baltimore! In first-rate order. Built for speed."

"Look there," said Will, gesturing. "Those three boats in a row, pray tell me what they are." He winced, embarrassed to sound like the landsman he still was.

"Aye, those would be feluccas," said Mr. Groves, "a small convoy of them. You'd see them all over the Mediterranean."

"Their sails look like bat wings," piped Jakob.

"Aye, those be lateen sails, that shape, and they do look like bat wings when the crew spreads the two of them wing and wing. Very observant, young master." Seeing their uncomprehending faces, he explained, "Wing and wing: on opposite sides."

"And is that also a felucca?"

Mr. Groves followed Will's gesture and shook his head. "She has two masts and lateen sails like a felucca, but take note of the oars. That's a xebec—the vessel Barbary pirates use for capturing ships and enslaving Christians. Having both oars and sails, it can maneuver when other ships are becalmed. A xebec has other uses, of course, like river work, but I don't like the cut of her jib no ways." He chuckled at saying it that way, since even the landlubberly Kästners could see that a felucca did not actually have a jib.

"Look! How pretty those are and how fast!" Amalie said, pointing to several slim, brightly painted sloops skimming the surface.

"Oh, indeed," said Mr. Groves. "Those would be private yachts from the Gibraltar Yacht Club, seeing as how fine they are decked out and how nimbly they sail."

Mr. Groves moved a little away from the children, which gave Katrina the chance she wanted to raise an objection with him about the captain's coarse demeanor.

"Oh, no, Madam," he said, "You are quite mistaken. He's not a hard master at all, as captains go."

She raised her eyebrows, but the loveliness of the day made her unwilling to discuss it further. She turned back to the view of Gibraltar. The harbor had a faded grandeur, with the British Naval station a powerful presence even in peacetime, and the pretty town a picture of sheltered, idyllic life, bedecked with flower gardens and leafy vines on pastel cottages with dark green shutters. The profusion of greenery and flowers contrasted boldly with the wilderness and gloom of the hills rising sharply up to the cliffs themselves.

CHAPTER 25

GÜNTER

Niklas found Katrina with the shocking news: "King Wilhelm has institut-
ed mandatory conscription. If we were still in Prussia, Hans and Will
would have to go to Arnsberg and report for duty."

"Oh!" Katrina breathed. "I am so glad to be away!"

"Nothing shapes a man like military service. I've always said as much.
But nothing is so likely to kill him, either."

They were silent, and then Katrina turned to him in alarm: "Could
the power of the Prussian Military Police reach into British Gibraltar?"

"It's unlikely," he said. "But let's just say I will be glad to put out to
sea again. If I had known we were stopping at Gibraltar..."

There was more bad news waiting for them: that morning, the dock-
master had given Niklas a letter from the Erlingers, and in the bustle of
debarking, he pocketed it. He recognized the sender's address and pondered with uneasiness how the letter had found its way to them. A sail plan
had been left with the harbormaster at Rotterdam, he supposed, and was
angry again that Izak Peterssen had seen no reason to tell him about the
stop at Gibraltar.

As they sat together after supper, Niklas opened the letter and read aloud:
"Günter never returned to Berleburg! The Schwarzwälder horses were
found by his brothers and then they found his body."

Katrina nodded sharply to Amalie, who rose and bustled the children
away. She could not believe he was reading the letter aloud, as thoughtless
an action as ever he had done.

"The Schwarzwälders were left still harnessed to the berlin wagon,
and they plodded on," he read to Katrina and the older boys, "until someone fed and watered and stabled them. When Günter did not return, three
of his brothers traced his route, located the horses and wagon and then
found the body. They supposed the horses had panicked and Günter fell
off the runaway wagon, broke his neck and rolled into the streambed. But

no. They saw his stockinged feet, and the gash in his shirt led them to a ragged knife wound. His pockets had been emptied, his boots stolen."

"What must this mean to Addie and her family!" Katrina's hand was at her mouth.

"Destitution," said Hans.

"Addie says here, 'The Trakehner was never found.'"

"Zimt!" said Hans. "It *was* Zimt."

"You," said Niklas slowly, "probably saw his murderer."

"Oh! Zimt might have been sold three times by then."

In the letter, Addie begged Niklas for aid. She had the letter from Katrina that left them food and household items. "These are of great value," Addie wrote, "and we are deeply grateful, a winter's worth of beer, cider, and foodstuffs. We can never repay your extreme generosity. However, as to the horses, wagon, and contents of the barn, I was given to think these were to be ours, but I have no proof of sale or evidence of whatever arrangements you and Günter made."

She said the bishop of the church, and old Otto Beckmann, Katrina's great-uncle, had put in competing claims for the abandoned property. With eight children to feed and no husband, Addie was desperate. The letter ended with a plea: "Please return to Berleburg and speak for me."

Hans: "Will you, Father?"

"I will not. As shocked and stricken as Addie must be, I am surprised she would ask."

"Apparently," Katrina said, "she did not know where Günter's political sympathies lay."

"She says this: 'Certain prominent people have been arrested, leaving no friendly ears to receive my appeal.' The names she lists," said Niklas, "make it no mystery to me."

"We sought only to save ourselves," Katrina said. "Now look what we have wrought."

Will: "Ordinary highwaymen would have stolen the horses—all three of them."

Niklas nodded. "The receipt I wrote out—since Addie doesn't have it—may still have been in Günter's pocket, proof to the authorities of our close ties."

"This," said Hans, "was no ordinary robbery. Attacking a man connected to the movement was meant to chill the spread of revolution."

"It would have been quick, such an attack," Niklas said, reaching out and taking Katrina's hand.

"I hope so," she said.

"Nevertheless," he said, "I cannot go back. There's nothing to be gained and a great deal to be lost."

Katrina: "Your life."

"Our being branded as deserters," said Will, waving to his brother and himself.

"You and the children," Niklas said to Katrina, "fending for yourselves in a strange country."

"Even sending a letter would be dangerous if its origins could be traced," Hans said.

"But I must write. Very carefully, to avoid implicating anyone more in Berleburg."

In the end, he decided to send a letter to Le Havre via ship, in the hands of a private courier paid to keep his mouth shut, never to mention Gibraltar. From Le Havre, it would be put in the hands of the French postal service and cross France to Prussia with no origin recorded but Le Havre. To anyone hunting them, this would suggest a destination of New York or Baltimore, where the long arm of Prussian revenge would never find a Kästner. Besides, they would be on the ocean before Addie ever opened the letter or showed it in court. It was the least—and the most—they could do for her.

CHAPTER 26

ALAMEDA

The next day dawned, and they were up early to see as much as they might of the town. As they stood together on the street, Niklas announced that they would conclude their exploration of Gibraltar at the clock tower of the Cathedral of Saint Mary the Crowned at noon. There, they would choose a café, led by their noses to whichever one declared itself most delightful.

"And in the afternoon," Katrina said, "we must find a market. The lemons, limes and oranges here are not to be missed, and besides, there's scurvy to think about." The ground seemed to take on a sudden tilt, and she reached out to steady herself on a white picket fence. This feeling had been worse yesterday, when she first set foot on land.

"It's your sea legs, Ma'am," Mr. Groves had laughed then as he caught her elbow. "You will be fine in a moment."

But today again, the land was still at sea, as far as her legs knew, and her heart was still sick with the news about Günter and with worry for his family. She wished she had assigned all of the household goods to Addie. Elizabet had no such need.

"Oh, look!" cried Amalie, gesturing to a pale latticed fence, "a fig tree!" The gate was overhung with big fig leaves fluttering in the breeze.

A few blocks on, the family stood staring at the entrance to the Alameda Gardens. They hurried inside, surrounded by an explosion of fantasy plants on every side: the dragon tree whose red resin, called sangre de drago or dragon's blood, was powerful medicine; the stone pine, source of the delicious pine nuts; and below them, candytuft and paperwhites in glorious bloom.

The Gardens, first dug in 1815 in the thin, red soil of Gibraltar, were well established by the year of their visit, having been filled by many natural philosophers who collected plants from around the world, the passion of the age. It was a magical place, an 'alameda' or open walkway, where one might take the air protected from the heat of the sun. At the top of Heathfield steps, a colossal statue of General Elliot towered over the Gardens. It was carved from the bowsprit of *San Juan Nepomuceno,* a Spanish ship of the line with seventy-four guns, and one of twenty-two vessels taken by the British at Trafalgar.

"We lost the Battle of Trafalgar," Niklas said, looking ruefully at the statue. "I wasn't in Spain yet or even in the army, but I heard all about it. Trafalgar left no doubt about Britain's superiority at sea."

"Which is why," Katrina said, "Napoleon relied on those of you in the cavalry." She took his arm and called his attention to one exotic plant after another, and before long, they were so engrossed that when at last Niklas looked up, he saw that the boys had slipped away.

"Oh!" Katrina said when he called her attention to it.

"They wanted to explore the waterfront," he explained.

"It's no secret they are both imagining a life at sea."

"I made them promise not to go alone," Niklas said. "I told them again about Metternich's long reach and about crimps and press gangs at seaports." The press gangs so common during the wars were mostly gone, but crimps were always at work, shanghaiing men and dumping them aboard for a price. Strong young men were always a temptation to certain unscrupulous captains, the worst sort, cruel petty dictators whose men deserted at every port and who were thus always searching for crew. It was a desperate fate, one to be avoided at all costs.

He shook his head. "They willfully misunderstood, taking 'not alone' to mean 'not without the other.'"

"We can hardly fault Hans, who can get himself out of almost any scrape," Katrina said, "but I do not appreciate his leading his younger brother astray."

Out of the gardens and on the street once more, as they walked and chatted, Niklas stopped to admire a particularly handsome example of old Moorish architecture. "Such sights," he told Katrina, "and the lovely cadence of Spanish—I'm surprised at how many words are familiar—these bring the Peninsular Wars back to me."

He was silent for a moment, and Katrina worried about his bad dreams. She heard him murmur, "I don't know why it was me," and then he turned to her and said, "When I arrived, I was a raw recruit, sorry to have missed the Battle of Trafalgar. It had happened in 1805, and I didn't get here until '08, but everyone still talked about it."

She could see he was lost in memory, and she shook his arm gently. "Nothing to think about on this exceptionally pleasant day with us by your side." These words reminded them of the boys' absence, and now it was his turn to comfort her.

"They are old enough to take care of themselves," he said. "Look what I was doing at their age! Besides, their stomachs will not let them forget lunch."

"Ja," Katrina said. "No one is ruled by his stomach more than Will."

"I'm not going to let them off easily," he said. "They put themselves at risk for a morning's fling, for shame."

By noon Jakob was riding on Niklas's shoulders, having told his father, "This road is too long for me, Papa." All of them were tired of walking. The shade of the cathedral's clock tower was a welcome sight, but as they approached it, Katrina glanced down and stopped abruptly.

"Niklas, what's this?" She stepped gingerly off a mosaic of old tiles in a Moorish pattern.

"You would see them all over lower Spain if we had time to look," he said. "The Moors were here for seven hundred years, you know. Just think of that, seven hundred years, and, let's see, it's two hundred or a little more, since they were swept into the sea."

"Why here, by a church?" she asked, aghast.

"My dear, you have it backwards," he told her. "The Moors didn't desecrate these grounds with their designs. They were here first, their mosques were torn down…" Niklas paused to consider the complexities. "And Christian churches were built on the ruins. In some places, the mosques were just rededicated, so the churches have Moorish designs all through them. What you are seeing here is just a scrap of nicely laid tile that didn't get ripped out."

At the sound of footsteps, they looked up to see not the boys arriving but Izak Peterssen striding into view. Niklas invited him to eat with them and asked, "Do you know a kitchen to recommend?"

Izak glanced at the sky before responding. It was clear, and the sun was indeed at its zenith. He pointed out a small inn off to their right, telling them a lovely courtyard lay in the alley behind it. "Order paella," he said.

Little Jakob had been lifted down and now began to drag Katrina toward the inn, with Amalie and Lisette holding hands as they trailed along behind. They ducked into the cool alley, Niklas urging them to go on ahead; he and Izak would prowl the docks for the boys.

Hans and Will were in on it together, having planned to separate 'accidentally' from the family. They had faded back as the family walked ahead and disappeared around a curve, and then they had turned back to the garden's entrance and walked briskly to the docks. Once on the streets of Gibraltar's sailor town, they began by inspecting the many small squares of paper flapping from nails on masts, bowsprits and rails. These handwritten or crudely printed notices announced departures, advertised for men, or put craft up for sale.

"This one," said Will, and he read: "'Exp. men sought. Departing Gibraltar 5 Apr for Canton. Bonus pd.'" He felt a thrill ascend his spine. "'Canton!' That's in China. China, Hans!"

They hunted for similar notices pinned to the doors and window frames of the many harbor-side haunts of sailors: taverns, inns and flophouses catering to tastes that would have shocked them both. It was a bright, cheery morning, but not too early for whores, several of whom called to the boys from the doorways or windows of boarding houses.

After three weeks at sea, it was easy for them to affect a sailor's swagger, and although the boys' clothing would have been a mystery to anyone inspecting them, it caused no stir; in a seaport, every garb was seen. In fact, if anything distracted the boys—besides a Barbary ape trapped by an enthusiastic natural philosopher for transport to England and yowling from its cage—it was the wild dress of men working on the ships or lolling outside the taverns, bright ribbons tying up old-fashioned pigtails, paisley or striped kerchiefs at the neck or forehead, straw hats with ribbons embroidered with a ship's name, weather-beaten blue jackets and the ubiquitous nankeen pantaloons. More exotic were Arabian robes and headdresses, Egyptian kaftans and turbans, and the oft-seen red fez.

They felt they had seen it all when four men rounded a corner carrying a Barbary lion in a cage. The boys flattened themselves against the wall. The beast turned to look at them, lifted its head and snarled. They gasped at the intense smell.

A grinning man in a blue-checked headscarf said, "Vous devriez l'entendre rugir, you should hear him roar." Gibraltar suddenly seemed a great deal more dangerous than they had thought. It would have seemed even worse had they known what was coming.

CHAPTER 27

SUDDENLY DANGEROUS

"They have him!" Will came steaming up the street, shouting, "They have Hans!" The women and children had just disappeared down the alley toward the café, and Niklas and Captain Peterssen had not taken more than a few steps toward the harbor. As soon as Will yelled, he turned and raced away, the men at a run behind him.

They had him all right, three burly sailors hustling Hans toward an unpainted barge pulling up to the wharf's edge. Hans was struggling mightily until one of the sailors beat him over the head with a cudgel. Hans staggered under the blow and was pushed along faster. Any moment now, the kidnappers would be past the quay and onto the barge.

"Avast, there!" Izak's voice boomed out.

Hans' captors looked back, startled. Their leader, a man in a black neckerchief, dropped his grip on Hans and grabbed for his cutlass. Hans ground his boots into the stone quay, bringing the other two to a halt. One of them, an ugly man with dirty black hair, clubbed the back of Hans' knees and dragged him forward. An instant later, the crack of Niklas's pistol rang out, and the ugly man collapsed.

Hans' wrists were tied, but he shook free and swung his clasped hands at the third man, smashing his nose and sending him reeling backwards off the quay and into the water. The man in the black kerchief, seeing the issue settled, ran. The men rowing the barge took note of the determined, professional pistol fire and pulled briskly away.

Niklas raised his second pistol. It was already trained on the fleeing man when Izak's low, authoritative voice said, "Don't shoot. We have enough trouble with one dead man."

He stepped a few feet forward and kicked the ugly man into the water. The third man was floating face down.

"Two dead men," Will said. He could hardly believe what he was seeing. His father had killed a man. So had Hans, with one blow. He was startled to find his dagger in his hand. At some point, he had, without conscious thought, pulled it out of the scabbard hidden at his waist. He slid it back in.

Hans stumbled a few steps and collapsed. Niklas and Will each took an arm and half-carried him up the street. They turned into an alley and braced him against the wall. He was stunned and badly bruised, with a swollen, bloody lip and a black eye.

"Let me take him to *Enigma* by the back streets," said Izak. He heard a whistle and saw Royal Gibraltar policemen running from far down the street toward the floating bodies. Erik Thorvald, *Enigma*'s master gunner, a massive, red-haired Icelander, suddenly appeared, and now he shouldered Hans, who looked the very image of every drunken sailor who had ever got the worst of a brawl, no uncommon sight in Gibraltar. Even England's King William, when a young midshipman, was once arrested in a drunken brawl in Gibraltar.

"We should get him cleaned up before his mum sees him," Izak said. "Collect your womenfolk and meet us at *Enigma*. The dead men may have friends, but they won't attack *Enigma*."

Niklas tucked his pistols into his waistband. He and Will brushed themselves off and emerged from the alley, sauntering away from the scene, acting casual. They heard Izak call after them, "We sail with the morning tide."

At four bells the next morning watch, with the first light of dawn a mere glimmer and the tide in the ebb, *Enigma* slipped quietly through the warm, dark seas of the Gibraltar Straits, for the wind had come a little south of east, and Izak Peterssen had given orders to unmoor. Once out of the harbor and into the bay, *Enigma* was prepared to set a proper course.

"Ready about," called Izak.

"Ready about, sir," came the response.

He waited to feel a little more way on the ship, waited to see the wind on the waves adjust itself in speed and direction.

"Helm's a-lee," he called out. The full-bellied curves of the sails luffed and collapsed; the bow swung smoothly to the starboard, further, further as Izak waited for her to come to the proper point of sail, and the sails to fill again.

"Sheet her in, now," he said in a big voice that carried all the way forward. "Trim her up sharp, do you hear me, trim her up sharp."

With taut lines all along, the crew now working as one, mainsails filling and then the topsails, the crew felt the ship find its way, and the course was laid for the Canary Current.

Katrina heard all of this and felt the smooth, sure movement of the ship; she knew herself to be one of several aboard grateful to leave Gibraltar, with its bony neck tying it to the Continent and with all the possible complications of the Old World far astern even now and farther astern every moment.

"We have escaped again," Niklas told her, "I believe this time we can truly say the whole lot of us are safe and clear away."

"Can it be true? I am just beginning to take it in. The boys were so foolhardy."

"We could have lost them both."

"And then what would all of this have been worth?" Katrina shivered.

"But we did save them, and we are all safely aboard, and Europe is fading in the distance with every mile we sail. Every knot," he corrected himself with a smile.

Katrina frowned. "We should have known—Günter paid for our first escape in blood. In our wagon, driving our team, he was likely mistaken for you."

"And yet, all unknowing," Niklas said, "I bade him goodbye at the tavern that night ruing how wealthy we had made him and thinking how little he deserved it."

Their words were overheard by two men standing downwind, who looked at each other with raised eyebrows. One was the ship's handsome young owner and the other a scrawny, older man wearing the black coat of a surgeon or physician. The owner was embarrassed to eavesdrop, however accidentally, and motioned his companion a few steps away.

"And now we have an ocean to cross," Katrina said.

"Only an ocean," Niklas replied, "between us and a new life in America."

Days later, *Enigma* picked up the Canary Current, which would swing her west as if the huge shoulder of Africa were a slingshot, north of the

Cape Verde Islands and into the North Equatorial Current. *Enigma*'s course was plotted to hug the top of this current as closely as the captain and the master dared, risking the doldrums of the Sargasso Sea in hopes of picking up the slender strands of current through the Antilles and along the south coast of Cuba, the fastest route to New Orleans, the Paris of the New World.

BOOK THREE

ACROSS

"If I … dwell in the uttermost parts of the sea,
even there shall thy hand lead me, and thy right hand shall hold me."
— Psalm 139:9-10

CHAPTER 28

FRANCESCA

When *Enigma* reached the horse latitudes and sailed west, it became apparent that she was in the doldrums. Many who had been seasick could eat again.

"It's a godsend," the ship's surgeon's assistant said in a low tone, since neither the captain nor the crew were at all content with doldrums. For days, they sailed very quietly indeed, sometimes with the water along the side sliding past noiselessly, but often utterly becalmed. The morning watch saw limp sails dripping with dew as the pre-dawn gray gave way to pale, cloudless blue skies. As the long days wore on, little could be done. The sails filled and wilted, filled and wilted. Sailors looked up in hope and listened for an order, then slumped back as the sails lost the air before anyone could take action. At last, the officers of the watch set them to reweaving loose ends.

The ship's surgeon's assistant was a cheerful Irishman named Sean Crowley, who was an old hand at sea, having first come aboard in '20 as an indentured servant to the surgeon of the *Erasmus*. He told darkly of *Niobe*'s crossing in '28 with strange, strong breezes and storms blowing her so far off course that several seasick passengers actually died of starvation, unable to eat for weeks. "Sure, and they were thin to begin with," he allowed, "but still, it's a hard fate to bear."

Among the sailors, the talk ran all the other way, with dire predictions of weeks of calm, no breeze to be had at all, so many unlucky women aboard, until everyone was put on half-rations and then on quarters, and then—. Among the more superstitious, rumors were told of ghost ships caught forever in the Sargasso Sea, endlessly becalmed, slowly rotating until the very oak beneath them rotted and their bones sank dead away or their furious spirits lifted their rotting ship to the skies like the fearsome *Flying Dutchman.*

"If ever you see it coming through the clouds," Sean Crowley said, "you're a dead man for sure."

In the afternoon heat, passengers lolled on the flat, nearly motionless deck, escaping the airlessness below, warm down to their bones, a good thing, most said, "an extra summer." It was still only March of 1836, when the ground in the Germanies might be frozen solid. The Kästners met the steerage passengers, an extended family from villages near Bonn, the Ackermanns. They were traveling with cousins from the foothills of the Italian Alps, Francesca and Franci Lenzini, a widow and her daughter. Francesca had married an itinerant Italian tradesman to the distress of her very provincial German parents but had lived happily, she said, never once missing the northern snows. It was she who had given the others the courage to travel.

Hearing this, Amalie blushed at the thought of marrying an Italian! And of eloping! It was a degree of disobedience she had never imagined, and when, in the privacy of the Kästner cabin, she voiced her disapproval, she was surprised that her mother did not condemn Francesca for such indiscretion. Katrina was amused at Amalie's naïveté and pleased to have Franci aboard, a seven-year-old who had instantly become Lisette's best friend.

Like Katrina, Francesca was a gardener, so they traded tomato seeds for feverfew and starts of oregano for those of tansy. When Katrina looked doubtfully at the tomato seeds, Francesca said the plant had come from the New World to begin with, so it should do well there.

"And don't believe any tales about tomatoes being poisonous," she laughed. "If they were poisonous, I would have killed my entire family. Which I didn't," she hastened to add, crossing herself. "Tomatoes are no trouble at all, and the plant is a grand producer, giving you bushels of fresh fruit in the dog days of August."

"I've heard that the foliage is suspicious," Katrina said.

"I won't speak to that, but you'll see for yourself why they say so," she said. "It looks like a nightshade plant."

"Oh dear!"

"I've never heard of anyone dying from touching it. The foliage and roots have no use that I know of as food nor poison."

Francesca was soon a favorite on board in spite of being a woman and a Catholic. She was almost always smiling quietly, a handsome woman to all and a motherly figure to the younger sailors. She always appeared on deck clean and well-brushed and besides, she spoke German, French, Italian and Spanish.

"No one speaks Portuguese," she said, "except those poor souls unfortunate enough to have been born in that godforsaken country. And of Catalans, the less said the better."

Like Katrina, Francesca could read and write and had taught her daughter to do so as well. Together, they helped those sailors who were illiterate read their old letters from home and compose new ones to be sent whenever possible.

Francesca's German cousins were poor farmers, Catholics, officially out of serfdom, but unofficially trapped in poverty quite impossible to escape. She said they were the lucky recipients of a certain local society providing one-way tickets to America, the money coming directly from their prince. At a mention of this, the Ackermann women crossed themselves in gratitude.

Later, when Katrina told Niklas about the steerage passengers, he commented that the Kästners had been serfs at one point, but long ago and never to be mentioned. Generations ago, he said, these Kästners had clawed their way up. But that was then, when it was easier.

"Gratitude is a fine thing," he told Katrina about the Ackermanns and their thankfulness. "We could all do with more of it."

"However," she replied, "as the source of their misery, their prince hardly deserves it."

"Ja, exactly."

They both knew that some German princes provided tickets to America for the poor, judging them more burden to their treasury than value as cheap labor. With no strategy for improving the lot of the poor, some hoped to slack the thirst for revolution by sending poor people away.

"Who got what the Ackermanns left?" Katrina wondered aloud.

"Consider the rags they wear," said Niklas. "It's likely enough, they left nothing, or nothing but debts."

Katrina nodded, "They may have had only this one chance to escape famine. How lucky they are to have Francesca's help."

"Ja, it took courage, when not one of them had traveled before."

"They must have had some measure of confidence that they wouldn't fall off the edge of the world."

Niklas looked thoughtful. "How did they get to Rotterdam?"

"They walked. Last summer. Francesca and Franci sailed from Genoa to meet them. They were delayed when the babies came, the two infants you've seen. And then they sailed as soon as they could in hopes of making a crop this summer."

"I doubt they will manage that."

Katrina and Niklas were silent for a moment before he asked, "The prince's generosity ends when they touch down in America?"

"Yes," Katrina said. "They were given only the price of a ticket. Then they are on their own."

A week of being becalmed went by, a stringy beard of doldrum weed growing, dragging along after the barque and slowing her more day by day. Francesca and Katrina took advantage of the calm to set up a brazier and kettle on the deck and make up a pot of cabbage and potatoes. Katrina contributed cabbage and potatoes; the Kästner goat provided milk; and Francesca provided onions and cheeses, Gruyere from Switzerland and a good, sharp Parmesan from Italy.

"Parma's a pretty city in the north, a quiet place, a university town," Francesca said, "but we like our duke, so no revolutionaries, not that we haven't heard of Rimini, and Murat, and the Risorgimento." She chopped some sage leaves and tossed them in. Katrina ground black pepper and added it. Francesca cooked slowly, letting the onions caramelize and then the cabbage, slicing the potatoes thin so they almost melted. When she stirred in the cheeses, the scent floated all across the deck and into the tops, a delicious aroma that inspired sailors to linger nearby.

In these lightest of breezes, the first mate's orders were endless, as he badgered the men to make constant adjustments, trying to make the most of whatever air might appear. This meant sailors moved all around the women, and a shanty arose again and again to keep the hauling in unison. Every sail-handling effort was incomplete until the many sheets, halyards, and various downhauls had been flaked neatly on deck or coiled elbow-to-palm and hung on a belaying pin.

"I've never known ordinary cabbage and potatoes to be used so well," Katrina told Francesca.

"If I had an oven, I would finish by baking," she said. "And then, when the cheeses browned on top, you'd see people running in off the street to ask for a bite."

Even as it was, the two women passed out plenty to their families and emptied the pot by giving a cupful to sailors who begged.

'Superb cabbage," Sean Crowley said.

"Good scurvy prevention," Doctor Ward agreed.

Off to one side stood the old man brought aboard by Thomas Segrave, scowling.

"They call him Methuselah because he's so old," said Katrina to Francesca in a low voice. As they watched, he said something to Cutlip, who glowered at the women, replied to Methuselah, and then turned away.

"Who is he?"

Katrina shrugged. "Niklas thinks he is a retired skipper, but all I can say for sure is that he isn't friendly."

Sailors lined up with cups or bowls, and Francesca filled one after another, her head down, focused on the ladling, until one of the sailors said, "Grazie."

The ladle in her hand jerked, and she looked up into a face half-hidden in shadow. She lifted one arm to shade her eyes, squinted, and made out a smile on the sailor opposite her.

"Grazie mille," he repeated.

"Oh," she said. "It's nothing."

"Al contrario, it means the world to me to have a taste of home."

Now it was her turn to smile as she said, "I'm glad you like it." He put both hands on the bowl, not to spill a drop, and she saw "Hold Fast" tattooed on his knuckles, the sign of a rigger, a sailor who climbed ratlines and scrambled along the yards to drop or gather in a sail.

When she glanced up again, he was walking away, and she could see nothing of him except the thick, ropy arms of one who spent much of his time aloft.

She knocked an elbow into Katrina's ribs and pointed with her ladle. "Italiano!" she said. Katrina smiled, having already taken note of their conversation, and was glad Francesca had found a countryman. His name, it would turn out, was Giovanni, and it was not the last they would see of him.

CHAPTER 29

OLYMPIAN ABOVE IT ALL

One short, worrisome, becalmed week seemed endless to Will, who used the long, empty hours to pester Niklas for permission to go aloft. When Niklas finally assented, Will begged Izak to let him work in the rigging. Soon he was high above the deck, to spell a lookout, his young eyes being put to good use.

Before the first time he climbed, Mr. Groves spoke to him, kindness replaced with ire at having to mind an incompetent whippersnapper without the sense to stay on deck when he could have. He gave Will one indispensable piece of advice: "Keep a hand on a shroud in case a ratline gives way and you fall where you'll be dead, splat on the deck, or if you're not so lucky, too maimed to be anything for the rest of your miserable life but a filthy beggar on the filthy streets of New Orleans."

"Aye, aye, sir, thank you, sir," Will said, and touched his cap, having already learned to keep a civil tongue in his head.

The shrouds held the masts in place, and he was glad to depend on these thick, tight-stretched lines rather than the wobbly ratlines that formed rope ladders to the tops. When he got to the bottom of the main-top platform, thirty feet up, he almost lost his nerve and squeezed through the lubber's hole. To climb like a true sailor, he knew he had to go out around the platform and reach it from topside. It was terrifying, but the thought of being labeled a stupid, cowardly Kraut was worse, and somehow, he found the strength in his arms to pull himself out and around the platform. The maintop, halfway up the mainmast, was where he had been assigned as a lookout. It was only a first step, but it was plenty for Will on a first climb. True riggers might rest here in their climb to the topsails or before they went out along the mainyard to drop or furl the massive mainsail.

Now, safe on the maintop platform, hugging the top mast, he allowed himself to look straight down through the lines. From there, the expanse of the sea was immense, and against it, the hull looked like a child's toy and their goal, to ride this toy across the ocean, an absurdity. He was amazed at what he had accomplished, but his muscles quivered and ached, and he did not know whether he could manage the climb down. He looked up into the topsail rigging and felt the world swim around him. And then he thought of doing this in a blow, when all hands were called and sail handling was at its most dangerous.

Despite the terror of his first climb, Will found he loved the thrill of it. Up there, it seemed he drew the first free breath of his life, of salt-sea air that would forever speak to him of freedom. Nothing brought him peace like being Olympian above it all, alone and free from the hubbub of deck work and domestic clamor.

Once, high up on the maintop platform, he saw Hans crossing the deck carrying a heavy slab, and he suddenly felt the distance between them. *I'm my own man at last,* he thought. *Not Hansi, not Papa. Up here, I can see farther than either of them.*

Then he lost the moment of confidence and said aloud, "Yikes! What am I thinking!"

If Katrina was ever on deck when Will climbed, she couldn't help but rub the wrist she had broken long ago and say nonsensically to whomever stood nearby: "That is not an apple tree!" Everyone thought she was going sea-crazy except Niklas, who knew the apple tree story. Most often, she hid her eyes whenever Will ascended, fixing them firmly on whatever stitchery was on her lap, rehearsing angry words for Niklas, words never to be spoken but never to be entirely forgotten either. When she agreed, back in Berleburg, that this trip would be a Bildungsreise for Will, she never imagined his travel education included being a rigger.

Hans could only look up, hammer or saw in hand, shake his head and say to Richard Billings, "Not for me."

Mr. Billings said, "Maybe we'll make a sailor of one of you yet."

"My little brother," grinned Hans, "has always been something of a monkey."

This made Katrina grind her teeth. *Does no one else understand the danger?*

When at last the doldrums released their grip and the barque entered the North Equatorial Current, sailing became smooth and lively. *Enigma*'s bow threw up a white-crested wave, and its stern left a wake where fish bounced while gulls and gannets and boobies dove for them. Now night followed day, marked only by the steady turn of the watches and the sounding of bells, everything set—square sails up to royals; outer and inner jibs; fore, main and mizzen staysails; and spanker. Nothing lay in sight from East to West or from North to South but blue sky and blue-green sea.

Niklas and Katrina were often in deep conversation, making plans for their homestead. Hans or Will sometimes joined them.

"What about," said Hans, "Duden's settlement in Missouri? He took Germans there in '32."

"So many that they are called 'The Thirty-Twoers,'" agreed Katrina.

"It's tempting," Niklas said, "but why leave Germany behind only to join a Little Germany?"

"Let's see how welcome or unwelcome we find ourselves and how much English is a problem—not for you, Niklas, but for the rest of us."

"We can always turn that way if we think it wise."

Hans: "The Missouri River is a temptation in any case."

"Ja," said Niklas, "Settling by a river of some size is essential; a tradesman cannot sensibly do otherwise."

Hans argued for going beyond civilization into unsettled, frontier territory in Illinois or Iowa, to work and live among the aborigines and their buffalo herds.

"Aborigines don't buy much," said Niklas. "But we'll go to the edge of civilization, where land is cheap. I'm not inclined to the soft, settled towns of America's East Coast."

"What's the big river?"

"The Mississippi," said Niklas. But America has everything, mountains, plains, huge lakes, many rivers."

"Do you miss our home?" Niklas asked Katrina once.

"Of course!" she said. "But the strange thing is how safe I felt in Berleburg before Werner was killed."

"We weren't really safe at all and hadn't been for some time."

"I know that now," she said, "But I still want to build a new home like our old one."

"Mother!" said Hans. "We couldn't replicate our old house even if we lived in Berleburg. The old growth is gone, timbered out, all the way to the remote corners of the mountains."

"I've heard there are virgin forests in America," Niklas said. "But it depends on what we find."

Besides their happiness at being free of Prussian conscription and secret police, it was not lost on them that on the edges of the America frontier, the price of land was attractive, unbelievably attractive. They would be glad to buy at unheard-of rates: $1.25 an acre for homesteading, that is, for buying land never before tilled or mined or otherwise worked, directly from the U.S. Government. At the frontier, so they had read, such land was abundant beyond all imagining and every acre of it at $1.25.

"It might be wild land," Niklas told Katrina and the boys, "but if there really is mile after mile of it, we can choose wisely. Finding land with natural advantages will go a long way to settling in comfortably and making a success of farming."

"But close enough to a town," said Will, "for us to set up a shop as well. Papa, what about this first winter?"

"It won't be easy. Maybe we can find work. We will have some things to trade, which will help, and with luck we will still have some..." Niklas looked around and did not want to say the word "gold" out loud. Instead, he rubbed his thumb and two fingers, and rest of them understood.

With this, Niklas began to tick off the natural advantages to look for. "First, there's the aspect of the land to consider. We want very gently rolling hillsides, neither steep enough to wash off in a heavy rain nor flat enough to puddle and drown a crop."

"Grape-growing hillsides," Katrina said, "south-facing. What an advantage to be there first!"

"Oh, yes! We will test the soil and look for what is rich and deep and friable. Years of topsoil, not overused or worn thin. Many overlook these things, but we will take our time and do it right."

"Think of the other riches of a perfectly chosen spot," said Hans, "a fresh creek running through for plenty of clear, clean water at hand and clay along its edges for caulking a house or barn or chimney and for making bricks."

"And a good, big trading river within easy reach," insisted Will, "filled with fish, but not so near a house or fields as to flood them."

"Grassland for pasture and straw for thatched roofs, timber for building: tall straight pine, fir or spruce," said Niklas, "maple trees for winter syrup, cherry trees for furniture, oak trees for hogs' acorns."

"And if possible," Katrina said, "a rock outcropping to mine for foundation stones and perhaps someday to use for a fine stone house."

"Maybe slate to split for shingles," said Hans hopefully. Slate mines near Berleburg gave the town its gray roofs and sometimes was used for siding, too. They all knew many good ways to use slate.

In their mind's eye they could see it all, how best to use the natural advantages of America, the gifts of nature, to make life rich and easy, "too fabulous to be believed," as Gottfried Duden had written.

"All of these riches are on land we can buy," Niklas murmured to Katrina, "in the land of the free."

"For us, our children and the children of our children," she said.

CHAPTER 30

STARS OF GOLD

Dr. Quentin Ward, the ship's surgeon, often ate with the family. He was a short, sallow Scotsman with very bad teeth and worse bad breath, as he was still recovering from a bout with scurvy.

"I could feel it coming on," he told them, "but we were too far asea, the lime juice all drunk up." Dr. Ward's high spirits made his daily smile as welcome as it was hard to look at. "As soon as we made land, which happened to be in Jamaica, I cured myself and half the crew with limes, lemons and sour oranges." One day, he told them, he would retire from the sea and buy land on the American Northwest Territories, which he knew only by reputation or tall tale, whichever it was.

Dr. Ward touched a front tooth and tested it for wobbliness. "At least they didn't fall out before we reached Jamaica." For this reason and out of nostalgia, his favorite food was oatmeal.

He explained that Great Britain was not like the Germanies: primogeniture laws kept family estates together, all the land going to the firstborn male. "As the fifth boy, I never had a chance of inheriting. Nor did I want to, since it would have meant my four older brothers had died. Besides, my eldest brother has been good to me, sending me to study with the esteemed Dr. John Burns—do you know of Dr. Burns?" he asked, looking at Niklas for an answer.

Niklas did not recognize the name and when he glanced at Katrina, she only raised her shoulders. "We do not," he answered.

Quentin Ward continued, "—and then on to the University of Glasgow. From there it was a matter of finding a ship, not an easy thing, but luckily, I was taken aboard and made a start before the wars ended."

"In the Germanies," said Niklas, who was a firstborn, "dividing tenancies every generation makes farms so small people fall into debt and the tenancies are lost. At best, farmers scrabble along, becoming poorer with each generation." *In England,* he thought, *I would have been wealthy.* The unfairness of it made him uncomfortable.

Then Amalie asked, "What about daughters?"

Doctor Ward looked off to one side. "Missy," he said, "We all know daughters marry and become mistresses of some other family's wealth." Amalie's cheeks burned. She could hear the disapproval in his voice, even though what he had said was as often false as true.

"Land may be cheap on the American frontier," Günter had once said to Niklas, "but you could be entirely isolated except for natives, who may welcome you or scalp you. You could be surrounded by American wisents—bison bigger than ours and in herds obscuring the horizon—not to mention bears and wolves. Or loneliness. It is lonely enough to drive women mad, some say." Günter had shaken his head at both the dangers of America and the weaknesses of women.

"Not Katrina," Niklas had told Günter. "She is strong, energetic and capable, as the frontier requires." Besides, as he knew too well, every opportunity has its price.

Enigma creaked day and night—they hardly heard it anymore—and above, lines clanked against the masts. In one particular black pre-dawn, Katrina heard not the hard throb or dangerous hum of heeling over in heavy weather, but the lazy knocking of lines in light air. Even on such a mild night, she never wanted to be aboard an ocean-going vessel again. It was either becalmed, with the captain furious and the crew testy, or running before a stiff wind while the crew dashed about and the passengers panicked. Like many aboard, she got her sea legs when the mal de mer passed and had to smile a bit when she saw the steerage passengers come up from below. The Ackermanns, about two dozen of them, were rarely allowed on deck. Several were lubberly still and wobbled like drunks across the polished planks of the deck. She kept her smile to herself, of course, out of Christian charity. Besides, she considered how she must have looked to the crew on her first few days aboard.

In rare moments of exhilarating freshness, waves from behind gave the barque a friendly spanking, and dolphins could be seen gamboling in the bow wave. Privately, Katrina called it glory sailing, though she had to admit the phrase sounded made-up and landlubberly; she would never say it aloud. Such glory came sometimes in snatches, sometimes in long, luxurious days and nights. Maybe it was worth the seasickness, close quarters, miserable rations, and occasional terror. Maybe not.

The ship quivered like a horse when the waves hit in a certain way. Once, when feeling this, Katrina said to Niklas, "You must like this. Or you would if only you had reins in your hands."

He smiled at her and nodded. "To a cavalry man, being aboard ship feels like home. Like riding a horse, you have to be in sync with it, muscles responding to its every move."

"It's a good feeling," she agreed. "And it strengthens you, leaves you tired at night and able to sleep even in our cramped quarters."

"I first sat a horse when I was a little tyke, no older than Jakob now. 'The boy's a natural,' my father always said."

"I've heard people say you have 'horse savvy.'"

"Yes, to me, it always felt right to handle a horse. Some people never get the knack of it, but I was in serious horsemanship training by eight, and by ten or eleven, I could manage all but the least predictable beasts."

"And then there was Zimt," Katrina said.

"I loved the first Zimt, a fine Trakehner, a great parade horse and fearless in battle. We trained in fancy maneuvers to delight a crowd, but the real goal was to sweep across the battlefield at a gallop, changing direction without losing formation. That was revolutionary, you know. No one had ever done it before."

"The Chevau-Légers, the light horse," Katrina said, "were the most feared regiments in the world and called 'unstoppable.'"

"I guess that's why I understand how some sailors are never at home on land. Being on board as part of a crew feels like being in a cavalry regiment: you are part of something big, something always moving and always requiring attention."

"We're not sailors, although maybe Will has become one, but we're part of something big," Katrina said. "For our family, but also for America. There's a whole country waiting for us to make it the way it should be."

He took her hand and said in voice meant only for her, "You mean, the home of liberty needs us to keep it?"

"I mean everything about America needs us to make a home, a family of wealth and culture. As for liberty, I hope we won't have to invent it or fight for it. I hope we can just breathe it in."

He looked deep into her eyes and smiled in a way she recognized. He wanted to kiss her right there in front of the entire first watch. Only propriety prevented him.

Then, on starry nights, came the nighttime glory. Every clear night brought out stars of extraordinary clarity, Polaris steady abeam or off the starboard bow, among more stars than they had ever seen. Niklas and Katrina loved the stars and their hint of a universe vast and mysterious.

Some of these warm nights even brought meeresleuchten, a sea shining with phosphorescence. It curled up where *Enigma* split the waves and flowed into the wake, surrounding them with sparkles and stars of gold, silver, purple, pink, and lime green, until the sea looked lit from within. Meeresleuchten was an otherworldly beauty. In their later years, they would tell others, landsmen and women, who would not believe them.

"Whoever imagined such a thing?" Katrina said to Niklas.

"It feels like an intimation, a hint, a promise of success."

"Oh, I hope so!" Katrina said.

Amalie and Lisette often found their parents in moments of glory sailing, sneaking up close to hold hands. The girls were their parents' good sailors. Neither had been ill since the beginning. This surprised Niklas, as he considered women the weaker sex and more inclined to be ill.

When he mentioned this, Katrina said, "And yet, it was Hans, our strong young man, who was most disabled by sea-sickness."

"Well, you gave him a run for that title, my dear."

"I suppose you're right," she said, but she wasn't happy to admit it.

One evening with hardly a ruffle on the surface of the water, they stood with Lisette at the rail in a deepening twilight, the evening star alone in the sky for a few minutes, *Enigma* cutting a long, straight furrow through the water, her wake brilliant with meeresleuchten shining far behind. They were as alone as anyone ever was aboard, with only the watch crew on deck. As their eyes grew accustomed to the dark, they saw a pair they recognized. Francesca and Giovanni stood far forward on the windward side of the bow. For some reason, Katrina thought of Odysseus's Sirens, irresistible beauties that made men crazy.

CHAPTER 31

ALMOST LOST

One splendid day, all the passengers quit their hammocks as if of one mind to savor a delicious change in weather. Will was off watch, so he took Jakob on deck, and it wasn't long before they were roughhousing. Katrina was busy braiding Lisette's hair, so Amalie, free of children for the moment, stood at the rail, enjoying the perfect sea breeze. Then she saw with trepidation Thomas Segrave, the ship's owner, approaching her spot at the rail, and she determined to ignore him. *A wicked Englishman!*

Will let his little brother chase and wrestle, while trying not to be too rough for the four-year-old. Thomas Segrave watched them for a moment, a smile playing on his lips, and then he turned to Amalie.

"Good morning," he said.

"Guten Morgen." She knew the English for it well enough, but she would not give him the satisfaction of hearing her use it.

Behind them, Cutlip glanced at Will and the little boy with his usual blank face. If he felt disdain for landsmen, he hid it well. The Kästners' status as cabin passengers and Will's pluck in the maintop gave the family a certain protection from the crew's contempt. Cutlip's eyes went back to the sails.

Just as Will looked out to the sea, Jakob dove at him, and startled, he swept one arm back, throwing the little boy aside. Jakob landed awkwardly on the slanted deck and fairly bounced up—onto the rail. He balanced there, his arms beating the air, a face of pure surprise. Amalie saw him there, flailing, and leapt to reach him. Thomas Segrave did the same and knocked into her. Will had already spun around and flung himself at the boy, grabbing.

Then Jakob was falling. They heard his high-pitched scream, and there was a desperately long moment before they heard the splash, a moment in which Amalie shrieked and Will stripped off his coat and dove overboard. Cutlip had already tossed a line overboard where the two would surface, grabbed a second line and barked out, "Man overboard!" At the wheel the master roared orders, and men ran to back the sails. Thomas seized the loose ends of Cutlip's lines and wound them around the base of the mainmast.

Jakob went far underwater and came up gasping and thrashing. Will saw the boy and grabbed at him, but Jakob slipped out of his hand and sank again. The rope end slid past them, but on deck, Cutlip had already grabbed a second line, flipped over the rail and raced down the strakes along the hull, feeding out line as he went. Jakob rose again, and Will snatched at him, got him and wrapped his arm around the little boy. They were far abaft by now, swept back by the waves, almost past the ship's stern. Then Cutlip was right above them, one hand reaching for them. He bounced off the strake at the edge of the water, aiming for the boys, and at the last instant, he grabbed Will's wrist. He yanked both boys up into the air and held on as Thomas Segrave and now Hans and others manned the rope and pulled the three of them up. Amalie heard Segrave shout, "Heave!" and saw the three of them go spinning upward as if they were weightless.

Many strong arms pulled them aboard, but Jakob was limp and lifeless over Will's shoulder. As soon as Will lay the boy down, Thomas Segrave began pushing on his chest. Footsteps pounded on the deck, and Thomas was swept aside by Dr. Ward, who grabbed the child and held him upside down.

"Hold him thus," the doctor demanded, handing Jakob's legs to Hans. As soon as Hans had Jakob by the ankles, the doctor squeezed the boy's chest. "Higher! Shake him!" Dr. Ward gave Jacob another powerful squeeze.

Amalie and Will had their arms around each other, watching in shock. Will shook with cold and fear, and tears ran down Amalie's cheeks. When it did not seem possible for things to be worse, Jakob's body twisted in the most horrible way.

"Stop! You're hurting him!" Amalie cried.

But suddenly great quantities of water spewed from Jakob's mouth, and he gasped and coughed. Hans needed no directions to turn Jakob around, as the child sobbed and gulped for air. With a grin, Hans held the child out as Amalie reached for him, and then Jakob was being handed around from one of the Kästners to another, being squeezed almost dry, as all about them the crew broke any sense of discipline, cheering and slapping Will on the back and shaking Cutlip's hand. Katrina and Niklas had heard Amalie scream and come running, and now both of them were hugging Jakob and over his head, shouting "Danke, danke, danke" to all. Amalie collapsed in tears, and Thomas Seagrave, the awful Englishman, helped her to her feet again.

That very evening, after Katrina and Amalie culled every delicacy in their shipboard pantry to make a dinner of celebration and thanksgiving, Cutlip and Dr. Ward were their honored guests. Captain Peterssen and Thomas Segrave hosted the party in the officer's dining saloon, an elegant, wood-paneled space with a polished table, a navigation desk, a large bronze skylight and neat bookshelves fitted with horizontal bars to keep books and maps from flying about.

"Cutlip" was introduced properly as John Cutler, forecastleman, larboard watch, at which Amalie and Will shared a secret smile. *How unexpected,* she thought, *that our "Cutlip" has a real name so like our nickname!*

Niklas presented the sailor a bottle of Kästner beer and a handful of gold coins, not nearly enough, since no amount was the true measure of his youngest son, but it was still more gold than John Cutler had ever held in his two hands. Dr. Ward accepted a bottle of beer but refused a reward.

"I was only doing my duty," he said.

"It was brilliant," said Captain Peterssen. "I have never seen a man—or anyone—saved that way."

"If it had been a full-grown man," said Dr. Ward, "I'd have had a halyard tied to his ankles and dragged him up that way."

Katrina looked attentively at John Cutler's face and wondered if his own mother would recognize him, emaciated, whipped brown by sun and wind, and with that deep scar across his lips and chin. She wondered how he had survived such an injury, and what his childhood had been like and what propelled him over the side of the barque, risking his life in a feat of incredible athleticism.

John Cutler said he came from Bosham on the south coast of England. "It's where King Canute told the tides to stop," he said, to which they looked polite but mystified. "It's where his poor benighted daughter drowned and is buried."

Their faces were still blank.

"In West Sussex," Thomas Segrave explained. "Directly south of London," he added, and their faces lit up.

But then John Cutler dipped them into too much detail again: "I was christened in the oldest church in England."

"The first one on that spot," agreed Thomas, "was built by the Romans."

Katrina looked down at the napkin on her lap, a wrinkle in her forehead. *Could our young hero and his fellow Englishman be correct about Romans being Christians? Hadn't the Romans fed Christians to the lions?*

Amalie seemed equally mystified. She whispered to her mother, "I had not heard they were ever in England."

From across the table, Thomas Segrave was looking with special fondness at Jakob, who sat at the table usually reserved for grownups, sharing his chair with Herr Kuschelbär.

"I lost my wife in childbirth," he told them. "One of our twins, a boy, survives and is now in London with his aunt. My little James is of an age with Jakob."

Amalie felt a rush of pity for little James, to have a father so wicked as Thomas Segrave. Then it occurred to her that he could not help being an Englishman.

Will was celebrated that night, too. His hand was shaken endlessly, and Izak Peterssen was not the only man to look him with new appreciation.

"You went right in after him!" said Niklas, who felt sure this would be a turning point in Will's life, a demarcation between feckless boy and responsible man.

"Not a thought for yourself!" said his mother. "But, oh, we might have lost you both!"

Will was immensely relieved to have his little brother alive. It was all too shocking. He should have known his brother was too small for rough-housing and the deck was too dangerous a place for horseplay. Still, he was pleased that in a desperate moment, he had no other thought but to go in after his brother. He also knew it had nearly ended in tragedy and would have without Cutlip's daring rescue of them both.

As if he could hear Will thinking, John Cutler leaned over and said, "There's a life preserver that hangs from the spanker boom. If you ever go overboard again and get swept past the boat, look for us to drop it."

"Thanks," said Will. "I will remember that." He could not help but shudder at the thought of going overboard again.

Later, below decks and to his surprise, John Cutler found himself feted again.

"More than one of us," explained Mr. Groves, "have dear wives and dear little children at home, and all would have been dismayed to see such a beautiful child lost to the waves."

After this, there was rather more respect paid to Will; to the captain's friend, Thomas Segrave; and to Dr. Ward. There was also rather more attention paid to Jakob than was to be expected from a weather-beaten crew and rather more forbearance of the child's natural high jinks than he deserved, and one might even have heard the word "angel" tossed about.

CHAPTER 32

CONDEMNED TO LIVE

In an inky black night after some weeks of sailing, Katrina heard a thump and then Niklas swearing. Moments earlier, he gasped for air and sat bolt upright, or tried to, and hit his head on a ship's beam so hard, he sank back into his cot, groaning and cradling his head with both hands.

"I was drowning," he told Katrina in a whisper, "falling through thick, soupy water, trying to save the children. All about me in the water were dead and dying soldiers, cossacks and horses, appearing and disappearing. Jakob floated away from me, just out of reach."

Niklas hesitated.

Katrina could see that he hated to say more, but needed to unburden himself. She listened to be sure the children were sleeping. "Tell me," she said. "Whatever it is."

"I saw Jan Emil, too, his face as dear to me as in life, and I saw his lips say, 'Papa!' but I couldn't hear him, and he was sinking. I dove down into even deeper, darker water, trying to reach him. Then I fell out of the water and landed in a Russian night with snow on the ground. Across a campfire was an ugly crone in rags, a Baba Yaga. She said I had killed her son. She pointed at me, and said, 'Ye, Soldier of the Devil, ye shall be condemned to live.' In a horrible voice."

He looked deep into Katrina's eyes. "Do you think someone like me ever escapes the mistakes, the horrors of his past?"

"I hope so," she said quietly. "Forget the old hag, and remember Jan Emil. I envy your having seen him."

"Yes, it was a blessing."

He was silent for a moment and then said, "Just before I woke, I wondered how a fire could burn under water, and that seemed to break the spell. That's when I sat up in this damnably tight ship's cot the size of a coffin."

"Made to serve as such should the need arise," she said. "With such wretched quarters for us, imagine what they suffer in steerage. Their hammocks are only twenty-eight inches apart. Did you know that?"

"I hit my head," he said, unnecessarily, drawing one hand away and studying it in the dim light. He was surprised to find no blood dripping through his fingers, no smear of blood across the palm, no blood at all. "How long," he wondered, "will such visions invade my nights?"

A preacher had once told Niklas his bad dreams were the work of the devil, that he needed a stronger faith, quoting scripture, "If you lie down, you will not be afraid; when you lie down, your sleep will be sweet." Katrina thought this an empty promise and it unkind to add guilt to torment.

"By day," Niklas told her in a very low voice, "I can dream of the future. By night, I am trapped in the past, like a weasel caught in a snare."

Katrina was almost asleep again and did not answer him. More than the children, she and Niklas understood the risks of the voyage. Danger was all around, and most of it more likely than drowning. Life could be cut short by injury, disease, or putrid food; such threats existed everywhere but were more deadly aboard, where one also faced the threat of storms, shipwreck, attack, and sometimes even enemies aboard or men made enemies by being squeezed into such tight quarters. It was so easy to fail at sailing that anyone might wonder what fool would undertake an ocean passage where a fluke of weather, a sloppy crew, a vicious privateer, a madman, or a single misjudgment by the captain could prove fatal.

At the same time, the difficulties and dangers of clinging to Europe were not to be minimized. Turmoil and tyranny were everywhere, war a regular state of affairs, opportunity limited in the extreme, and even a position in a community and some degree of wealth, such as they had, were little protection and no license to do or speak as one might think right or wise. And by staying, one gave up the shining possibility of America.

After a few days, Katrina took her little ones in hand along with Franci and three young Ackermanns, and with Amalie helping, began teaching them to recognize German letters and say a thing or two in English and French. One Ackermann child was a round-faced girl with wide blueberry-blue eyes like Lisette's. She was a lovable, silly goose who instantly adored Lisette and Franci. To judge from the amazement in those blueberry-blue eyes, she had reached the zenith of her young life when Lisette shared a zucker zweiback, so far superior to a ship's biscuit as to cause her to trail after the older girls in hopes of crumbs.

What, Katrina wondered, *would the child do for a gingerbread cookie?* She decided to make the next day's treat a cookie.

Amalie took pains to keep the children out of the crew's way. When she sat perfectly straight on a small, black, brass-studded trunk, reciting poems to the children in a voice both sweet and strong, everyone from Captain Peterssen to forecastleman Cutler set to a dozen unnecessary tasks to keep themselves on deck, working quietly so as not to miss a word. Amalie could not help but notice her many admirers, and it made her pink cheeks pinker. Even their new passenger, the English owner, listened, smiling at the lovely cadence of Amalie's voice. When something made her laugh, it was an infectiously happy sound that cheered everyone.

Days later, on a warm, sunny deck, Katrina set her knitting needles to flying, and Francesca asked her to slow down and show them how the stitch went together.

She laughed. "I don't dare slow down. I'm like the caterpillar with a thousand legs. If I stopped to think about it, I would trip over my needles!"

Francesca often joined Katrina on deck, her female cousins sitting alongside. Two Ackermann sisters were remaking one of Francesca's old skirts for their girls. One of these girls was a shy young woman named Hannah, strikingly beautiful and newly married. Amalie looked sideways at her, this girl who was only a few years older. Her blonde hair, delicate features and pink skin were perfect.

Amalie, whose knitting needles could move almost as fast as her mother's, whispered, "Hannah could be a princess."

"Don't be silly," Katrina told her daughter. "And go get a bonnet. No one wants a girl who looks like a milkmaid."

Most weeks with fair enough sailing had a make-and-mend day, when the deck was crowded with sailors darning socks, repairing rips and tears and embroidering ribbons along the seams of their trousers or on their shore-going straw hats. The sailmaker and his helpers often sewed on deck as well, for the sake of the light.

Almost all of the sailors had a superstitious bias against having women aboard, but it did not restrict their interest in the fine work Katrina and Amalie could do. They looked on and asked questions, while Katrina and Amalie in turn studied the heavy materials and sewing tools needed for sail-making.

"Look, Amalie," Katrina said, as she turned over an edge of sailcloth in her fingers and noted the awl and the stout needle needed to work it. "A length of sail canvas might make a good shade for a porch or for animals."

"An excellent idea," said Amalie. "We could use Papa's leather tools to work it. Even the grommets and grommet-setter are similar." She motioned to her father, saying "Look, Papa," and explained their idea.

Niklas was happy to be called away from the conversation he had been having with Methuselah. He had begun talking to the old man imagining their age would give them something in common, but it had soon become clear that they had both been in the Napoleonic Wars, and then that both had been at Waterloo—on opposite sides. *This ship*, Niklas thought, *carries too many Englishmen for comfort*. He was glad John Cutler and Thomas Segrave were both too young to have fought with Wellington,

Now Niklas showed Katrina his drawing of a log cabin. He had once been part of a crew building a hunting cabin for the duke in the Red-Haired Mountains. "It will all depend on what we find to build with," he warned. "We will hope for tall, straight trees like the spruces of the ancient Berleburg Forest. On the Russian steppes, I saw vast grasslands with never a tree, excellent for an enormous mounted army to cross over, but a hard, lonely place to live."

"Like America's Great Desert, maybe." They had read about great stretches of grasslands where nothing could be grown, it being impervious to the plow.

Later, in the evening hours, Niklas took out his violin and handed Amalie a harmonica.

"Look here," a big, rawboned sailor exclaimed joyfully when Niklas opened his violin case, "we got ourselves a catgut scraper!"

"Silence!" said the officer of the watch, but not even his stern face or angry frown could hide the way his eyes smiled at the sight of the instrument.

As Niklas and Amalie played, the family sang along, and the Ackermanns and some of the crew soon joined in. Niklas played a tune he had learned in Spain, and to everyone's surprise, Francesca began to sing—in Italian—a song none but Giovanni understood, though everyone clapped and smiled.

On this charming evening, as a sailor brought out a tin whistle and played along, another grabbed a friend and tapped a lively dance on the deck. They were soon joined by another and another. Even Izak Peterssen, at the wheel, seemed to smile. A happy ship was valuable, given as it was to working together when threatened by storms or battles or any of the dangers of the open sea. Besides, this was joyful music, even if he, as captain, could not join in. Even on a loose, democratic merchantman like *Enigma*, the idea was absurd.

CHAPTER 33

NORTH SEA CAPTURE

Enigma sailed under the British flag, regardless of her captain's nationality, because the ship was owned by a conglomerate of British aristocrats and industrialists. The majority owner was her new passenger, Thomas Segrave, a younger son of a mine owner and one of England's nouveau riche. Niklas knew something of this, but was to learn much more one morning while he shared breakfast with Izak Peterssen, Thomas Segrave, and Katrina. They lingered over a pot of coffee, and O'Malley, the captain's steward, had to refill it several times as Izak and Thomas grew nostalgic, if one could call such harrowing memories nostalgia. It was obvious these two had a friendship rare between captains and owners. When Katrina asked how they came to know each other, it turned out that a shocking experience had thrown them together, and later they had shared their training aboard a series of Royal Navy ships.

Izak Peterssen said he had been at sea since he was ten, but it was what happened to him at twelve that made him loyal to the British. "I was on *Hagen*, a Danish knarr of the old style, my grandfather's. *Hagen* was a small merchant vessel carrying walrus ivory, wool, wheat, furs, honey, and weapons, when it was attacked and overpowered by *Ibrahim*, a Barbary xebec."

"*Hagen*," interrupted Thomas Segrave, who had obviously heard this story before, "had carried a few Russian slaves to Iceland in earlier days but even those unfortunate souls would have considered being taken by a Turk a fate a thousand times worse."

"On the terrible day we were captured," said Izak, "those who did not die in the fighting were chained to a bench as galley slaves, where we were expected to row, eat, and sleep until we died of exposure and exhaustion."

"Galley slaves," explained Thomas, "were never unchained unless the ship came under attack, and then Barbary pirates were not above making their ship lighter and faster by throwing the slaves overboard."

"Which is in fact what happened. After twenty hours' chase, the British *Isolde* attacked *Ibrahim*. We had pulled under the whip until a breeze came up and made oarsmen useless. *Ibrahim*'s crew came down the benches with axes and cut our chains, tossing us overboard like sheep. We were still in chains," said Izak, "and most sank and never rose, never breathed air again."

"Except Izak," said Thomas.

"Aye, I survived. The icy waters of the North Sea were a terrible shock, but I was skinny and not yet grown. The cold water let me slip out of my shackles, and besides, I could swim. As I broke the surface, my lungs bursting, *Isolde*, God bless her, had already put a boat down."

"There were only two other survivors," said Thomas, picking up the story, "and one is here aboard with us, Erik Thorvald, our master gunner."

Katrina must have looked confused, because Izak explained. "He's a large man like your first son." He nodded to Hans. "An Icelander with a flaming red beard."

"Ah," said Katrina. Erik Thorvald could not really be missed, even in a crowd of men.

"Thorvald had the strength to swim even while shackled," said Thomas, "pumping his joined legs like a seal. So heavy and awkward was he in chains that trying to get aboard, he nearly swamped the rescue boat we sent."

The third survivor was Izak's grandfather, a strong swimmer who had taught Izak what to do if he fell overboard. He was picked up by *Isolde* but was too exhausted to survive.

"Grandpa never spoke a word after his rescue, but lay warmed by *Isolde* blankets until he died. He knew me at the end and smiled to see me alive and rescued."

"Long quiet hours when Izak never left his side," added Thomas.

"Aye. It was hard to lose him."

Tears sprang to Katrina's eyes to think of an old man suffering so vile a fate.

"Izak was speaking English in no time," Thomas said.

"'My mum was Frisian, and it's an easy jump from Frisian to English. And my other Opa was German, so I spoke four languages and could translate, which brought me to the captain's attention. He was a hard man but a fair one."

"It helped that you were a sailor already, and as agile as a monkey."

"I had been properly trained on *Hagen* and had sailed on my father's fishing boat, *Signe*, since I was in breeches. She was a solid oak ketch, gaff-rigged for a steady, comfortable motion in any sea, the picture of strength from her beautifully varnished spars and her anchor windlass to her brass-bound wheel."

Thomas laughed. "He cannot recall that old fishing boat without singing her praises."

Izak smiled for a moment and then continued his story. "Thorvald and I will bear the marks of our enslavement for life, he quite literally; on *Isolde,* they cut off the spiked iron cuff around his neck. It had been used like a ring through a bull's nose to tame a creature of extraordinary strength. The scars from it mark him today and will do so for life."

Katrina and Niklas had remarked on the ring of scars on the big man's neck.

Thomas said, "Our rescue gave you a lasting admiration for the English hatred of slavery and of Turks most especially."

"Aye, it's true. By the time I might have rejoined a Danish ship, I felt at home in the Royal Navy, and having seen the tropics, I was not averse to sailing further south than most Danish ships had right or reason to go."

"He's not telling you all," said Thomas. "He's been through several actions, including on a frigate with fifty-four guns—boarding a French ship-of-the-line in fierce hand-to-hand combat that left scars he will always carry, earning enough prize money for a right handsome captain's house in Copenhagen."

"Not nearly as handsome as your father's house in London," said Izak.

"Is your boy there?" Katrina asked Thomas, "the one you say is little Jakob's age?"

"Aye, he is. James is a sight safer there than on board with me."

Like most English ships, *Enigma* had adopted Royal Navy habits, precautions and traditions, some essential for the orderly running of any ship, some reasonable precautions that gave a predator the impression he was approaching a man-of-war, and some silly and pretentious, and even more so when performed in loose imitation of the original and unhinged from any purpose they might once have had. Times were dangerous, enough so that seamanlike captains continued the practice of giving the crew regular gunnery exercise.

Thus, on one particular calm day, Izak stood on the quarterdeck, timing Erik Thorvald's gunnery crews' ability to hit floating targets—empty water barrels with a staff and a scrap of fabric attached. Thomas Segrave stood by him during this exercise.

No one could have been more pleased with the captain's martial spirit than Niklas, and he easily won Izak's permission to continue the boys' training in pistols and swords. When the Ackermanns saw this, they asked to be trained as well. Izak approved and sent the word around to the crew: they were not to laugh. Very soon, Niklas saw to it that they had no cause to. He began the Ackermanns' training with hunting knife drills, and when Richard Billings outfitted a half-dozen Ackermann men and boys with batons, cudgels and fighting staffs, Niklas adapted sword and knife fighting to these crude weapons. The Ackermanns were strong farmers, accustomed to handling an axe or a plow, and glad to be on deck learning more of the arts of defense.

Strong but minimally skilled, men like the Ackermanns were most dangerous as an angry mob, and privately, Niklas told Hans and Will never to be part of such a melee if they could avoid it.

"Put some distance between yourself and your opponent," he said, "so your skill counts."

Katrina was fervent in her hope that the boys heard.

CHAPTER 34

PROPHESYING WOE

For ballast, *Enigma* carried limestone blocks, stacks of iron cannonballs, casks of fresh water, and cases of French wine. Everyone aboard kept using the water, of course, even after it took on a wretched taste from the oak barrels, so the barque became lighter as it crossed the ocean.

"Pissing away our ballast," a midshipman giggled. This boy, Gideon Groves, was a nephew of the first mate. He had not grown tall yet, and his voice still piped like a child's. The British Royal Navy knew the importance of training boys early, and *Enigma*, like many merchantmen, followed the tradition. They considered a boy ruined who had not been to sea by age ten, so Gideon thought himself lucky to have found a place aboard at the advanced age of thirteen. But he was homesick. He could not quite help himself from keeping close to the Kästner family, especially Katrina, whenever she was on deck.

"How old are you, Gideon?" she asked one bright day.

"Sixteen."

She choked for a second. "Child, tell me the truth."

"Fourteen," he lied.

She let it stand, so as not to embarrass him. "Coming to sea late in life, is it?"

"Oh, no, ma'am, I've been around the sea most of my life."

Yes, she thought, *standing on a dock somewhere looking out at it.*

The officers, including those as young as Midshipman Groves, drank a few bottles of wine, but most were to be sold in New Orleans, along with the limestone ballast and the cargo stowed above it. This included the Kästner chests of Dutch pottery, great wheels of Edam encased in red paraffin, crates of French furniture, and clocks made in one of the Germanies. There was even a shiny, black fortepiano made in Meissen, on order for a Madame Robergé of New Orleans. In Delfshaven, the Kästners had watched it go aboard in a sling like a great fat cow. Spare canvas and spars, extra iron fittings and line—fine African hemp—filled every crack and crevice below deck.

The food stores were mostly below as well. Three hundred pounds of ship's bread awaited—large round crackers of water and flour baked so hard they almost broke teeth, impervious to weevils for a month or so. Salt pork and salt beef filled barrels, as did twenty gallons of molasses, two hundred pounds of flour, a few small cartons of sugar and butter, two bags each of dried peas and beans, fifteen pounds of coffee and tea in tins, and four barrels of potatoes. Soft, round loaves of Dutch bread and sweet apples were eaten on the first coastwise leg and replaced in Gibraltar with traditional Spanish flatbread and baskets of oranges, lemons and limes. Now all of the fruit and even the flatbread was gone.

The Kästners kept their chickens and goats forward with the rest of the little floating farmyard: cows, sheep, chickens and pigs, continually diminishing as the ship needed meat. Katrina made it a point to have Amalie milk the nanny goat and collect the eggs while they were still warm from the hens. She knew the ship's galley crew would consider a theft of eggs or goat's milk entirely justified: "Why, we're the ones to carry them across, ain't we?"

"We are lucky to have a captain who provisioned the ship so well," said Amalie one day. She and her parents were watching ship's boys handing up sacks of potatoes and lugging them to the galley.

Niklas looked at their sensible daughter with some surprise. "I certainly hope so," he said. "We shall see."

"It's not luck, Amalie," Katrina said. "One of the most important questions your father asked Captain Peterssen was whether *Enigma* would be well stocked. And whether attention was paid to keeping her water sweet. It's sulphured, you know."

"Oh," said Amalie, "of course you would inquire."

"And we are responsible for our own provisions," Katrina added. "That's what we've been eating all along."

"Certainly," said Amalie, but she looked surprised.

As Amalie left, Niklas and Katrina exchanged glances. "Our children," he said, "have been coddled, never to have felt the pinch of famine."

"We wanted to save them from it; any parent would."

"Naturally, and I am forever thankful that we could. But she's usually so sensible."

"Perhaps she and the others have been made just a little foolish on account of such a soft life."

All of this was as nothing compared to what had happened below. It was a shock and a sad story and not finished, as far as Izak Peterssen was concerned, but an intimation of a wretched future. Niklas quoted him to Katrina.

"They say immigrants are flooding Liverpool, Hamburg and Le Havre, lured to America by stories of easy wealth, low taxes, free land, absurd freedoms."

"We really didn't see that in Rotterdam," Katrina said. "And besides, to us the freedoms of America are not absurd."

"We can't compare what we saw with past years in Rotterdam, and besides, they aren't really talking about people like us but those in steerage."

She nodded. "But why are they worried? Aren't passengers just another source of income?"

"I asked much the same," said Niklas. "Thomas—" and here Katrina noted that the Englishman was now on a first-name basis— "Thomas said *Enigma*'s owners had congratulated themselves for their grasp of the changing world, seeing trans-Atlantic passenger traffic ticking up, promising easy profits and diminished risks. They even pointed out that human cargo loads and unloads itself."

"And passengers pay up front," said Katrina. Passengers of any rank paid upon embarkation, no waiting until the voyage's end to find buyers and sell cargo at a price unknown, and so long as the ship did not wreck or otherwise fall prey to the thousand dangers of an ocean crossing.

"Le Havre, especially, is up in arms about the immigrant influx and all the talk is about restrictions, they say."

"It's hard to imagine many will give up civilization in Europe for barbarism on America's frontier."

"They both say we are an exception to concern ourselves with anything like freedom or culture. Cheap land is the main attraction, so steerage is where the trade's headed."

Katrina did not answer him, but she had gotten to know Francesca and her cousins, and she knew they cared about more than an immediate need to escape poverty. Besides, she had been below and seen the cramped, airless space converted from cargo bays, where the Ackermann family suffered. It made the Kästners' small deck cabin look luxurious, finished as it was with portholes and a skylight and polished paneling.

"I wonder if those miserable quarters of theirs had anything to do with it."

"Miasma, maybe. But how could that be true out here where the air is clean."

"Only if you're allowed on deck," Katrina said.

Their speculation was about the recent death of a steerage woman. It was Hannah, the extraordinarily beautiful young woman with blonde hair and fair skin, the one Amalie thought an unrecognized princess. She was barely more than a girl, an Ackermann by birth and newly married to a young man now wild with grief and isolation.

That afternoon, with the flag lowered to half-mast and sails braced to all but stop the ship, everyone on board gathered on deck. The captain, prayerbook in hand, said a proper service for the poor girl, his face solemn and his voice deep. He spoke first in English for the sake of the flag and then again in German for the family. "Thus we commit her body to the deep," he concluded, "So zum tiefen verpflichten wir ihren Körper."

He nodded to Mr. Crowley, who began to tilt the plank on which the canvas-wrapped body was laid, a hint to her family's men to lift with him. A woman stepped forward, her hand raised to pause them, and she sprinkled ashes from head to foot of the canvas. The men lifted with Mr.

Crowley then, and the soft scrape of sliding canvas was followed by a gentle splash. The sailmaker had prepared properly, having sewn her into her hammock and weighted it with a cannonball. It disappeared below the waves at once.

The young woman's sisters and mother had been crying all along; now the mother's intense sobbing escalated into a wail, a long, aching, unnerving sound piercing the heart of everyone on board. Her husband shook her, and she dropped back into plain hard sobbing.

Amalie, who had so envied Hannah, seemed in shock. The Kästners stood together and watched respectfully. Katrina and Niklas held firmly to the children, Katrina's head bowed to hide the tears on her cheeks. No Kästner had gone anywhere near that body, and now they all would avoid the Ackermanns for some time to come.

Captain Peterssen stood ramrod straight, his eyes raised to the heavens. *It may look like piety,* Katrina thought, *but in this hard moment, he is not at all happy to have passengers at all, especially women.*

The sound of the Ackermanns' grief rose again, and Katrina saw the group shuffle forward, struggling. They were holding the young husband back. He was shouting something, and then the family tightened around him and held him. A few of crewmen were at the ready, their faces tense with the possibility they would have to touch an Ackermann. Among them, in his black suit, was Methuselah, who smacked a belaying pin against his palm. His face was twisted into what looked almost like eagerness, and Niklas frowned to see it.

"Stand down," Mr. Groves ordered Methuselah.

"Eh?" he said, bending his good ear to the first mate. The other ear was not so much deaf as missing, sliced off long ago.

"Stand down!"

No one knew why the young woman died, or if the family did, they were not saying. Dr. Ward, who generally knew everything happening above and below decks, said he had seen nothing but whispers being told behind handkerchiefs. Typical Germans, the Ackermanns were obsessively clean, but he had smelled blood and vomit, he was sure of it.

He would not speculate, but Katrina worried about typhoid or cholera. Had Hannah vomited blood? Did she abort? She studied the Ackermanns, going through a list of possibilities. Disease could sweep through the close quarters of a ship. Then another thought struck her. Through swollen eyes, she surveyed the men aboard. *Was Hannah raped?* It was a shocking speculation, but while young women should always be properly guarded, being aboard ship made it difficult. Everything about this death made her nervous, as it did everyone, especially the superstitious sailors. Which was all of them.

Izak had said to Niklas that no Christian sailor liked this business of taking on women, and now one of them dead and another making that most unnatural wail and a besotted husband ready to follow his love into the deep. Izak was worried about loose talk of a doomed ship and the need to find a Jonah, and some fanatic starting to prophesy woe: a whale would hit *Enigma* or a plague would strike, and she would run into New Orleans a ghost ship with none left alive.

"When I looked out at the sea today," Izak told Niklas, "it was in the dear hope of seeing anything but plague aboard: the green clouds of a hurricane forming or a privateer with its topsails set or the *Flying Dutchman*, making straight for us. Anything but plague."

Katrina said nothing. Her throat was too closed up to speak anyway. She worried about whether another woman would be next, and she vowed to keep Amalie nearby at all times.

CHAPTER 35

FIRST SIGHT OF LAND

The morning began hot and slow, with almost no wind and *Enigma* picking up an uncomfortable sloshing that threatened to make Katrina, Hans, and Jakob sick again. Amalie was on deck with Jacob, playing a game of cloud shapes to keep the child's eyes on the horizon, as Dr. Ward had advised. Will was in the maintop, watching for islands and shallows. A low bank of far-off clouds came ever closer, and the wind began to build. Soon *Enigma* was flying down the waves, in her element in twenty-five or thirty knots. Izak had taken over the helm from Mr. Groves, and he looked perfectly happy there, severe and alert, with smiling eyes.

On Day 45 out of Gibraltar, *Enigma* lost the wind again for watch after watch, and Katrina worried about the food supply. The ocean crossing had been slow, and the fishing uncertain, although a porpoise had recently been caught and shared. Forty-five days was all a crossing should require. Some time ago, she had cut her own rations to leave more for the children and stretched every meal with oats and hardtack. So far, the family had not complained. When she unwrapped the last slab of Westphalian ham, she found that half had been stolen.

Katrina told Niklas in confidence, "I am worried about the Ackermann's food supply and whatever Cook still has."

"Ja," he nodded.

"At least we still have the nanny goat and the last few chickens. If Thomas did not like milk in his coffee, or the chickens quit laying…"

On Day 46, Will spotted a brig in the distance, too far away to hail, and today there were terns gliding around the sails and dipping into the wake, where *Enigma* kicked up small fish. Far away, another ship appeared, a barque like themselves, and then it slipped below the horizon.

Methuselah told Will, "It's the nearness of South America, naught but jungles, wild beasts and cannibals, ruled by the papist Portuguese." He turned and looked hard at Will, "You all ain't papist, are you?"

"No," said Will.

"Well, that's something."

The great excitement aboard at the first sight of land faded as islands became common. The wind sometimes carried a whiff of land, but they had not seen fishing boats. More than one wondered where the people were.

Will was in the maintop long hours, as Mr. Groves now posted lookouts day and night against the dangers of islands, reefs and shallows. To Will, it seemed years since he had first gone out along the mainyard to help lower or raise a sail. His first time, he thought the footropes would be the death of him, they jumped and pitched so as he and others moved along the yard. He was terrified when they were expected to brace themselves, bellies on the yard and feet horizontal or hooked there to reach down and gather the sail. Now he could do so with confidence, but he still dreaded the order's coming in a blow, as he knew it must, and Katrina shared his dread.

Mr. Groves warned everyone: "Don't be getting excited. It's a weary long passage yet to be made." He showed them on a map how the Caribbean Sea stretched from east to west with New Orleans on its northwest shore. "It will be at least a fortnight," he said.

"Two more long weeks," Niklas said.

"Ja," Katrina said, "three weeks longer than we planned, and that assumes we are not lost." She had not realized that Amalie was listening until the girl spoke.

"Could we have passed America by, Papa? Simply missed it?"

"No, of course not. It stretches from the north pole nearly to the south pole, so there must soon be land in sight. In the middle is this huge bay filled with islands—think of all the islands we've seen.

"And until we arrive, we still have a few potatoes, onions and zucker zweiback," Katrina said, "while the crew is down to little more than hardtack and salt pork. Though Cook tries to make something of it."

"With what he calls lobscouse and dandyfunk," said Amalie. "I know 'lobscouse' is a stew with hardtack—he wants our goats for it—but what's 'dandyfunk'?"

"Hardtack, soaked, then fried with molasses on top."

"Ugh."

"Better than plain hardtack, Daughter," said Katrina. "And far better than nothing."

When Niklas saw what little food Katrina was giving herself, he swore to eat less, too. The very next meal, which came after a long watch at the wheel, he forgot to do so, not thinking of it until the last bite was on his fork. Katrina saw him stop suddenly and push it off onto Jakob's plate. The child ate it without a thought.

Later, Mr. Groves traced a wide swath of ocean on his map as he told them of the Antilles Current: "It might sweep us away to the north, into the Gulf Stream, up the coast of North America and out to sea again. We must cross it safely and get into the Loop Current." On a return trip, he assured them, prevailing westerlies and the Gulf Stream would take a ship quickly across the Atlantic, but sailing west was difficult. It was made more so because they had entered dangerously shallow waters, threatened by hurricanes and alive with pirates and privateers to whom a merchantman like *Enigma* looked a fat, easy prize.

Even before the sun rose one day, it was clear that the weather was turning uncommon dirty, but only those reading a barometer had any idea how quickly it might be upon them or what a rough patch they might be in for. The wind had shifted to the sou'-sou'-east and ran with the prevailing northerly current, now confused by rollers from the east and steadily picking up force. Captain Peterssen put the ship into a run before the wind, which with luck was going approximately where he wished to go, and she flew along, making truly remarkable distance.

On deck, every sailor watched the sails intently. Orders came sharply, and over and over the crew ran to adjust the sails, for fear the most minor tweak, unmade, could lead to a broach. It was the rule of the seas, whether a man was mending a sail or tending one, that the slightest shoddiness could begin a slide, perhaps irreversible, into disaster. Everything required total attention, and each task must be done to perfection.

Lightning glimmered in the clouds to the north, and waves washed across the bow, some aft as far as the capstan, when suddenly *Enigma* was hit by a violent adverse wind. It carried off the foretopgallant sail, which though furled tight, was caught by a loose edge and ripped open. The sail was torn to ribbons, and the lines, cut loose, sliced through the air, threatening to carve through any man caught in their arc. From then on, the gale played out in a succession of heavy squalls. At two bells, Mr. Groves called all hands to shorten sail in pitch blackness. Izak was at the wheel with two others, it requiring three men to hold and turn the wheel. On this dark night, they steered by the wind on their faces.

Hans and Will were off watch but had slept in their clothing. When orders came, Hans was first to step onto the main deck and was immediately up to his knees in water and bowled away as a wave swept the deck. The line he grabbed at that moment became his lifeline.

"Hans!" Will yelled. He was on deck himself and holding a line. He saw Hans caught in the nets at the rail, getting to his feet, and heading for the bow, where the idlers would manage the jibs and bowsprit. Thomas was ahead of his time in insisting on nets, and now these had saved Hans.

"Lay aloft, me boys! Main course first." Mr. Groves somehow made himself heard over the screech of the wind. Will seized the ratlines and began to climb, hanging onto shrouds for dear life, while the ship rolled and pitched. He hauled himself through the lubber's hole onto the platform, no acrobatics on a night like this, and stepped out onto the footropes of the larboardside mainyard.

"Farther out! Spread yourselves out!" Mr. Groves could still be heard.

Will was in the middle, a sailor named Davey nearest the mast, and John Cutler on the outside. As he and the others spread out, the order came. "Haul away, Haul up!"

At his first grab the wet sail flipped out of his hand. In forty knots of wind, a flick of a sail could send a man overboard.

Davey yelled at Will. "Keep ahold, you goddamn Kraut!"

"Gott im Himmel!" Will shouted back, as if that helped.

From below, Mr. Groves: "Lay out there, Gideon, you useless lump." The boy was on the yards above Will, helping furl the mainmast topsails.

The barque tipped from side to side and pitched forward and back, swinging men in the rigging like kites on a string. Below them, the sea was a fast-moving line of cresting waves, foam spinning off the tops. Rain came at them sideways, peppering their cheeks. Then *Enigma* heeled starboard to forty-five degrees, and those on the larboard side, including Will, were raised out over the water. They could do nothing in that moment but cling to the yard. From far above, Will saw something fall in a graceful arc.

He thought it was a spar torn loose, but no, it was flailing as it fell. It seemed impossibly small, like a dog or a doll, and then Will heard a scream, more of surprise than terror, and suddenly the sound was cut off and gone, lost in the waves.

"Man overboard!" Will yelled, and Davey did, too, at the same instant, as if they were a chorus.

From the deck, the captain's voice: "Heave to!" For the second time on this voyage, men ran to back the sails.

"Furl! Furl! Furl!" bellowed Mr. Groves, and they furled for all they were worth and slid down the shrouds.

Will hit the deck in time to see, in the ocean, the slight body of Gideon Groves bob to the surface, not alive, not gasping for air nor making any attempt to swim, the neck bent at an impossible angle as if it had no bones at all. And then it slid beneath the waves.

A boat had already been swung free of its davits and was ready to lower.

"Belay that," said Mr. Groves, his voice dead flat. They watched, all of them on deck and those who had come up at the shouting, but nothing more was to be seen of Gideon Groves.

When at last the storm began to blow itself out, the wind still howling above and sending wafts of foam across the deck, the crew set to work repairing *Enigma* feverishly, in the knowledge that a much-abused ship can founder and send all aboard to a watery grave. The sea was still violently agitated, the pumps kept going watch in and watch out. Richard Billings and his carpenter's crew were hard at work. Hans was lowered over the side in a bosun's chair to lay in new lapboards where the waves had battered the starboard bow past the copper, the headrails gone and the bowsprit unable to carry its sails, it being little more than a stump. Riggers were hard at work above and below, knotting and splicing, though Izak would not send anyone up the ratlines to the uppermost reaches quite yet.

Hans returned to the deck and climbed out of the bosun's chair, saying to Will, "It ain't half as bad as crawling out on the bowsprit in the storm, and me about to upchuck at any moment. Nor you up on the yards."

Will shuddered. He could not think of being on the yards without remembering Gideon and the graceful, awful arc of his fall.

"It was so loud," Hans said, who could see how upset his little brother was.

"Yes," Will said. "I knew a blow would be, but the shrieking of the wind, and the keening of it through the rigging—"

"Aye, and the ship itself, creaking and moaning, fittings popping like she'd come apart."

"No wonder she needs so much loving care now."

"It's just that we're out here..." Hans waved an arm at the surrounding sea, "with no idea how far away a harbor might be."

"We know it's the hard edges that are dangerous, but even so, land would be a sight to see just now. You know what they say, 'Give a sailor a knife and a forest, and he can build a ship.'"

"Master Billings could, that's for sure."

"Had we a forest," said Will.

All this time, Katrina had worked amid Stygian darkness and stench, sick herself and caring for Jakob, not a good sailor in any storm. The child was cranky, weak, pale, and frightened, and so was Katrina. For long hours she held him, cramped and exhausted with Lisette draped over her shoulder, taking comfort in her children piled in here and not sunk below the waves and gone forever, like poor Gideon Groves, who slid off the topmast yards, a boy who would never become a man.

CHAPTER 36

DIAMANTE

Izak Peterssen hated piracy and slavery as do only those who have been its victims, but he was no fool for a fight, so through long hours of rough seas following the storm, *Enigma* tried to outrun her attacker. The masthead lookout confirmed what Mr. Stephens had said earlier.

"It's *Diamante*, sir," the lookout told Captain Peterssen. "Once *Diamond*, when she was ours. My cousin Gavin, he sailed her one cruise, gunner's mate; said she was passably quick but took twice the men as should have. Not much danger to most, but out-gunning *Enigma.*"

Izak stared at him: "Well?"

"Ten twelve-pounders, sir, a long-range bow cannon and four eighteen-pound carronades."

"Fifteen to our thirteen, then."

All that the lookout told the captain was true. Spanish-built as *Diamante*, taken by the British, who rebuilt her from ship-rigged to schooner and renamed her *Diamond*, then retaken, presumably descending from trading in smuggled rum as a semi-respectable privateer into true and evil robbery on the open seas: piracy. She was likely crowded with men being kept below deck in hopes of deceiving *Enigma*'s lookouts. By the time the moon was well up, she was coming up on *Enigma* seven knots to its six.

Still, she was under short sails, her yards all ahoo and her deck littered with rubbish. Izak Peterssen could not be sure she was dedicated to action. Was she wavering, indecisive, shoddily sailed, or waiting to set-to in the light? His own decks had long been cleared for action, the gun crews ready to take their positions and well supplied. Like most merchantmen, *Enigma* was sadly shorthanded, one of the owners' economies. Izak had kept all able-bodied men, sailor or landsman, on deck for the last watch, even feeding them there, to confuse *Diamante* about the crew size. Many merchantmen had little choice but to beg for mercy in such a situation, but Izak Peterssen had fought with the Royal Navy too long to be one of those. Despite *Enigma*'s slowness and weight, despite her having women and children aboard, who were of no use and got in the way—and land-lubberly men as passengers—he intended to fight.

"*Enigma*," he told Niklas, "carries more guns, powder, and balls than most merchantmen; you can command our small cadre of 'marines,' your-selves, and the Ackermann men, and I have exercised our gunnery crews, perhaps not as often as I should have, but often enough, I hope."

That night, Niklas sharpened his sword and talked at length to Hans and Will, as Katrina listened. The boys' inexperience was a worry. Not even Niklas, who had trained them since boyhood, could predict how they would stand up to the fury of action. Niklas slept soundly that night, but the boys were too keyed up, and this morning, the last thing Katrina told them was, "Stay calm and confident, boys. If those around you panic, meet panic with its opposite; make yourself calm and steadfast. Wipe doubt from your mind. You will hit your target. Beginning to end, one shot after the other, be sure of it." She had been taught this for shooting competi-tions in Berleburg, and she had found it good advice in almost any situation.

Niklas looked at her in surprise and said, "Yes. Your mother is exact-ly right. Confidence and a calm mind will pay off every time. From now on you can call her your little colonel."

Hans and Will grinned, but their grins faded when they looked at her.

"What?" said Niklas. "I said you were right, didn't I?"

The early morning watch was filled with steady, anxious preparation. Decks were cleared, hammocks rolled and lashed to the rails, splinter net-ting raised, shot and balls brought up, sand and sawdust sprinkled to help the men keep their footing. Scuttlebutts of water were placed at the ready, and the surgeons laid out their instruments.

Mid-morning, Will sidled close to Niklas and asked in a low voice, "Have you seen my second pistol?"

"What! I gave it you."

"When? I don't think so."

"You idiot, where did you put it? Think, child!"

The tips of Will's ears turned pink. He did not like being called an id-iot or a child, today of all days. But the greater his irritation, the smoother he kept his voice: "We have hours yet, Father. I'll find it."

An ugly puce glow crept up Niklas's neck, and for an instant, Katrina thought he might throttle Will. *How could the boy not know his father's impatience with anyone failing to prepare?*

Through the forenoon watch, a tense silence ensued, everyone on deck alone with his thoughts, noiseless stem to stern but for the rush of water alongside, the creaking of the hull and the rustle of sails filling and luffing. Second pistol found, Will climbed the ratlines in silence and crouched in the maintop. It was quiet enough to hear the scrape-scrape of Dr. Ward's sharpening knives for surgery.

Below decks, Amalie and Katrina had long ago riffled through their trunks for lengths of calico, the only clean cloth left aboard, and set about tearing it into strips for bandages. Katrina's lips were set in a tight line of anger that *Enigma* should be attacked; that three of the family should be called into action at the risk of their very lives; and especially and particularly that Izak Peterssen this whole long voyage should have refused to allow anyone on board to use fresh water for washing clothing; thus, in these dire straits, they were tearing up perfectly good dressmaking materials. The look on her mother's face worried Amalie, and the two younger children crouched in a corner, too frightened to play.

Shortly after six bells, the wind having backed two degrees, *Diamante* set her royals and larboardside stunsails and bore down on *Enigma*. She ditched a tattered Dutch flag flown as a ruse de guerre, and now flew the wicked black flag of no nation. Minutes later, *Diamante*'s long-range gun fired a warning shot across *Enigma*'s bow, and then the broadsides began, aimed squarely at *Enigma*'s rigging.

Even below decks, Katrina could smell the cannon smoke. She shooed Amalie and the two little ones through long, narrow, musty, filthy passages, going down and down, lifting Jakob down the ladders they came to, hurrying to the Lady's Hole, a secret compartment Mr. Groves had shown them, there to hide with the children until all was quiet, and even after that, until someone came to get them, friend or foe.

"Never come out," Mr. Groves had warned her, "until someone comes for you. Someone whose voice you recognize."

The Ackermann women and children were already inside, and Katrina, the last one in, closed the hatch, but not before she saw the terror on the young women's faces and felt it rising in her own throat. She was the only woman with pistols, and now she sat with them on her lap, looking up at the trapdoor, wondering what good her few bullets would do. The girls were on either side of her, and Jakob clung to Amalie's neck. Katrina shifted a little so she could dig into her apron pocket. There her fingers found it, her father's carving of a fiddler. She brought it out and held it up so the children could see it in the faint light.

"Opa," whispered Amalie.

Katrina nodded. "We need his blessing now more than ever." She was deeply afraid and upset that it had come to this, angry with Niklas, with Izak Peterssen, with the stupid pirate captain, and with the way the world was arranged, from boys fighting on playgrounds to men who could not seem to find another way to live but to rise up periodically and kill each other. But if there were to be a fight, she despised having to hide. *Where is a sword when I need it?* Then she called Francesca to her.

"Francesca," she said, "We can talk now. The battle above us rages quite loud enough to cover our voices, but the very moment the guns go quiet, we must become absolutely silent. Be sure everyone in your family knows this. Sit shoulder to shoulder, and be ready to stifle anyone making any noise at all." A movement to one side caught Katrina's eye, and she stared, and then realized it was a rat. No, not one rat but several clustered together. She shuddered, but then she steeled herself, drew breath, and turned to Francesca again: "If a shout or a knock comes at the hatch, no one—no one at all—is to call out or answer. Not a peep, you hear me?"

Even from their hidey-hole far below, the women could hear the thunderous roar of cannon and the screech of guns recoiling, and now a terrible crash and the faint echoes of a scream.

CHAPTER 37

SOMETHING LIKE A BERSERKER

Three decks above the women came a shout, "That's the maintopgallant yard's come down!" Shattered wood littered the deck. The yardarm tore straight through the ship's splinter netting. The bosun's boy writhed in pain, a long wedge of wood lodged in his skinny calf. The third gun crew had him by his shoulders, lifting him to the aft cockpit, where Dr. Ward and Sean Crowley had been set up to work since dawn.

By now the sails were shot through, the mizzenmast had been hit repeatedly, and the foremast was a blasted stump. Izak Peterssen was on the quarterdeck, his firm voice giving orders relayed instantly along the deck. "Thorvald," he said to his master gunner, "wait for my signal of 'Pistols!' That's when we bring her about. We will go only so far in the tack as to amuse them, then abort. Wait for my signal," he warned. "Timing is all."

Thorvald growled in assent, his focus utterly on wreaking all the destruction he could.

To the small crew of marksmen, the captain said, "Wait for them to begin boarding, not before. At my command, fire directly into the first wave of boarders, the greedy buggers."

To Niklas and the boys, of whose skill he could be sure, he added, "Take out their captain, if at all you can. Nothing will cause more confusion and dismay than losing their leader."

"Aye, aye, Captain," Niklas nodded, his eye already on the figure of the pirate captain, clearly visible in a uniform both glittery and confusing, cobbled together of several nations.

A smile flickered across Captain Peterssen's face to hear Niklas use the naval expression. He had always had a man or two skilled in rifle or pistol if needed, but now there were true marksmen on deck and in his tops, crack shots, a luxury. To have Thomas Segrave aboard was good fortune, and to have Niklas Kästner, an experienced military man, bring his own trained crew of boys on as passengers, was a true stroke of luck, and his being able to command the Bonn farmers in their own language another lucky stroke. By now every man aboard, passenger or crew, knew a certain truth: they pulled together and survived or none of them did.

Enigma's guns were firing methodically now, with a gun crew of five or six at each cannon and shot boys hurrying to carry twelve-pound balls to them. They had aimed well and inflicted serious damage on the *Diamante*, but it was no more than a privateer or pirate could expect to sustain in an attack, not at all disabling. The next step, the boarding, would come soon. Boarding nets had been stretched along *Enigma*'s starboard side, and men were still at work securing the last of them.

Diamante was the faster ship and no surprise: schooners were faster than barques. They required more crew, too, a disadvantage until moments like this, when their numbers, probably more than sixty men, were a decided advantage.

"They could easily overwhelm us," Mr. Stephens said quietly. He was counting on Thomas Segrave, who was a powerful fighter, never shy, and the Kästner three: Niklas a superior swordsman and the boys excellent marksmen. Thorvald and his gun crews could be depended on in whatever extremity *Enigma* faced, and the Ackermanns had knives and boarding axes. A few of the Ackermanns had pikes, and two were armed with crowbars from the carpenter's toolbox. All could have wished for a plain solid oak club. Among them was a man named Johannes, a bear of a man, whose red face and bulging muscles made it clear that, landsman or not, he was ready for a fight.

The first wave of the pirate's crew—its true size now apparent, enough to make any man blanch—was lined up at her gunnel, jeering the Enigmas. They would share the booty, a fact making them both vicious and eager.

Niklas was in uniform and on the poop deck, staying out of the captain's way but sword in hand and prepared to fight. He saw sharpshooters in *Diamante*'s mastheads and knew his uniform would make him a target, but this did not weaken his resolve; he had been a target before this and would rather draw their fire than have them fire at Hans or Will.

Hans was more than ready for action, every muscle hardened, his eyes narrowed, and his face transformed into something like a berserker's. He felt a focus and strength like he had never known. In spite of terrible odds, in spite of frighteningly high stakes, he could hardly wait for the fight to begin. He was on one knee, his pistol drawn and aimed at the pirate captain. Strapped on or tucked in were his second pistol, his sword and an eight-inch shiv to use like a razor-sharp claw in close fighting.

Will was thirty feet above the deck in the maintop, his pistol braced on the maintop railing, and like Hans's, aimed at the pirate captain. Will's eyes were slits of determination, and he had firmly in mind a plan to slide down a backstay to attack boarders from above.

At a shout from the Spanish captain, the first line of Diamantes threw their grappling hooks and began to climb. Captain Peterssen roared, "Pistols! Boarders, repel boarders!" and the front men aimed for the borders and fired. A half-dozen men dropped into the sea, instantly replaced by those behind them.

The sharpshooting Kästners fired on command, and they saw the Spanish captain stagger backwards, clutching his chest, and then steady himself on the mizzenmast and seem to recover. In the bow where the ships were most closely joined, Johannes Ackermann stood with one foot on the rail, foaming at the mouth with rage, and swung a massive crowbar with extraordinary strength and precision, sweeping men into the sea to his left and his right.

Enigma shivered and swayed to larboard in a false tack. Johannes Ackermann had not entirely understood the plan or its nautical explanation and was taken by surprise. He was in mid-swing when the barque heeled sharply. He lost his footing and went flying over the side. In the confusion, Niklas thought he saw Methuselah take a swing at Hans, but in the same moment Hans was jerked backwards, hit by a bullet. Far above, the ship's sudden jerk caught Will by surprise, and he grabbed the rail of the maintop, nearly dropping his pistol. For a half-second, he was more afraid of falling than being shot. When a few Diamantes scrambled aboard, Thomas Segrave plunged into their midst, his sword singing. He cut a man open with one hand, and, a pistol in the other hand, he shot a second.

The false tack happened so fast, an entire wave of Diamantes fell into the ocean. The ships swayed back together, crushing the next group of boarders. *Enigma*'s front men pocketed their pistols and grabbed pole-axes or pikes to knock off the grappling hooks. In the midst of it all, *Enigma*'s boom smashed into *Diamante*'s mainyard with a shudder down to the keel, and the falling mainsail cloaked the pirate's bow-chaser. The false tack had been shockingly effective.

Diamante's captain moved her ahead of *Enigma*, maneuvering away to regroup. On *Enigma*, Izak raced to the bow, grabbing Thorvald as he went: "The bow-chaser! Before she can wear!" They used the long-range gun mounted in the bow to devastating effect, smashing *Diamante*'s rudder and holing her at the waterline. A slight shift to larboard and *Enigma*'s broadside guns fired, tearing rigging apart and by sheer luck bringing down *Diamante*'s mizzenmast in one deafening roar. Amid it all, Izak Peterssen saw the pirate captain sink to his knees and then disappear in the melee.

The *Enigmas* erupted in cheering, and the shot boys danced with joy. "She's sunk, she's sunk, she's sunk," they sang. Izak Peterssen grinned as Niklas had never seen him do.

"How did you—" Niklas began.

"I saw it done by the *Orient* in '28," Izak Peterssen said. "It was our best chance. Now, the yardarm, the mizzenmast, that was sheer luck. Could as easy have been us."

"I refuse to think it," Niklas said, pumping his hand, "You have our congratulations, sir."

"And you have mine, my captain of marines. The bullet that slew that vile pirate leader came from you or your sons, like as not." He turned to Thorvald and ordered, "Reload starboard with grape."

Diamante was lying dead in the water, her sails shredded, her hull grievously holed. *Enigma* drove abeam of her and played havoc with men and rigging with a broadside of deadly grapeshot, tearing great lengths of *Diamante*'s rails away, killing another swath of her men. *Enigma* pulled ahead, swung around the schooner and dealt a death blow, firing from larboard so close that through-shot holes appeared at *Diamante*'s waterline. A few Diamantes were still firing their pistols, but their mates knocked these out of their hands, and *Diamante*'s horrid black flag was pulled down.

As a white flag got part way up the *Diamante* mainmast, the Enigmas let out a mighty cheer, oblivious for the moment of the blood on their own decks. Thomas Segrave strode up to Izak and clapped him on the back, saying, "A most impressive performance, sir. I give you joy of your victory. You have saved us all from grisly death."

CHAPTER 38

SO CRUEL AND GREEDY

Three decks below, Mr. Groves opened the Lady Hole hatch, announcing the victory through the cover first, having been warned of Katrina's pistols and not wishing to become an accidental casualty. Now Katrina emerged from a hatchway onto the main deck, blinking at the bright light of day and at the thick cannon smoke drifting away. When she saw Niklas and Will whole and unbloodied, she went directly to the surgery, a stack of pretty calico bandages in her arms, stepping briskly across decks still littered and bloody, ignoring the shrieks and moans of men as they were lifted and carried to the surgery. Hans was already there, holding his bloody left arm close to his chest and grinning. He was as happy as she had ever seen him. *I must ask Niklas*, she thought, *if he was happy in battle.*

The Ackermanns, yelling and pointing, were wild for saving Johannes, who could be seen far below, having clasped onto a fallen spar and now holding on with one massive arm and swatting frantic Diamantes with the other. They appealed to Niklas, who seemed larger with both victory and command, but they did not need to beg; he was already in action. He was not inclined to lose a good man. Seeing all of this at a glance, Izak gave one nod, and the Enigmas put down a boat.

At the last moment Johannes took pity on two young *Diamante* lads and threw them into the rescue boat before pulling himself aboard. Now everyone, Johannes, the young lads, and the rescue crew, were coming up the side. As the last of them stepped aboard, the water below erupted in bloodcurdling screams, sounds not even Niklas had heard the like of. The screams stopped as suddenly as they had begun, the water now full of blood, frenzied sharks heaving about. He looked down to see a last man, his face contorted with horror, disappear beneath the waves. He searched the deck for Katrina, hoping to shield her from the gruesome sight, but of all aboard, only she and the surgeons had not looked up from their work, itself grisly enough.

In victory the Enigmas marveled, slapping each other's backs and exclaiming, "What merchantman takes a privateer and a schooner at that?"

"Not every merchantman has a captain like ours."

"At least it wasn't *Queen Anne's Revenge* with forty cannon and Blackbeard at her helm."

Below decks, Amalie had the children in tow, and even they felt the general relief and joy aboard. Jakob was leaping about, swinging an imaginary sword, and Lisette dodged and feinted amid peals of laughter.

Shortly, the schooner's pirate captain was carried aboard, grievously wounded, a Kästner ball lodged deep in his chest and another having gone through his thigh, from which blood poured. He was determined to present his sword as a gentleman. With men carrying him, he did so and died promptly. Izak Peterssen was a fair man, but now his face was clouded with anger and disgust. "This scab," he said as he surveyed the bodies on his own deck, "is a devil I would happily have hanged, a bandit, thief, and fiend who asked to be treated as a gentleman. Goddamn his black soul to hell."

Diamante was sinking fast, and her crew were quick to abandon, having grabbed such provisions as were at hand. The Enigmas stripped the schooner as quickly and methodically as they could. *Diamante* had recently taken a heavily laden trader, poor devils now at the bottom of the sea, and there were riches enough in her hold to make any sailor, captain or owner smile.

Aboard *Enigma*, the Diamantes not badly wounded were herded to one side, a motley crew, downcast to be beaten by a merchantman and deeply fearful of what the victors would do next. Among them were several Englishmen professing joy to be aboard an English ship. They had been taken as captives, they claimed, not a deserter among them.

Deep in the dark of that night, with little sound on the ship but the wind humming through the rigging and the cry of "All's well" from the watch, the acrid smell of cannon smoke still in his nostrils and his ears not yet recovered from the roar of cannon, Will rolled quietly out of his hammock. Katrina heard him and wondered if he was to go on watch; she still had not learned the bells as well as he had, and besides, this was no ordinary night. But no, she saw him kneel in prayer: "Danke, Mein Gott. Thank you for saving us, and for a father who knows how to fight and who taught me how." He knelt there for a while, though whether praying silently or unsure what more to say, Katrina did not know, and then he slipped back into his hammock.

Katrina recalled Niklas's praise for the boys and what he said of Thomas Segrave. "I didn't think such a pretty boy could be so quick or ferocious or brave." Now Niklas was groaning, and she thought he might be dreaming again. In fact, it was the briefest flash of the day disturbing Niklas, a moment of chaos when Methuselah seemed about to strike Hans. *He bears watching*, thought Niklas and was asleep again.

The next day, after the children were seen to and Hans's wound rebandaged, Katrina unfolded a piece of foolscap and dipped a pen in ink. She had written faithfully to Cousin Elizabet, keeping all the letters wrapped in oilcloth, to send when they reached America and considered themselves forever out of reach. Now she began again:

"My Dearest Elizabet,

"I hope to take advantage of the next ship we meet bound for Le Havre, Rotterdam, Bremen, or any other Christian port to send these few hurried lines.

"We are across the Ocean and passably near the most easterly of the West Indies or Antilles, if what I seize of the officers' talk is truth. What happens now is in God's hands, however, as we were set upon by pirates, wicked Spanish pirates whose faces were never so cruel and greedy as when they thought they could board us and kill us altogether.

"By the grace of God, our own good captain, Isaac Peterson, executed a devilish sea maneuver of his own, running up to the pirate with all possible vigor, then swinging the ship in some way I cannot in truth describe in a seaworthy way, the upshot of which was that great numbers of these aforementioned wicked pirates dropped into the sea and yet more were crushed between the hulls of the two ships.

"This drained the spirit of the remaining villains, who attempted to flee, but our captain and the godly crew that brought us across, never shy of action, showed their true seamanship, chasing the pirate, blasting her until her colors came streaming down. The pirate captain came aboard to surrender, mortally wounded, and barely managed it before he died. Our crew took what it could from the sinking ship, it having shortly before and evilly enriched itself by robbing some poor merchant ship. God rest the souls of those they killed to do so.

"Niklas, Hans, and Will were on deck throughout this dreadful action (I hope you never see the like for thundering of cannon, thickness of smoke and pitiable loss of life and limb), surviving unhurt except for a pistol ball straight through Hans's arm, which wound looks clean. They acquitted themselves handsomely, the boys, says Niklas, and it was one of their balls, most likely, he says, that killed the pirate captain.

"He seems more settled or even happy to have seen battle again. Perhaps it's the victory itself or that he is well pleased about the boys, that they have seen action and stood up manfully to it. For their parts, Hans is exceedingly pleased with himself, and Will can hardly wait to spin the tale into some pretty young ear. He was in the tops as a sharpshooter. Just his climbing up there is a more frightening sight than I can bear.

"The children and I were kept well below stairs, where we and the other women took refuge in the Lady Hole, a secret compartment in the bow, dark, smelly and filled with rats. I need not tell you of the terror we felt while so concealed or our relief when the ship's first mate came to free us. By the men's valor we were saved a horrible fate, but I am still angry! If only to have been a man myself! Oh, to have had a sword in hand!

"When we women were released at last, I went immediately to assist the ship's surgeons, a bloody awful business, I will tell you, and leave it at that.

"Our stalwart captain says he shall land wherever possible on the nearest island rather than go on directly to New Orleans, ourselves being smartly damaged and our rigging cut to pieces. God save us from a storm until then. Where and when we shall land, I do not know, but we found more food in the pirate ship, thank the Lord, and for everything else I shall endeavor to trust to Him and pay no mind to the whoosh-whoosh of the pumps manned through every watch. Now here is Niklas, urging me to attend to Lisette and Jakob, who send their love.

"With my dear love to you and your children, your most affectionate cousin, Katrina Beckmann Kästner"

Katrina leaned back with a sigh and felt the soothing rhythm of the ship in motion. She patted the ink dry, folded the foolscap precisely into quarters and sealed it, fatigue washing over her in the aftermath of excitement and anxiety. From somewhere below she heard an Ackermann child cry out.

BOOK FOUR

EMANCIPATION

"O brave new world, that has such people in't!"
— William Shakespeare, *The Tempest*

CHAPTER 39

LA PUNTA Y EL MORRO

A crippled *Enigma* crept along the south shore of Cuba, rounded the tip of the island, caught the Gulf Stream and sailed in its easterly current, away from New Orleans and towards Havana.

"It's the wrong direction, but brings Havana's safe harbor closer," Mr. Groves said. *Enigma* had no choice, being damaged, overcrowded and thirsty.

On 11 May 1836, *Enigma* ghosted into Havana's well-protected harbor as the evening stars winked on. Almost all souls stood at her rail, crew and passengers alike, Izak Peterssen having not the heart to order anyone save a prisoner below on such a night. The white of gulls caught the fading light, and off to larboard a flutter of white ibis rose chattering from their nests.

"El Morro," cried the mainmasttop lookout, and soon all could make out the famed lighthouse and its twin tower, La Punta, of bleached coral, incandescent in the twilight, as if lit from within. It was their first glimpse of civilization in the New World. White beaches gleamed against lush tropical forest, palm trees waved gently against the darkening sky, and lanterns blinked on in the distant city. Breadloaf mountains made Havana easy to identify, and from them came the scents of land, first the musky green odor of dense vegetation and flocks of nesting birds and then the tantalizing smells of the city: food being cooked for the evening meal, tobacco smoke, sugar rotting on the surrounding plantations, and the sweet top notes of blooming flowers.

Enigma glided between the towers of the ancient forts, built in 1589 on pincers of land that gave the huge bay a narrow mouth and sheltered it from the sea. The forts, Castillo San Salvador de la Punta and Castillo de los Tres Reyes Magos del Morro, were home to Spanish troops and no friend of an English-flagged ship, but in these peaceable modern days, no threat either. Thomas Segrave said Spain had declared the port free and open to trade, and as far as anyone on board knew, it still was. They were relieved when no cannon fired from the shore. *Enigma* had no desire to engage a fort and was certainly in no shape to do so. She already flew signal flags indicating her peaceable intent, her status as disease-free, and her need for help.

Mr. Groves was the center of shipboard conversation, when all the talk was of this city of mystery laid out before them, unknown to most aboard, including the Kästners. He had sailed the Caribbean a number of times, and he told them Havana was an old city for the New World, settled almost by Columbus. "It has a fine natural harbor, which made it a refuge for the Spanish treasure fleet, the same as was full of silk and spices and pearls and jade and china as fine as you've ever seen, and thus a target for marauders of every nation."

"Pirates?" asked Will.

"Well, that's a matter for some discussion," Mr. Groves replied. "A captain might have a letter of marque—a commission from his king—during war, making him a privateer. The same man might be a pirate during peacetime or a smuggler in between. It's men such as that as sacked Havana." Several looked confused, and he assured them: "Now the Diamantes that attacked us, that's another story. Those were true pirates, evil incarnate."

Seeing his listeners still attentive, he went on. "Once, pirates captured Havana, demanded ransom of seven hundred gold ducats, and sailed away. The next day, two great Spanish treasure ships, heavily laden and heavily armed, arrived from Mexico. The governor of Havana, not being a seaman nor having any sea sense at all, demanded the ships leave their treasure in Havana and give chase to the pirates. They followed orders and was themselves taken. After few lashes, they told their captors all about the treasure left in Havana, who sailed back here and took that as well!"

His listeners shook their heads at the foolishness of governors and powerful men in general, and then Amalie asked him, "Pray, what exactly is a treasure ship?"

"A Spanish galleon, Missy," he said, and seeing her blank face, he explained. "They are all sunk or broke up for brass now, but I saw them as a youth. Massive fat cargo ships, Spanish, built to carry Mexican silver to the Philippines, trade with the junks down from China, and circle back to Mexico. Each circle took a year, using the Pacific current." Mr. Groves traced a circle through the air.

"Once in Mexico, and once the Bolivian silver was laded as well—you've heard of Cerro Rico, now ain't you? In Potosí?"

Amalie shook her head, and she was not the only one.

"It's a mountain of silver, the biggest in the world—it, the silver, I mean, and the China goods was carried across Mexico by donkey cart and sailed to Havana. It got so bad with attacks from rogue ships, the Spanish treasure fleet was ordered to assemble here, in Havana, and sail in convoy to Spain. They came in all summer to Havana, to rest and reprovision before sailing east. Everyone took shore leave, with money to burn, and left their mark on Havana in every which way you can imagine."

This last Mr. Groves said with a wink at Will and no thought that fourteen-year-old Amalie was listening, too, and wondering what the first mate meant.

Katrina, however, understood perfectly, and had an urge to cover her daughter's ears. She looked with deep disapproval at Mr. Groves. Since the attack of the *Diamante*, the crew and passengers had become friends of a sort, or at least had developed a mutual respect, but she was glad that most of the voyage had passed with little communication between them. *A rough sort, to be sure*, she thought. *Except for Cutlip, who had proven there could be nobility hidden in sailor's clothing. And except for the doctors and Thomas Segrave. Even Captain Peterssen might be a gentleman. But not First Mate Groves, no matter how useful and kindly.*

Havana was a walled and heavily fortified city that boasted the largest dry dock in the New World. The wounded barque was one of many coming in weary and battered by storms, dying of thirst or hunger, but few had done as she had: outrun storms and fought off attack. By the time she ghosted into the harbor and picked up a mooring, several small boats were ready to meet her with calls of ¡Fruta fresca! ¡Pez! ¡Panecillos calientes! The Enigmas bought eagerly and feasted on their first taste of the tropics.

At dawn, on the quarterdeck usually reserved for the captain alone, Niklas stood with Izak Peterssen, Thomas Segrave, and Mr. Groves. Dr. Ward had climbed to the maintop with a spyglass slung on his back and Will to assist him.

"On deck there, if you please," Will called down. "Doc gave the all clear."

None of those on deck saw any hint of the dreaded yellow flag of contagion: not on a single ship, not at the hospital island, and not at the port itself. Only the flag of Isabella, the six-year-old Queen of Spain, fluttered in the breeze. No fewer than a dozen members of the morning watch were listening. They saw the nod their leaders exchanged and the quick flash of Izak's smile.

"Liberty, it is!" the whisper went 'round. After a long crossing and glorious battle, some could hardly wait to regale a crowd with their story. Now they were sure this delightful harbor town was to be theirs, and not only that but with prize money in hand or as like prize money as a merchantman sailor ever had. This was a tired crew, but one whose recent victory had them thinking fairly highly of themselves. From the murmurs Niklas was hearing, they were filled with clear ideas of what to do the minute they stepped ashore: the joys of white sand beaches for those who have never lolled upon one, excellent rum as cheap as water, and the most beautiful women east of the South Pacific and particularly obliging. So sure were they of their coming happiness that several members of the watch below gave up well-deserved sleep to undertake to beautify themselves.

Niklas leaned on the rail, thinking of how good it had been to be in charge of a cadre of fighting men again. He had turned them into a passable 'marines.' Now, watching the flag of Spain flutter in the breeze and catching a scrap or two of Spanish, he had only to blink to imagine Bonaparte's colors flying there instead, as they had in 1808 in the quiet days before Madrid's Dos de Mayo rebellion. For a while it seemed France had done Spain a favor by forcing its imbecilic king, Charles IV, to abdicate, and his son, another foolish despot, to flee. There was talk of the royals escaping to Mexico or Argentina, he recalled vaguely, as the Portuguese royal family had to Brazil. Spain came to its senses in the aught 1800s and remembered it would always prefer a Spanish king to a French one, no matter how incapable or tyrannical.

Katrina came to stand beside Niklas. In the cool morning air, they could smell food cooking.

"I must be hungry," Niklas said. "My mouth is watering just to think about jamón serrano, which is a Spanish dry-cured ham, and pimentos de padron, blistered peppers.

"I will be so glad to put my feet on land," Katrina said.

A clatter on the quay made them turn. Angry voices gave orders. The harborside was full of black men carrying, pulling carts, stacking barrels. It was one of those stacks that slipped.

"Niklas, just think of it, we are about to enter a strange land, so full of Negroes—" Katrina waved a hand at the docks. "And besides that, a Catholic monarchy, where we are not only strangers but no closer to freedom."

"Ja," he nodded. "Like Gibraltar, but with the Spaniards in charge this time."

"Gott im Himmel! Do we need to worry about the Inquisition?"

"Not sure. It may still be a force, whatever they tell us."

"I'll warn the children again."

Izak Peterssen came back on deck, having tucked a pistol into his best waistcoat, the yellow one, a tradition in the Danish Navy and his private nod to his homeland. He had buckled on his sword and collected his papers. The natural deep-water harbor and magnificent dry dock were exactly what *Enigma* needed, and it was a blessing that she had come gently to a place that bore no sign of contagion. However, no one envied the captain his duty of reporting the unwelcome news of encountering a pirate ship in a sea thought cleared of them nor the difficulty of dispensing with captives in a country that did not want them. There was also the question of how an English-flagged ship would be received and what a Habanero harbormaster would want in the way of documents. And bribery.

O'Malley turned to those on the quarterdeck and announced, "Captain, Sir, boat's approaching. The harbormaster, I suspect."

CHAPTER 40

EZMERALDA

When the Kästners arrived, Havana had everything to surprise and delight a middle-class, provincial German family. It was a thriving, civilized, walled city with churches, a hospital, a university already celebrating its hundredth anniversary, streets lined with fine shops and fine mansions, newspapers being published, and a botanical garden. The President's Palace was newly rebuilt, and a viaduct under construction was all the talk. It would soon bring the clean, sweet water of the mountains to Havana.

The tropical softness of the air was enchanting, laden with the scent of jasmine and lemon. Equally enchanting were the elegantly dressed Habanero society girls. The streets felt both different, with overhanging balconies to shade passersby, and similar in their medieval plan and closeness. Craftsmen and merchants occupied thick-walled homes with shops and warehouses on the first floor, slave quarters on the second floor and elegant third-floor apartments where the family lived.

"Slave quarters!" Katrina said when Mr. Groves told them this.

"Oh, yes, ma'am. It's a sugar island, and sugar requires slaves."

Mr. Groves was leading them to the home of Señora María Paloma Ruiz Iglesias, a widow who accepted boarders. They went quickly through the harbor town and the grand plazas into poorer, more crowded neighborhoods, where there were no caballeros in leather or senoritas in lace. Instead, they found themselves among people dressed in little more than rags who were never still but always at work, driving laden donkeys or rolling cigars, or minding mostly naked children. It was a relief to turn onto a neatly kept street where Mr. Groves knocked at the solid wood door of a whitewashed house.

Señora Ruiz was a smiling, round-faced, young woman, with tiny black eyes sparkling with friendliness. When she said, "Llamame Paloma," Niklas translated, "She says, 'Call me Paloma,'" surprising himself to have a reservoir of Spanish after so long.

Her modest home was on a quiet side street. It had a deeply shaded front porch, a roof of interwoven palm fronds, and a walled garden, where fabulously bright parrots flashed their colors and a few coffee trees were in bloom, their fragrant white flowers sharing branches with last year's bright red coffee cherries.

When Will admired these glossy green trees, she scoffed and waved to the mountains behind the town. "There, in the hills," she said, "the real coffee plantations grow. These just keep us from having to buy beans."

Will got a dreamy look in his eyes, as if he wanted to climb into the hills and seize one of these plantations. Katrina smiled to see him already imagining himself the owner of a coffee plantation. Then Niklas yanked him from his daydream: "Will! The baggage."

The oldest of Paloma's four children, Pepe, helped the Kästner boys drag the trunks into modest rooms lining one side of the ground floor. Slaves lived on the other side, with the Ruiz family on the second floor. Pepe's full name, it turned out, was José Alejandro Garcia de Cadiz Ruiz. He wrote it in the dusty floor of the courtyard, looked shyly at Will and asked, "Habla usted Inglés?" Will shook his head, and Pepe tried again: "Do you have English?"

"Ja," said Will. On the ship, they had all learned as much English as they could. Having to speak English in America was a constant worry. "Sprechen Sie Deutsch?"

"No," said Pepe.

"Well then. English it is."

The two boys were still smiling at each other when Paloma called out: "¡José Alejandro Garcia Ruiz! ¡Ándale!"

"Oh!" she exclaimed, when she heard that the family had touched down in Gibraltar, "both sides of our family came from Cadiz—very near Gibraltar—in our grandparents' time." She was eager to hear every detail of their recent visit to the peninsula, and wisely enough, she did not ask how Niklas came to know Spanish. Perhaps she could guess what might have brought him to Spain.

The next morning, the three adults sat down to a table spread with a brightly embroidered white cloth in Paloma's front parlor, the pleasantest room in the house, especially as it was now lit by morning sunshine. Katrina was in her dressing gown of fine white muslin, which looked splendid against the bright blue wall behind her. The boys had eaten early and gone out with Pepe to the harbor, the busiest edge of Havana with endless comings and goings. The younger children, much loved and petted as they were in both households, were eating in the kitchen with the household's cook, Missus Gaby.

"I looked in on them," Katrina told Niklas. "They are being reminded about using their forks and spoons properly and not speaking unless spoken to."

"My Gaby is so good with children," Paloma said. "If they are lucky, she will treat them to a ghost story at the end."

Katrina laughed, "No doubt with gasps and hand-holding under the table and concluded with much laughter and not a few nervous glances!"

They were all grinning now, and then Niklas could wait no longer and turned his attention to breakfast.

"My dear hostess, you have outdone yourself," he exclaimed, at the sight of sausages, scrambled eggs with guajiro cheese, and an excellent black coffee steaming on the sideboard with a pitcher of fresh cream and a pot of very dark muscovado sugar. The sausages were soon dispensed with, and the first pot of coffee very much lowered as Paloma listened raptly to Katrina's detailed portrayal of Continental fashions, including those to be observed just now at Gibraltar. Niklas sat listening with half an ear, savoring the best coffee they had tasted since Gibraltar and engaged as he was in a second helping of eggs and cheese.

At that moment, Will burst in. Paloma looked down at her cup, but not quickly enough to hide the disapproval in her tiny black eyes. Katrina turned to Will with a smile. *This boy,* she thought, *was the baby who worried us because he was late to start walking. Then he skipped walking and went right to running. And he has not stopped running yet. Will is a rambunctious boy for a rambunctious new world.* Katrina only hoped America was ready for Will.

To Will, this second day in Havana was the beginning of an utterly new life abroad, because he had just seen and talked (in halting phrases, Pepe translating) with the most beautiful girl in the world. Her name was Maria Ezmeralda Sofia O'Farril y Núñez de Castillo. Like him, she was fifteen, but there the similarities ended. She was petite and buxom, with laughing green eyes, glossy black hair glinting red in the sunlight, and a musical voice. He longed to hear her sing.

She had stared unabashedly at his blue eyes and the way his blond hair curled over his ears and fringed his forehead. She was reminded of the faceplate in a book of Greek myths her tutor once loaned her, Apollo come to life before her. She had not known such male beauty could be real.

With one look at the adoration playing across her face, and at the high-fashion cut of her dress, Will was hers forever. Pepe stepped discreetly behind them, listening and translating like an unseen spirit, watching the two of them walk on ahead, their footsteps in synch as if they were soulmates. For a few precious steps along el Malecón, the city's magnificent seaside boulevard, the two successfully impersonated long-lost lovers with a sophistication that would have astounded their parents.

Ezmeralda twirled her parasol in the most ladylike way, with only the slightest suggestion of a tease in her delicate handling of it, and Will bowed like one accustomed to royalty and handed her up a step as gently as a feather. When Will touched her fingers, a shock went through him, and he held these delicate fingertips a moment longer and then lifted them to his lips for the most chaste of kisses, glancing up at her lovely face.

"Señorita mio!" he said slowly, freighting the words with meaning, since 'señorita' and 'mio' required a fifth his Spanish vocabulary. He switched to French to speak from the heart, "Je vous adore."

Her face lit up, her eyelashes fluttered, and she replied, "Ah, monsieur, vous m'embarrassez."

It was a breakthrough: she spoke French!

Before either of them could say another word in any language, the moment was ruined. Ezmeralda's chaperone, a fierce-looking woman with black whiskers on her chin, glanced up from haggling over a truly astounding turtle for the family's evening meal. The chaperone was already rehearsing a recipe for instructing the houseslaves when she saw the pair of them, a complete unknown and worse, an impertinent foreigner, daring to talk with her darling Ezmeralda.

It did not require any translations to chase off Pepe and Will. They ran from the raised voice, the raised parasol and the big, angry-looking turtle-monger instantly enlisted by the chaperone. Will followed on Pepe's heels, who ran a convoluted path meant to confuse and dismay the turtle-monger and any sheriff's posse he might have gathered. When they finally sank to their haunches, their backs against a wall of crumbling pink stucco, Pepe gasped out something he should have told Will much earlier: girls like Ezmeralda are spoken for almost from birth. Outsiders are not welcome to court them and certainly never to wed into Havana society. Limpieza de sangre, pure Spanish blood, ruled Havana now, had ruled it since the beginning of time and would rule it forevermore.

Will was not listening with the close attention the situation deserved. Ezmeralda's delicate complexion, her dainty figure, her musical voice, and more than all else, the look of adoration she gave him filled his weak masculine mind with a totality that amazed and delighted him.

"Tell me her name again."

"Maria Ezmeralda Sofia O'Farril y Núñez de Castillo."

"Ezmeralda. When can I see her again?" Will asked.

"¡Nunca!" "Never!" Pepe looked at him with incredulity. "And the sooner you leave Havana, the better for us all."

A few minutes later, when Will broke in on his parents' breakfast, his nerve deserted him, and he did not tell them what seemed inevitable truth moments earlier: he was going to stay in Havana forever and marry the beautiful Ezmeralda. Instead, he looked a little shamefaced, made up a tale about how very hungry he was, and on being invited to join them, wolfed down everything left on the table, finding he was, in fact, quite hungry.

In the midst of feasting, he looked at his father and asked quietly, "Lecker?"

"Delicioso," Niklas translated, and Will turned to Paloma with his most winning smile, "Delicioso, Señora," using another twenty percent of his Spanish vocabulary.

She nodded in acknowledgement, a smile played on her lips, and her eyes regained some of their natural friendly sparkle.

CHAPTER 41

MOROS Y CRISTIANOS

In Cuba, said Mr. Groves, most free Negroes owned slaves, and craftsmen in Havana were mostly black, mulatto or quadroon, whether slave or free. Niklas and Katrina saw the truth of this as they strolled along Calle Tejadillo, near the old market square, where all—masters, slaves, and families— were of various hues from glistening coal to fawn.

The girls were with them, and now Lisette tugged Katrina to one side, looking about to burst into tears.

"Oh, Mama," she said, "what an awful rash these poor souls have! Even the children! Does it hurt them? Will they die of it, do you suppose?"

Katrina sat the little, soft-hearted girl down on an upturned half barrel outside one of the shops and told her the truth of the matter, to the child's shock and relief. Their skin, such a different color, did not hurt them! A different "race"! Lisette had not been aware of the existence of Black people or of races at all, Berleburg being something of a backwater in that way. Katrina knew very little herself, but she had at least heard of Negroes. Niklas had told her about them from his time in the '08 Peninsular Wars in Portugal and Spain, and besides, she knew they were the wretched victims of American slavery, and now, they were daily reminders of the slavery all around them in Cuba.

Enigma's galley crew included a tall, thin Ethiopian, a handsome, cocoa-brown man called Jim, a freeman, but Katrina could understand how, among so many sun-toasted sailors, Lisette had entirely overlooked Jim. No one in the family had known slaves of any color, unless one counted the serfs from whom their own families descended (a shocking thought), but they knew that in Roman days, slavery had filled Europe.

"Today, the Germanies, and indeed, all of Europe," explained Katrina, "are exceptions in the world; slavery is otherwise universal."

"Oh, dear," said Lisette as her tears dried.

"Really, Mother?" asked Amalie. "Is it truly otherwise universal? What about England?"

"Well, I was quite wrongly counting England as part of Europe." She stood, shook off her skirt, and hoped Amalie would ask for no greater precision. "But otherwise, I do believe it is universal."

The girls followed their mother's example, standing and shaking their skirts. They trailed behind Niklas along the wide Alameda de Paula, a tile-paved promenade with stone benches and leafy green poplars lining either side, then turned up into la Plaza de la Catedral. The Cathedral of Havana was only fifty years old, but in this tropical climate, it already wore the patina of age. They stared at it. Its asymmetrical towers reminded them of the cathedral in Cologne, though on a much smaller scale and with ornate Baroque detailing replacing somber medieval lines, carved in whitish coral instead of gray stone.

"Really, it's nothing to compare with Kölner Dom," Niklas said quietly.

"A miniature, to be sure," Katrina said, "But it does catch the light in a certain way."

"And it's good to see any church at all."

Katrina breathed in the rich new scents of the market stalls on either side of la Plaza de la Catedral. "What impresses me is this marketplace with its bananas, coconuts, mangoes, and cigars."

Niklas looked at Katrina with more appreciation and enthusiasm than is quite typical among long-married couples. "Yes," he said, "these humble gifts of Nature are as important in their own way as the cathedral."

"Better keep such heresies to yourself," Katrina whispered with a smile.

They strolled away from the cathedral, browsing among the market stalls in Cathedral Plaza, overhearing as they went a priest haranguing his companion about the evils of Lutherans, by which they knew he meant all who rejected the Roman Catholic Church.

Said the priest in outrage, "They call our sacred Mass an 'abominable superstition,' and blind themselves to truth. They love reason, deny God and abhor the saints!"

"At the core of it is denying the authority of the Church," his companion agreed, "encouraging common folk to read the Bible, as if such as they were able to construe the scriptures properly."

The priest sputtered in anger, "Heretics, all! Hell is too good for them!"

Katrina glanced at Niklas with raised eyebrows, but neither of them was martyr enough to speak out in this hotbed of Catholicism. He turned Katrina and the girls aside, and the four of them studied mangoes as if their lives depended on it.

They walked away, Niklas with the superb posture, broad shoulders and solid musculature that make a man's clothes look better than they are, clean, pressed and expensive. Here in Havana, where Napoleon was universally despised, a few looked askance at Niklas's crisp, military-blue coat, and discerning eyes might have suspected its origins, even though Katrina had stripped it of insignia and epaulettes. Other eyes fixed themselves on Katrina and the girls with their wide necklines, puffy leg-o-mutton sleeves, and Katrina's very fashionable jade green shawl, gloves and ribbons. Habaneros were nothing if not fashionable, and the Kästner women were living, breathing fashion plates from the heart of Continental Europe. The very blond men and children with them were exotic to Habanero eyes—altogether a sight not to be missed.

Until recently, Havana had been a center of luxury, rich with Chinese silks, spices, pearls, and porcelain overflowing from Spanish galleons sailing the Pacific in year-long voyages, following the current in the gigantic Pacific Gyre. The treasure fleet sailed this route for almost three hundred years, enriching Spain beyond anything it deserved or imagined, and leaving Cuba with a thousand shards of this once-proud trade.

Even now, when they visited the shops on Obispo Street, they could see that Havana still had silk and pearls from the Far East and rubber, vanilla, nutmeg, cloves, allspice, and cinnamon from the Philippines and Spice Islands.

"Look at this," Katrina said, pointing to a finely worked silver-handled cane.

"Ah, Señora, you have good taste," said the clerk. "It's a Gregorio Tabares—of Petosi silver, of course."

"This is the silversmith Paloma raved about—who made the tray I admired," Katrina told Niklas in an aside. "She called him Cuba's founding silversmith and her silver tray the only object left from better days when her husband lived. It pains Paloma to speak of how far she has fallen."

"And wasn't 'Petosi' the silver mountain Mr. Groves mentioned?" asked Niklas. Katrina shrugged, so he tapped his cane on the countertop and asked the attendant, "The silver mines are in Bolivia, I understand?"

"Sí, Señor."

"Yet another instance of how valuable it is to be on a trade route," said Niklas. "And here, the trade route stretches halfway around the world."

Katrina whispered an idea to Niklas, and he nodded. "My good man," he said to the attendant, pointed out a silver belt buckle, and explained their idea.

"Sí, Señor, Señora. It will be as you wish and ready for you next week."

On the street again, Niklas nudged Katrina at the sight of two men delivering baskets to a shop. They looked like they were wearing pajamas, and a long braid fell down each man's back, longer even than those *Enigma* sailors wore.

"Nicolás Cabrera, one of Captain Peterssen's friends, told me to watch for Chinese slaves and freemen as well as indentured servants from the Philippines."

"How exotic they look."

"With trade open again, people are coming from Europe, too—I mean Frenchmen, Germans, Englishmen, not to mention sailors."

"Who may have originated anywhere," Katrina said. "It makes Köln look positively provincial."

Niklas gave her an odd look. "My dear, Köln *is* provincial."

They had been in Havana almost a week and were used to its afternoon showers when one caught them out and they dashed into the shelter of a doorway.

"Donnerwetter!" Katrina exclaimed, shaking her skirts and stamping the mud from her shoes.

A stranger taking refuge with them laughed, "How à propos." He begged their pardon and said he couldn't help himself, he was that glad to hear the sounds of his native tongue. He introduced himself as Herr

Kleimbach, a banker, formerly of Dortmund, bowing and saying, "How do you do, Herr, Frau?"

Niklas replied, "Your servant, sir."

"My dear sir," said Herr Kleimbach, "please tell me the news from the Germanies, Hamburg, Dortmund, everywhere."

As they talked and talked, he rubbed his hands together in glee, so delighted was he to hear about the price of flax, last winter's weather, Carnival in Cologne, and every other innocuous bit.

Before they parted, Herr Kleimbach had a warning for them, lowering his voice to tell them what they already knew. "The Spanish Inquisitors have officially been disbanded, but it would be well to avoid the slightest conflict and certainly any talk that might reek to them of Lutheranism. It is only a few years since Protestants of any sort were permitted to enter the Spanish Lake."

As it happened, they had gathered the children before they disembarked in Havana and reminded them: outward evidence of piety was all well and good in their hometown, but this was a Papist country, and nothing would arouse the authorities faster than a challenge to the official faith. Even before they had strolled amidst the denizens of the most casual, welcoming, and thoroughly cosmopolitan Gibraltar, Amalie had sewn her plain silver cross to the inside of the deepest pocket in her brown linen traveling frock, where she could touch it unseen for courage.

Indeed, at dinner one evening, Paloma innocently served them a dish of black beans and white rice and called it Moros y Cristianos, Moors and Christians, a reminder of Spain's many battles against heretics.

"She means nothing by it," Katrina said quietly to Niklas.

"Yet, we too would be thought black beans: foul heretics. Lumped in with Turks!"

"Shh," she said.

CHAPTER 42

AS SUSPECT AS SPIES

At a café along el Malecón, Niklas joined Izak Peterssen, Thomas Segrave, and their friend, Nicolás Cristóbal Cabrera, captain of the Bermuda-built schooner, *Augusta Ann*. Like Izak and Thomas, Cabrera had been a boy aboard a British ship-of-the-line. Now, as the four of them drank excellent, bitter coffee, Niklas asked Cabrera, a Havana native, about the city's latest improvement, a railroad.

"It's a marvel," said Cabrera, "but Cuba is already so different."

"Do you mean what happened on Hispaniola?" asked Thomas.

"Yes," said Cabrera. "When the slaves there rebelled, Hispaniola—"

"Which they now call 'Haiti,' a native word, I think," Thomas explained in an aside to Niklas.

"Haiti is the half that rebelled," said Cabrera. "It supplied almost all the sugar in the world, and when it fell, Cuba grabbed the sugar market. The Haitians were inspired by Bonaparte," Cabrera said, crossing himself, as if the extreme horrors of slavery on Haiti were not perfectly adequate to inspire bloody revolt.

"Slavery is the rule almost everywhere," Izak said with caution. "And yet, in our modern era, how can we justify it?"

"Or as Christians," added Niklas.

"Well, let's be realistic," said Cabrera. "Freeing the slaves would ruin the nation."

"So Hispaniola's demise was a windfall for Cuba," Thomas said, to bring the conversation back on track.

"Exactly," said Cabrera, with a knowing tap of a finger alongside his nose. "And now, the railroad is the last improvement, a fast way to carry sugar to the harbor. And new slaves back out to the plantations."

Will dragged Hans out to the construction site at the Havana-Bejucal railway, where they stared agog at the locomotive and five brightly painted railway carriages parked on the one finished end of the tracks. It was an inspiring sight, especially to forward-thinking Cuban merchants, bankers, and landowners.

For several days afterwards Will worked earnestly at figures, looking up to exclaim things like, "Should it be the grower who pays for a railroad, or the ship's owner?" Or again, "It's a shopkeeper along the route who stands to make the most! Wherever the contraption comes to a rest, people will embark and disembark, buying all along. He makes little investment but reaps fat new opportunities!"

He tried enlisting Hans into his schemes, but his older brother sat stony-faced even when Will insisted, "It's a new world, Hans!"

Hans held up one hand and pushed back his chair. "We sail within the month, and then where will your grand schemes be?"

"What works here will work in America!"

"Do whatever you must in America, but leave me out of it, little brother. I need some air."

Watching this, Katrina said nothing, but she looked at her middle son with new appreciation. He had new muscles from his work on the rigging, but he would always lack the size and muscle that made Hans turn heads wherever he went. *Does it matter*, she thought, *when he debates investments and profits and is positively enthralled by new machinery?* For the first time, it occurred to her that Will might have the makings of a rich man.

They had not been in Cuba long when, with his first glimpse of el caballo Criollo Cubano, Niklas abandoned all morality and desired nothing more than to become a horse thief. He could see that these small, handsome, spirited horses were related to Andalusians, Spanish horses now almost worth their weight in gold in the Germanies. They were not recent imports, Habaneros said, but descendants of horses brought by the conquistadors in 1511.

Niklas admired these horses more than he could say, and he spoke to Izak about bringing several of them aboard, legally purchased, of course. Izak acquiesced, but Niklas could see he was not happy about the idea, and ultimately, reluctantly, Niklas decided against it, there being too many unknowns about America to undertake an importation of horses.

Izak nodded when he heard Niklas's decision. He could not have turned Niklas down, not a man who had stepped in so brilliantly to become the captain of *Enigma*'s marines, but he was happy not to face a crossing with horses in the hold.

To Amalie, it was los Blanquitos de la Habana, the little white dogs of Havana, that were irresistible. Small dogs with long silky hair, los Blanquitos were so obviously happy, curious and devoted to their owners that Amalia looked longingly at her father and asked, "Can't we? It's not sensible, I know, but just this once? I will take care of them, I promise."

Katrina looked away when Niklas turned Amalie down, she who asked for so little. These sweet dogs were tempting, but the frontier was no place for a lapdog born and bred in the tropics. Laughable as was the idea of buying un Blanquito de la Habana, had Niklas decided to import horses, he could not have refused Amalie. Not for the first time, Katrina wished Niklas was rich and could indulge himself and his family with every luxury, including fancy lapdogs and admirable horses.

But as it was, and with the exception of buying goods to trade, the Kästners indulged in little more than what they ate, gorging on oranges, lemons and limes as protection against scurvy, exploring the astonishing flavors of pineapple and chocolate and gagging at the sweet, gummy taste of cassava, a root Cubans ground in place of wheat. Seafood of every kind was abundant, and even poor Habaneros had fried plantains and their day's catch to sustain them and rum to comfort them.

One lovely cool morning at Paloma's, Niklas and Katrina talked quietly over a breakfast of spectacularly good oranges and hot chocolate, very good hot chocolate.

She helped herself to a second cup and remarked, "What if Brillat-Savarin was correct when he wrote, 'Dis-moi ce que tu manges, je te dirai ce que tu es,' 'Tell me what you eat and I will tell you what you are'? Will my skin become a lovely shade of chocolate while we sojourn here on this sugar island?"

"Oh, yes," Niklas said, "you might melt in the afternoon rain, being mostly sugar by now." They chortled together at their mutual wit and had another cup of chocolate.

In Gibraltar, they had seen North African Arabs, but few black Africans, and the Spaniards here were altogether different from those in Gibraltar, far wealthier and flashier. Gibraltar Spaniards formed the underclass, merchants at best and a few disreputable doctors. Here, elegance surrounded the Kästners, señors jangling in silver and dark leather, señoras and señoritas in white, black or ecru lace accented by bright red cochineal and flashes of silver, gold and rare stones, among them turquoise, coral, and a lovely cool green jade. The stones were sometimes carved in exotic ways revealing Mayan, Aztec or Zapotec origins.

Cuba was the queen of the Sugar Islands, and she meant to keep this crown, despite the horrors of sugar slavery. This lovely month of April, the sugar harvest was going on all around, men and women at work in the fields from dawn to dusk, the sickening scent of rotting sugarcane mixing with the sweet scent of juice bumbling in cauldrons until it was poured thick into wooden molds to yield pure, unadulterated dulce.

"Just yesterday," Captain Nicolás Cristóbal Cabrera complained when they met him again at the café, "we were Spanish under the Queen. Now we are Cuban under Tacón. And the taxes! Are they trying to ruin us?" Like many Habaneros, Captain Cabrera blamed Las Águilas Negras, the Black Eagles, and the Cadena Triangular, the Triangular Chain.

"And now the Soles de la Libertad, the Suns of Liberty," said Izak Peterssen.

Cabrera lifted a finger to his lips. "Even saying their name aloud…"

Izak nodded.

"The Crown wiped out Las Águilas a few years ago, and you would have thought that settled it, but Spain only became more despotic," Cabrera said. "Now she oppresses all, loyal subjects and proud families of limpieza de sangre."

"Since losing one territory after another," said Thomas Segrave, "and after last year's antislavery treaty with us." Cabrera raised an eyebrow.

"I have lived in the Gibraltar colony for some time," Thomas reminded him, "where Spain and her lost possessions are constant subjects of discussion, especially when something like a treaty touches us Brits."

"It's true," said Captain Cabrera. "Cuba and Puerto Rico are now the only Spanish islands in what had been a Spanish lake."

"Is it something askew in the times," Katrina mused, "everywhere, cruel tyrants usurping thrones?"

Captain Cabrera looked at Katrina as if she should know better than to speak on such matters. "It's just another way," he said, "to steal our sugar harvest."

Under the table, Niklas took Katrina's hand.

In the elegant salons of Havana, everyone whispered about General Manuel Lorenzo, the governor of Santiago, who, to the ire of Tacón, supported the liberal Spanish Constitution of 1812. Covert rebels lurked everywhere, who knew how many? Making Cuba a twenty-fifth state of the U.S. was a cause célèbre for Southerners who wanted slave states to outnumber free ones. Here in Havana, showing the slightest support for independence had become all the more dangerous.

"The trouble is mostly foreigners," Captain Cabrera said, glancing about.

"But think of your own Padre Varela y Morales," said Izak, "escaping just before arrest."

"Just yesterday," said Thomas Segrave, "we saw a revolutionary seized in broad daylight and beaten to within an inch of his life. Izak and I saw it."

Captain Cabrera nodded and looked meaningfully at his listeners, "Foreigners are always as suspect as spies." He inclined his head to Niklas and Katrina. "It's good your family is quiet, respectful and well-to-do."

"And leaving soon," Niklas replied.

"When you do," said Captain Cabrera, "be careful. The mouth of the Mississippi can be hard to find. La Salle missed it time and again. And stay well away from Texas and its war."

"Mexico has them on the run, I've heard," said Thomas. "I mean, Texians are a rabble, aren't they? Up against the great General Santa Anna?"

"Si, but Santa Anna is behaving badly, that mission-fort, Alamo, and then that massacre at…"

"Goliad," Izak supplied.

"Four hundred executed after an honorable surrender. Disgraceful."

"Still, Mexico's probably won it by now," said Thomas.

"I don't expect to go anywhere near Mexico or its rebellious province," said Izak.

"Cuba is so well situated," mused Niklas, "with its fabulous natural harbor and more sugar to ship out than any other island."

"Aye," said Cabrera, "but the old treasure galleons are no more, and Cuba is no longer Spain's "Pearl of the Antilles." Antislavery and independence movements threaten everywhere."

"We were glad to make land in Havana," said Izak. "Many ships going east are thankful to pause here before a voyage across the Atlantic. Havana is America's richest, largest and most heavily fortified harbor."

"I don't think a Cuban revolution likely," said Niklas.

As he and Katrina walked home, he explained his thinking. "It's hard to be a revolutionary when you are prosperous, no matter how cruel a tyrant."

CHAPTER 43

COMFORT IN DRINK

Observing the many shades of skin betraying parentage, Will found it hilarious that Habaneros should consider themselves limpieza de sangre, pure Spanish blood. It was equally inconceivable that he himself should not be good enough for Ezmeralda, with no allowance made for the high culture and education in the Germanies, let alone the couple's instant mutual attraction (he was convinced it was mutual) or the power of true love. Whenever he was abroad, he kept a sharp eye out for her, sure she might appear at any moment. He described her to his parents and implored them to do the same.

Just yesterday his heart had skipped a beat at the sight of a small, well-dressed girl whose black hair shone with a red glow, but when he called out, she turned, and he saw she was not Ezmeralda. What was true, though only Pepe knew and Katrina guessed, was that Ezmeralda's family agreed with Will about the power of young love and were imprisoning the girl, preventing another chance encounter. What not even they knew was that the negotiations for the girl's marriage to an elderly uncle were being pushed forward with new intensity. In the meantime, Will wrote her love letters in French, laboring to perfect each phrase. The letters lay undelivered, however; Pepe said he was unable to find her address.

Hans knew enough to take pity on his little brother and distract him. Every evening at nine o'clock, the great fortress of El Morro fired a cannon shot, a tradition running back seventy-four years to the British capture of Havana, when the city was opened to trade for the first time and the cañonazo announced a nightly curfew. By 1836, the cannon was no longer for curfew but for indulgence. Habaneros were lovers of late-night drinking, gambling and whoring, a situation Hans discovered and appreciated almost instantly.

One night, at the nine o'clock cannon, Hans crept quietly out, not at all surprised when Will followed him, or that, as he was noiselessly opening the gate in Paloma's garden, he heard a hoarse whisper: "Hans!"

Hans turned to Will and said, "Come on then, if you must."

That's exactly it, Will thought, *I must.*

Soon they were striding down el Malecón, heading for the dicey end and listening for the most raucous music and laughter. With pleasure they heard English voices. This was not a surprise; el Malecón was seaside, and most sailors went no further than local sailor towns, cheap, disreputable neighborhoods of boarding houses, taverns and bordellos lining harbors everywhere. They had found la Piña de Plata and the Enigmas.

Hours later, it was Richard Billings and the red-bearded Erik Thorvald buttressing Hans and Will as they stumbled back to Paloma's. The group was guided by Rafael, the tavern-owner's handsome young slave, sent along to make sure these customers were not robbed blind while they were drunk and found floating in the harbor the next morning. Until *Enigma* set sail again, they were "regulars," and the owner wanted to be sure their money wound up in his pocket, not some thief's. Rafael opened the garden gate, and the two other men managed to push Hans and Will inside.

"There you go now, mateys," said Billings, as he braced Hans inside the garden fence. Neither Billings nor Thorvald was especially steady on his feet. "And next time, stay away from Methuselah."

"What was it he called you?" Will asked.

"He thought I was Papa, every Englishman's enemy." Hans slurred this, and they all laughed, remembering Methuselah's clumsy attack, both men too drunk to kill each other.

Hans gave them a bleary smile, tried valiantly to bow and slipped into German: "Danke, meine liebsten Freunde, Thank you, my dearest friends." Only Will understood German, and the last three words ran together, but Hans's warm feelings were clear to all.

Erik Thorvald nearly fell over as he tried to return the sentiment, bowing as he replied in his best Danish, "Vi er beærede over at hjælpe dig, We are honored to be of assistance."

"Dors bien, Sleep well," said Rafael in oddly inflected Haitian French, gesturing to a little stone step in the garden, "et fais attention, cette étape, and mind that step."

"Promise me, we meet again tomorrow night," said Billings, as the newly dear friends parted.

Katrina worried that such nighttime revelry must wake half the neighborhood. She watched them stumbling over each other, bowing and embracing, having found comfort in drink. The next morning, Will could not face breakfast, and Hans was late to arise. His red eyes and close-lipped irritability did nothing to hide their escapades from their parents.

Hans needs to be on his own, Katrina thought, *in someone's army, but will Niklas ever let him go?* As for Will, he was not ever likely to find Ezmeralda, and Katrina did not know what desperate thing he might do about that.

Day after day, the botanical world seemed to explode around them. Palms of all sizes and shapes swayed around and above, fronds clattering in the breeze. On every side, great swaths of fuchsia bougainvillea and waxy white, fragrant jasmine bloomed. Jacaranda trees set a glory of blue, like a fantasy of overgrown lilacs. Katrina consulted with Paloma about aloes, known to sooth burns and cuts. She introduced Francesca, and they added aloe starts and begonias—for colds and poor digestion—to the plants and seeds that had crossed the Atlantic with them.

Along the road outside Paloma's house, bent men and women carried huge bundles of tobacco leaves wrapped in bark from the Blue Mahoe tree on their way to long, open-air factories. There, and along the streets, men and women rolled cigars on their thighs with a practiced twirl and a final twist. Will spent most of his small horde of coins to buy these cigars.

"There will be eager buyers further north, where cigars are all the fashion," he told his father.

Niklas agreed. He rolled one between his finger and thumb, studying it. "They are replacing pipes." The two of them admired the aromatic boxes made of Spanish cedar to serve as humidors and bought several.

"This is a real find," Will said.

"We'll see how well they survive an ocean crossing," said his father.

Another find was Plaza Vieja, where many ship owners lived, with its glorious fountain: four dolphins of Italian Carrara marble spouting water.

The plaza had a newly built, covered market named la Mercado Cristina in honor of the Spanish child-queen. It was filled with fish, poultry, vegetables and fruit of every description.

Niklas and Katrina, returning to the Ruiz house from the market, rested for a moment on Paloma's garden bench, putting down a heavy sack of tropical fruits. Later, a crate of humidors and cigars would be delivered, a questionable use of their pirate prize money, but much better than los caballos Criollo, to Katrina's thinking.

CHAPTER 44

FAR FROM FREE

Hans was in the garden, picking ripe coffee cherries from Paloma's trees. "Keeping my hands busy," he told his parents when they arrived. "It's too nice to be inside." The three of them sat in peace for a few moments, Hans on the ground, cross-legged.

"Father, you were once imprisoned?"

"You know I was." Niklas was surprised to hear a question to which Hans obviously knew the answer.

"And you were a member of Berleburg's Antislavery Society?"

Again, Niklas nodded, wondering where Hans was going with this. His membership in the Antislavery Society reflected his genuine beliefs, but it had also been a cover for illegal revolutionary activity.

Hans lowered his head and looked around cautiously. They leaned toward him, and he spoke at just above whisper.

"We may be able to help a man, a good, young man, escape the prison of slavery."

Katrina glanced at Niklas. *Did he hear?* He nodded and motioned for Hans to continue.

Hans told them then about Rafael, whose family had come from Haiti with their owner, who was a physician, not a planter, and now also the owner of a tavern, la Piña de Plata. Havana had seemed a good choice when they escaped Haiti's revolutionary turmoil, but over the years, Cuba became a sugar island, with the violence and repression that required.

"Now Tacón wants the last of the Haitians out," Hans said, "and the protection Rafael's master provides grows thinner every day. At one time, he talked of taking the family to France and freeing them, but now he is too ill. Raphael is desperate for freedom and has devised a plan. It's risky, but he thinks it will work. His sister and one brother want to make the attempt with him."

"How does this involve us?" Niklas asked.

"You know Missus Gaby, Paloma's cook?" They nodded, and Hans continued. "She's Raphael's mother. She heard that we leave soon, and she overheard you disparaging the curse of slavery. This gave Raphael the courage to speak."

Niklas held up his hand and whispered, "I think someone's coming." He waved to the left. Hans rose and stole noiselessly to the garden wall. Niklas went the other way. In a few moments they returned, having done a search of the streets and alleys on all sides of Paloma's walled garden.

"You know, don't you, the penalty for helping a slave run?" Niklas asked.

"Ja, sure. Hanging."

"And your head on a pike."

Katrina gagged at the thought. *Such Medieval cruelty.* "Should we go inside?"

Niklas shook his head. "Let's sit by the fountain instead." At the center of Paloma's garden was a small fountain, which would put them as far from the walls as possible and with the sound of the water to muffle their voices.

"Und sprechen Sie Deutsch," Katrina said.

"Ja," said Niklas, "Good idea."

They settled themselves on the edge of the fountain, their heads close together.

"It's a simple plan," said Hans. "We buy Rafael and the others, Annie and Jan-Jak, take them aboard with us and then, after the harbor pilot is gone, we lower them in a boat. After that, it's up to them. Their hope is to make it to the free Bahamas."

"Izak and Thomas must agree," said Niklas.

"Which they will in their hearts, but will they act? There's always a gap between what one says and what one does."

"Even if they are willing, the crew will be disgusted at such an illegal action. They are very traditional."

"Ja, but it won't signify. They won't be able to report it until New Orleans, and then they'd be reporting it to Americans, who have no legal truck with Cuba."

"Besides, we would simply deny it. It would be us and the captain and the owner against the others. They'd never be believed."

"We could provision an escape boat ahead of time," Katrina said.

"The barque's boats have sails, and Rafael and Jan-Jak know how to sail. But it would depend on the weather."

"Everything at sea depends on the weather. They could be blown back to Cuba and find themselves in a much worse position, being worked to death as sugar slaves."

Katrina nodded and asked, "Are they willing to risk it?"

"Yes. Their master grows older every day and crazier. They trust him less and less."

The Kästners had heard of people being caught and re-enslaved. They sat silently for a few minutes, weighing these horrors against the desire for freedom.

Niklas looked at Katrina. "It adds risk for us."

"But it's also a chance to do something substantial against slavery."

"Yes," said Hans, "It's only one thing, but it is in our power to do it."

"And to them, it is everything," Katrina said.

Niklas was still silent. Then he put his hand in the middle of their small circle, and Hans and Katrina understood. She put her hand on top of Niklas's, and Hans put his on top of hers.

"It is decided," said Niklas, and Katrina could hear the resolve in his voice.

The next morning, Paloma looked aghast when they told her none but Niklas had ever seen a beach. She said, "You must go. My Pepe will take you, and I will pack a picnic."

Soon, they were following behind Pepe for what seemed a long time through marsh and grasslands and sand dunes where seagulls swooped and cawed and long-billed curlews plucked crickets out of tufts of beach grass. Katrina thought it quite different and interesting, but then they crested the most seaward dune onto the seashore itself. It was a revelation of soft white sand, translucent turquoise waters and life on every side. Sandpipers raced along the edge of the water, sea turtles lumbered across, and tiny clams disappeared into the sand.

Pepe departed after Paloma's picnic was eaten, and the Kästners lay about on the warm sand in various stages of delight, lulled by the cool sea breeze, absorbing the gentle rhythm of waves that barely crested before running up the white sand like miniature horses. The children waded in and laughed when bright blue and yellow fishes swam between their legs.

Lordly coconut palms swayed above, and the long view across the turquoise-blue expanse of the sea stretched their eyes. Once having found the beach, they came back to it as often as they could while *Enigma* was being rebuilt and rerigged.

Many days at the beach were like the first when they marveled at sand dollars and starfish, startled at crabs creeping along the sand, and found shells of every strange configuration and subtle hue, including the miraculous mother of pearl. They came early to see the morning star cradled by a sliver of moon and late to emerge from the surf dripping, wringing their clothing onto sand that lay in ripples below their bare feet. They wondered at the tides, skipped through the seaweed strewn on the strand, licked salt off their skin, and absorbed sunlight as if it alone would save their lives.

One day they arrived to find a stiff northerly wind whipping up a white-capped sea, more teal-black than turquoise, sending fierce breakers with wind-driven crests to pound the sand. They stood well back, admiring this show of wicked force, the very sand at their feet sweeping along in wide arcs ebbing and flowing in imitation of the waves. They were glad not to be aboard ship for this. When the wind strengthened yet more and blowing sand bit into their cheeks, they turned away and slid down the back of the dunes, heading for home.

The next day they returned to a beach with ten- or twelve-foot waves, big rollers crashing in under a bright blue sky, a sandy world that seemed always changing. The men bounced, slid and laughed among the big waves; Amalie and Katrina went out as far as their knees; and the little ones built sandcastles all afternoon. They were packing to leave when Katrina looked far out into waves now backlit by the sun and saw sharks silhouetted in the water, many sharks.

"Look, look!" She pointed, but she need not have hurried; the sharks kept coming and coming.

"This," said Niklas, "is a feeding frenzy, like the one I saw after the battle."

"I'm glad to be witnessing it from afar," Katrina said with a shudder. Lisette came over and put her arm around her waist. At last, they turned their backs on the wild beauty of the beach and walked home.

Niklas and Katrina weighed their plans for homesteading in America against the beach and the university and the other attractions of Havana, considering whether the family should try to stay.

"We are free," Katrina said. "No one waits for us in America. We can make our home anywhere, and Metternich will never think to look for us here."

"That may not be quite true," said Niklas. "All of the monarchs support each other, and we do not know how far-flung their spy networks are."

An excess of caution, Katrina thought.

"But the real issue is that this country is far from free," said Niklas. "We may be free to go or stay—perhaps, if they will have us—but here we would have to accept a Catholic monarchy and abandon our hope of a free country."

"You're right," Katrina said. "I don't know how I could have suggested we stay."

"We would have to convert."

She blanched at the thought.

"Besides," said Niklas, "I would be persona non grata again. Those here who remember Napoleon hate him. We don't even know if Herr Kleimbach would be so friendly if he knew."

"That alone is enough to stop us."

"There's more. Cuba is long settled, every inch of land owned."

Katrina agreed: "Our nest egg would be worthless here compared to the American frontier."

"Not to mention that most livelihoods depend on slave-owning," said Niklas.

"Besides all of that, although we are free, Hans's Rafael is not." She looked down, studying her bare toes. "I couldn't bear to leave him stranded, beach or no beach."

"But will carrying them from Cuba to some empty spot on the ocean be any favor? Or will it be the death of them?"

"We'll never know," Katrina admitted. "That underground river—"

"The Gulf Stream—"

"may sweep them out to the ocean."

"We might be able to get them within sight of a Bahamian island."

"That would be a great relief to me."

In the end, there was no question of staying in Cuba. Their hope of land, liberty, and the freedom to speak and worship depended on stepping aboard again.

Still, Katrina promised herself: *I will never forget the tropical paradise of a beach in Havana.* As it turned out, for the rest of her life, the beach would be what she dreamt of on cold winter nights, but sometimes she would dream of sharks and be glad to open her eyes in her own house far away from a salty, sandy beach.

CHAPTER 45

SECRET DANCES OF JOY

Years later they would think of those sultry days in Havana as if a dream, even seemingly ordinary moments like meeting Izak and Thomas Segrave at the café on el Malecón. One bright morning when Niklas and Katrina were there, a long row of brown pelicans swept by the embankment, and gulls kept up a battle of raucous calls while the small group of friends drank good coffee and rum punch as they listened to *Enigma*'s owner and captain discussing repairs and provisioning.

"The quality of Cuban timber is considered excellent," said Thomas Segrave, "for the construction of first-rate ships, and this has led me to have rather more extensive repairs done."

"Much of this—masts restored, hull plugged and re-coppered, rigging replaced—would have to done anyway when we land in New Orleans. Cheaper and safer to have it done here," Izak explained to the Kästners.

Niklas listed the goods he had purchased, proof of the unexpected trade advantage gained by landing in Cuba. Then, with singular discretion, he drew the others' eyes to a treasure he had wrapped in a length of embroidered red silk.

"Look here," he said, as he showed them a green jade necklace, handling it most discreetly. "A neighbor of our landlady traded it for delftware. It's from China, can you imagine? Once exchanged, no doubt, for Mexican gold." Even in this dim café, where he did not dare turn the necklace to the sunlight for fear strangers would see it, the stones glowed.

"Amazing, fabulous," said Segrave. "If you should ever wish to sell it, please offer it to me first."

Niklas nodded his assent, but Katrina hoped he would seek her opinion in the matter. "More importantly," he said, wrapping the necklace up again, "I may want to bring servants with us, three young Negroes." Katrina watched the others' reactions closely.

Izak stiffened. "Servants? Or slaves? No man will be a slave on a ship of mine."

"Nor is it legal to carry a slave," said Thomas Segrave. "The ship is British, and Britain outlawed slavery, what? Three years ago? I am sure you know this. A slave would become free the moment he set foot on my ship."

"Gentlemen, gentlemen," Niklas said. "The freedom of these three young people is our dearest hope." He went on to tell them of Rafael's situation and that of his sister and brother, feeling fortunate to have fallen in with such like-minded men. Aboard their ship, they ruled the world.

They ended pleased at the prospect, despite its risks, and they assured the Kästners that if the three young people sailed with *Enigma*, they would have protectors for as long as they were aboard. In this surprising way, Niklas and Katrina learned that Thomas Segrave, a rich man's son, had something important in common with them; he, too, had been a member of an antislavery society.

"They've been around in England for, what? Fifty years?" Thomas said.

"The societies are well established in the Germanies, too. And yet here…" Niklas shook his head sadly and then cautioned them: "Nothing is settled. Hans knows Rafael well, but we have not even met the young man, and I don't know if his master will sell them."

"Be careful," Thomas warned. "It may be a trap. The master may want cash, and even if not, he may bear you ill will for…what? For being a Protestant? For putting wicked ideas into a slave's head?"

"Aye," agreed Izak, "He may want you arrested. If he accuses you of stealing his slaves, his property, you could hang for it. Sound him out carefully." Before they went their separate ways, Izak pushed a sack of coins across the table: "In case you need more to buy their freedom."

"Good idea," said Thomas. He reached into a pocket inside his boot, motioned for the sack, and added some gold to it. "Give us an accounting, if you'll be so kind."

"Of course," Niklas said. He was glad to have generous partners.

Sugar required slaves, many slaves. Almost all of Havana's great wealth rested on the often-bloodied backs of slaves, one in twenty of Cuba's population a generation ago and now one in two. This is what Paloma told Katrina and Niklas, shuddering to be among so many dark faces.

Just now, in the lovely spring, she said the harvest was on, requiring huge shipments of *tasajo*, sun-dried beef from Argentina. "The work on Cuban plantations is too hurried for slaves to tend their provision plots during harvest. Only during *el tiempo muerto*, the hot "dead" season of July through December, do sugar slaves have time to grow their own food."

Katrina nodded. "From what I understand, sugar depends on slave labor in vast numbers."

"This is true. When the British-Spanish Mixed Commission Court was formed, we thought it might change things, but it's weak—no real barrier to the slave trade. And the profits can be enormous." Paloma excused herself, and the Kästners sat in silence for a moment.

"Consider the profits possible," said Will, "whenever one can extract something of value for next to nothing, cross an ocean and resell at a satisfyingly high going rate."

"As true of gold or diamonds as it is of slaves," Niklas said. He was impressed that Will had such a grasp.

They sipped hot coffee as they thought. Then Hans said with some surprise, "If people are willing to enslave others, even when they know how it kills, absolving themselves of torture and murder and every other depredation of slavery, simply for profit and without so much as a blink, they will stop at nothing."

Niklas nodded, and his reply was grim. "Considering this, no one, no one at all, should be surprised when the ethics of certain other business practices are found to be questionable."

It had always been true that some slaves took their lives in their hands and escaped. This was widely known, but officials minimized it, the better to claim both its impossibility and a lack of responsibility. One reason slavery was on so many tongues was the authorities' recent failure to destroy a hideout of escaped slaves, what the Habaneros called un palenque. It was near Santiago, at the other end of the island. The raid was a disaster, and while distant five days by horseback, slaveowners spoke of it in terrified whispers.

Paloma said, "They blame the 1833 British abolition of slavery and even the specter of the Pirate Republic once in the Bahamas."

"These are inspirations to those still enslaved?" Katrina asked.

"Sí," said Paloma, "that's the fear."

An odd thought occurred to Katrina. "Do these palenques shelter those who inhabited the islands before Columbus?"

"¡Oh, los Taínos!" said Paloma. "They're long gone. They died off rather than work—God's way of giving us the islands."

Later, in private, Missus Gaby scoffed at that. "Los Tainos still alive up in the mountains, and they help us when they can." She said a captain of the Mayari district led a posse of armed volunteers to find and crush the palenque. When they reached the top of a ridge, they saw a settlement at least three miles across. Lookouts spotted them, blew horns, and a force of about three thousand rushed the posse. It retreated, but not before more than half—eighty or so—had been killed or captured.

"The whites," Missus Gaby said, "they whisper, but they don' know nothing."

She said no more, but Rafael told Hans about celebrations far and wide, whispered poems, secret dances of joy, and clandestine plans for escape. It upset him. "This makes everything harder," he said to Hans. "It will put everyone on alert."

"He's right," Niklas said. "The authorities will be looking for someone to punish." As it happened, at the same time, Spain tightened rules, raised taxes and rescinded rights. Slaveholders, like hens in a pecking order, turned on their slaves with a new and awful severity.

The next morning after breakfast, Katrina smoothed a piece of foolscap on the cleared table. She dipped her pen and wrote,

"My Dearest Elizabet,

"We are, all of us, alive and safe in the most fascinating and curious harbor of Havana, Cuba. Imagine our delight when our brave and stalwart captain found this refuge, though how he uses his arcane instruments and the very stars at night to find anything upon a sea which looks as endless and empty as eternity is a mystery I shall never plumb.

"The people here go about in lace and satin finery on fine horses and carrying pretty little lapdogs called silkies, as proud and haughty as if they were a great nation, though it is but a weak echo of Europe. The little cathedral is made of coral rock embedded with seashells, quaint and fanciful, fairly glowing when light touches it, but looking insubstantial to any inquiring eye. Will had to poke it to believe it was solid. Even the horses, though beautiful, are small.

"The harbor is impressive, with a long promenade. Several fine squares and a university enrich the town, but in any direction the streets turn into dirt roads, on which urchins of every description race around parents leading donkeys piled high with vegetative burthens. Most are enslaved Africans, our first sight of that horror, which is everywhere here, so one hardly knows what to think or say. We fear what more we may see of this horrid practice in America."

She lifted her quill and debated how she might tell Elizabet about Rafael and his family. She did not doubt Elizabet's sympathy for the cause, but in the end, she decided to say nothing. After all, there was nothing but talk to report now. Instead, she decided to tell Elizabet about the beach.

"In spite of all I have said, Havana has especial delights for weary travelers such as we are. First and foremost are the safety of its harbor and its other astonishing gifts of nature, tropical fruits surpassing even what we partook of so gratefully in Gibraltar, tropical birds and lizards delighting us with their quickness and color, and the most amazing room of nature I have ever visited, the sandy beach, where roam massive turtles amid scuttling crabs and sandpipers (like miniature cranes) stalking every little thing at the very edge of the water. If ever you can perchance visit a tropical beach, my dear Elizabet, do avail yourself; my weak grasp of the language prevents me from describing its many delights in any fullness. Were it not for the sweet inducements of land and liberty, I could not give it up.

"Niklas is busy buying cigars and other Habanero specialties, including cups and bowls made of the hard shell of the fruit of a native tree known as calabash or higuera, very handy indeed. Hans goes off by himself for long periods of time and tells no one, so that his father and I shall be glad to have him aboard again, and Will has been in love and (we hope) is out of it again.

"Amalie is now fifteen and has become a woman, to her surprise and dismay. Her shape is now that of a young lady, and I can see something of you in her face. Lisette is a pleasure as ever, and is being dragged along by Jakob to share his immense joy in all things that crawl or shine and thus amaze and delight little boys.

"With my dear love to you and your children, your most affectionate cousin, Katrina Beckmann Kästner

"P.S. We met a Herr Kleimbach of Dortmund, who spoke as if he might know our northern cousins. He came here some time ago at the behest of his employer, a certain German bank, the precise name of which escapes my mind at the moment. He attached himself to us like a tick, so pleased was he to hear the sound of our ordinary German voices. I wonder, shall I become so sick at heart for home?"

CHAPTER 46

MOST SINGULAR PASSENGERS

Stepping out into the street, blinded by sunlight, Niklas and Katrina saw a young man who seemed to stand in their way. Katrina shaded her eyes, and at the same time felt Niklas's arm release hers. She knew he was reaching for the dagger at his belt.

"S'il vous plait, Monsieur Kästner," a polite voice pleaded in strangely accented French. "Hans begs your attention pour un moment, as do I and my master."

The speaker was a young man, cocoa brown and handsome with close-cropped hair. He stepped back and to one side. Katrina recognized him as the one who had brought Hans and Will home. His expression was blank and submissive, with no glimmer of emotion, an ancient, empty slave expression giving nothing away, telling nothing, claiming nothing.

She guessed: "Rafael?"

"Yessir, Ma'am." The young Black man had not missed Niklas's hand on a weapon. "Hans awaits you, and my master, Doctor Alejandro Miguel Suárez Martinez, requests your presence."

The street seemed quiet. One might even say deserted. "Lead on," Niklas told Rafael, his hand still on his dagger.

Rafael hesitated. "If I might suggest—" He glanced at Katrina. "It's in sailor town."

"She comes with us," said Niklas.

Where Rafael led them, the streets rapidly deteriorated until Katrina was glad to have two strong men with her and glad their guide kept up a good pace. Very quickly, they reached la Piña de Plata, and Rafael held the front door open for them. The room, which smelled of liquor and stale cigars, was empty except for an old man at the bar.

The bartender bowed and asked, "Monsieur Kästner? Madame Kästner? The master awaits." At Niklas's nod, he waved them to a back room, a private chamber, better lit. At a gambling table, Hans stood with an old white man in a wheeled chair.

The man in the wheeled chair spoke in a French with the same strange Haitian inflection as Rafael's. He introduced himself, pointedly ignoring Katrina, whose presence seemed to surprise and then insult him.

"I am Alejandro Miguel Suárez Martinez, a physician trained at Madrid." He drew himself up straighter in the chair, as if to mollify the ragged circumstances in which they found him. "The medical school at Madrid is not as old as Heidelberg's." Here the old man inclined his head to Niklas in deference to his German roots. "Or for the love of God, Bologna's," and here he crossed himself. "But it is a gray-haired institution nevertheless and prepared me well for these misbegotten islands, where I have lived my life and where I will die." This long statement seemed to have exhausted him; he collapsed back onto his pillows, coughing.

They waited for him to recover.

The old man looked at Niklas with significance. "Rafael has had no formal medical schooling, but he has been assisting me for years, and if he weren't Black, that would make him a decent doctor."

The three Kästners looked with greater appreciation at Rafael, who bowed in acknowledgement.

"You want to buy him?" the old white man asked.

The blunt question went to Katrina's heart like a knife.

He continued. "I no longer need him. I cannot practice, and no one wants him except as my assistant. But I know his worth and will insist on a good price." He coughed again, holding up one finger to let them know he had more to say: "But why I should sell him to heathens?"

Niklas stood and said, "I will not answer that question, because we are not heathens."

"Then we have nothing more to discuss," said the old man, motioning to the bartender to move his wheeled chair.

"I am here," said Niklas, "on behalf of two Englishmen, a ship's captain and a ship's owner."

Doctor Martinez waved the bartender away. "I have always liked Englishmen, they who caught the Corsican monster."

Niklas ignored this slur against Napoleon and lied without compunction: "Aboard ship, Rafael would serve as surgeon."

"What will the Englishmen pay for this prize, a surgeon?"

"Enough to please you, I believe." Niklas set a bag on the table with a thump. "We want Jan-Jak and Annie, too."

The old man hefted the bag, looking doubtful. When he emptied it, gold coins rolled onto the table, and then the jade necklace fell among them. He stared. "This makes it possible."

"I will need papers." Slaves without papers had no freedom of movement. They could be captured and re-enslaved before they had gone twenty steps. A bill of sale would get them past harbor inspections and keep them from being easy targets.

"Oui," said Dr. Martinez, but something in his voice alerted Niklas to the vast distance between going to meetings in Germany and taking action to help an actual enslaved person. He looked hard at the old man. Rafael had told Hans his master wanted to see the three of them freed and gone, but Niklas found this hard to believe. Perhaps Rafael's master wanted to recapture the three of them and sell them again. Or, for some obscure reason, he wanted to punish Rafael. If the old man claimed it was an attempted escape, Rafael and his brother would hang, their sister would be soundly whipped and re-enslaved, and even that might not be the worst of it. They might be decapitated, their heads on a stake as a warning to all inclined to run. Niklas might be shot or hanged for aiding a felon and maybe Hans and others as well. Why wouldn't General Tacón make an example of interfering foreigners— damned-to-Hell-Protestants! —with no one to object?

"We," said Niklas, "expect possession at once."

Doctor Martinez nodded. "Of course."

It took most of an hour for a bill of sale to be drawn up and the tavern door to close soundly behind them. When it did, Niklas told Rafael and the others, "I will free you as soon as manumission papers can be drawn up."

"If you will forgive me, sir, such papers are fine," Rafael said; "I would sew such papers under my skin if I had them. But our real hope lies in escaping to a free state."

When they reached Paloma's garden and were safely inside, Katrina reassured their three new companions, "Our ship's captain knows what it is to be enslaved. He was taken as a boy."

"Besides, the ship's owner, who sails with us," said Hans, "is himself a member of an abolitionist society." He had already told Rafael of Niklas's belonging to an antislavery society.

"You will be safe on board with us and with such good men."

A loud knocking sounded at Paloma's front door. Annie gasped, and Katrina put her arm around the girl, who shivered with fear. Niklas drew his sword, and Hans raised a pistol. They turned to face Erik Thorvald and Richard Billings coming for them, their weapons drawn. Thorvald swiped an arm across his bloody nose.

"Quickly! This way, to the ship."

"The children!"

"Already aboard," said Thorvald. He and Richard Billings seized their arms and pushed them forward. Billings glanced behind them.

"He sent his thugs to retrieve his property," Billings said, nodding at Rafael and the others.

They ran through the streets to the docks, where Will was carrying the last of their trunks on his back as he went up the gangway, and Pepe was leading a donkey away. At the rail, Lisette waved from where she stood with Amalie and Jakob.

"Did you know he would come after us?" Niklas asked Hans.

"I suspected." Hans was grim. "He wanted both his slaves and the money. And seeing a few Lutherans hang would have been a bonus." Hans turned to Billings. "Is the pilot aboard?"

"Aye," said Billings, as he ran up the gangway.

Katrina paused to speak to Pepe. "Give your mother our thanks."

Niklas took her arm. "Let the boy get away. There's not a moment to lose."

Captain Izak Peterssen ordered the anchors hove to and soon the solidly rebuilt *Enigma* was under sail, happily re-watered and re-provisioned and carrying fresh beef, molasses, sugar, rum, oranges, and cigars, as well as three new passengers, Rafael, Jan-Jak, and Annie.

Enigma headed out to the mouth of Havana Bay while the harbor pilot barked orders. When at last she was beyond the twin towers of the ancient forts and breasting the swells of the turquoise sea, *Enigma* rounded into the wind and put herself in irons, sails flapping as the pilot scrambled over the side and dropped safely into the cutter that had followed them out; two of its crewmen, fore and aft, hung onto *Enigma*'s forechains.

"Vaya con Dios," the pilot shouted from below. He hesitated for a long moment, waiting for Izak Peterssen to sweeten his fee with a few more coins or a bottle of rum.

"¡Vete contigo!" shouted Izak, "Begone with you!"

The pilot shrugged; the crew released their hold and shoved off. The pilot cutter's sails filled, she tacked and soon disappeared.

As on the evening they arrived in Cuba, passengers of all classes lined the rails for another beautiful evening, a "red sky at night, sailor's delight." Standing a little behind the Kästners were the *Enigma*'s new, most singular passengers, tiny smiles evident, had anyone looked closely.

"We have only a week to New Orleans," said Mr. Groves, "an easy week if we are lucky."

Thomas Segrave nodded, and Katrina smiled as she glanced over at him, a member of the British nouveau riche and of an antislavery society. She could not have imagined it of him.

"Here we are again, Niklas," Katrina said, "escaping!"

"We were lucky. In other times, we might have been caught up and forcibly converted."

"Even now, Doctor Martinez's brutes might have caught us.

"Our sons did well, Hans especially, to spirit Rafael away and plan it all."

"Yes, they did. We are fortunate to be clean away."

Will was among the few not to thrill with the general joy of a voyage well begun. He was pleased to have managed—in a great rush—to bring the youngsters and trunks safely aboard, but his heart still stung with the loss of his beautiful Ezmeralda.

Only a few hours had passed when Rafael approached Niklas. "Monsieur, the sooner you can put us down, the better. The current will take us east and run us up to San Andreas or one of the other Bahamian islands. Where is no matter, so long as it's soon."

Mr. Groves, an enthusiastic member of the scheme, agreed with Rafael. "The Lesser Antilles Current will take you east, but as soon as it begins to curve north, or becomes weak and confused, row for all you're worth to get in among the islands."

"Or else it might sweep you out to the Atlantic," Izak warned. "The current is strong here, squeezed between Cuba and the tip of Florida." He looked up to the sky. "Besides, right now, the weather promises you the fair days you need.

"Can you send us a letter?" Katrina asked. "Is there mail between the Bahamas and New Orleans?"

"Maybe," Rafael told her. "If it is at all possible, Madame, you will hear from us."

"Are you ready? Is the boat provisioned?" Mr. Groves spoke quietly to Will, who nodded. The moon was full, the sky filled with stars. The second watch was on deck, looking forward to an easy time of it.

Suddenly Mr. Groves shouted, "Put her in irons!" Sailors, hard-bitten men ready to obey orders without question, looked at each other in surprise. "Now!" he shouted. "Lower a boat. We're putting these scoundrels off!"

This was part of the plan, the first mate's seeming anger giving a reason for this unusual but not unheard-of action. Now they acted fast before there were questions or anyone took the first mate's anger to heart and struck one of the three.

In moments Rafael, Annie, and Jan-Jak were bundled into the boat amid a stream of invective from Mr. Groves. Annie touched the fine new woolen shawl from Paisley Katrina had given her and smiled gratefully at Hans. With a jerk, the boat was raised over the rail, swung out and down. It hit the water, and the three siblings pushed off, raising a sail as soon as they cleared away from the ship. They did not dare wave, but Annie looked back, and Katrina was sure she mouthed, "Merci."

"Good riddance!" yelled Thomas Segrave with false but convincing anger.

Niklas heard men behind them complaining about wasting a boat. "Should have dumped them overboard for the sharks," Methuselah said.

As the little sail faded into the distance, Hans said softly to his father, "This may have been the best thing we ever did."

Katrina was in tears. She could not have said why it mattered so much to her, these three, no older than her own children, setting off across the ocean for a new life.

At a signal from Mr. Groves, the conspirators marched aft to the dining saloon, where, when they were safely inside, Izak held up a finger to his smiling lips and poured a celebratory brandy for each. They silently toasted each other, and then Niklas said a whispered prayer for the emancipated family's safe arrival in the Bahamas.

Now *Enigma* would swing south and pick up the loop current that would take her around and deliver them to New Orleans and America at last.

BOOK FIVE

HOME AGAIN

"It's all God's will: you can die in your sleep,
and God can spare you in battle."
— Leo Tolstoy, *War and Peace*

CHAPTER 47

THE BLIND HAND OF GOD

It might be said that the storm began during the night of 7 June, when after days of good sailing, the wind died completely. The black water below shone like polished granite and the full moon appeared with multi-colored rings encircling it, first a fine line of bright white, then a wide ring of ghostly white, almost as bright as the moon itself. Outside that, rings of color began—yellow fading to orange and pink, then bright blue and even green, repeated several times. Altogether, the image was massive and extraordinarily bright.

Niklas, unable to sleep, saw the odd phenomenon and woke Katrina. They looked up in awe and listened quietly to the sailors' talk. Mr. Groves called it a lunar corona, the most spectacular and rare of rings around the moon.

Like most highly unusual sights in the sky, it was thought to portend something dangerous, some extreme change almost upon them. To the master of the watch, the rings were strange enough to order the mainsail reefed. This turned out to be entirely unnecessary, since the next day dawned preternaturally calm. The sails filled for a few moments, and the ship sailed a mile or two and then everything flopped, sagged, and hung limp again. When a morning shower passed over, it tattooed the glassy-flat surface with overlapping dots.

While the barque was becalmed, Mr. Groves knocked at the captain's cabin.

"Come."

"I don't mean to disturb you, sir, but you should know that Methuselah brought a new knife aboard, a proper sharp sticker."

"Well, Groves," Izak said, annoyed, "he probably bought it in sailor town. Dull the point."

"I have done so, sir. But sir, this is what I wanted to tell you—he tried to talk me out of it, saying we had a foreign devil aboard and ranting on about Waterloo and plots to kill the king."

"Hah! The king? It's not like there's a king aboard!"

"Aye. I don't like it, sir."

Izak frowned. "Keep an eye on him, Groves."

By now, Izak Peterssen had had enough of superstition and caution, and set the crew to hanking on everything it could. By the middle of the first dog watch, with the sun already low in the west, *Enigma* had made a decent day's sail of it, but the barometer was falling fast with everything horrid such a drop signified. By the second dog watch it was dangerously low. Huge thunderheads gathered across the southeastern horizon in a mass of green and violet-black clouds, illuminated now and again with flashes of lightning.

"A black squall," Methuselah told Niklas.

Niklas looked up in surprise. The man had avoided him since Gibraltar.

Methuselah continued. "It comes on fast, lightning all 'round. But we are not far from New Orleans."

Mr. Groves disagreed. "New Orleans ain't no safe haven," he said. "We are still too far away, and besides, a ship is safer at sea than in port during a storm. Some few ports give a boat shelter alee, it's true, but the very opposite is true of New Orleans." He stomped off.

Ominous clouds filled in across the sky and then a sudden blast of wind hit the barque straight out of the south, shoving it forward, then settling in at a steady thirty-five or forty knots, heeling *Enigma* over sharply with starboard chains buried deep in the waves and wind whistling through the rigging. As yet, however, this was nothing the Enigmas could not manage. They ran before the gale with all they had, bringing New Orleans closer by the minute.

To the east-southeast, a massive storm was taking shape, slowly building to its full force. At dusk on 8 June, the sky turned purple and green and then pitch black except where a thin band of light on the western horizon picked out a ragged silhouette of heavy seas. Lightning reached them first, slicing through fast-moving clouds with dazzling regularity. Even below decks, the crash of thunder was so loud, passengers and sailors alike started and trembled.

In the Kästner cabin, everyone worked furiously, lashing everything loose to the bulkheads. Katrina tied Jakob and Lisette into one hammock, while Lisette cried and Jakob chimed in. She left Amalie to comfort them and with line enough to tie herself to their hammock.

"He will be sick," Katrina told Amalie, nodding to Jakob. "Tie this bucket to their hammock so you can bring it up to him." She turned to help the men secure everything possible. In a few moments, she and Niklas would tie themselves to their cots.

Then the rain began. A hard, nearly horizontal rain peppered the watch on deck and soon dripped through the roof of the cabin. Even when those on watch could shelter in the waist, men had to turn away from the rain to breathe. Everything but the spanker and a trio of storm jibs had long since been lashed to the yards, and the ship ran before the wind on almost bare bones.

As the first watch began, the second mate, Mr. Stephens and Methuselah took the wheel with the captain, it requiring three men's strength. Blinded by constant flashes of lightning, they struggled to keep *Enigma* dead on before the wind, pointing its bow directly into the immense waves. The ship pitched through the waves, surged forward, and then dropped down into the trough, where she endured a truly awful hesitation before pitching forward again. She came rushing back up into the black waves, foam burying the waist four foot deep, the forecastle vanishing as she plunged again.

Again she rose, water sheeting off the deck and rushing from the scuppers. Aloft, yards strained and shuddered. Rigging snapped, and lines cut through the air like cracking bullwhips. Then, just as a deafening flash of lightning blinded them, Methuselah jerked the wheel the wrong way, flung his arms to heaven, and screamed, "Let the heathens die!" He was tossed headlong across the deck. Izak and Mr. Stephens fought to bring the wheel back on course, but it tore free of their grasp. Izak slid across the deck and smashed against the rail. The rudder swung free, and the barque fell off her course, coming broadside to the waves.

A towering wall of water hung above her for an instant and then smashed down, shaking *Enigma* to her core. The roof of the Kästner cabin split with a thunderous crack, and water poured in. Niklas and Katrina's cots pitched them out, and they hit the bulkheads hard. Niklas scrabbled to his feet and was flung out of the cabin.

"Niklas!" Katrina screamed, but over the roar of the sea, no one heard her.

The boys struggled to stand, trying to find the cabin door, knowing that whatever had happened, all hands would be called. Katrina grabbed at them.

"We are sunk!" Hans shouted.

"Let me go, goddamn it, Mama." This from Will.

They waited, waited, waited. Hans had joined arms with Will around Katrina, holding her so hard she could hardly think. In that breathless moment, all aboard, man or woman, sailor or landsman, knew what was at stake. Would *Enigma* rise with the rising swell? Or was she sunk?

After a terrifying moment, *Enigma* rose. She surged forward, dropped into the trough between the waves, and rose again as the same horribly exaggerated pitching motion resumed. They did not know that on deck, Mr. Stephens had grabbed the spinning wheel, Izak had crawled back through fallen spars and snarled rigging, and Niklas had fought to get to the wheel. Together they took it in their hands and struggled to bring the barque up to the wind. These three men, against all odds, saved all on board and gave them a second chance to make a life for themselves, a good life with children and grandchildren to come.

Izak Peterssen, who understood as clearly as anyone else aboard that a broach was an imminent threat to their lives, shook the water off his head. Niklas's legs nearly gave out against the shock of the ship's rolling and pitching. The hull groaned like a sick animal, splintering and cracking as all around, wind and waves raged. Methuselah was gone. He had been flipped overboard as soon as he let go the wheel.

"Go below," Izak roared to Stephens, whose head was bleeding profusely. The master looked at him as at a specter and refused to let go the wheel. "We have it," the captain lied, still yowling above the screech of the wind. Groves was now on deck, loosening Stephens's grip and leading him below.

Hans saw what was happening at the wheel and leapt to help.

Izak: "Up the helm hard!" Hans added his strength. It took all three to bring the wheel into position. Sailors streamed up out of every hatch, Will among them. A cacophony of voices sounded.

Groves was back on deck: "Aft to the spanker sheets! Heave away!"

Another voice: "Hang on now, or we're all goners!"

Izak: "Lay forward and check the hatches! Get the carpenter if they are breached!"

In the cabin, Katrina pulled herself hand over hand to the children's hammock, where Amalie threw a loose end of line around her waist, and together, they managed to get it tied. Lisette and Jakob wailed in fear or pain, Katrina did not know which.

"I had no idea," Katrina said to Amalie.

"I thought we had seen the worst when we lost Gideon."

Katrina surveyed the children, watching for any loosening ties, any object about to fly into them, the horror rising in her throat and her heart filled with despair. *How could he have brought us so far,* she thought, *only to die nameless, lost and forgotten in some foreign ocean, doomed by the blind, omnipotent hand of God? I was a fool to agree.*

Amalie struggled to comfort Jakob, who seemed injured or frightened or both.

"Mama!" cried Lisette.

Katrina felt a great wave of panic and guilt. *If we go down with the ship, where Niklas and I brought our children, God will take us to account for our stupidity, our hubris. Was Hannah's death a warning from God? Was Gideon's?* For an instant, in her mind's eye, Katrina saw her kitchen in Berleburg, fresh bread on the table, clean blue and white plates, her family around her, safe and innocent, their smiling faces warmed by candlelight. She blinked and was back on Enigma, in the dark with the wind howling and Jakob crying piteously. *Never again,* she swore, *will I put my children in danger such as this.*

All through the night the storm raged on, with a mysterious break when the men tumbled into the cabin, lying exhausted wherever they could.

"It's the eye of the storm," Niklas said, "and will get bad again."

"Maybe worse, according to Groves." Hans said this with his eyes closed.

"We'll be ready this time," said Will.

"Father saved us," said Hans.

"And Stevens. And Izak." Niklas's voice was almost a whisper. "Methuselah is gone. Overboard."

The other side of the hurricane came and went, exhausted men managing somehow to keep their grip on line and wheel. Hours later, after the wind and rain had abated, the seas were still horribly confused, coming in huge swells from the south-southeast and in crosscurrents from every quarter. Niklas and the boys helped clear the decks and begin repairs, while Katrina and Amalie set about restoring the cabin.

Mr. Groves mustered the crew at the edge of the quarterdeck and reported to Izak, "All present and accounted for, sir, except Methuselah, who was drowned, sir." Not a man standing in front of them was free of bruises or cuts. "Dr. Ward has five in the surgery." Mr. Groves began to count again, just to be sure.

"The passengers, Mr. Groves?" asked Izak.

"All's alive, sir. Though an Ackermann child's hurt bad."

"We are down six men, then."

"Aye, aye, sir."

Izak knew Methuselah had tried to kill them all. He was glad not to have to hang him.

It would be another eight hours before the rain subsided, before Captain Peterssen dared take a strong hand off the wheel for even an instant, before anyone dared light a galley stove or set anything more than a miserable scrap of patched canvas as a storm jib.

CHAPTER 48

ST. ELMO'S FIRE

When the seas smoothed and the captain had a welcome cup of coffee in his hands once more, when Mr. Stephens had been bandaged and lay sound asleep under the influence of Dr. Ward's laudanum, when the ship's carpenter's crew was at work, and all first-watch hands were knotting and splicing as fast as ever they could, when the second watch had been sent below to begin their recovery, the bosun's boy shouted, "Look up, the masthead there."

All on deck peered up to see blue fire, St. Elmo's fire, dancing off the ruined tops of the main and forward masts. Smiles went 'round the crew, their shared happiness erasing class, rank, and exhaustion. St. Elmo's fire meant the worst was over, and indeed the hours blossomed into one of those clean, beautiful days that sometimes follows a storm, nothing but blue skies, high white clouds racing along, and the water rushing against the hull suffused with innocence.

In that post-storm moment of joy, Katrina helped to care for the injured Ackermann child. She thought of the little family they had put off, Rafael, Jan-Jak and Annie, who had had a week to reach land. If they had not done so, they were surely lost. She remembered Niklas's desire to bring aboard el caballo Criollo Cubano, Cuba's Andalusian-like horses, and was glad the hold was not full of a half-dozen horribly injured horses needing to be shot. She thanked God for deliverance and asked His forgiveness for her doubt at the moment of crisis. She was humbled when she thought of the courage and strength Niklas and Hans had shown in that moment and how this had saved them all. *I must thank them both*, she thought, *and I must never forget to be grateful.* She was oddly elated, as if surviving such a trial must be enough to qualify them for a new life. *America*, she thought, *must be right around the corner*, and then she laughed at herself for imagining an ocean with street corners.

All the Kästner men had been at work on deck for hours before the rest of the family escaped the cabin to breathe in the fresh Caribbean air. The little children were right behind Katrina, with Amalie bringing up the rear, guiding each around the coaming, wood trim around each hatch, the better to keep out water out. *Enigma* lurched to starboard, and Amalie herself stumbled on the coaming.

"Mind your step, Missy," cried Thomas Segrave, seizing her arm and deftly lifting her to one side.

"Oh, my!" she said. They looked down through an open hatchway and saw how she might have dropped straight down. "Thank you, sir! I should surely have fallen to my death without your quick action."

"Such a charming exaggeration," he smiled. "Let's never imagine such a disaster after what we have been through together."

Katrina had turned at their voices and now saw that Thomas Segrave held Amalie's arm a moment longer than necessary. It might have been the most innocent of touches, but it was not, Thomas would later admit. He felt a shock such as he never thought to feel again and suddenly understood the French phrase, "C'est le coup de foudre." Literally, it meant, "It is a strike of lightning," but figuratively, "It's love at first sight." That's how it felt to them, like a strike of lightning. For a confused moment, Amalie told her mother later, she wondered if it could be the St. Elmo's fire, having come down the mast and taken up residence in this man, the tall, handsome Englishman she had watched, first with anger and then with admiration. He had touched her.

"You are quite steady, now?" Thomas still held her arm. "Do you have your sea legs again, Missy?"

"Oh, yes, Herr Segrave. Merci. Danke Schön. Thank you." Amalie was genuinely happy to have been saved from a terrible fall, but there was much more to her feelings than that. She smiled up at him, her eyes lit with gratitude and wide in innocent surprise.

He looked at her, and Katrina, watching, knew this was when he saw for the first time a woman instead of a slip of a girl. Her round face still hinted of the childhood she was leaving, but when she lifted it to him, it also showed the young woman she was becoming, one who could lay a hand on his and smile with equanimity. With all of his much greater experience in such things, Thomas did not know whether she felt the same electricity.

Amalie, however, was sure of it, but it was followed by a sudden spike of fear of what the future held and whether all Englishmen were wicked, but mostly, of what her mother would say. She bowed her head to this particular Englishman, withdrew her arm, and stepped away. She wobbled a little, and Katrina took her hand.

A few long, difficult days later, Mr. Stephens said, "We shall see land by and by, I expect, sir," He had taken his noon observation, and he knew the hurricane had blown *Enigma* significantly off course. She was now very near the coast of Texas. "We shall see land by and by, sir," he repeated.

"And glad of it," the captain replied.

This was not quite true. Izak Peterssen was not entirely glad of the prospect of land, although *Enigma*'s new spars had been ruined and master carpenter Richard Billings was reporting eight inches of water in the hold. Izak's own sightings suggested the nearness of the coast of Texas, which was in the midst of a war marked, as all wars are, by chaos and atrocity.

Habaneros were generally on Mexico's side in this war, but there was a problem. Mexico had outlawed slavery in 1829, but if Texas became independent, would it be a slave or free nation? Many Habaneros thought no country could do without slaves, and besides, if freed, slaves would murder their former masters. "Look at Haiti," they said. Others pointed out that this had not happened in Mexico and besides, slavery's inhumanity must sooner or later doom the practice. To those aboard the *Enigma,* little about a fight in this obscure corner of the world mattered. Their first hope was to avoid landing in the midst of a war.

"It has been a long voyage," Izak said to Thomas Segrave. His voice showed the strain.

"Aye, and costly."

"There's nothing to be had for it but to land, if we can find a refuge, and put ourselves to rights. You know what they say."

"Give a sailor a knife and a forest—"

"But look, there's no sign of a forest." Sandy beaches now stretched off the larboard side, and the grassy dunes of barrier islands. Even ashore there seemed to be only marshlands.

"At least we have the crew we need at this point, battle-tested, and an experienced marine corps, which no one could have predicted."

"And even the women have proven themselves not entirely useless," Izak said.

Katrina's cheeks burned. She thought him unkind to say such a thing in her presence. *Not entirely useless. Indeed!*

"Most important," said Mr. Groves, "we need water."

Several of *Enigma*'s water barrels had been stove in or contaminated during the storm, and besides, she needed spars and canvas, and her boats had been swept away when she broached.

Below decks, the Ackermanns were in various states of distress. They had not known Texas existed, and now its appearance off the larboard bow made them think they had indeed sailed to the end of the world, and worse yet, a war-torn end. They worried that Captain Peterssen might declare his responsibilities at an end and abandon them in a wilderness.

Francesca was on deck with Katrina, and now she asked, "Is this place America?"

"I guess so. In the same sense that Havana and Mexico are part of the Americas. But it's not the United States."

"Our tickets say 'New Orleans or elsewhere in the United States as the captain determines.'"

"Then I think you are safe here, or at least as safe as any of us might be."

"Unless Mexico considers us captives."

"Yes. Unless that."

In the waning breezes of the hurricane, *Enigma* was still sailing fairly lively nor'-nor'-west along the curve of Matagorda Bay, in spite of the storm damage. Master Billings' report of water in the hold was remarkably good after what she had been through, the result of the good repair done in Havana. Men were on the pumps, watch on watch, and the water was already down from eighteen inches to eight, so the hull was sound. The rigging needed far more repair. Lines on one side and then the other stretched and strained as the barque rolled from side to side. Even Katrina could hear the difference in their hum, and no seaman aboard missed this.

"Another roll like that and a mast will go." The low, grumbling voice skimmed over the deck to her ears, as did the snappish reply, "So it's a brig we'll be, and what's it to you? We float; that's all that matters. We float."

Enigma was indeed not in imminent danger of sinking. Her crew continued to improve the jury rig of her sails, and Will was aloft as a lookout in spite of the topmasts above him being blown away. In a fair wind, she could stay safely off shore. The shoals, sandbars and rocks of an unknown coast presented a greater danger than the open sea, but, if the wind continued to die, *Enigma* would slide helplessly into them.

CHAPTER 49

MATAGORDA BAY

From the maintop platform, Will hailed Mr. Stephens at the wheel, "The deck there! A settlement. Five points off the l'ward bow. On the rise there beyond the barrier island."

"How big?" shouted Mr. Stephens.

Will studied it. "A village, no more. Docks and vessels, nothing big. Lighters, fishing boats, barges, and a cutter or two."

Mr. Stephens passed the word along, and Captain Peterssen left his breakfast and came on deck.

"The mainmast lookout there," Izak called, directing his voice upward, "do they see us?"

"Sir, not that I can tell, sir," came Will's answer.

"Mr. Stephens," said the captain, "Raise a signal flag: *We wish to communicate.*" The flag, half yellow, half blue, soon flew at the masthead.

Shortly afterward, a faint boom was heard across the water, and a puff of smoke appeared. "On deck there, they see us, sir," Will reported, quite properly, though unnecessarily.

Izak Peterssen slung a spyglass around one shoulder and climbed to the mainmast crosstrees to study the shore for himself. Nothing in the harbor appeared to be a threat. He saw nothing like a fort. The coast looked flooded from the storm, making it hard to say whether there was deep water at all. A long barrier island lay between *Enigma* and the harbor, if it could fairly be called that. A change in color, from the deep turquois of the Caribbean to a paler blue warned of shallowness beyond the barrier islands. It would be impossible to cross without a local pilot, especially now, with the storm bringing in heavy surf and a strong undertow.

However, the inhabitants of this village, probably Mexicans, could see how damaged *Enigma* was. They were unlikely to think her a danger to the town. Instead, they might be salivating at the opportunity to take such a ship and convert her for battle. Or, they might be desperate to hire her or seize her for escape. If the locals wanted *Enigma*, they would have a distance to come, all of it in full view and in reach of *Enigma*'s cannon, before they could even get close. They could not know her current weakness or that most of her powder was wet.

"If this coast is at war," said Niklas in a low voice, "We can be sure of nothing. *Enigma* might be a tempting target."

"Given our weakened state—" Katrina hesitated, and Niklas finished her thought.

"We could be surrounded by a dozen small craft with armed men."

Izak slid down, landed with a thump and gave an order for Thorvald to fire an answering half-charge. "What irony," he said quietly to Mr. Groves, with no idea that Niklas overheard, "if we were now to be taken by small craft."

The boats in this harbor might be small, but they would be fast. *Enigma* could easily outdistance them, given a fair breeze and decent canvas, but as the air continued to fade, she had neither. The only perfectly clear thing was uncertainty. Was the town controlled by Texians or Mexicans? Would they see *Enigma* as friend or foe? Even if they were friendly, could they help? Did this desolate spot have timber or a blacksmith?

The Enigmas needed water and a safe place to make repairs. They also needed translators. Several English-speakers were aboard, though Americans were said to speak a barbaric version. Niklas could be an interpreter in French or German; any of the family could be. And Francesca was the best aboard for Spanish.

The crew had been armed since first light, and gun crews stood at the ready, though it was for show; they would be lucky to have enough powder for a single salvo. *Enigma*'s small corps of marines was on deck as well, adding to the visible count of men, their arms lying discreetly on the deck or hidden on their persons, and their eyes on Niklas, who was once more their commander. To any ordinary eye, they were a pitiful group, a half-dozen half-trained, poorly armed peasants, but they had fought with desperate bravery against *Diamante*, and they had the confidence of that memory to bolster their considerable farmer's muscles. Niklas was surprisingly proud of them. Besides, he had the skills and courage of Thomas Segrave, Hans, and Will to rely on, battle-proven as they now were. As he walked quietly among them, he heard a low rumbling growl coming from Johannes Ackermann.

Katrina and the younger children were below deck with all of the Ackermann women except Francesca, out of sight and crossfire, but not hidden away in the Lady Hole, it being half full of water. On the mainmast platform, Will waited and watched, his pistols now more important than his eyesight. To a careless observer, all looked peaceable.

They had taken soundings all along this barrier island, and Mr. Groves reported a bottom of only three and half fathoms, sandy and shelly. With a floodtide bearing *Enigma* toward even thinner water, Izak gave orders to set an anchor. The anchor's flukes dug into the bottom and held; the curve of thick anchor line straightened, and *Enigma* rode securely at anchor, becalmed, all power gone from her sails.

When at last a boat came from shore, it was a cutter, fast and sleek, whose nameboard read, "*Aeneid.*" Its home port was Bath, Maine, a town whose boat-building yards were legendary. American-built—that was promising—but flying an unknown flag. Niklas stood on the deck with Peterssen and Segrave, his right hand lying casually on the hilt of his sword with the self-assurance of one who has often used a weapon. Several of the largest and most threatening of the crew were clearly visible, among them Hans, Johannes Ackermann, and Erik Thorvald.

"At least," said Niklas in an aside to Hans, "we are not being set upon by a dozen vessels intent on doing damage, no questions asked."

"Aye," said Hans, "but this cutter can approach, learn what it wants to know, then turn and run with a speed we cannot match through waters too shallow for us."

Francesca was there, too, in boy's clothing and with her hair stuffed into a cap. She tapped Niklas's elbow and asked, "They will most likely be speaking Spanish, don't you think?"

"Ja," he said.

"Or French," she said, "la lingua Franca."

"Or island French," said Niklas, recalling Rafael's Haitian. "If it's English, the captain will answer." He was beginning to be annoyed by Francesca's chatter. He had tried to explain the Declaration of Independence to her and Giovanni one recent evening, but neither of them seemed to grasp its importance.

"What if it's a native language?" she asked.

"Anything's possible. I have no idea what Indian villages look like."

"I wish I knew Portuguese," Francesca fretted.

Niklas studied the cutter's occupants. The headman was easy to identify. He stood aft on a small deck in a bicorn hat and an odd uniform: double-breasted dark blue with a gold sash tied, oddly enough, on the left, and with epaulettes—perhaps those of a general? A sword, of course, and black boots. Its peculiarity put him in mind of pirates, although it was not at all flamboyant. Rifles, pistols, and swords would lie at the feet of the sailors, of course, but at least the weapons were not in their hands.

"Hola el bergantin," came the hail, but Izak Peterssen was not falling for that.

"Ahoy, the *Aeneid!* We are *Enigma* out of Bristol," he shot back in English. "Sailing under the British flag as a neutral merchantman."

"Your purpose here?" The headman spoke this time in English.

Izak took a deep breath and told the truth. "A storm blew us here. We need repairs and water."

There was a moment of conference on the cutter as the headman spoke to the man at the tiller. Then the headman turned to Captain Peterssen, grinned, and said, "Welcome to city of Linnville, sir, in the newly independent Republic of Texas!"

Across the deck men cheered, and hearing it down below, the women of *Enigma* breathed a sigh of relief. They may have been willing to fight to the death, but they were tired and bruised, more than one of them with a sling or bandage, the joys of peace apparent to all.

It was not just Izak Peterssen's honest declaration making the cutter's master so friendly. He was Major John Forbes of the Army of Texas and recently Sam Houston's commissary general. The Texans had been studying *Enigma* since she was first sighted, and they had already seen to their relief that the ship was British built, too badly damaged to be a threat, and quite alone. The residents of Linnville were war-torn and flood-weary at the moment, only weeks past the Battle of Coleto. Besides, their town had been founded as a port for the New Orleans trade, and they were traders at heart. If the ship could be made seaworthy, they had goods waiting and travelers eager for passage.

But most important, they had big news the world needed to hear: Texas was free.

CHAPTER 50

THE PROMISED LAND

Ashore again, in a place not even Mr. Groves could tell them about, the Enigmas found themselves among friends. Mr. Elijah Bennett, enterprising village founder, welcomed the ship's passengers and officers to his newly built hotel in Linnville. News of the arrival sped through the miserable wooden shanties making up most of the village, and people lined up to see the ship's doctors, two being such an embarrassment of medical men.

Soon after they landed, a man well dressed in the continental fashion asked to see the Kästners. Apparently, he had heard German being spoken. He introduced himself, Herr Lennart Mueller, as a friend of Johann Ernst, writer of *The America Letters*, and had they read these letters? Niklas and Katrina had, in fact, read several of Johann Ernst's letters. One had been published in an Oldenberg newspaper not far north of Berleburg and passed along to them. Niklas had given the paper to Günter—he winced at the memory—in hopes the Erlinger family, or at least Edzard, might someday follow them to America.

Ernst was now a rich man with more than four thousand acres, Herr Mueller told them, to a softly murmured "ah" from Katrina and significant looks exchanged between the boys.

"Johann Ernst," said Herr Mueller, "was a gardener, an important estate gardener for the Duchy of Oldenberg, and now Stephen Austin—" He paused and explained: "Austin is an empresario, a land developer, who helped win the state's recent war."

"Ah," said Niklas.

"Austin gave Ernst a grant of 4,428 acres to attract his fellow countrymen." Mueller added, with a small bow to Katrina and Amalie, "and countrywomen."

It seemed to them an unimaginable amount of land. Mueller explained that Ernst landed in New Orleans in '31—just five years ago—meaning to go to Missouri, but Texas looked even better.

"Mexico's 1825 law set the price at four cents an acre," said Herr Mueller. "Four cents! And forgave taxes for six years."

The Kästners stared at him in disbelief.

"An oath of loyalty was required," said Herr Mueller, "to Mexico and the Catholic church, but now that's kaput. Who knows what else will change? Sometime soon, the Republic of Texas will write new laws." He looked meaningfully at them and added, "They will surely set new prices, but until then—"

Mueller called Texas a land without winter, like Sicily, but with game, fish, and fertile land to be had for little more than a surveyor's fee. "Besides," said Herr Mueller in a voice lowered for their ears only, "there may be a German colony to come out of this settlement. Think of it—a colony in America could change everything for the Fatherland. Wealth and liberty go hand in hand."

Niklas said nothing in reply, but his doubt must have shown on his face, because Lennart Mueller sputtered as he went on: "It will only require pushing the natives west, which should not be difficult. We could open America for German colonies, maybe a new German state."

"I will consider your proposal, Herr Mueller," Niklas said.

As they turned to go, Katrina said in a low voice, "Four cents an acre! Herr Ernst was in New Orleans and decided here was better." It had not escaped Katrina's attention that the very long barrier islands on Matagorda Bay seemed to have beaches like Havana's.

Later, as they stood by a stack of trunks and bags to carry to their hotel rooms, Lennart Mueller looked longingly at Niklas's violin case. "I myself do not play," he said, "But, oh, to hear that sweet sound again, once more before I die!"

Niklas agreed to play for him once supper was finished. The moment arrived, and they all waited for the violin to be unpacked and tuned. Soon the music transported them, perhaps Niklas most of all. Hans tucked Lisette in the crook of one arm and Jakob in the other, twirling them around, the little children shrieking in delight, while Will and Amalie spun even faster. Francesca and Giovanni were especially graceful on the dance floor. Even Katrina was on her feet, dancing with Izak Peterssen. Sailors and ship's officers and Texas Army soldiers and townspeople seized the moment and filled the little dance floor.

When he finished a particularly energetic piece, Niklas could see the dancers were near collapse. He let a long moment of silence fill the room, but before conversation could rise from an ongoing flutter to a din, he lifted his violin again, and with it whispering along a single note, he began the last piece, which Katrina knew to be his favorite, *Napoleon Crossing the Alps*. People hushed each other so they could catch each soft suggestion.

As the tempo picked up, they found dancing irresistible, no matter how rubbery their legs or how breathless they were. And when, moments later, the violin rose to a concluding crescendo and then a wonderful, shocking end, the children crumpled all about Niklas and Katrina in delight, to smiles and clapping from every nook and cranny in and out of the room, people smiling around doors and cheering in from the windows.

Niklas had been lost in the music and looked up now in surprise, seeing everyone within earshot of his violin gathered to listen, and now he realized he had heard the stomping of boots and the soft thudding of moccasins and bare feet. People had been dancing outside, too! Katrina smiled up at Niklas in pride. She saw the little children laughing and begging Hans for more and Franci in Francesca's arms with Giovani at her side. Thomas Segrave bowed to Amalie. They had apparently danced together, which did not please Katrina. Segrave may have saved Amalie from a bad fall, and he may be rich and cultured, but he was British nevertheless.

Lennart Mueller thanked Niklas profusely and begged him again to join the German colony in Texas, "such talent and culture, exactly what we need. Schöne Musik, beautiful music! It was the most satisfactory evening," Mueller said, "So zufriedenstellend, most satisfactory. It does the heart good."

Niklas bowed, smiled, and demurred.

Neither Niklas nor Katrina was surprised the next day by a visit from Major Forbes. He was clearly interested in the whole family: three strong men, one of whom could bring a very welcome level of military training to the war-worn, infant Texas cavalry, and three handsome females in a new country with far more men than women.

"How strange," Katrina said, "to be considered valuable simply for being here and alive."

"Ja. Although I suspect he's more interested in my knowing the Drey Wunder of German sword fighting, than in me."

Katrina said nothing, but privately, she thought she and Amalie might interest Major Forbes even more.

Forbes was an Irishman like John Joseph Linn, the founder of Linnville, who came to join Martín De León's 1829 colony. De León's Spanish family still hobnobbed with the royals of Europe, but the man himself had died of cholera in '33, a great loss for his Mexican colony. Major Forbes introduced George Erath, who spoke German with an Austrian accent that set Katrina's teeth on edge.

"Texas was a land rush of wondrous proportions," George Erath said, "and even I, a tanner's son from Vienna, now own a league and a labor of land."

Erath told them he had arrived in New Orleans in 1832 and traveled to Cincinnati and then Mobile, Alabama, "where I would be a tanner still if I had not come on to Texas. I was two years at Vienna's Polytechnic Institute, so I became a surveyor in Texas."

Listening, Katrina worried about finding a school so fine for Will. With their traveling days almost over, she wondered how much his travel education had taught him. *Whatever else it has included, it has not improved his Latin, Greek or mathematics,* she thought. She did not notice with what homesickness George Erath glanced at her and Amalie, remembering his own mother and sisters in Vienna.

Then George Erath shook himself and told them about the Battle of San Jacinto, where Santa Anna surrendered and which gained independence for the new Texas. Erath said Forbes was one of the four *alcaldes,* or mayors, of Victoria, just upriver, and the owner of warehouses in Linnville.

Forbes said, "I move cotton, wool, pecans, hazelnuts, and mustang grape wine from the interior of Texas to New Orleans, so I must say, my warehouses are sweeter smelling than Linnville's others, the ones for cattle, hides, tallow, and horns."

It was that other trade, and its origins, however, intriguing Niklas. He wanted to see a Texas rancho, and Mr. Bennett wanted to encourage his interest. He could make such arrangements, he said, and after breakfast, he introduced them to young Juan José De León.

"He's a nephew of Plácido Benavides," said Mr. Bennett, at which Juan José looked abashed and the Kästners looked mystified. "One of the heroes of the recent war," he explained. "And owner of the big ranchero near Victoria, along with the heirs of Martín De León."

"Ah," said Niklas.

"I'm riding home tomorrow," Juan José said. "Would you like to accompany me? I'm going to the rancho at Zorillo Creek, part of the twenty-two thousand acres my family owns."

Katrina's eyebrows rose at the astounding size of the ranch. She had been amazed at four thousand acres, and now this young man before her spoke of twenty-two thousand acres! Juan José was dressed decently for a cowboy, but he wore nothing fancy. *In Texas,* thought Katrina, *wealth apparently does not mean a gold-plated saddle or a jeweled collar or a retinue of slaves.*

"In the Germanies," she said, "that would be a principality."

"Or maybe two," agreed Niklas.

"Oh, yes, ranchos are big," said Juan José. "The Franciscans got them started near a hundred years ago, to support their missionary work." He crossed himself. "Then peace with the Apache came, and impresarios, like my grandfather, started filling in between missions."

"I don't mean to be impertinent," asked Niklas, "but why are the ranchos so big?"

Juan José smiled as he said, "Grass is sparse, and land grants is free, so the ranchos grew big." He saw the questioning look on Katrina's face and admitted, "And ours is bigger than some. Well, the biggest, I think."

"Is all this your land?" she asked, waving a hand about.

Juan José De León nodded. "Pretty much. Linnville was in the Spanish province of Santander, and I suppose it still is, until the new republic says different."

"How far a ride are we talking about?" asked Niklas.

"Not far," said Juan José, "It's about thirty miles to the town of Victoria, settled in 1748. But our part of the ranch is by Zorillo Creek, as runs down toward Matagorda Bay, and the ranch house is a morning's ride."

After he left, Katrina said to Niklas, "Maybe this Texas is the promised land."

"Maybe. But Herr Mueller said pushing the Comanches and Apaches off their homeland would be easy. I have seen with my own eyes that it is not, no matter poor and benighted a people may be."

Katrina nodded but was mystified. And then she understood, "Oh, you mean Russia!"

"Yes." He was annoyed that it took her a moment to understand. "I have seen as few others have how hard people will fight for their homeland. Also, it's nonsense to say the politics of Germany would improve if it possessed colonies."

"Yes. And might not a German colony have Waterloo veterans?"

"Indeed. Would a revolutionary be welcome? I don't know."

"But I don't think we have to join a colony," Katrina said, "to buy this four-cent land." They left it at that.

CHAPTER 51

THIS TATTOOED TRIBE

Katrina and Amalie could not help but watch the strangest people they had ever seen. A young Indian woman waited with her son on the wide plank porch of the Bennett hotel. She played with her son, a boy about Jakob's age, almost naked. Their game involved tossing stones into a maze she had scratched into the dirt. Katrina knew Jakob longed to join the Indian boy, but instead, he clung with one hand to her skirts. In the other hand was Herr Kuschelbär, dangling by an ear. At intervals, whether the Indian child or mother appeared to win their game or to lose it, they dissolved into muffled giggles.

The Indian woman wore a pale deerskin skirt—scandalously short, barely past her knees—and a tunic embroidered in a wide curve from shoulder to shoulder with stones or seeds or shells in turquoise, orange and white, and multiple necklaces of the same beads, among them a silver crucifix. Swirls of white wool embroidery marched down each sleeve with little balls interspersed.

"A crucifix?" Amalie whispered. She was astonished.

"And French knots?"

A triangle of tattooing decorated the woman's forehead, above which her hair was parted into two long, thick, lustrous braids. Katrina blinked hard: the mother and child's head were oddly flattened.

Amalie had noticed it, too. "Is this head shape natural to American Indians or a strange affectation?"

"Or an affliction?" Katrina could only shake her head. When she turned to speak to Amalie, she thought she saw the other woman lift her eyes from the child and study her. Presently a tall, muscular man, a fine specimen of a man, heavily tattooed and with a long bow slung across his back, came out of the hotel, looked hard at the two European women and said two or three unintelligible words.

Just then, Niklas came across the wide porch with Will and hailed Katrina. The Indians turned, the warrior stiffening as he studied Niklas's pattern of scars. To this tattooed tribe, Katrina supposed such markings had meaning. Then the warrior apparently decided they did not. He nodded to Niklas, said "Hola, Señor," and strode away. The Indian woman rose effortlessly and followed, the child in her footsteps and skipping to keep up, their bare feet raising puffs of dust but making no sound.

Mrs. Bennett wiped her hands on her apron as she came to the doorway. She was a short, fat woman with white hair, a ready smile and a nose remarkable for a large mole. She radiated motherliness.

"Karankawa," she said, shoving up her white cotton sleeves. "Those three are from the Ebahamo village down the coast. White Bear, he's is a good 'un, fought on our side in the war against Santa Anna, and though there's only a few of them to be had, they are mostly big strapping fellows like him, as good as two of our own." She lowered her voice as she said this last part, woman to woman, not to be disloyal.

"She was wearing a crucifix!" Amalie exclaimed. Neither she nor Katrina could know they had seen three of the very last of the Karankawa, including a little boy who would become a famous warrior before he was killed in the massacre that would wipe out the curious tribe.

"Oh, yes, some is Christian. The mission priests are wild for converting them," Mrs. Bennett said. "But others are true wicked heathens, actual cannibals as like to eat you up as not."

Katrina remembered the man's hard look and gagged. Mrs. Bennett apologized, and Amalie took her mother's arm to steady her.

"Let's get her a cup of tea," Mrs. Bennett said, "and talk of anything else." She had some calico, she said; Mr. Bennett brought it from New Orleans, the Paris of the New World, the Queen City, a lovely blue calico, she would show them, she said.

That night, as Katrina fell asleep in a small, dark room tucked under an eave, the faces of the Karankawa family rose up before her, rushed forward and then shattered like glass, the parents impassive, the boy's mouth open in a soundless scream. Katrina woke with a gasp, and Niklas stirred and asked, "Are you all right?"

"Ja." She thought a moment and said, "I didn't expect this place to be so primitive."

"No. But what could we know of all this?"

In a moment he was snoring again. She saw his profile against the moonlight, remembered the strains of his violin, and forgave him everything. *He was right: what could they know of all this? Of all the places in the world to be!*

A cloud covered the moon, and she was unable to make out anything until heat lightning broke across the sky and she glimpsed the shape of Jakob's skull in his makeshift crib. As she watched and listened, he cried out a little without waking.

The next morning, with the boys on the carpentry crew and Amalie looking after the little ones, Niklas and Katrina set out with young Juan José De León, who, as it turned out, was a pleasant, talkative guide. He took care to lead them along the easiest route through the swamps and marshes feeding the bay and then into the scrub brush and past broad stands of post oak trees lining the creeks.

At Juan José's insistence, they went well-armed. Besides the recent war and the possibility of a flare-up, Karankawa, Tonkawa, and Comanche lived all around the bay, the last of these, at least, notorious for savagery. Before they left Linnville's coastal region, Niklas saw ruins along a distant shore and asked about them.

"Oh, that's el Nuestra Señora de Loreto de la Bahía Presidio, the Bahía Presidio, built on La Salle's fort," said Juan.

"Here?" asked Niklas. "Of all this long coast, we happened to land where La Salle did?"

"Sí," said Juan, shrugging his shoulders. "Matagorda Bay is a natural harbor, an obvious choice."

"For us," Katrina said, "it was where we ran out of wind and water."

Niklas asked, "The French explorer La Salle landed about two hundred colonists here—was it 1685, perhaps?"

Juan José laughed. "Before my time, that's for sure!" A glance at Niklas's unsmiling face subdued him. "A long time ago, anyway. But after La Salle left, the rest mostly starved, and then they were finished off in a massacre. There's no Frenchmen left from that time."

"A massacre," Katrina said. "Which tribe was it, Juan José?"

"The Karankawa, same as still live here and are probably watching us at this moment," Juan José said, looking around.

Katrina looked with raised eyebrows at Niklas. "Perhaps we shouldn't have left town."

"Oh, Señora," said Juan José, "they are pretty much tame now. Except the Comanches."

"One of the boys escaped the massacre, didn't he?" Niklas asked.

"Not exactly. He was taken captive. Several were captured and then rescued. One of them," Juan José continued, "wrote about it."

"Yes, I read his account."

"The Karankawa were cannibals or maybe still are," said Juan José, "and the different tribes are as likely to hate each other as us and always killing and then making up with each other. But the treaty Mr. Linn got them to sign last fall made the folks in Linnville feel a lot safer."

"Will we pass a village?" Katrina asked, wanting to turn the conversation away from cannibalism. "Or perhaps see warriors hunting buffalo?"

"Tener cuidado con lo que deseas," warned Juan José, and Niklas translated: "Be careful what you wish for."

Presently, however, they did see an amazing sight—a herd of lean cattle with immensely wide horns, six feet from tip to tip of the horns, and the bulls with the humps of their thick necks more fearsome yet.

"I saw cattle like this in Spain," said Niklas.

Juan José looked him with curiosity. "Tell me about Spain."

"It's a country like any other," Niklas said. "Tell me about the cattle."

"Longhorns," Juan José said, "run wild here, and an enterprising rancher can pick up as many as he dares."

"They are not owned?" Katrina asked in amazement.

"Well, no Señora, they ain't," he said, "at least I don't think so." Juan José stood in his stirrups and squinted. "Nope, I don't see our brand. But branded or not, they ain't exactly tame." He laughed. "If anything threatens them, man or wolf, they make a circle around the calves, horns out, and then it takes some ingenuity and grit to get them corralled and fed up."

"How strange!" was all Katrina could say. She wondered how many more strange treasures America might offer up for free.

"And wonderful," said Niklas. "Naturally, Americans are rich. Free land. Free cattle."

"The Indians will eat anything, but they prefer buffalo. And it ain't one bit easy to drive them to all the ways to New Orleans."

They rode in silence for a long while, and then Juan José looked at Niklas and asked, "Is it true what they say, Señor, that you were with Napoleon in Russia?"

"It is. Why do you ask?" Niklas squinted at the sky to hide the suspicion bubbling up: *How had this boy heard of it?*

"The Alamo, Señor. There was a veteran of the Russia campaign at the Alamo, one Moses Rose. Do you know him? Real name of Louie, only called Moses because he was so old."

Niklas demurred: "It was a big army."

"Oh, certainly, Señor. This Moses Rose, anyway, survived the Alamo attack. When Captain Travis drew a line in the dirt and asked, 'Does anyone want to leave?' Moses Rose stepped over. Only Moses Rose. Said he had faced death too often to do it again."

"This man, he was a coward?" Niklas spoke cautiously.

"Oh no, Señor, I would never say so, Señor! He fought bravely all along, and Travis let him go with no hard feelings. He was a friend of Jim Bowie's—maybe that helped. Turned out, the rest were all killed." Juan José paused. "Don't know where Moses Rose might be now, but I expect you might run into him, if you stay in Texas."

If we stay in Texas! Katrina thought. *But it is so very different from Berleburg. Flat, gray, and primitive.*

The De León ranch house was a long, low edifice visible from a distance. It took time to approach, and as they got closer, they could see it was as much fort as house. It had high walls and only a single, dark, carved wooden door with a smaller door cut into it for everyday use.

"Was it built as a fort against the Mexican army?" Niklas asked.

"No, Señor. It was built against Indian attack, long before the war. My uncle who owns it, Plácido Benavides, was a hero of the war. He fought in many battles and led a regiment of settlers. My family are Texans now, all of us!"

"It's not really a different idea from the castles on the Rhine. In a few years, you may add towers and battlements and ramparts and moats."

"Ramparts? And moats?" laughed Juan José.

The compound seemed too quiet to Niklas, and he commented on it.

"A big group has departed for New Orleans, Señor, something to do with deeds. They went overland."

Katrina looked meaningfully at Niklas, but he shook his head. Tired as they might be of life aboard, their passage was paid to New Orleans, and if anyone knew the pain of traveling overland, it was Niklas. Besides, a land trip would mean buying horses and wagons and hiring guides, at least.

"Overland is a long, weary trip in the best of times," said Juan José, as if confirming Niklas's opinion, "but until your ship arrived, it was the only way."

As they approached the buildings, a pretty young woman pushed open the door-within-a-door and came running toward them, her face lit with happiness.

"Mi hermana," Juan José explained with a smile, as he swung down from the saddle.

"His sister," Niklas translated for Katrina.

"Bienvenido a nuestra casa!" Juan José's sister exclaimed, "Welcome to our home." In the glow of these happy, handsome young people, Niklas and Katrina enjoyed a dinner of beef and beans and admired the substantial De León compound. Like Juan José himself, they were blessedly unaware of the family's future.

CHAPTER 52

INDEED, SIR

While her parents were gone, Amalie had a wonderful afternoon, all because of Jakob. If she had not been racing through the Bennetts' store after him, with Lisette and Franci running after her, giggling wildly, and if Jakob had not turned a corner at top speed, he would not have run into the Englishman. However it had happened, Amalie thought it was the loveliest encounter.

"Whoa, son," Thomas said, and scooped up Jakob. She heard his voice for one instant before she rounded the corner and almost ran into him herself. She stopped just in time, and Lisette and Franci piled up into her, still laughing at the mischievousness of the little boy.

"Oh, do stop, Jakob," Lisette ordered, and then she saw the dreaded Englishman. "Oh, sir! You have him!"

"Yes, I do have him," Thomas said, and he look sternly at Jakob and asked the child, "Are you going to behave for your sisters now? They can't run after you all day, you know, so take pity on them."

Jakob looked abashed for a moment and put his head down on the man's shoulder, and then he began to wiggle.

Thomas set the boy down in front of Lisette, deftly reaching around Amalie to do so. "You are to walk, I say walk, not run, with your sister, back that way." He waved off to one side, so Lisette took one of Jakob's hands and Franci took the other. They turned the boy as the Englishman had directed and walked off that way.

"I do so apologize, sir," Amalie said, smiling up at Thomas. She swiped the back of her hand across her forehead and wished she were not quite so warm from running after Jakob. The memory of being in Thomas's arms while her Papa played the violin nearly made her faint, but she breathed in deeply. Much later, she would tell her mother, "I was determined not to faint away and miss this serendipitous meeting."

Thomas was quietly studying her face. She was already pink from exertion, and now she blushed, suddenly aware of a tendril of hair that had escaped her bonnet. She reached up and tucked it in. He turned and bowed ever so slightly, extending his elbow to her. She lay a small hand on his arm, and they walked in stately silence through the door and out to the Bennetts' wide porch. He guided her a distance from the door to a shady spot by the railing.

We are quite alone, she thought with a thrill, but it was not true. She did not see Mrs. Bennett moving silently to the end of the long counter where she could watch them through the open doorway. It was not a gossip's curiosity but something more serious and more maternal.

"I have a son about your Jakob's age," Thomas said without preliminaries, and she thought her legs would buckle. "In England. Your little brother makes my heart ache." He saw the stricken look on her face, and was surprised to understand it. It was as if she were transparent, and he could see straight through to her deepest feelings. She had lifted her hand from where it lay on his arm, and he placed his on top of it, settling hers again, and gently reminded her, "My son's mother died at his birth."

"Oh," she said, "oh, my, oh." She remembered her friend Hetta in Berleburg who was afraid of exactly that: one pregnancy and death. Then she remembered her manners. "I am so sorry. Please accept my condolences."

"It was four years ago, now, though never long enough." He let some respectful time elapse. "Did you leave someone…important…when your family left Europe?"

She looked down shyly and thought of Henrik Laufenberg, her childhood sweetheart, who now struck her as the most insignificant puppy love. "No," she said, "only friends."

There was another pause, after which Thomas spoke with studied casualness: "Is your father thinking of staying here, in Texas, our happy accidental landing?"

She was surprised at this. "I'm not sure, sir. Are you staying here?"

He smiled. "I have goods to deliver to New Orleans. We sail in a few days. But," he said, at the look on her face, "I own a ship. I can take *Enigma* anywhere, including back to—" he waved an arm at the town, "Linnville. Or wherever you are."

"Sir!" she said, blushing again.

"Forgive me if I have been forward," he said, and then he changed the subject: "I admire your love for the children."

"They are a delight to me, most of the time."

"We have that in common, then," he laughed, "a delight in children, most of the time." He took her hand from his arm and lifted it to his lips and kissed it. "I hope it is one of many shared interests we shall discover over time."

"Indeed, sir," she said. She watched as he bowed and walked away, admiring everything about him, the strength in his arms and shoulders, the set of his jaw, the energy in each footfall. Her hand was tingling where he had kissed it.

Inside, Mrs. Bennett retreated to her usual place in the center of the long counter. A moment later, when Amalie danced past and nodded, her cheeks were pinker than usual and her smile irrepressible. She had no idea how much her joy revealed. This was the moment when Mrs. Bennett was persuaded that she must report the event to Katrina, brief, innocent, and proper as it had appeared.

Out at a nearby creek, Hans and Will regretted being part of the carpenter's crew. They suffered from Texas heat and humidity, and besides, the first task of the day was to whack the grassy shores free of snakes. Yellow pine logs had been floated to the coast, and when these were shaped into spars, they were raised into place under the guidance of Izak Peterssen and Richard Billings. The raising was an amazing maneuver watched by almost all of Linnville's two hundred souls, even though it meant trekking up a hillside overlooking the one deep water inlet.

In the end, it was the Ackermanns and Francesca Lenzini who stayed in Texas, talked into it not so much by Forbes or Mueller, but by Francesca herself. Katrina did not know whether "four cents an acre" or "like Sicily" was more convincing to her friend.

"Herr Mueller told us how expensive New Orleans is," said Francesca, "and my Ackermann cousins can ill afford more delay. Half the spring is lost."

"They need to sow crops," agreed Katrina.

Going off with them was Giovanni, the Italian sailor who had become Francesca's dear friend and a precious link to her past. They were packing a covered wagon for the long trek to Ernst's four thousand acres, the wagon pulled by longhorns.

Katrina was surprised. "We saw them wild and didn't know they could be driven."

"They can even be trained to the saddle, I'm told," said Francesca. "They're smart as a dog, it's said, so I'm not sure what to watch out for."

Niklas and Katrina bade the Ackermanns good-bye with genuine regret. Katrina already missed a true friend, and Niklas was sorry to see Johannes Ackermann's strength go. Besides, they knew Lisette would lose her only friend.

Francesca was apologetic. "We lack your resources. I have a little money left, but my cousins have nothing but their strong backs. We voted," she said with pride. "Most felt, with so little, it's wiser to be in a colony that will feed us through the coming winter."

"Perhaps Texas does not have a winter."

"Aye," she agreed, "like Sicily." Katrina could hear the homesickness in her voice.

"If worse comes to worse," said Niklas, "you can sail to New Orleans."

"Or go overland," Katrina pressed a muslin-wrapped gift into Francesca's hands, a wool shawl from Paisley. "Maybe this will help if it's ever chilly here."

Francesca peeked at it, touched the softness of it, and restored it to the safety of its muslin wrapping. She smiled and gave Katrina a kiss on each cheek. "It's beautiful! I will never forget you, my dear friend." Her eyes were bright with tears.

CHAPTER 53

PERFECTLY SUBLIME

Niklas had purchased two large bales of tanned hides, but after tasting the local mustang wine, he decided it was better left in Texas. They had Mr. Bennett's lovely blue calico packed, and at Katrina's insistence, Hans loaded a barrel of pecans. She had never seen this sweet nut available in such quantity or so cheaply. In Texas the trees grew wild, their delights to be had for the picking and shelling. As a baker, she could hardly wait to explore the possibilities: pecan shortbread, pecan sweet rolls, pecan pie, pecan bread, toasted pecans with cinnamon and sugar. Amalie longed to replicate the fried chicken with pecans and honey Mrs. Bennett had served.

Niklas looked askance at this quantity: "Perhaps a sack would do?"

"It would not," Katrina said.

Herr Mueller, there to see them off, asked them to carry a few letters to New Orleans for him. He also gave them an introduction to a German friend, one Karl Schneider, an émigré Bavarian, a resident of New Orleans. "Karl is rising quickly to fame as a brilliant banker, and like you, he's a violinist." He gave them a second letter of introduction to Samuel Hermann. "Herr Hermann is a German immigrant, a Jew before he married a Catholic girl. He's one of the richest men in New Orleans." Herr Mueller handed his letters to Niklas but did not quite release his hold on them.

"I could always send them with someone else," he said, with a wave toward *Enigma*. He smiled, "If you've come to your senses."

"I'll be the first to admit, you make Texas sound very attractive. And you have persuaded the Ackermanns."

"We won't forget Texas," Katrina added, "or Linnville, especially if Texas lives up to its promise and proves to be a republic."

In the end, Herr Mueller bowed to Katrina, shook Niklas's hand vigorously, and told them to go straight to Karl when they landed. "There are tricksters—false German agents— at every port. Well, not here," he admitted, gesturing to tiny Linnville, "where I'm the only German but Erath!"

He grinned again. "But everywhere else, New York, Baltimore, New Orleans, even Cincinnati! Be wary!"

Izak Peterssen took aboard a local army captain, a Major Slattery, an Irishman who came to fight for Texas and was now eager to return home and perfectly happy to be paid for doing so as the captain's local guide. The rest of steerage was quickly filled with Louisiana volunteers, Cajun French, mostly, although it was hard to tell, since even the Irish New Orleanais spoke French. These included several officers of the Texan Revolutionary Army. Two peace treaties signed at Velasco on May 14 gave them the confidence to move on.

Among the new passengers were merchants who filled the hold with stores of beef, wool, hides, and pecans. There was also an emissary from the new Texas government with orders to re-supply the rapidly dwindling army with rifles and ammunition in case fighting should erupt again.

Niklas and Katrina had some things to stow, and when they came back on deck, *Enigma* had already made sail, inner and outer jibs sheeted home and the minute, doomed frontier settlement quickly falling astern. Above, a clear sky brought a fresh breeze, a true tonic after the hot, humid air of Linnville. Off the bow, dolphins played, and to the south a flock of snowy egrets skimmed the surface, their long black bills and legs penciled against the pale sky.

All of the family, especially Hans, looked back with some regret as the long barrier islands of Matagorda Bay dropped into the distance, but in the end, they agreed with Niklas: "We left a country we love because it was politically confused, dangerous, and poor twenty years after a war. What is the wisdom of settling in a strange country having just concluded a war and mayhap back in battle any day?"

Katrina had added very quietly, "Not to mention the savages."

Out of Matagorda Bay they had perfectly sublime weather with blue skies, soft breezes, and an afternoon shower to cool and clean the air. There was none of the treachery of hurricanes, but instead, a most welcome following sea whose great swells pushed *Enigma* gently across, fine fresh fish aplenty to be taken over the side, with never a black night when all hands were called, pitched from their hammocks to face shrieking winds and horizontal rain.

The waters were alive, the whales of the Atlantic replaced with leaping dolphins or the ominous fins of sharks. The Louisiana men hung out their fishing lines whenever they could, bringing aboard groupers and amberjacks to add to the table fare and once a spectacular blue espadon voilier, a sailfish, which on the plate, proved to be tough. Thomas Segrave, a fishing enthusiast, made fast friends of these fishermen. They often waved to broad-beamed fishing boats and small trading brigs and sloops, evidence of the richness of the waters and the proximity of the coast.

During five hundred miles of sailing from Matagorda Bay and across the Gulf of Mexico, they were never far from land.

"These waters are thin," so Mr. Groves said, and with that in mind, *Enigma* sailed as far out as she could and still keep an eye on the coast, there being no one aboard, not even Mr. Groves, who could be trusted with dead reckoning in these waters. Wherever they sailed, in their wake squawked gulls and terns and shearwaters and cormorants and gannets and boobies. Soaring far above they saw the Magnificent Frigatebird.

"Really, that is the species' name," Major Slattery told them, "though 'magnificent' is also a fair description."

Niklas looked at him with new appreciation. "How do you come to know so much about this remote part of the world, sir?"

He laughed. "I don't think of it as remote! I grew up hereabouts. My family escaped the Éirí Amach, the 1798 Rising in Ireland." He looked closely at Niklas to see if he would be repulsed to be in the company of a rebel.

Niklas was not. "The Irish struggles inspire the German resistance even today." Then his face fell as he recalled Günter reciting the Irish loyalty oath in the tavern.

Major Slattery saw this and asked, rather obliquely, "Do I detect a military bearing, sir?"

"Yes," said Niklas, surprising himself and Katrina. "I served with Napoleon. In the cavalry, the Chevau-Léger. The Peninsular Wars, Egypt, Russia, Elba and Waterloo." He did not remember a time when he had answered so openly.

Major Slattery let out a long, low whistle. "That's quite a record, sir."

"It is," admitted Niklas, a smile playing about his lips. He happened to be holding Katrina's hand, and now he squeezed it. He knew without looking at her that she was smiling. "Enough of such talk," he said as he pointed to a black bird in *Enigma*'s wake: "Now, what's that one?

"Ah," said Slattery, "that's called a water turkey." He stuck his finger in his mouth, and held it up to test the breeze. "Sou-sou-west," he declared, "perfect for New Orleans."

The prevailing wind and the loop current swept *Enigma* to the east, and the air was warm, pleasant, and fresh, as if the Gulf of Mexico were apologizing for its hurricane and urging them to put it out of their minds.

CHAPTER 54

MISSISSIPPI DELTA

Far out in the poorly charted waters of the Gulf of Mexico, long streaks of mud marred the clear turquoise waters, marking strips of crosswise current. River current. Izak Peterssen wisely followed the widest of these strips toward what he hoped would be the mouth of the Mississippi. When it became clear this was indeed river current, Mr. Groves said they might be only a few broad reaches from the mouth of the river, if they could make it out.

"It's a delta," he said, holding up his hand with fingers outspread, "with five or so big currents, and more small ones than I—or anyone—can count."

Enigma was lucky, though, and before long she did a touch-and-go at La Balize on San Carlos Island to pick up a river pilot and sail onward through the amazingly wide and seemingly endless delta. Along a sand-fringed island to the east lay a sign of danger clear and present: the wreck of a sailing ship, the tips of its masts still visible above the waves, tilted crazily. As the delta channel became more defined, the current strengthened and sandbars threatened.

The pilot told Izak Peterssen and Mr. Groves, "No one can know where sandbars are from day to day. Your crew has to be at the ready to change sails or fend off. Don't sail at night without a full moon." He recommended a two-boat river crew, and Izak agreed to it. At the pilot's signal, four strong men came out rowing a lighter, equipped with pikes, boathooks, and oars. They would accompany *Enigma*, which put down its own boat and crew. The boats were tied to the ship to guide and pull her. Thomas Segrave could do nothing but sigh, and Niklas could only imagine the expense, one of many unexpected.

Seeing this, Izak nudged Thomas in the ribs: "Remember the riches of the *Diamante*."

Katrina whispered to Niklas, "Imagine the wealth needed to float this ship under any circumstances. Much delayed and twice rebuilt, will there still be a profit?"

Niklas shrugged. "I have no idea. But even an owner must feel rewarded to be here alive."

The river was broad, but as *Enigma* began to run up the delta, life pushed in all around, swimming below in muddy water, crawling along verdant shores, and filling the humid air with everything from whooping cranes with seven-foot wing spans to no-see-um gnats that flew up the nose and attacked the eyes and burrowed into the ears. After a day of this, Jakob screamed in frustration, rubbing his ears. As Katrina picked him up, swatting all around, Amalie ran for a piece of lace. Soon, with lace draped over him, the child fell asleep in Katrina's arms. After a little while, she handed him to Niklas, who lowered him onto a deck chair so gently he did not wake. He had been a good little boy, but he was, after all, not yet five.

Along the shore, they saw alligators, like knobby floating logs, perfectly still, perfectly treacherous. Once, while Katrina stared at an alligator slipping into the water, a long branch dropped almost on top of it with such grace that she realized it was not a branch but a snake. She shuddered at the size of it and was glad *Enigma* was a good distance from shore.

"And this is only May," Niklas said to her, as sweat dripped down his spine. He had loosened his shirt collar as much as was decent. Neither of them had imagined heat like this. With New Orleans sure to appear one of these days, and after ice storms, doldrums, pirates, hurricanes and savages, they did not wish to voice the slightest ingratitude. In fact, they were filled with thankfulness to be so close at last to America itself. This was the United States on either shore, Niklas said, though mostly uninhabited jungle and recently French and before that, Spanish, and before that, French again for several hundred years.

Mr. Groves told them, "Should be only eight or nine days to the city, even with the current against us, nothing at all compared to the long, long voyage already behind us."

Katrina fanned herself as they watched the trees go by, massive trunks with their feet in the water and drooping branches hung with long, gray tassels and now celebrating summer with bright clusters at the tips. "Are those new needles or perhaps green flowers?" she asked.

"I could not say about that, ma'am, though the tree is cypress, and the gray beards are called 'Spanish moss.'"

Soaring to a hundred feet or more into the sky, the trees dwarfed petty concerns. Here and there, in swampy coves, patches of vegetation were lit by the bright white of water lilies.

"Niklas," asked Katrina, "have you ever seen a place like this?"

"No," he said. "It's swampland, I suppose."

"This is dark, tangled and hostile."

"A jungle," he agreed, "strangely crowded with verdure, creeping things, and insects."

"Yes. And birds. The birdsong alone forms a canopy over the river. But if we are in America, where are the people? Even at La Balize, there were only a few wretched fishermen." She swatted at a mosquito.

"Ja, the air teems with life and fairly drips, unlike anywhere else."

By evening, when they were deep into swamp, they heard the first of the gators roar. The whole family was in their cabin at the time. Niklas grabbed Hans and Will and went to ask whether *Enigma* was under attack.

A few minutes later, they returned. "It's just an alligator," he said, shooing the boys in and closing the cabin door. "But you should see the swamp at night. Fog. Mr. Groves says we'll likely hear the gators all night." Almost immediately they heard another. Jakob decided it was safer on Amalie's lap, and Lisette scrunched up by them.

"Donnerwetter!" Katrina said. Before dawn, they had another alligator surprise. When the creatures began feeding, their huge jaws snapped closed with a bang almost like a pistol shot.

"First they roar," Katrina moaned. "And now this." She had been charmed yesterday by a bullfrog's guttural chant, startled by the screech of a heron, and oddly comforted by the distant hammering of what Mr. Groves called a Lord God Bird. But the scream of a panther at dusk made her cringe, and now a night of roaring alligators had been the last straw.

Amalie patted her mother's shoulder. "At least Lisette and Jakob slept through most of it." Her own face was shadowed with exhaustion.

By mid-morning, Katrina stood on deck, shading her eyes, staring at a strange pair of towers almost overgrown.

Major Slattery greeted her. "Morning, ma'am. Curious, ain't they?"

"Oh, yes! Are they part of New Orleans?"

"No, ma'am," said the man with Major Slattery, another Texan army officer, Lieutenant René Gravier. "Those were built by the Bayogoula. 'Bayou people' the Choctaws called them. Monsieur d'Iberville met the Bayogoula. When would that have been, Slattery?"

"Hmm, a hundred years ago, maybe?" said Slattery.

"Likely more than that," Gravier said. "Anyway, the Bayogoulas provisioned d'Iberville and his men for the voyage upstream. He said it was a friendly village of two clans and two temples, but what they worshipped!" Slattery shook his head in disapproval.

Katrina looked appropriately mystified, and René Gravier exclaimed, "The possum! Bayogoula worshiped the possum! Bears, wolves and birds, too, but the possum was their particular god."

"I believe the natives of Cuba, the Taíno, worshipped the frog," Katrina said uncertainly. A whittled frog in a Habanero shop had been explained that way. "Pray tell, what's a possum?"

"A nasty gray thing," said Slattery, gesturing its size. "Like a giant rat. Out to here with its tail."

"Does this tribe still live here?" Katrina stared hard at the undergrowth, trying to make out a figure of a man or woman.

"Well, now, that's the surprise," Gravier said. "Not long after d'Iberville called them 'friendly,' one Bayogoula clan murdered the other."

"Oui," Slattery said, "and then the murderers welcomed in the Tonica tribe, and like in Troy, the guests murdered their hosts."

"Mon Dieu!" Katrina said.

"Smallpox may have played a part, too, and maybe cholera," René Gravier admitted, "but today, not a Bayogoula man, woman or child exists. The savages on the river today are the ones from Barataria."

"What?" Katrina asked, alarmed.

"The pirate stronghold," he said. "Jean Lafitte and his gang."

"Lafitte's long dead," Slattery scoffed. "And his son died of yellow fever. Though whether all his men are gone—"

Katrina excused herself and went to warn Niklas and the boys of pirates on the river.

CHAPTER 55

THE PARIS OF THE NEW WORLD

Niklas asked Mr. Groves: "Is there a church with German services in the city?" One thing Niklas and Katrina wanted to accomplish as soon as they reached New Orleans was to go to church. They wanted to thank God for their safe passage, and while they felt a prayer of gratitude or penitence could be sent heavenward anywhere, it was time the children saw the inside of a church again.

"It's a Catholic city, but there's a German synagogue on Rampart Street," Mr. Groves said, "and at least two Protestant churches, Christ Church and First Presbyterian. Louis XIV's *Code Noir* forbade Jews and Protestants, but it's not official anymore."

"Ah," said Niklas, squinting at the sun, reluctant to be particular. "These may not be especially close to the church we hope for." He knew Protestants of a different strain would be little comfort to Katrina.

"There may be services in a private home. Weren't you given a German contact?"

"Yes," said Niklas, "two contacts." He dug in his pocket for the scrap of paper Lennart Mueller had given him and read aloud: "Karl Schneider. Samuel Hermann."

"Look for them in the Third District," said Mr. Groves. "It's called 'Little Saxony' or La Faubourg des Allemands, the German suburb."

"Des Allemands," repeated Niklas with satisfaction. "I see that in the address."

René Gravier had overheard. "You might inquire at the Hermann mansion. Monsieur Hermann made his fortune on the German Coast before he built a fine new house on St. Louis Street."

Major Slattery disagreed. "I wouldn't ask there! He was born a Jew. A good Catholic he may be now, but he won't want to help—" He asked Niklas, "What sect are you, Sir?"

Niklas was shocked to be asked so directly. "Calvinist, Sir."

"Hmm," said Slattery. "What about the German Coast?"

Niklas and Katrina had heard about the German Coast, which had been settled before the American Revolution and made famous by Samuel Hermann's great success.

"Too far," said Mr. Groves. "It's a day's ride above New Orleans."

As Mr. Groves walked away, Major Slattery took hold of Niklas's sleeve. "I wouldn't mention being Calvinist, Sir."

Several days later, the humidity had coalesced into fat, lazy drops of rain, but even that could not dampen anyone's excitement. It may have been well enough to luxuriate in tropical Havana and to land in a Texas safely out of war, but this at last was the actual, official, authentic United States of America. After the interminable crossing of ocean, gulf, delta, and bayou, being about to traverse *Enigma*'s gangplank and step onto American soil was a source of great excitement.

As more buildings began to appear along the shore, Katrina asked Major Slattery, "Is this it?"

"Oui, the outskirts," he said, "Jefferson Parish."

The shoreline showed fields, the occasional house, and clusters of villages with mills, modest church steeples, and the clang and fire of a blacksmith's shop. This was hopeful, but nothing like a great city. Nevertheless, Niklas looked almost gleeful, as he had when *Holsatia* pulled away from the dock in Cologne. In the sunshine of this new day on the edge of New Orleans, the Old World's never-quite-resolved conflicts seemed to have melted into the muddy waters of the Mississippi. Gradually, they came in among taller, finer buildings with more people, and then *Enigma* made a tight turn, was pulled along by its boats for a little distance, and turned again, and suddenly they could see the city spread along a grand, curving ridge of land.

Ahead, the great white dome of the St. Charles Hotel appeared, and then masts in clusters, sailing vessels with flags of all colors, including the Blue Peter signal of imminent departure, followed by a crowd of steamboats, four deep along the wharf, and then clusters of fishing vessels, flatboats, ferries, lighters and small working boats of every description, including dugouts. They heard the beat of hammers and the voices of many people, busy, loud, impatient people. A great farmer's market came into view, a riot of smells and colors, and then Mr. Groves barked orders, dock lines were thrown and caught, the gangplank was lowered, and Mr. O'Malley called to the Kästners quite civilly, bidding them disembark.

"Bienvenue à la Nouvelle-Orléans!" he said. Niklas's eyebrows shot up. He had not known until that moment that Mr. O'Malley spoke French.

Now at last they went down the gangplank and found themselves on the wide New Orleans levee, laughing at their own wobbliness, their sea legs betraying them, and they stood at last in America. They could not help but hug one another, the men clapping one another on the back and then turning to their new friends from Texas, who gave them hearty congratulations for their long, safe journey, wide smiles and handshakes all around.

"Remember that old church in Rotterdam, the Pelgrimvaderskerk?" Will crowed. "We made it all the way here, all of us, even our little fiddler! And it's not even November!"

Jakob held his hand out to be shaken, and it was, but then they walked away and he looked back at the crew, still aboard and waving to their passengers. "Mama?" he said, a little quiver in his voice. He pointed to the men in the crew, rough, hardened sailors who had taken him to heart.

Katrina had no answer but to lift him into her arms as both of them waved to the sailors. As they walked away from *Enigma,* Jakob was the last to wave goodbye, tears glistening on his cheeks. Katrina wondered if he remembered when home was anywhere but *Enigma,* and she swore to make a home for him that would show him something of what Berleburg had been. She kissed him on the cheek and handed him his stuffed bear. The poor thing had lost a button eye by now and needed a long soak. "Let's go see if Herr Kuschelbär likes New Orleans, shall we?"

They made a long, polite goodbye to Captain Peterssen, Thomas Segrave, Erik Thorvald, and Major Slattery, expressing many thanks for their safe delivery.

"We might have lost *Enigma* to the hurricane but for you," Izak Peterssen said to Niklas. "Not to mention your command of the marines."

"We have plenty to thank you for," Niklas said as he and Katrina presented Izak a silver buckle. They had had it engraved with his initials in Havana before they even knew how he would carry them through a hurricane and a harrowing arrival in Texas.

"May Thomas and I call upon you when you are settled?" Izak asked. "We will have days or perhaps weeks to re-fit *Enigma*."

"Of course," Niklas said, "It will take at least a week to secure a steamboat to go north, and then we will have to wait until its departure date."

"I feel sure we shall see you before then," Izak looked around. "Shall I hail a hackney for you?" Niklas was carrying a valise, but most of their things were still aboard.

"We'll explore first and send for the rest," said Niklas. "Will you walk with us?"

Izak Peterssen bowed his assent, and Thomas glanced at Amalie. Niklas did not see this glance, but Katrina did. Amalie lowered her face, but a smile showed below her bonnet. *Ah,* Katrina thought, *I'm not wrong. There's something between them.* She smiled. *They will soon be separated, Gott sei Dank.*

CHAPTER 56

A PROPER HOME

Carriages, wagons, men on horseback, and many people on foot made their way through an excited hubbub, the signature of any city.

"Now this is better," Niklas said.

"It's amazing to be back in civilization," Katrina agreed.

"Such a relief after the swamps," said Amalie.

"Such a relief after everywhere," said Will. "Linnville was barely more than the most backward of Hoch Sauerland's villages—"

"But with savages and longhorns," agreed his mother. Katrina shuddered at the memory of the hard stare of the Karankawa man.

"Havana was another world," said Hans, "where things looked something like home but turned out to be so different—tropical, slave-driven, Catholic."

Katrina glanced at Will as a moment of grief flickered across his face.

"Except for Havana's beaches," she said. "I won't hear a bad word said against the beaches."

"Or the coffee," said Niklas. "Now, Gibraltar, there was an odd mix."

Katrina agreed. "With all the ancient threats of pirates and Turks."

"Here, instead, the sweet, civilized sound of French," said Hans. "It's not German, but still, a relief after all that English aboard." The scar from Gibraltar still showed on his forehead, and he touched it without really thinking of the men who tried to kidnap him. "Listen!" he said, cocking his head to one side. They smiled as they heard strains of a violin and harpsichord. "That's the sound of home!"

Katrina felt tears start, though she could not have said whether she was happy to have the family safe in the civilized world or sad to be on the other side of the world from Berleburg.

They were at the riverside just outside the Vieux Carré, and everywhere, longshoremen loaded cotton bales, canvas sacks of rice, hogsheads of sugar, and ship's stores of every kind. Carpenters plied hammers, officers barked orders, steam stacks blew, and somewhere, a bugle sounded. Flatboats floated downriver, laden with corn or wheat or potatoes or hay or whiskey or cows or chickens or hogs, none quiet, but mooing, clucking and squealing. Homespun-clad Americans poled flatboats, and frontiersmen in buckskin with long knives at their sides called out in English or French. Further downriver, Cajun fishermen cast off from docks where nets were stretched by men and women repairing them. It all smelled strongly of fish and offal and sweat. Amalie and Katrina put handkerchiefs to their noses.

New Orleans had none of the cliffs of Gibraltar or the pearly beaches of Havana, but it had all the heady scents, clatter and confusion of any port. It rang with noise and secrets, wisdom and foolishness, anger and joy at once, a place where people mixed and multiplied, where ideas sprang up and revolutions seemed possible. Its houses, glinting gold in the sun, spoke of trade and prosperity.

Katrina swayed, almost falling.

Niklas caught her and steadied her. "Is it just sea legs, my dear?"

She shook her head: "It's disorienting being in a city so civilized, but at the same time, so crude." An odd, lightheaded feeling washed over her, past, present and future swirling together. She saw stevedores stripped to the waist, black skin shiny with sweat. Indians paddled silently from ship to ship, selling the day's catch from bateaux like those used for millennia.

"So many different people!" she exclaimed.

"Cities are always full of different sorts," said Niklas, patting her hand.

"But this! Thank God we did not bring Rafael here."

She saw a handsomely dressed family on its way to a steamboat, with a little girl holding a stuffed bear as she peeped over her mother's shoulder.

"Look, Mama," said Jakob. "She has a Kuschelbär."

The family was trailed by a beautiful Black woman, slender and young, with a red cloth tignon and a basket balanced on her head. On one raised finger, a little songbird perched, and she smiled at it.

The other faces in the crowd paid little attention, but a short, dark man happened to jostle this beautiful young woman's raised arm, and as he did, he glanced at Niklas. He was a strange-looking man in shabby, foreign clothing, and when his eyes stopped on Niklas, Katrina saw him register first surprise and then a startling malevolence. She looked up at Niklas, but he was talking to Hans; he did not see. She spun back to the short man, suddenly afraid he might pull a dagger, but he was already limping away into the crowd, a large bear-like man following him. *Russians?* she wondered. *Here?* When they were out of sight, she did a slow circle, looking for other threats. No one else was paying them the slightest attention, except a little Black boy holding out a banana he wanted her to buy.

Niklas smiled at her, and Katrina felt her world steady itself. "Here indeed is another Paris with all its élan and graciousness in miniature, exotic in its jungle setting."

She nodded. "Here, there will be music and dances, newspapers and books, tutors and scholars, haute cuisine and haute couture."

"Do you feel our freedom, Katrina? Where are the kings and queens, the ancient animosities?"

"Left far behind, I hope," Katrina said.

His arm was around her waist, and she looked up at him with admiration. They watched as sugar, cotton, indigo, hides, tobacco, and molasses was loaded. Out of ships coastwise came coffles of slaves to do the hard labor of wringing wealth from the land on cotton and sugar plantations. Out of ships from the Old World came crates with goods meant to enrich New Orleans and civilize the vast remoteness of America's Northwest Territory. Katrina recalled the fortepiano in *Enigma*'s hold and imagined it being lifted onto these docks.

"I believe this part's done and over. We got them all here alive."

Katrina saw the pride on his face as he looked from one child of theirs to another. There was a commotion far down the levee, and Katrina heard a high-pitched voice speaking Italian.

"Did you—" she said.

He was looking off the same direction. He had heard it too.

"Lasciami andare, Signore! Unhand me, sir!"

"Francesca?" *Could it be?* Katrina wondered. Now they heard another voice, a low growl, perhaps Italian.

Katrina signaled the children to stay put, but the older ones were having none of it. Hans and Will and Amalie were right behind them, the two young ones handed off to the care of ship's officers trailing them. The little knot of Kästners took a few hurried steps toward the voices, and then

Francesca herself burst out of the crowd, with Franci and Giovanni on her heels.

"Katrina!"

"Francesca! How did you—I am so glad to see you!"

"We came by Lake Pontchartrain on the *Aeneid*, a week shorter! We have been haunting the docks every day, watching for *Enigma*."

"But your cousins?"

"I decided they don't need me anymore. Not as much as my daughter needs dance lessons!" She opened her arms wide as if to take in all of New Orleans. "It's glorious, Katrina! Wait 'til you taste it."

"Better than cabbage and potatoes?" Katrina laughed.

Izak and Thomas and Thorvald and Major Slattery had caught up with them, and Lisette ran to embrace Franci.

Will looked around at them all, Germans and Italians with an Englishman, a Dane, an Icelander and an Irishman, and laughed, "What a motley crew we be!"

Niklas answered him, "That's the way we like it!"

"Ja, ja, ja," said Katrina, smiling.

Her friend, Francesca, was saying something to Niklas: "Besides, with all your talk about the Declaration of Indipendenza—we decided America needed us."

"It does indeed, Signora!" he agreed.

"Let's leave off travel," Katrina smiled, "and get a house built."

"One more trip," he answered her with a grin. "We will go up the Mississippi to the frontier. But once we're there and we have in our hands a deed, we will make a proper home for all of us, including our little fiddler."

"Never to move again."

"Ja, never to move a single inch," he said, and he thought, *Here at last, in New Orleans, le nouveau Paris, with you at my side and all of us safe, we never need to go anywhere again.* Niklas sighed in satisfaction.

FROM THE AUTHOR

Hard choices and cruel surprises are always part of an immigration journey. Laughter, too, if we are to tell the truth, and rejoicings. By an accident of birth, I heard more about my great-great-grandparents' 1836 journey than anyone could expect. Their teenage son, my great-grandfather, was sixty-seven when his daughter, my grandmother, was born, thus I am only four generations from 1836. I became a bona fide, living, historical link, because their lives are to me what nautical fiction writer Antoine Vanner called the Victorian era: "'the day before yesterday,'...history you can almost touch."

Their story, as I tell it here, is fiction, but it is true in some way for many thousands of unnamed, unrecorded immigrants. From 1840 to 1910, about ten million Europeans left for America, pulled in by freedom and opportunity and pushed out by war, famine, political repression, and a great many personal reasons. Millions of immigrants told their children the happy story and left the other one unspoken, unheard and forgotten.

By the 1880s, the largest number had come from German-speaking regions stretching from the eastern edge of Holland to multilingual Austria, which alone had seventeen official languages. What is now Germany was not united for a generation after the failed revolution of 1848-49, when Prussia, the largest of many Teutonic countries, began absorbing others. In America, all of these ethnicities, dialects, and languages were simply called "German," and thought of as one.

After 1840, the failure of potato crops across Europe caused famine and created a crush of immigrants, especially from Ireland, where millions starved while England looked the other away. Something similar happened in Sweden. Almost as many Irish immigrated as Germans, to be followed by immigrants from Slavic countries and Russia as steamships made cross-ings faster and cheaper. By the time the third largest group came, the Italians, many went to and from, bringing wages to the Old Country and family to the New World.

Early immigrants, like those in this book, were on their own getting to a harbor, finding a ship, and feeding themselves for a crossing that took forty-five days on average. By the 1860s, things were easier, with combination tickets available for purchase. These typically took one by rail from wherever was home to Hamburg to catch a steamer across to Hull, England; rail across to Liverpool; sailboat or steamship from Liverpool to New York; and either a steamship across the Great Lakes, or later, a train to Chicago, Milwaukee, or Minneapolis. However they came, and long after it was "easy," it is fair to say that most immigrants found their lives torn forever between two worlds.

Like my real family, the fictional one came from the little town of Berleburg, east of Cologne, in Wittgenstein, which, in 1795, was part of Napoleon's first conquest, an area he gave to his little brother to rule.

My great-great-grandfather apparently left Berleburg in Napoleon's cavalry sometime before the 1812 Russian campaign. He survived that disaster, as only one in forty did, and came home after Waterloo. When he and his family emigrated in 1836, they aimed for what was then the American frontier, settling in northwest Illinois four years after the Black Hawk War had pushed the Meskwaki (Fox), Sauk, and other tribes across the Mississippi. His son became one of the richest men in Illinois and lived on the farm he would give to my grandmother, but that was much later.

When Napoleon invaded Russia in 1812, he was almost to Moscow before the czar decided to put up a fight, and that was when two men related to me may have met for the only time.

One was the Russian Count Ostermann-Tolstoy, whose grandfather came from my Ostermann grandfather's hometown of Essen and replaced the czar for a time, which made him deeply unpopular and nearly cost him his life. On his mother's side, Count Ostermann-Tolstoy was a favorite cousin of the Tolstoy who wrote a book you may have read about the war. By 1812, the count was already famous for several things, including courage in battle, as well as being handsome and dissolute.

Fighting against Count Ostermann-Tolstoy was another relative of mine, my maternal great-great-grandfather, the intrepid cavalryman fictionalized here as Niklas Kästner.

Rose Osterman Kleidon, 2022

ACKNOWLEDGMENTS

First, I thank my students. For years I taught college students to write in various ways—for other classes and for careers in the sciences or in marketing communications. All that time, they were teaching me, too, giving me the courage to take on an extreme writing challenge, historical fiction. Luckily, I had taught how to make one's research reliable, so when I began telling a story of 19th century immigration, I could delight in the required research and whiz through it.

Writers need a spark of inspiration, and for me, it came from a small, admittedly obscure writing group in the Estancia neighborhood in Surprise, Arizona. Friends, your amazement at whatever I wrote encouraged me to think I might have something of value to say.

Others who kept me on track include Barbara Ellis, a fine editor who became a friend, Jan Kardys, who had confidence in me, agent Emily Kim, and the always friendly, helpful, and capable team at River Grove Books. I also thank Christopher Norris, who read with sensitivity to PTSD, sharing his own experiences and those of veterans he treated; and Steve Ellis, who brought his sailing expertise to bear. Then there were the language experts, including Chris for Spanish, Ewa Kapera for Polish, and Rebecca Barnum for French. My German experts included Dr. Barbara Fischer and Dr. Paul Riedesel, whose unrivaled knowledge of the Berleburg region, its local language and customs, and the politics of the era did much to keep this fictional tale within the strictures of historical accuracy.

I owe a special thanks to Nancy E. Turner, *New York Times* bestselling author, finalist, The Willa Literary Awards, Arizona Author of the Year, *These is My Words, Sarah's Quilt, The Star Garden, The Water and the Blood, My Name is Resolute,* and *Light Changes Everything.* Her encouragement and sensitive, sensible editing suggestions came at just the right time.

Nothing was more encouraging than author Pete Beatty's endorsement, an amazement when I think of how much I admire his hilarious and groundbreaking *Cuyahoga,* which reaches deftly into the spirit and myth of

American frontier towns to bring us both those distant times and an exhilarating, entirely original perspective on today.

I am thankful also for the kind encouragement and support of Steve Vogel, a classmate in high school and college and the *New York Times* best-selling author of *Reasonable Doubt* and *The Unforgiven.*

My friends and family read for me, especially Judi Sanna Kleidon and Pamela Sharpe Osterman, who said this story deserved readers far beyond the family. My brother John found an amazing cache of documents. My deep thanks go to William Zucker, who did brilliant translations of Carl Ewald's stories for children and who was my cheerleader from the beginning. Also cheering me on were good friends Beth Livingston Hakes, Clint and Karen Hakes, Doris and Errol Baxter, Gurinder and Sandy Rana, Mike Kolsky and Barbara Rosen, Mike and Shurley Stumpf, Rose Richardson, Quentin Maguire, Diane and Henry Lynch, Irish genealogist Tom Crowley, Mike and Kathy Lehr, about a thousand Fosseys, and the plant experts among my garden club friends, especially Claire Purdy, Pam Reitz, and Mary Ann Slattery, who also let me borrow her last name.

My Osterman, Hakes, Kleidon, Sauer, Smith, Sandhu, Ballos, Jungknecht, Nishigaya, and Rokusek relatives have watched both the fictional and genealogical sides develop, offering photos, documents, maps, and much enthusiastic support. Among them are direct descendants of the family who inspired this story, those who knew the family, and kissing cousins. Behind them all are my father and mother, who could tell stories of the family in great and loving detail, speculating on mysteries about who and why and when. This story is for them and for the long-gone grands, great-grands, aunts, uncles, and cousins whose courage, love, loyalty, and wit outlast them and inspire this story.

Most of all, I thank my sister, Linda, who read tirelessly, one draft after the other, seeing strengths in each; Joan, with her reliable enthusiasm and kindness; and Steve, who just plain likes the way I write. My son, Kurt, daughter-in-law, Megan, grandsons, Ethan and Emerson, and especially my husband, Dennis, deserve big, solid gold Oscars (or reasonable facsimiles) for keeping the home fires burning while I ignored everything in the 21st century. Perhaps most of all, I am thankful to Dennis for his relentless optimism and his masterful methods for encouraging creativity. Thank you all, dearest family, friends, and colleagues.

www.ingramcontent.com/pod-product-compliance
Lightning Source LLC
Chambersburg PA
CBHW021504110726
47899CB00001BA/283